Giri

"LUDLUM, LOOK OUT, MARC OLDEN IS HERE!"
—Walter Wager, author of *Telefon*

"FAST-PACED THRILLER . . . The book gallops along, with a large and vivid cast of characters, all of them deftly and interestingly drawn . . . The ending has a nice touch of ambiguity. Fast and juicy!"
—*Publishers Weekly*

"ACTION . . . DOUBLE-DEALING, KINKY SEX, KUNG FU AND JAPANESE CUSTOMS."
—*The New York Times Book Review*

"*GIRI* HAS BLOOD AND GUTS . . . We learn a good deal of Oriental philosophy, and it is to Marc Olden's credit that these discussions never get in the way of his fast-moving plot."
—*The Washington Post Book World*

"Anybody who loved *SHIBUMI* and *THE NINJA* shouldn't miss it."
—James Patterson, Edgar-winning author

"Powerful stuff, and the action scenes are taut and convincing."
—Lawrence Block, author of *A Stab in the Dark*

"Marc Olden writes with the quick, slashing motions of a karate chop!"
—Gerald A. Browne, author of *19 Purchase Street*

MARC OLDEN

BANTAM BOOKS
Toronto • New York • London • Sydney

GIRI

*A Bantam Book / published by arrangement with
Arbor House Publishing Co.*

PRINTING HISTORY

Arbor House edition published November 1982

Bantam edition / March 1984

*For information address: Arbor House Publishing Co.,
235 East 45th Street, New York, N.Y. 10017.*

ISBN 0-553-23922-8

Published simultaneously in the United States and Canada

PRINTED IN THE UNITED STATES OF AMERICA

H 0 9 8 7 6 5 4 3 2 1

For my beloved Diane

Giri

Japanese, meaning obligation,
loyalty, duty

Now indeed I know
that when we said "remember"
and we swore it so,
it was in "we will forget"
that our thoughts most truly met.

a *tanka* by Saigo Hoshi

ACKNOWLEDGMENTS

My mother, Courtenaye Olden, and my agents, Arthur Pine and Richard Pine, for their unwavering belief; Dick Martin and Harry Batchelder, Jr., for sharing their expertise; Joe Q. for data and a point of view that's never ceased to be of help.

Prologue

> Youth is justice and vigor. Vigor is simulated by *bu* (martial arts) and overflows into good or sometimes bad actions. Thus if *Karate-dō* is followed correctly, it will polish the character and one will uphold justice, but if used for evil purposes, it will corrupt society and be contrary to humanity.
>
> Gichin Funakoshi,
> father of modern *Karate-dō*

New York

He had stalked her for over three hours. Twice she had passed his hiding place and he could have reached out and touched her. His training, however, had emphasized *wazo o hodokoso kōki,* the psychological moment to execute a technique. Never strike too soon or too late. Wait for the opening, then seize it. If no opening appears, create one. Feint. Distract. Then attack, quickly, decisively.

Give no warning. Birds of prey, when attacking, fly low without extending their wings. The attacking beast crouches low with his ears close to his head. The shrewd man, before striking, takes care to appear harmless and inoffensive.

On the other side of the wall, only feet away from him, someone leaving for the day slammed an office door, then tried the knob before walking to the elevator. Seconds later the elevator arrived, which meant that he and the woman were now alone on the floor. His breathing became more rapid and for the first time in minutes he moved. The movement was limited to his fingers; he kept his gloved hands at his sides, fingers stretched, and held for a count of five before curling back into white-knuckled fists.

Bringing the heel of one hand to his lips, he peeled back the glove, letting the amphetamines drop into his mouth. He worked saliva around them, then swallowed. When the rush came he shivered with pleasure and after that came the heat of the whirlwind and then he felt the absolute power within him.

The telegram annoyed Sheila Eisen because it forced her to make a decision she wanted to avoid. Tonight she would have to choose between two men, one with the power to give her everything she wanted, the other a man who had betrayed her and whom she loved.

From her Fifth Avenue office facing Central Park and the Plaza Hotel, she looked down on a street wet with the first snowfall of November and fingered an antique watch of French enamel and gold hanging from her neck. It was a gift from the man waiting for her in a limousine parked below; he was her lover, an Academy Award–winning film producer twenty-five years older than she and married. He was also the second largest stockholder in a major Hollywood studio and today had offered to make Sheila a staff producer, providing she moved to Los Angeles.

But on the desk behind her was a telegram from her ex-husband. Last night, for the first time since their divorce two years ago, they had slept together and the sex had been mind blowing and fulfilling, leaving Sheila too weak to deny what she had known all along, that she had never stopped loving him. This afternoon he had sent her roses, and then a telegram came asking her to marry him again. She had left her office and walked across the street into Central Park, where she had sat and cried. Some part of her wondered if she shouldn't be angry at him; he had walked out on her and now he was back and doing *this.*

Who was it who had called a decision a timely cruelty? Closer to home the producer, whose sense of survival had taken him from a Budapest slum to a Bel Air mansion with its own heliport, had told Sheila, "Never give people a choice. They inevitably make the wrong one."

She was in her early thirties, a small, pretty woman with an unlined face encircled by drooping strands of fashionably permed red hair. Her job as the East Coast story editor for her lover's studio called for her to stay alone in the office until 8:00 P.M., when a vice-president telephoned from California. He was a treacherous closet queen whom Sheila loathed, and he had gotten where he was by taking credit for other people's work, Sheila's included. He preferred calling at five, Los Angeles time, and expected Sheila, three time zones away, to pick up the phone herself—no secretary, no answering service.

Her watch read six minutes to eight. Turning from the window she walked to her desk, piled high with books, scripts and galleys, sat down and pulled the telephone toward her. The only thing worth filming she had found in weeks was an off-Broadway play, but if the studio was interested it would have to act fast. The producers of the play were thinking of moving it to Broadway; when that happened the price for film rights would triple.

She leaned back and tapped her teeth with the edge of her watch. That play would make one hell of a debut for her as a film producer. She smiled, wondering if that didn't constitute a choice between her ex-husband and her lover.

A gentle tap on the reception door made her go rigid in her chair.

"Yes?"

"Police. Detective Sergeant Ricks, Manhattan Midtown." The voice was gentle, flat with the bored courtesy of all New York cops. "Hope I didn't frighten you."

Eyes closed, Sheila touched her pounding heart. "As a matter of fact, you did. I'm alone here and waiting for an important phone call."

"I'll try not to take up too much of your time, Miss—"

He paused, waiting for her to fill in the blanks.

"Mrs. Eisen. Officer, I don't mean to be rude, but can't this wait, whatever it is?"

" 'Fraid not, Mrs. Eisen. Precinct got a call from security downstairs about a prowler in the building."

Sheila was out of her chair. And scared.

"We think the guy sneaked in through the freight elevator entrance on the Fifty-eighth Street side of the building," the man said. "We're checking all floors, toilets, broom closets, fire exits, you name it. You have automatic elevators in these buildings and sometimes a nut case sneaks in after everybody's left for the day, and rides up and down waiting for some woman who worked late to get on by herself."

He never raised his voice. But his dispassion—some would call it professionalism—hinted at things best left unsaid.

She crossed her office on the run and jerked open the reception door to a lean, smiling man wearing a dark blue topcoat and gray hat. He held a detective's gold shield in one gloved hand. He kept his smile in place and waited patiently until she realized she was blocking his way. Then she stepped back into the reception area and he followed her.

He closed the door behind him, placed a monogrammed attaché case on the receptionist's desk and looked around. Then he pushed the hat back on his head and scratched his forehead with a thumbnail. Alan Ladd, Sheila thought, calm and collected.

He unbuttoned his topcoat, removed his hat to reveal frizzled blond hair and looked Sheila up and down with a thoroughness that she found disturbing. And then he became professional again, his green eyes sweeping the reception room, missing nothing. He couldn't have been more than thirty and was clean-cut and wholesome, traits she had never found attractive in men, but he wasn't here for that.

He pointed with his hat to the front door. "That lock's bad news. Spring latch with a tapered bolt. Anyone can use a credit card or a piece of plastic and open it in two seconds. Lock it again and on the way out I'll show you how easily it opens."

"Yes, yes. Of course." Sheila locked the door.

"Funny thing," said Detective Ricks. "Half the break-ins don't involve a break-in at all. They happen because of an unlocked door, an open window, key under the doormat, the sort of thing that shouldn't happen at all."

"What kind of lock should I have?"

"Deadbolt, no two ways about it. It's not spring actuated. The bolt stays in a locked position and you can't pry it back so easily. You have to remember no lock is impregnable. The best you can hope for is to delay the intruder. Make him think it's going to take a while to break in so he'll move on to an easier target. Most burglary is an on-the-spot occurrence, a crime of opportunity. Hit and run. If there's going to be trouble getting in, the perpetrator doesn't want to be bothered."

He dropped his hat on top of the attaché case and flexed his gloved fingers. The initials on the case, Sheila noticed, were R.A. Something else, too. Detective Ricks was wearing a gold stud in his right ear.

Behind her the telephone rang and she snapped her head in its direction, then looked back at Sergeant Ricks and he saw all of it in her face. Suspicion. And hope. Because the telephone was ringing and she had only to pick it up and cry out for help.

Tsuki no kokoro.

As the moon shines equally on everything within its range, so should the fighter develop such consciousness that will make him always aware of the totality of the opponent and his moves.

He attacked. Quickly, decisively.

His left hand snaked out, knife edge crushing Sheila's larynx and ending forever her power to speak, but not killing her. Not yet. Her eyes bulged. It was a joke, of course; it wasn't happening to her. For a few seconds she was both observer and participant, standing outside of herself and watching the beating, but the awful pain crept closer and trailing it was panic and fear with a stench of its own.

She held her hands to her throat and backed away from him. He followed and when *maai,* distance, was correct between them he struck again. He drove the heel of his right hand into her nose, crushing it, and she staggered into the receptionist's desk, still not accepting this attack. But the pain was increasing; she couldn't breathe and her skin was clammy.

He closed in, kicking her in the thigh, buckling her leg and dropping her to the floor. With no wasted motion he crouched over Sheila and expertly punched a series of piston blows into her kidneys. A strangled noise came from her throat as she stiffened, clawed at the carpet and willed herself to live, because she had not yet chosen between the two men who loved her.

Suddenly the man stopped. With surprising gentleness he pulled Sheila away from the desk and as the telephone continued ringing he lifted up her skirt, took down her panties and tossed them aside. He parted her legs and smiled lovingly down at her before removing his topcoat and jacket and unbuckling his pants. He inhaled deeply, feeling the pleasure of being fully aroused. He entered her, balancing himself on his elbows and knees, taking care to keep himself away from her bloody face.

He rode her briskly, losing himself in her flesh and feeling control slip away. In seconds he was groaning, pushing deep in his race for ecstasy and then he abandoned himself to that supreme pleasure, so close to death itself.

He collapsed on the carpet beside Sheila, lying quietly, breathing through his mouth and feeling a love he could not put into words. The two of them were united in *Chi-matsuri*, the rite of blood which was a thousand years old and which required that combat be preceded by a human sacrifice to the god of war.

Combat.

He sat up quickly and looked at his wristwatch. In less than an hour he and his enemy would be face to face.

He heard a death rattle from the woman's throat. Her eyes pleaded for mercy, but all he could give her was release. Driving his right elbow into her temple, he demolished Sheila with a single blow.

Three men, two of whom were conversing about a marketing plan they had been working on for the past twelve hours, walked from the elevator across the empty lobby to a desk where a uniformed security guard sat watching television. All three signed out for the day. The guard looked up briefly, saw businessmen in topcoats, carrying attaché cases, then returned to the hockey game. The guard did not notice that the third man, whose scarf covered most of his face, took the ball-point pen in a gloved hand and traced the preceding signature.

On Fifth Avenue the third man pulled the scarf from his face, touched the gold stud in his ear and looked up at a rust-colored sky, feeling the chill of the falling snowflakes and night air on his heated skin. He felt invincible; his *ki*, energy, was growing and his senses were so keen that he could hear wind and water from another time. Tonight when he stepped into the arena he would stamp his feet and shake the earth. He was protected by the rite of blood and by *Hachiman Dai-Bosatsu,* the great Bodhisatva, god of war. He was a sword, forged by the four elements of metal, water, wood and fire.

He was true *bushi,* an invincible warrior.

One

Gojo-Gyoko

Principle of five feelings and five desires, character flaws to be taken advantage of in your enemy

1

The Cayman Islands lie one jet hour south of Miami and 180 miles northwest of Jamaica. Measuring only one hundred square miles, the islands have a population of twelve thousand, descended from Scottish farmers, Europeans, Africans and shipwrecked buccaneers, who once terrorized the Caribbean under Sir Francis Drake, Henry Morgan and Blackbeard. They supported themselves by fishing and exporting shark skins, turtle products and dyewood. Grand Cayman is the largest island, a thin, flat splinter of coral, white sand and mangrove swamps.

In 1962, the Caymans, a dependency of Jamaica, refused to follow her lead and become independent of Britain. Instead the three islands—Grand Cayman, Little Cayman and Cayman Brac—voted to remain a British Crown Colony, governing with its own constitution; foreign policy and defense were to be directed from London. Following the Bahamas, which had prospered by offering tax exemptions to foreign banks and multinational corporations, the Caymanians decided to turn their tiny and isolated community into a Caribbean Switzerland.

With the passage of a new trust law in 1966, the Cayman Islands became an international financial center, offering foreign companies a tax-free haven and allowing world banks to operate in the islands with a secrecy unmatched in the Bahamas or even Switzerland. Fifteen years later almost three hundred banks and over eleven thousand companies were registered in Georgetown, the capital of Grand Cayman, a presence representing hundreds of billions of dollars, all of it free from taxes and surveillance.

Or questions regarding origin.

* * *

The counting was almost completed. Eight million, three hundred thousand dollars in cash, hand carried from New York to Grand Cayman in three suitcases and placed on the desk of a Georgetown bank manager who was also a lawyer and one of seven members of the islands' "executive council," or cabinet. This allowed him to make the laws that assured his prosperity and confounded his rivals. He showed his clients old-fashioned courtesy, served them long Cuban cigars and Vieille Rhum from the French islands and, most important of all, kept secrets very well.

But there were indications that he was not without his own secrets and Trevor Sparrowhawk, sitting in the banker's paneled office under a framed color photograph of Queen Elizabeth II, took note of them. A look had passed between the married banker and his much younger secretary, a sloe-eyed, voluptuous Jamaican who wore African blue lilies in her hair and a Lucien Picard wristwatch. Slap and tickle going on there, thought Sparrowhawk, who was more observant than most. The bridge of the banker's nose sported dark indentations, a sign that he had recently given up wearing eyeglasses in favor of contact lenses and a more youthful appearance.

Sparrowhawk also knew that this man's salary as a banker, while comfortable, did not match his earnings as an attorney, in which capacity he received a thousand dollars for each registration of a multinational corporation, most of which then included him on the board of directors. In ten years he had registered over a thousand companies, leading them into the shadowy world of offshore banking and tax avoidance. Framed certificates arranged on a bookshelf proclaimed that the banker, who wore the Eton public school tie, was also a member of several prestigious London clubs.

Of the five men in the banker's office, only Sparrowhawk was not counting money. He was a mere observer, bored by the long hours of waiting; he spent most of his time at the second floor window, looking out at the Georgetown harbor and the unloading of a cruise liner from Caracas. And when that paled, he returned to his seat to read *Poems, Chieflly in the Scottish Dialect,* a Robert Burns first edition given to him by his wife as an anniversary gift. Closing the book, Sparrowhawk stood up and placed the book on his chair, then stretched before touching the floor, fingertips on the thick carpet. Not bad for a lad of fifty-five.

Trevor Wells Sparrowhawk was a stocky, red-faced Englishman whose needle-thin nose jutted out over a thick black mustache, with ends pointed and waxed. His full head of silver hair hid the remains of a right ear mangled in the Belgian Congo by a drugged Simba wielding a panga. His dark gray eyes were narrowed in a squint, suggesting a permanent suspicion of mankind. He wore the SAS lapel pin on his tweed jacket, proudly regarding his service in that elite British commando unit as the most satisfying of his long military career. These days Sparrowhawk lived and worked in America, where he was chief operating officer and a director of Management Systems Consultants, a private intelligence service.

On one side of the large black oak desk the Caymanian banker and two assistants stopped counting to enter printout totals from individual calculators into a ledger kept by the banker. Opposite them, and with a calculator of his own, sat Constantine Pangalos, a high-powered New York attorney whom Sparrowhawk and two of his agency guards had escorted with the money from New York to St. Petersburg by car and from there by jet to the Cayman Islands. Pangalos was fortyish, a dark and hairy little man, with thick eyebrows over a hooked nose and a decided preference for other men's wives. Sparrowhawk was convinced that the man's lechery and abominable table manners would have found him quite at home with Rasputin. Pangalos had once been a noted federal prosecutor, in charge of a task force investigating organized crime. But now he worked for organized crime, for the Paul Molise family of New York. As did Trevor Sparrowhawk.

Another cruise liner arrived in the harbor. Sparrowhawk heard the three blasts of its deep horn and the answering whistles from the fishing boats.

"Finished."

A tired Pangalos flopped back in his chair and massaged strained eyes with his fingertips. He spoke to Sparrowhawk, whom he disliked—the feeling was mutual—without turning around. "You can call New York now. Tell our friends three days."

The Englishman rose from his chair, the Burns poems under one arm. Paul Molise, junior and senior, would be delighted to hear they were getting the eight million back so soon. Washed, of course. This particular laundering scheme was the brainchild of Paul junior, a financial wizard who had graduated from Harvard Business School and was responsible for his family's move into legitimate investments: nursing homes, shopping centers, savings and loan associations and real estate.

Management Systems Consultants also laundered its share of dirty money, but that was not its primary function. Under Sparrowhawk's shrewd direction it gathered information vital to Molise interests. The information came from the police files, congressional committees, corporate board meetings, union bargaining sessions, the IRS, FBI, secret court testimony and the federal witness protection program. It came from former lawmen now on the company payroll, who used their contacts to secure computer tapes, data bank information and copies of memos, dossiers and reports.

Sparrowhawk had turned Management Systems Consultants into a profitable company. It had legitimate security contracts with leading corporations ranging from hotel chains to fast-food restaurants. It performed investigations for top law firms, politicians and foreign businessmen. It furnished bodyguards, in-house security for banks and federal plants, performed debugging and wiretapping and made employee background checks. Most of its clients thought the company was legitimate and efficient; they didn't know that private information about each of them was accessible to a crime family.

Though backed by Paul Molise and his father, Management Systems Consultants was Sparrowhawk's domain. He insisted that wet work, killing, be left to the wogs, so as not to bring MSC under scrutiny. The company was to restrict itself to washing money and collecting intelligence.

"Men see wrong even in the righteous," he had said to Paul Molise. "The suspicious mind has only to know a little to suspect much more. American law enforcement is that suspicious mind. It surely has both of us under surveillance, you more than me. In any case, a corpse draped around the company water cooler is apt to discourage business and cause our board of directors to leap up and down like a fiddler's elbow."

In the Georgetown banker's office Sparrowhawk said to Pangalos, "I'll telephone from outside. Gives me a chance to stretch my legs. By the way, should anyone inquire, when may I say you'll return to New York?"

"When I get there. I have things to do in Miami."

"I'm sure."

Pangalos slowly turned his small dark head to lock eyes with Sparrowhawk. The staring contest ended with the Greek snapping at the banker, "Let's keep it rolling. We finished the counting, but there's paperwork to take care of. I'd like it done while we're young, okay?"

Sparrowhawk watched Pangalos indulge in a protracted fingering of his crotch. Insatiable bastard. One of Pangalos's clients, a producer of television news in New York, had been too busy to accompany his wife to Florida, where she had fled to escape a November snowstorm. She was now waiting for Pangalos to join her at a Spanish villa in Key Biscayne.

"I shall take Robbie with me," said Sparrowhawk, referring to one of the two agency guards waiting outside the door. "Martin can stay behind. Should you need a runner to bring a message to me I daresay he'll have no trouble locating me in a town this size."

Pangalos smirked. "Maybe you can find some bimbo down here to sit on Robbie's face."

"Perhaps I shan't be around the next time you annoy Robbie."

Frowning, Pangalos chewed a thumbnail, remembering how close he had come. Sparrowhawk had stepped in between the two of them and calmed Robbie down, but it hadn't been easy. A remark about Robbie never going out with women had set him off and almost cost Pangalos his life. Robbie was lethal.

He was expert in Tae Kwan Do and Okinawa-Te, in Kung Fu and Shotokan. In knife fighting and Bo-jitsu, stick fighting. He and Sparrowhawk had first met in Saigon, where Robbie was a SEAL and Sparrowhawk had worked for the CIA. Both also worked for the Mafia, which had managed to make a big profit out of the Vietnam War. At Management Systems Consultants, the thirty-year-old Robbie worked as bodyguard, as courier for cash and vital papers and as martial arts instructor to company personnel. Sparrowhawk was proud that Robbie successfully competed in major karate tournaments, where he had become a nationally ranked competitor. With only one child—a daughter—Sparrowhawk saw Robbie as the son he would have liked to have, and the lad showed his respect by calling Sparrowhawk major.

In Saigon, where Paul junior and Sparrowhawk had first discussed forming Management Systems Consultants, the major had made it clear that Robbie was to be part of the deal. This was not merely a gracious gesture to a comrade-in-arms; the lucrative contract and wide latitude of freedom offered Sparrowhawk did not rule out the possibility of treachery from the Italians. Robbie would be a handy chap to have around.

Sparrowhawk was suddenly alert. Something was wrong at the other end of the phone in New York.

Paul Molise was supposed to have answered. Instead Sparrowhawk heard another voice, mockingly polite and barely suppressing laughter. An alarm went off in the Englishman's mind. As arranged, he was using a public telephone in Georgetown to reach a public telephone in Manhattan, one that should have been free from wiretaps. The voice that greeted Sparrowhawk seemed to know he was out of the country.

"Paulie says he's sure you did a good job down there. He wants you to pass the information on to me."

The information. Molise's eight million, now untraceable in a Cayman bank, would return to America in three days as loans to businesses controlled by Molise. Also, Molise would be allowed tax deductions for interest payments on the loans.

And in the telephone call fifteen minutes earlier Sparrowhawk had arranged for someone—not an employee of Management Systems Consultants—to carry out a contract killing for the Molise family within the next forty-eight hours.

The silver-haired Englishman, receiver to his ear, drew deeply on an oval-shaped Turkish cigarette and stared at a Pride of Burma, whose scarlet and gold blossoms made it one of the world's most beautiful trees. Two American college girls, made giggly by *ganja,* cycled past on their way to Seven

Mile Beach, fins and snorkel masks dangling from handlebars. One, the blonde, reminded Sparrowhawk of Valerie, his daughter, and suddenly he remembered his promise to bring her some coral jewelry.

"Hey, I know you're there," said the voice. "I can hear you breathing."

Bloody bastards are on to us, thought Sparrowhawk. One bloody bastard in particular.

He put a hand over the mouth of the receiver and with his head signaled Robbie to come closer.

"Manny Decker," whispered Sparrowhawk.

Robbie's eyebrows rose. "That's him on the phone?"

"Keep your voice down, dammit. Whoever it is, is trying to disguise his voice with a handkerchief over the mouthpiece. But I'll give you cards and spades it's Decker."

"Son of a bitch. How did he find out which phone we'd be calling in New York? How the hell did he even know we were down here?"

Sparrowhawk, struggling to control his anger, stared at the setting sun, a bright red ball that had turned the sea into crimson glass. Jesus in heaven, how he hated to be hunted.

"Doesn't matter how he came to know. He's a police officer."

"Come, come," urged the voice, "time's a-wasting. Give me numbers, dates, something to tell Paulie."

The look on Robbie's face would have chilled the blood of a lesser man than Sparrowhawk, who had seen it before: in Saigon just before Robbie tortured and killed, and at karate tournaments before he annihilated his opponent.

The Englishman, his hand still covering the receiver mouthpiece, violently shook his head. "Unpurse your lips and listen to me. You've twice had a go at Decker. Leave it at that. This isn't Vietnam, do you understand?"

Chastened, Robbie hung his head.

Like Robbie, Manny Decker was an accomplished *karateka.* Twice they had met in tournament competition, with Robbie winning both times. In their last fight, which had gone into overtime, Robbie had savagely broken the knee of the New York City detective. Only skilled surgery and months of special exercise had saved Decker from being permanently crippled.

After that, Decker had never fought in another tournament, leading many, Sparrowhawk included, to assume he was afraid of Robbie. Decker continued to train and instruct and was in top shape, but he avoided all tournament competition. Unfortunately, he was still a good cop, too good. Sparrowhawk and Robbie had run up against the man in Saigon and knew how efficient he could be. Decker was assigned to a federal task force investigating Management Systems Consultants; to date, the investigation hadn't gotten very far. But any murder that could be blamed on MSC would naturally be welcomed by the task force. And by Decker. Especially by Decker.

Damn Paul junior for even considering the idea of Robbie or anyone else at MSC for a contract killing. But what could one expect from wogs, spaghetti eaters. They suffered from a revolting desire to control and manipulate everyone in their employ. The instant Robbie or Sparrowhawk or anyone at MSC killed on Molise's orders, the Italian would forever have them by the balls. Sparrowhawk wanted outsiders for this sort of work and if Paul junior didn't like it, tough.

At the moment it was back to the bank for a quick conference with Pangalos on how to go about contacting Paul junior, if it was wise to do so at all. It might be better to return to New York and deliver the news in person. In either case, Sparrowhawk planned to meet again with the bank manager and other Caymanian cabinet members to discuss installing a new security system at the Georgetown airport, a deal worth one million dollars to Management Systems Consultants. That was another reason why Sparrowhawk had personally accompanied the money to the islands.

"Paulie," began the voice in New York, but Sparrowhawk had tuned him out. He distrusted the voice at the other end and, without uttering a word, he hung up.

2

Detective Sergeant Manny Decker stepped out of a snowy New York night and into Japan.

He was in the Fûrin, a private Japanese club on East Fifty-sixth Street in Manhattan, named for the delicate hanging bell that tinkled in the wind. *Gaijin,* outsiders, were not welcome here. The Fûrin was a place where lonely Japanese men could hear their language spoken, flirt with professional Japanese and American hostesses, drink Awamori, the sweet potato brandy from Okinawa, and close deals by imprinting documents or correspondence with *hanko*s, their personal seal.

To get inside, Decker had flashed a *meishi,* the business card of a Japanese he was to meet upstairs in a private room. Not presenting a *meishi* was considered by the Japanese to be the height of bad manners.

Decker handed his hat and topcoat to a hostess in a kimono and wooden clogs. He kept the attaché case and followed a dark-suited maître d' through a restaurant designed around a rock garden, with a miniature waterfall and dwarf trees. Food smells—sliced raw fish over vinegared rice balls, delicate sparrows charcoaled over steel plates, cold buckwheat noodles—triggered memories. Of Saigon. Of Michi. If the pleasure of their love had lasted only a moment, its pain had lasted much longer. Michi Chihara was dead.

The detective was stared at, first by men in one corner, who played go in shirt sleeves and cooled themselves with hand-painted fans. And by men at the bar, who sat reading newspapers flown in daily from Tokyo or watched video cassettes of sumo matches from Tokyo's Kokugikan Arena. Decker, not upset at being eyeballed, considered staying to watch one sumo match. They never lasted over sixty seconds;

a 350-pound sumo wrestler wasn't built for endurance, but, oddly enough, the huge men had agility, balance, speed. They were Japan's most popular athletes.

Decker, however, decided to keep walking. Good manners said be on time, especially since he'd been the one to ask for the meeting with Ushiro Kanai.

Manny Decker was five foot ten, broken-nose handsome, with dark brown curly hair and matching mustache. He was thirty, slim and hard muscled and his eyes were sea green. He had been a cop since his marine discharge six years ago, winning his detective's gold shield in less than two years. The broken nose was a reminder of an early karate tournament when an opponent, wearing a class ring, had failed to pull a punch to the face.

Decker was also a field associate, a shoo-fly, part of the Internal Affairs Division of the Police Department. Field associates were recruited out of the Police Academy and their identities kept secret. Their job was to spot police misconduct and report it. For this they won the hatred of just about every cop on the force. It was life on the edge. Decker enjoyed it.

Which is not to say he wasn't careful. Associates had a single contact at headquarters, a lieutenant or captain. Associates and contacts used code names and met in out-of-the-way places. Decker improved on that. He and his contact never met face to face; they stayed in touch by phone, and Decker initiated all calls.

On the second floor of the Fûrin, the man leading Decker stopped in front of an *o-zashiki*, a private dining room with tatami, rush-covered mats changed frequently to retain the sweet smell of straw. The entrance to the room was covered by a shoji screen, a sliding door of translucent cream-colored paper. From inside a voice answered *hai*, yes, and then the detective was alone.

"Please come in, Sergeant Decker."

Decker removed his shoes, placed them on the floor beside Kanai's, then slid the door open.

Ushiro Kanai, dressed in the dark suit favored by all Japanese businessmen, sat on his heels in front of a small, lacquered square table holding a cup of warm rice wine. As head of the New York office of Murakami Electronics, a

Tokyo-based multinational corporation with branches in thirty-one countries, the boyish-looking Kanai, still in his forties, was being groomed as company president. He was intelligent and enigmatic, the product of a highly competitive society.

He motioned for Decker to sit on the other side of the table. The bad knee prevented him from sitting on his heels, so Decker sat as he did in the dojo, on his buttocks, feet in front but close to his body. Kanai gave Decker a smile that was hard and cold. The smile didn't mean shit. Kanai thought damn little of New York to begin with, and less since the stabbing of his son-in-law three days ago.

Decker handed the attaché case to the Japanese and watched the smile disappear. For once Kanai, whose life had been one of stern self-control, was caught off guard. His mouth dropped open. But he recovered quickly. He recognized the case; he'd given it to his son-in-law as a gift. Kanai thumbed it open, lifted the lid and carefully examined every sheaf of paper inside. This time, when he looked at Decker, there was no smile.

Gratitude.

Kanai closed the case, placed both hands palms down on the top and shut his eyes. From me to you, thought Decker. I've just handed you back your future and I expect to be paid.

"Dōmo arigato gozai mashite, Decker-san," Kanai said, with a bow. Thank you very much.

"Dō itashi-mashite, Kanai-san." You're welcome.

"Dōmo osewasama desu." I am much obliged to you.

Decker sensed Kanai's meaning. But since his Japanese was at best rudimentary, fragments picked up from fifteen years of karate and the bittersweet affair with Michi, he decided to make sure. He waited until Kanai opened his eyes and then stared at him.

"Giri." Kanai breathed the word. Though Decker had just returned a stolen report that could have damaged Murakami Electronics and pulled Kanai down from his high position, the Japanese executive disliked being obligated to a *gaijin,* a foreigner. But he was, and pride demanded that he meet that obligation. Pleased with himself, Decker did the polite thing. He followed Japanese custom and poured rice wine into Ka-

nai's cup. With Kanai's admission of *girl,* all that remained for him was to tell the Japanese how he wished to be paid. He wished to be paid here and now. Tonight.

Three days ago, in a cheap hotel on the West Side, a Japanese male had been found badly knifed. He had been robbed of cash, personal jewelry and an attaché case containing valuable company papers. The man was Ushiro Kanai's son-in-law, an accountant for Murakami Electronics, and he had been carrying papers detailing a proposed takeover of a California electronics firm, one with American defense contracts. The proposal was one that Kanai wanted kept secret until he had dealt with the sticky problem of Pentagon objections to foreign nationals buying defense-connected businesses.

Single Japanese men in New York had problems finding women. Not only were there few single Japanese women, but the language barrier prevented the men from socializing with American women. Some of them turned to prostitutes, a dangerous alternative. The Japanese were sometimes robbed, beaten, murdered.

Kanai's only daughter had hated America. She found it violent and dirty. Nor did she enjoy being left alone by a husband who worked long hours to please a father-in-law he feared. When her illnesses, real and imaginary, pushed her to the brink of a nervous breakdown, Kanai ordered her back to Japan. Within weeks of her leaving, her husband's loneliness became unbearable.

"As I told you over the phone," Decker said to Kanai, "we made the arrests this afternoon. Three people: the prostitute who solicited Mr. Tada, along with her pimp and his friend, who had been waiting in the hotel room. The watch, the one you told me and my partner about the other day, was seen around town. Gold band, rubies for hands. The pimp had been flashing it in discos and after-hours clubs. Has the name Yoko on the back."

"My daughter's name. And the watch, where is it now?"

"It's with the property clerk. You'll find a receipt for it inside the attaché case. We'll need the watch for evidence against Mr. Tada's attackers. It'll be returned as soon as possible. How is your son-in- law?"

"Still quite serious. He remains on the critical list. My

daughter flew in from Osaka last night. She is quite upset." Kanai tapped the attaché case. "Please, why is this not being kept, as you say, for evidence?"

It was Decker's turn to be caught off guard. He stopped, a cup of sake in front of his mouth, and he wondered what the hell had made him think he could run a game on this man. Kanai was clever. If he hadn't yet figured out that the detective was trying to use him, he was about to. He supposed he could always tell him the truth, for the truth was mighty and would prevail. Decker wished he believed that.

The detective put down his sake, sucked in air and gazed at his stockinged feet. "The case is here, Kanai-san, because it is important to you and because I wish to trade it for something that is important to me. Something you have." He looked up. "Information."

Kanai used the fingertips of both hands to make slow circles on top of the case. "You have read what is in here."

"Yes. It means nothing to me, nothing to the police. That's entirely your business, you and the American government. What I wish to ask you has nothing to do with Murakami Electronics."

"And what you wish to ask has value to you, so much value that you have been allowed to choose what you will hold for evidence and what you will return to its rightful owner."

Beautiful. Right for the jugular. Decker nodded, half in admiration, half in embarrassment at having been found out so quickly.

And Kanai waited. One learned not to rush. Patience, said the Chinese, and the mulberry leaf becomes a silk gown.

Decker massaged his bad knee and wondered how much of the truth to tell Kanai.

Since October, the detective had divided his time between precinct duty and an assignment with a federal task force investigating Management Systems Consultants, the private intelligence and security company. Decker was assigned to the case because two men he had known in Saigon, while serving there as a marine embassy guard, were now task force targets: Trevor Sparrowhawk, the Englishman who had founded MSC and was its head; and Dorian Raymond, a New York detective suspected of passing police files to Sparrowhawk. Raymond was also a suspect in three contract murders ordered by the Molise crime family.

Funded by Washington, the task force consisted of two dozen men, FBI, DEA, IRS, New York City detectives and investigators for federal prosecutors, all under Charles LeClair, himself a federal prosecutor. LeClair, son of a black air force general and a German actress, was an ambitious man who lived for his conviction rate, one of the highest in the federal court system. Outwardly genial, he was a master of the political aspects of his job and a spellbinding performer in and out of the courtroom. Decker had distrusted him on sight.

Decker had one other qualification that interested LeClair: he was sleeping with Dorian Raymond's estranged wife.

At their first meeting LeClair had said to Decker, "I'll touch on this lightly. I am aware of your relationship with Mrs. Raymond. And, as I'm sure you know, she does see her estranged husband from time to time. So this brings us to pillow talk."

LeClair managed to look embarrassed, as though reluctant to do this to Decker. He was almost convincing.

"Bear in mind that we have a purpose in being on this task force, and so long as we maintain that view, we maintain our usefulness in law enforcement. You have your career, I have mine. We can help each other or we cannot help each other."

Decker considered himself warned. Everybody in law enforcement, Decker included, had an eye out for the main chance. Advancing your career was the name of the game. At the same time one had to avoid stepping on the wrong departmental toes or getting crushed in the numerous power games surrounding police work. LeClair was simply being up front with Decker by telling him that on the task force, LeClair's career came first and everybody else's came second. In law enforcement, the power and all of the money were with Washington. LeClair was Washington. And he had warned Decker.

Management Systems Consultants was under investigation because it had sabotaged an inquiry into the crime connections of Senator Terry Dent, New York's most powerful congressman. If LeClair could bring Dent down, his own career was made; he would end up in Washington, the center of attention at embassy parties and the object of constant media exposure. LeClair also wanted to bring down Constantine Pangalos, the lawyer for Dent, MSC and the Molise family. When Pangalos had been a federal prosecutor and LeClair had been a member of his staff, the two had been friends. But it was now time to show who was the better man.

LeClair leaned back in his chair, hands behind his head. "Relax, Decker. Cross your legs or loosen your tie or dig the wax out of your ears or something. Your file says you're into karate. Always wanted to try that myself. Never got around to it. How long have you been practicing?"

"I've been training fifteen years."

"I'd better treat you with respect. Fifteen years. Still keeping it up?"

"I train two hours a day. Every day."

"No shit. Where do you find the time?"

"I make time. I run at four in the morning or midnight or when I can. I jump rope and do stretching exercises at home. A lot of times I work out on my own, usually when the dojo's empty."

"A man who flies his own flag. I like that. Ever use it on the street?"

"Yes."

LeClair was impressed. He studied Decker; that kind of persistence made the detective special, a man with certain strengths and weaknesses. LeClair would have to learn what they were and how he could use them.

LeClair then turned conciliatory. "Sorry about bringing Mrs. Raymond into this, but I don't have to tell you that guys in our line of work don't have a private life. Our marriages, bankbooks, sex lives, personal mail can all be poked into by inspectors and there isn't a damn thing we can do about it. Anyway, Decker, I'm here to make it as easy on you as I can. I need you and I need you working happy. Singing and dancing on the old plantation."

In spite of himself Decker smiled at that one. But when it came down to the short strokes, LeClair could hurt him more than he could hurt LeClair and they both knew it.

"You're on board now, Decker, so I think it's fair to say

we are entitled to a certain loyalty from you. This might bring you into conflict with what you think is best for Mrs. Raymond. They say when you serve two masters, you have to lie to one."

LeClair's grin was pleasant. His eyes were not. "Please don't let it be me."

Across the table from Ushiro Kanai, Decker began telling the truth. "Yesterday, my partner and I came to see you at your office. When we got there, two men were just leaving: Constantine Pangalos and someone else. Could you please tell me the name of that other man?"

The Japanese looked down at the attaché case a long time before answering. Finally, "He is Mr. Buscaglia. He is the president of a union that represents security guards. Mr. Pangalos is his attorney. My company owns the building that houses our New York office and we must have security for our workers and tenants. We are thinking of dismissing our current firm and hiring Management Systems Consultants, which Mr. Pangalos also represents."

Kanai removed the attaché case from the table and placed it on the floor beside him. "Recently we had some difficulty when our building was picketed by an affirmative action group. They claimed we had not hired enough black and Puerto Rican guards. At one point, the demonstration threatened to become violent. Some of our people were afraid to enter or leave the building. It was then that we heard from Mr. Buscaglia, who told me that he would speak to the group and fix things. He kept his word. The blacks and Puerto Ricans left. I was most impressed."

Decker decided not to tell Kanai that he had been tricked. Buscaglia had probably sent the "affirmative action" group to the building himself and called them off when it suited him. A grateful Kanai was bound to be more receptive to a sales pitch from someone who had done him a favor. If Buscaglia was connected with Pangalos and Management Systems Consultants, that also linked him to the Molise family. Like other legitimate businessmen, Kanai's fear of crime and desire for labor peace had led him into bed with some very bad people.

"Mr. Buscaglia has offered us an attractive package," said

Kanai. "The guards in his union work cheaper, the pension plan will cost my company less and he guarantees no strikes for the length of the contract."

Promises written on water, thought Decker. But who could blame Kanai for believing? Crime and vandalism were everywhere, making the security field the third-fastest-growing business in America. Fear had put Management Systems Consultants at the top of this growth industry, in a class by itself with a multimillion-dollar income from private intelligence as well as security services. Decker now had a new name: Buscaglia, plus his union. That should please LeClair for at least ten minutes.

"Mr. Pangalos and I discussed one other business matter," said Kanai. "My company has begun a program of diversification in America. Already we have real estate interests in three states, and next year we will break ground on a new hotel in Hawaii, on the island of Maui. We had planned to purchase an interest in a new Atlantic City casino hotel that Mr. Pangalos represents."

Rather than appear too anxious, Decker poured more sake for Kanai, then waited until the executive had poured for him. Both men practiced stern self-control. The pauses in their conversations were in the tradition of Japanese deliberation and sensitivity to the feelings of others.

Decker took three sips of sake before speaking again. "Could you tell me, Kanai-san, the name of the new hotel casino represented by Mr. Pangalos?"

"It is called the Golden Horizon. The new owners are the Marybelle Corporation. I believe they deal in video games, vending machines, slot machines and home computers."

"May I ask why your company no longer wishes to buy into the Golden Horizon?"

"There had been an agreement in principle to purchase a ten percent interest for a certain figure. However, that agreement was based on the Golden Horizon being in possession of a certain file, a list of major gamblers. Every casino in the world has one. I believe you Americans call them high rollers. Men who gamble for very high stakes, who can afford to lose as much as five million dollars in a single night."

"It's called a pigeon list," said Decker. When a casino changed hands, the pigeon list was sold separately. One list

Decker knew about contained the names of three hundred gamblers and had sold for three million dollars.

"Before buying into the Golden Horizon," said Kanai, "I insisted on seeing its pigeon list, as you call it. I wanted to see the names of men the casino considered favored patrons. I regarded that list as part of my company's investment. Unfortunately, Mr. Pangalos and Marybelle Corporation could not show me such a list. I can only assume that they do not have it and whoever does wants a high price for it."

The Marybelle Corporation and the Molise family won't stop until they get that list, thought Decker. No outside investor will put a dime into Golden Horizon until they see it, and the hotel casino needs outside investors to keep up the appearance of being legitimate.

The Molise family would not be happy with what Decker had done to Sergeant Aldo LoCicero either. LoCicero spoke Sicilian and had been assigned to translate wiretaps placed on Molise's people by LeClair's task force. LoCicero was not on the task force; he worked out of Decker's precinct and it was there in the locker room that Decker noticed LoCicero's new teeth and what appeared to be a persistent chest rash.

For a long time the Sicilian-American had suffered from bad teeth. Suddenly he'd had them filled, cleaned, capped; overnight LoCicero's mouth had turned from coal to pearls. And with his proud new smile had come the habit of constantly scratching his chest. Once Decker had come upon LoCicero alone in the precinct locker room, huddled close to his locker in an almost childish attempt to hide while he frantically rubbed lotion on his itching chest.

At the sight of the detective, the patrolman grew twitchy with nerves. He paled at Decker's suggestion that he remove his blouse and undershirt, the better to get at the itch.

Decker often walked the twenty blocks from his apartment, on West Sixty-fourth Street, to the station house for exercise, and it was on one of these morning walks that, unobserved, he watched LoCicero's wife let her husband out of a car several blocks away from the station house. The car was a Chrysler Imperial, long and black, new and expensive.

While increasingly disillusioned by what he encountered every working day, Decker still found a cold satisfaction in kicking a hole in other people's vision of themselves. In his heart he knew what all cops knew, that power was pleasure.

Decker moved in closer on LoCicero. He telephoned "Ron," his anonymous contact at police headquarters, and told him about the man's new car, new teeth, chest rash. A day later Decker learned that the car had been purchased in Nassau County and registered in the name of Mrs. LoCicero, who paid eight thousand five hundred dollars in cash, a third of her husband's yearly salary after taxes.

The LoCiceros had also paid cash, five thousand seven hundred dollars, for an upcoming Caribbean cruise aboard an Italian liner, and had contacted real estate agents about a new house, far out on Long Island and away from their "changing neighborhood." LeClair had to be notified, but Decker didn't want the information to come from him. Should he turn out to be wrong, the prosecutor would have one strike on him. Ron agreed. The information was passed to the task force through Internal Affairs. And Decker had guessed right about LoCicero.

LoCicero, while translating Molise wiretaps, had made copies to pass on to the crime family. He had shaved the hair from his chest and worn a recorder taped to his skin each time he stepped into task force headquarters at Federal Plaza. One telephone number found on him was that of a public booth in Manhattan. Word of LoCicero's arrest, however, reached the street in a hurry, so that no one in the Molise family would go near that phone booth. Decker, backed by two FBI agents, had only been going through the motions when he answered the ringing telephone on the corner of Seventy-second Street and Columbus Avenue. Whoever was at the other end wouldn't talk to a stranger. Later it occurred to Decker that LeClair might have been toying with him. Assigning him to stake out that booth was practically an admission that the prosecutor knew who had tagged LoCicero. Or was it?

In the private room of the Fûrin, Kanai said to Decker, "At the hospital we talked briefly of *Karate-dō*, when I mentioned that my son-in-law once trained, but had been forced to stop by the pressures of work. Had he been more experienced, he might have done better against his attackers. Did you learn Japanese through the martial arts?"

"I speak only bits and pieces, Kanai-san. Enough to embarrass myself."

"We Japanese appreciate hearing even a little of our language. We are warmed by the efforts of strangers, no matter how small."

Kanai seemed more relaxed. His obligation to Decker had not involved betraying his company or his self-respect. It was something he would remember.

"I expect to come to an arrangement with Mr. Buscaglia regarding new security guards for this building. It is sad, but one cannot live in New York without such services. Just a few days ago, there was a horrible killing on Fifth Avenue."

"I know," said Decker. "A woman working late was raped and murdered in her office."

"Oddly enough, a similar murder occurred in San Francisco two months ago. I was there to meet the architects for our proposed Hawaiian hotel. A woman working late in a nearby building was also attacked and murdered in the same fashion."

"The police here think it was the work of a maniac. They're not sure if he used a weapon."

"This killing does not come under your jurisdiction?"

"No. Different precinct. I read about it in the papers and saw it on the green sheet, the list each station house gets every morning of all the crimes that occurred in the city during the previous twenty-four hours."

"I see. Just from newspaper accounts, one could almost say that the same man did both murders."

"With respect, Kanai-san, I would say that this is a coincidence. A sad coincidence."

Kanai did not disagree with Decker. "I prefer to call it destiny, Decker-san, and destiny is the sum total of our actions, the adding-up of all our days. Destiny is a ruthless justice. I would say that the dead women were judged and sentences passed, perhaps by the same man. Perhaps. In any case, please to honor me by joining me for dinner. I will have food cooked in this room. Forgive me for not having planned a more suitable meal. I ask you to accept what little I can offer you on such short notice."

Remembering the department rule about freebies, Decker shook his head. Ignoring his refusal, Kanai rose to his feet, walked across the mat and slid back the door. He spoke rapidly in Japanese, then returned to the detective and looked down at him. "It is my obligation, Decker-san."

Giri. Decker had set that wheel in motion. The dinner invitation was the result of something he had done, an inevitable consequence of his scheming. The sum total of our actions, Kanai had said, the adding up of all of our days. To leave would be an insult, making it difficult to return with further questions about the Marybelle Corporation, Buscaglia's security guard union, Management Systems Consultants.

The sake was making Decker hungry. When had he last eaten? Eight hours ago? Ten? He watched the Japanese chef enter, followed by men carrying a portable stove. It occurred to Decker why his refusal had been brushed aside; Kanai had assumed he was following the Japanese custom of *enryo,* a polite refusal that actually means the opposite.

"Kobe steak," said Kanai. "It is kept here for me personally." Decker raised both eyebrows. At $150 a pound, Kobe beef was the most expensive in the world. Kobe cattle, raised in western Japan and sold for $125,000 per cow, were hand fed beer and given daily rubdowns with plum wine, which supposedly tenderized the meat. Decker's mouth started to water.

And there was the beauty of the meal. The detective watched with fascination as a fish was carved into the shape of a flower and fried seaweed woven into the shape of a beautiful bird. *Sara-kobachi,* dishes, cups, bowls of a subtle loveliness, were arranged on the counter, along with blue and white porcelain, bowls of bamboo and black pine, reddish brown earthenware plates and *hashi,* chopsticks.

Decker ate.

Sometime during the meal Kanai mentioned, politely, that he would be willing to discuss Pangalos and Buscaglia whenever the detective wished. The remark passed almost unnoticed. But Decker was not the type to let anything pass unnoticed if he could help it. Instinct overruled him. He thought about what he had just heard, then realized how clever Ushiro Kanai was, and realized, too, that this meal had been a part of that cleverness.

Kanai wanted Decker to keep him informed of any danger to his company. It was the Japanese nature to get to matters in their own good time, and in a way that benefited them. It was Kanai's nature to use, not be used. Absentmindedly, the detective poked at a bowl of rice with his chopsticks and allowed himself a smile. Some men were wise; others were cunning. Ushiro Kanai was both.

Decker reached for a beer and suddenly, as though stabbed from behind, Kanai stopped eating. His eyes bulged. Decker couldn't believe what he was seeing.

Fear.

Kanai reached across the table, scattering dishes and bottles and yanked Decker's chopsticks from the bowl of rice, where they had been standing upright.

"Death," said a breathless Kanai. "In Japan, a bowl of rice with chopsticks sticking up is offered to our dead in the family shrine."

"Sumimasen," said a chastened Decker. "I apologize, Kanai-san. I have done something very stupid. I beg your forgiveness."

Silence.

Decker felt like crawling away and hiding. Damn. In Saigon Michi had told him about that custom and he had simply forgotten. *Baka.* Stupid.

There was a gentle tap at the paper and bamboo door. Kanai got to his feet, walked across the room and slid back the shoji. It was the maître d'. He and Kanai spoke in whispers and then the maître d' bowed longer than usual before leaving.

Kanai kept his back to the detective and when he turned, he spoke in a choked voice. "*Sumimasen,* Decker-san. I beg your forgiveness, but I must leave immediately. I go to my daughter. My son-in-law has just died."

He left Decker, guilty and confused, alone in the room.

3

Cold and edgy, Detective Sergeant Dorian Raymond arrived in Atlantic City shortly before 8:30 P.M. He parked his used Chevrolet on the outskirts of the oceanside resort, away from the boardwalk with its string of gaudy hotel casinos, and away from the center of town, where lovely Victorian and Edwardian homes stood surrounded by crumbling slums.

The drive down from Philadelphia had been tiring. Dorian had started out in fog, heading south toward the sea, slowed by roads covered with snow and ice. An hour later, he was stuck in highway traffic backed up over a mile, but he stayed outwardly calm. The last thing he needed was for someone to remember his face.

A trailer loaded with sewing machines had collided with a busload of senior citizens. When Dorian finally drew abreast of the accident, his reaction at the sight of old people wrapped in blankets, waiting for medical treatment, was disgust. They had delayed him. Why didn't the old farts move to Florida?

To make matters worse, the heater in his car didn't work. He hadn't brought a scarf with him, so he pulled the hood of his sweatshirt over his head and wrapped a sweater around his neck. His nose was runny, his throat scratchy. Blame it on the guy in Philadelphia who had fixed him up with this four-wheel disaster. Fuck him.

Despite everything, Dorian arrived in Atlantic City in plenty of time to kill Alan Baksted.

The Chevy rolled to a quiet stop on a deserted stretch of Brigadier Boulevard. In the distance he made out the fog-shrouded lights of Harrah's Marina Hotel Casino. Here, just blocks away from the ocean, the fog was heavier and Dorian had to turn on the windshield wipers. One worked, one didn't. Beautiful.

Still, he could see well enough to make out the corner apartment house. Six stories, on his right facing Harrah's. Baksted's car, a gray Porsche, stood out among the three parked in front of the building. Dorian blew into cupped, gloved hands. Nice car, a Porsche, but you couldn't take it with you.

Behind him, a half-empty city bus rolled out of the fog, its lights spearing the darkness, and then it was gone, red taillights growing smaller. A man, coughing and spitting, passed, pulled by a collie on a leash toward Harrah's. Minutes later an empty cab cruised by.

The New York detective left his car, locked it, then walked the few yards to the Porsche, where he used a cigarette lighter to check the plates. *ALAN B*, front and back. Nothing like a little flash to impress the broads.

Dorian walked to the front of the Porsche, looked around to make sure he wasn't being observed, then crouched beside the left front tire. He stabbed it three times with an ice pick, and the Porsche settled closer to the ground, angling slightly to the left. Dorian stood up, tucked his hands into the front pockets of his sweat shirt and walked back to his car. Too bad he couldn't spend some time in Atlantic City. The casinos didn't close until 6:00 A.M. and he knew a couple of warm ladies, a black croupier in particular, who loved to party. Next time.

Back in the car, he lit a cigarette and settled down to wait. He was in his early thirties, a large man with a meaty handsomeness and receding red hair. He wore a jogging outfit, which was a joke because he hated running, hated all exercise. He wore dark trunks over gray sweat pants and a down vest over a hooded sweat shirt. His eyes were watchful behind pink-tinted, rimless glasses and his hair was covered by a green woolen ski cap. Before leaving the car again Dorian would exchange the cap for a black and yellow ski mask.

In New York, he worked out of an East Side precinct not far from Gracie Mansion, where he sometimes pulled special duty at official functions. Dorian Raymond was shrewd, a seasoned survivor in a world of weaker men. He was a confirmed gambler and womanizer, traits that had ended his marriage to the woman he still loved.

As a gambler, he was a consistent loser and rarely out of debt. To a gambling addict like Dorian Raymond, losing was almost as satisfying as winning. In all things, he lived for the moment and distrusted the future.

Love frightened him; the more you loved, the more someone wanted from you. And he felt there wasn't that much to him. Sooner or later he feared someone would find that out. A series of meaningless affairs was designed to hide this vulnerability. Unfortunately, they also destroyed his marriage.

Only at the end did he tell Romaine how much he cared for her.

"You don't love me," she said. "You love your version of me."

"No shit. And what version is that?"

"The one you get from fucking every woman you can lay your hands on. The one you and your cop friends have of all women. Madonnas or whores, nothing in between. I'm talking about the version that hasn't a damn thing to do with what I really am."

He suddenly realized that what truly mattered about his wife were those things he had never wanted to know.

In the Chevrolet, Dorian snapped his fingers. He had forgotten that today was Romaine's birthday. Separated or not, he should have sent flowers, a card or telephoned. He hated himself for having let it slip his mind. Another mistake to be paid for. Angry, he beat the steering wheel with the heel of his palms. Wasn't losing Romaine payment in full for everything?

Lighten up. Now wasn't the time to get bent out of shape; he had work to do. He reached for the flight bag beside him, took out a pair of jogging shoes and put them on. They were a size too small. No matter. Dorian wasn't planning to run a marathon. He reached into the bag again, this time removing the piece, a Hi-Standard .22, the smallest and one of the deadliest-caliber handguns made. A .22 caliber bullet traveled a thousand feet a second. It was the CIA's preferred handgun, as well as the favorite of professional hit men. It also took a silencer.

There was a photograph of Baksted in the flight bag, not

that Dorian needed one. He had met the casino owner a few times in Atlantic City and liked the man. Baksted had a sense of humor, had fixed Dorian up with a few dancers from the line at the Golden Horizon, and given him a line of credit at the casino. Dorian had even eaten at his house and played with his children. None of which stopped him from accepting a thirty-thousand-dollar contract to kill him.

Handsome and in his late twenties, Baksted wore the frizzed hair and drooping mustache that made him resemble the Philadelphia Italian hoods he ran with. He was sharp, good with numbers and good at putting deals together. Somehow he always found the money to cover his end, no matter how big the deal. And he never owed money. He showed respect, which the "Mustache Petes"—the mob guys left over from the days of Capone, Luciano and Genovese—appreciated. He would do favors, but often he was too greedy for his own good. He played around, flaunting his infidelity in front of his wife. Tonight he was with a seventeen-year-old dancer from one of the boardwalk resorts.

Baksted had it all: money, good looks, family, women, a future. But he wanted more. It was Dorian Raymond's job to see that he didn't get any more—ever.

"I thought Alan was protected," a shocked Dorian had said to Sparrowhawk when the Englishman telephoned him from the Cayman Islands to inform him of the contract. Baksted fronted legitimate business for Carlos Maggiore, the Mafia don who controlled Philadelphia rackets and had interests ranging from Atlantic City to Florida to London casinos.

"He was, dear boy. But it's now time to settle his account. An accord has been reached between Molise and Maggiore factions and Mr. Baksted, Alan, is redundant."

"Since when?"

"Dorian, please don't get your knickers in a twist. This isn't exactly the end of civilization. Baksted's made enemies, which carries with it a rather severe penalty. Your pay envelope for this one is thirty thousand."

Dorian whistled. He turned his back to the crowds trudging by in the snow and slush on Lexington Avenue and jammed a forefinger in one ear. He listened carefully.

"I sense I have your undivided attention," said Sparrowhawk. "By the way, how's the weather up there?"

"Sucks."

"Yes. Well, it's quite nice down here. Sunshine, salt air, rum punch. Marvelous, really. Anyway, on to Mr. Baksted, God rest his soul."

Through Marybelle Corporation, the Molise family had bought the Golden Horizon from Alan Baksted and six partners, all legitimate businessmen. Price: just under twelve million dollars. Baksted decided to keep the pigeon list for himself, letting his partners divide the twelve million. When they complained, he threatened them with Carlos Maggiore. A mere mention of that name was enough.

Baksted then proceeded to act tough with Paul Molise, Jr. To impress New Jersey's gaming commission, the Molise family wanted Marybelle partnered in Golden Horizon with legitimate businessmen. In a world of tight money, only Murakami Electronics seemed willing to buy a 10 percent interest in the casino.

"However," said Sparrowhawk, "the Nips insist on seeing the casino's list of freewheeling gamblers before handing over any yen."

"What's the big deal?" said Dorian. "Paul buys the list from Alan and that's that."

"Not quite, old boy. Paul offered the bugger two million for it, then three. Alan accepted three, then changed his mind. He upped the price to five and said take it or leave it. I should add that the name of Don Maggiore was bandied about to scare young Paul."

Dorian whistled. "Schmuck. Didn't Alan know he was risking a war with that kind of talk?"

"Ignorance is bold. Mr. Baksted's selfish behavior jeopardizes the acquisition of a major casino and manages to insult the wops into the bargain."

"Fine and dandy. That's the why of it. Now let's hear the how. I want to know how Paulie got Maggiore to dump Alan."

"Simple. *Auri sacra fames,* says Virgil in *The Aeneid.* The accursed hunger for gold."

Closing his eyes, Dorian nodded. It had to be. What Alan forgot was that in the underworld guys who despise each other will sit down for money. And money was the reason that nighttime was about to fall on Alan Baksted's dreams.

Maggiore was to have points in the Golden Horizon, nothing big, but an interest nevertheless. His corporations were to furnish the casino with insurance, cigarettes, croupiers and he could wash money through the casino if necessary. Paul would get the pigeon list, paying Maggiore a "finder's fee" of one million dollars. And there would be no full-scale war in Atlantic City to scare away the tourists. Only one hit. After that, business as usual.

Paul junior played one more trump; that card sealed the deal.

"There is the matter of a certain file," said Sparrowhawk. "It's in the office of a commission set up by the governor of New Jersey. The file deals with a secret investigation into Maggiore's dark kingdom. He would like to have a copy of it. Paul junior has promised him that Management Systems Consultants will deliver the file two days after Mr. Baksted gets the chop."

"Can you?"

"Dear boy, we've had that file in our data bank for the past month. Information is the most valuable currency of all, something every police officer should be well aware of."

"No argument there. What about the pigeon list? I assume you want me to bring it back to New York."

"I strongly recommend that you do. Mr. Baksted will have it on him."

"How can you be sure?"

"By agreeing to Mr. Baksted's terms. By arranging a meeting he will rush to, list in hand. You will intercept him near the home of his latest paramour and prevent him from reaching journey's end. Don Maggiore's minions in Philadelphia will aid you in your task. Car, weapon, the address of Mr. Baksted's current morsel and so on. Attend to this matter immediately. We don't want the Nips to lose interest, do we?"

"Wouldn't want that to happen," said Dorian. "Too bad. Alan's not such a bad guy."

"The meek shall inherit the earth, but not its pigeon lists. Oh, incidentally, Robbie's going to be fighting in Atlantic City in four days. Full-contact karate, no holds barred. Some champion or former champion is coming out of retirement to challenge him. Should be a jolly good show. Can't be there myself. Have business in Dallas."

"If I'm in Atlantic City, you'll pardon me if I don't go near the fight. Lots of New York people go down to gamble and I don't want to be recognized. I just want to burn Alan, then split."

"Of course, dear boy, of course. Just like Vietnam. Hit quick, then melt into the bush."

"Tell Robbie I said good luck."

It was just as well that Sparrowhawk kept Robbie away from contract killings. Dorian needed the money; he was fifteen thousand in debt to the shys, not counting the vigorish. The thirty thousand for whacking out Alan would pull him out of a very deep hole.

As for Robbie killing to order, he had done that in Vietnam, sometimes too well. Sure it was war, but Robbie put his heart and soul into it, doing things that even Dorian and Sparrowhawk wouldn't do. If Robbie ever started blowing people away in the States as he had done in Nam, there would be sleepless nights in quite a few places.

Dorian outweighed him by almost forty pounds but would no more think of fighting him unarmed than he would of turning queer. In a Saigon bar, Dorian had watched him destroy four Green Berets, two of whom had k-bars, combat knives, and knew how to use them, or thought they did. One had been crippled for life.

Dorian and Robbie ran into each other occasionally, but no longer had the closeness found among men in combat. Nam was in the past. These days it was a good thing Robbie got his jollies from karate competition. Sparrowhawk or no Sparrowhawk, God help the world if Robbie didn't have a private war to wage.

Dorian stood in front of the Chevrolet, ski mask on, the .22 in his waistband and hidden by the down vest. His watch read 9:10; Alan's "appointment" was at 9:30, downtown in a suite at the Golden Horizon. Business is business, Alan. No hard feelings.

Dorian began jogging, his big body leaning forward, toes turned in, elbows tight against his sides. He ran flat-footedly, mouth open, fists high. Christ on a cross. One block and he was out of breath.

He leaped on the sidewalk, out of the path of an oncoming

panel truck, then back in the street again. For the life of him, he couldn't see why anybody ran if he didn't have to. One more block, only one and then he turned. Baksted was at his Porsche. It had to be him, though in the fog it was impossible to see from this distance. What if it was somebody trying to break into the car, a nigger working the lock with a coat hanger. Terrific.

He ran, feet slapping the asphalt, wet fog licking his face. Another car came up behind and caught him in its headlights, then passed and lighted up Alan by the Porsche, kicking the tire and cursing.

He heard Dorian. He waved, flagging him down with a brown envelope. "Hey, got a flat here. Give me a hand, okay?"

Dorian withdrew the .22 from under his vest, stopped running, crouched, both hands cupping the butt, and from only four feet away fired a head shot. The .22 made a gentle *pop*, nothing louder than opening the top on a can of beer. Alan bounced off the Porsche and went down, one leg under him. The envelope lay on the hood of his car.

His throat burning from the three-block run, lungs on fire and adrenaline pumping, Dorian looked down at Alan. He fired two more shots into his head, then two more into Alan's heart before shoving the .22 back into his waistband. In the dim light, the blood on Alan's face appeared to be glittering strips of black cellophane. Dorian was fucking depressed already.

But he wasn't finished. He had to leave a message behind.

He reached into the pockets of his sweat shirt, took out several fifty-dollar bills and tore them in half. Deliberately, he tucked halves of the torn bills in Alan's jacket pocket and under the gold chains around his neck.

The message was clear. Greed.

Dorian stood up, took the envelope from the car hood and felt the hard shape of a notebook inside. He tried not to think of Alan's twin five-year-old sons.

Minutes later, in Ocean City, Dorian hung up the phone, stepped from the booth and brought the bagged vodka bottle to his mouth. Empty. Disgusted, he flipped the bottle over his shoulder into a snowbank. Romaine had been polite, thanking him for calling on her birthday. But she had also been cool, withdrawn, obviously not wanting to be hurt anymore. Finally she said she had to go; she was busy.

From Atlantic City, Dorian did not drive straight back to New York. First, he had to change cars, which meant driving fifteen minutes south to Ocean City, a quiet little town on the Jersey shore. Here he parked the Chevy on a side street, changed back into his own clothes, then crossed the street to a dark Ford. The .22 was in one overcoat pocket, the silencer in another. Let the Philly people dispose of the Chevrolet; Dorian disposed of the guns. From inside the Ford he watched a young man in an army overcoat and Phillies baseball cap leave the restaurant, get behind the wheel of the Chevy and drive off. The Chevy, like the Ford, was a stolen car and would end up in a chop shop, broken down into dozens of pieces and sold in Europe and South America.

Dorian needed a drink. He went back into the restaurant. Fucking unbelievable. Ocean City was a dry town. He would have to drive across a bridge to find a liquor store.

When he had his bottle, he sat in the car in a deserted area and drank. He thought of Romaine and of Alan, poor bastard, and Dorian knew he couldn't make the drive back to New York without speaking to Romaine. There was a public telephone booth in front of the liquor store.

But she had been *busy*. Hearing her say that word tonight, when he really needed her, was like being kicked in the heart.

Back in his Ford, Dorian slammed the door and was about to turn the ignition key when ahead of him he saw a man leave an isolated house and start jogging toward him, moving in and out of patches of moonlight and darkness. He almost dismissed the man, but something about the runner caught his eye. The man glided, moving with a practiced stride. No strain. He looked familiar, but how could he be out here in the middle of nowhere? And he carried an attaché case in one hand. He was in very good shape.

Robbie.

Shocked, Dorian acted reflexively. He hid, ducking down in his seat. A count of two and then he straightened up, turned around and stared at the runner after he had passed. Definitely Robbie. But what was he doing in the boondocks when he was supposed to be fighting tonight in Atlantic City, in front of a sold-out house? Was he running to get there on time?

It made no sense. There was nothing around but scattered houses, trees, wide sandy beaches and down the road a bridge leading to Ocean City. Robbie usually carried his *gi* and protective gear in that attaché case; each year Sparrowhawk got him a new one from London, monogrammed, with a combination lock.

Dorian watched Robbie get into a car, make a U-turn and speed toward the bridge and Ocean City. And, he guessed, Atlantic City. Swiveling around, he stared at the one-story wooden house Robbie had just left and shook his head. Strange. Tonight was a big night for Robbie in Atlantic City.

So what the hell was he doing here?

4

Atlantic City

"Rob-bie!"

"Rob-bie!"

"Rob-bie!"

They chanted his name rhythmically, clapping on each syllable and filling the arena with screaming sound. But *zanshin*, concentration, demanded that a fighter watch his enemy with eyes, mind, spirit, searching for any weakness that could be used against him. Robbie Ambrose denied himself to the thousands who called for him. He sat in his corner, his breathing even, and from under hooded eyes stared across the ring at Carl Waterling.

Waterling bled from a cut over a swollen left eye and there were angry welts on his left side, the target of Robbie's kicks. A ring doctor leaned over and gently touched Waterling's ribs. The fighter stiffened and winced, inhaling through clenched teeth. I bet it does, thought Robbie.

A card girl, blonde and pretty, mouth wet with lip gloss, began her walk around the ring, arms overhead holding a white card reading Round Three. Through the whistles and obscenities she continued smiling, but to Robbie the smile was genuine. "Good luck," she whispered. Her eyes told him something more.

Robbie concentrated so hard on Waterling that he scarcely heard the thousands of voices shouting for a knockout. Instead he heard another voice, the warrior voice. *Namu Amida Hachiman Dai-Bosatsu.* Hear, o great Bodhisatva, god of war. I am your sword, your will, your deed. The four elements—fire and water, metal and wood—are in me.

I am strong in your strength.

I have performed *Chi-matsuri,* the rite of blood.

I am the true *bushi,* the thousand-year-old samurai.

I am strong in your strength.

"Rob-bie!"

"Rob-bie!"

"Rob-bie!"

He blinked, pushing from his mind what he had done earlier tonight to the woman in Ocean City; he had performed the ritual murder that would ensure his victory here. Like the others, she had been easily fooled by the detective's badge and in the end she had given her body to the god of war.

He felt a tap on his shoulder. It was Seth, his cornerman, holding the mouthpiece. Robbie took it, feeling the rubber hard against his gums and teeth. He bit down hard. And as he stood, the roar from the crowd warmed him. He was Robbie Ambrose, with the uncanny ability to find his opponent's weakness and exploit it. He stood poised, expectant, the adrenaline moving in him, with seconds to go until the bell. . . .

It was professional full-contact karate, America's fastest-growing sport, a combination of Western boxing and karate techniques. In less than ten years it had emerged as the modern version of the historic Japanese fighting form, offering contests that outdrew the traditional karate matches (point fighting), where the techniques stopped just short of the target. Also called kick boxing, the young sport had adopted several safety measures: instead of striking with bare fists and feet, the fighters wore gloves and foam rubber kicking pads and were forbidden to strike at the groin, throat or joints.

Attacks were limited primarily to the waist and above, with strikes permitted to the thighs and calves. Each round was limited to two minutes. A fighter lost points on fouls or by failing to meet the minimum of eight kicks per round. Wins were scored as in Western boxing, by knockout, technical knockout or decision.

Tonight's fight, sold out weeks in advance, was a grudge match between two of the most glamorous names in full-contact karate. Before retiring, former champion Carl Waterling had been the only man who had ever defeated Robbie, taking a split decision from him in a close match. In his heart, Robbie knew he had won. But Waterling had been the champion and the fight had taken place in his hometown.

Two years later, Waterling, avid for the higher purses paid professional full-contact fighters, decided to come out of retirement and meet the number-one challenger, the golden boy Robbie Ambrose. Robbie was overrated, said Waterling. He was going to cut Golden Boy down to size. The popular ex-champion, with his record of sixty wins, no defeats and forty-three knockouts, was going to make a comeback against the charismatic fighter with a record of thirty wins, twenty-eight knockouts and only one defeat.

The fight generated money. An Atlantic City hotel casino underwrote the bout. Scalpers asked and got eight times the face value for tickets. A television network paid to film the fight. The martial arts press published ratings lists of fighters and covered the hundreds of tournaments held yearly worldwide, but only a handful of fights held the excitement of this one. The promoters called it "the Seaside Shootout."

As light heavyweights, the fighters weighed in between 167 and 175 pounds. Robbie Ambrose drew the most attention with his lean, handsome, blond looks and the golden stud in his right ear. Several Hollywood celebrities came to his dressing room to wish him luck. He was a star, too. Waterling was sought after, but by fewer people, none of them famous. His hatred of Robbie increased.

The crowd groaned when Waterling entered the ring. At thirty-two he was beefy, balding, noticeably out of shape. A hairy stomach hung over the black belt tied around the top of his blue silk *gi* pants and he breathed through open lips, his mouthpiece loose in front of teeth. It was obvious he had not trained. Robbie knew it and was going to make him pay for it.

In the first round Robbie attacked with a flurry of kicks, going for the soft, flabby body. He spun, turned his back to Waterling and lashed out with a kick that caught the ex-champion in the stomach and drove him into the ropes. The kick took the wind out of Waterling, and he backpedaled on rubber legs. Pursuing, Robbie shoved his right hand into Waterling's face, driving his head back, and then lashed out with a front kick, the leg fully extended, which again caught Waterling in the stomach.

He backpedaled, but Robbie caught him in a corner. A fake of the head, then two uppercuts, and the ex-champion rolled along the ropes. The audience smelled blood; it leaped to its feet and roared. Waterling counterpunched on instinct, caught Robbie high on the cheek, but did no damage. The round ended with Waterling bleeding from the mouth.

In the second round Robbie dropped Waterling twice, first with a roundhouse kick to the head, opening a cut near his eye. Waterling took an eight count, then clinched with Robbie. Near the end of the round, Robbie spun around and lashed out with a vicious backfist that staggered Waterling, who finally sat down on the canvas. The referee ruled it a knockdown, but before counting could begin, the round ended.

Round three.

Both men shuffled forward, faces hidden behind forearms and gloved hands. Waterling was out of breath. He was also afraid.

Ichibyoshi. When close enough, strike quickly, in one breath, making no prior movements, no fakes, no hesitations. Strike before the enemy escapes.

Robbie led with a right hand, hitting the cut over Waterling's eye and opening it again. Waterling, trained in Tae Kwon Do, retaliated with two high kicks common to the Korean style. Robbie blocked one, ducked under the second and before Waterling could escape, kicked him in the right thigh. As Waterling moved back, Robbie kicked the inside of his left calf and, with the same leg, kicked him in the ribs.

Waterling's hands came down to protect his body.

Now.

Ni no koshi no hyōshi. In two beats. When the enemy attempts to withdraw, fake a strike and hesitate. The enemy will tense and, for a fraction of a second, relax. Then strike without delay.

Lifting his right leg, Robbie faked a kick to the ribs, then dropped the leg. Waterling froze in place.

In a move that brought the house to its feet, Robbie leaped high in the air, spun around and, still airborne, kicked backward with his left leg, catching Waterling flush on the temple. The ex-champion's mouthpiece flew out and his arms were spread to either side. He fell into the ropes and toppled forward, falling facedown on the canvas.

There was a tidal wave of cheers from the audience. They had gotten what they had come for.

The referee didn't bother to count over Waterling. As doctors and cornermen rushed to the unconscious fighter, the referee motioned Robbie to the center of the ring, and taking his gloved right hand, he raised it in victory.

"Winner. By kick knockout. Third round. Robbie Ambrose."

Robbie smiled, turning to all four corners of the ring, acknowledging the crowd for the first time.

Minutes later in his changing room, Robbie fielded questions from the press, well-wishers and promoters intent on booking future dates. He was relaxed, answering in a quiet, almost shy manner.

"Robbie, it didn't last long. Did you follow any particular plan and when did you know you had him?"

"My plan? Keep pressing, is all. Feel him out early, see what he likes to do, how he reacts to certain attacks, but mostly stay on him. When did I know I had him? First round. I'm being honest with you when I say the man hadn't prepared. Got to prepare, got to be ready for war. That's what you face in the ring, a war."

"Robbie, do you think Morris is ducking you? I mean, he's the champion and—"

"Hey, you said it, man. I didn't. I'll fight anybody, anytime. Whether he's got a rating or not. Doesn't matter."

"Any truth that Waterling got the lion's share of the purse and you got stuck with what was left?"

He waved the question away. "Talk to the promoters about money. I got a lawyer in New York handles contracts and money. Let's just say I'm satisfied with the way things turned out."

Laughter.

"Robbie, I hear Manny Decker still trains. They say he's in great shape. Any chance of you two meeting again? Some people say that was your greatest fight, until Decker broke his knee."

Robbie picked at the protective tape around his hands. "That was my last point fight. Decker's not into full contact, so I guess he and I aren't going to meet anymore. I took him twice. Nothing left to prove there."

"Robbie, what about the World Open Championships in January?"

"You mean for the *suibin* trophy."

"Yes."

"I'll be there. Man, everybody will be there. Should be some kind of war."

Suibin was a square-shaped vase used in flower arrangements in Japanese temples, shrines and homes. The January tournament, to be held in Paris, was a world-class competition open to all black belt *karateka*s between the ages of twenty-one and forty, professional or amateur, any style, any weight. Sponsored by Japanese and European businessmen, the tournament was not only the talk of martial arts circles but had attracted the attention of the world press.

To discourage the foolhardy, contest rules required each contestant to sign a release absolving sponsors of liability in case of injury or death. In addition, each contestant had to post a nonreturnable entry fee of $700. That money was to cover transportation, hotel and living expenses of those ten *karateka*s who survived the grueling eliminations to qualify for the finals.

There was a single prize. It was a beautiful *suibin,* a replica of a priceless 1,200-year-old original on display in Japan's Imperial Palace. Like the original, the bronze replica was a square-shaped vase whose four corners rested on a miniature dragon, a fox, a gnarled tree and the shoulders of an ancient fighting monk, all in exquisite detail. A skilled workman had spent two years creating the replica, worth over fifty thousand dollars. With it came two gifts from Emperor Hirohito: a handwritten scroll and a small gift from the palace, a secret. And also to the winner went the honor of being acknowledged as one of the finest fighting men in the world.

"Morris, if you're listening," said a grinning Robbie, "I'll be at the Sports Palace in Paris, come January."

"Robbie, I've got a date in January in Los Angeles and I'd like to match you with—"

"Sorry, no business tonight. Contact Management Systems Consultants in New York. My lawyer's there and he handles bookings and contracts. If I'm free, maybe we can work something out."

"Robbie, you were dynamite out there tonight. Really took care of business."

"Thank you."

"Doctors say Waterling's jaw is broken in three places and he's got a couple of cracked ribs."

Robbie shrugged. Right now he didn't feel shit about Waterling one way or another. The man didn't exist for him any more than the woman did, the woman Robbie had sacrificed tonight to ensure his victory.

"Robbie, I'm with the network. I just want to say you were the Second Coming out there. This is my first full-contact karate fight and I'm hooked. I mean it was *Star Wars,* World War Three and the Bolshoi Ballet all in one. Robbie, we'd like a couple of quotes to use when we televise the fight over Thanksgiving weekend. We're told that something like ten million men, women and children in America alone now practice karate in one form or another."

"Hey, I guess so."

"Most, I assume, do it for self-defense. Some for exercise or whatever. What's the secret? How does one go about becoming another Robbie Ambrose?"

Robbie scratched the back of his neck. "Confidence. I mean don't just think you're going to win. Know you're going to win. Skill, technique, experience. You've got to be on a confidence level that's so high there can't be the slightest doubt about winning."

"And how does one go about getting that kind of confidence?"

"Hey, it's simple. You prepare. Conditioning, sparring, running, stretching, whatever. Do them. And above all, believe they'll work for you."

The network executive held his tape recorder closer to Robbie. "Like developing your own ritual, sort of."

A grinning Robbie looked up at him. He aimed a forefinger at the network executive's chest. The hand trailed unraveled tape. "Exactly," he said. "Exactly."

5

It was dark when Decker began his morning run in Central Park, but in minutes a red sun would appear from behind East Side high rises and tinted glass towers. He jogged toward the Seventy-second Street transverse, keeping to the middle of the road, away from the blackened snow and ice along the asphalt. The park was officially closed to traffic for a few more hours, so Decker had it to himself. At least he hoped so.

Decker was a loner, unable to commit himself to anyone. His ex-wife Marla had said, "Jesus, Manny, I wish to God I knew whether that wall you have around yourself is keeping me out or you in."

It would only have hurt her to say what she already knew, that commitment was Michi and Michi was dead. Since then his sole commitment had been to karate, a pursuit demanding loyalty only to oneself. Karate was a strengthening of the human spirit, the acquiring of confidence and peace of mind, a world he could turn to and close out all other worlds. To immerse himself in it was to be at once a part of two cultures, East and West, and yet not really a part of either.

So, Decker's was a life without obligation. He was an observer, a traveler passing through, fulfilling himself in the dojo, blessed because living in solitude allowed him to make his own laws. And that's why he had become a field associate, to make the laws himself.

At Seventy-second Street he spun around to run backward for fifty yards, lightly throwing elbow strikes with both arms and inhaling the cold air. Then he turned back, to run parallel to a frozen lake dotted with THIN ICE signs. That's me, he thought. Tap dancing on thin ice. I don't want to hurt Romaine. And I don't want LeClair to hurt me.

Romaine Raymond lay sleeping in Decker's apartment. Before leaving he had looked down at the beautiful twenty-five-year-old dancer, who slept with the same heart-stopping sensuality that made her dancing special. Her long dark brown hair fanned out on the pillow. A slim hand, fingers curled, lay on the pillow near her head. Her knees were slightly drawn up, as though executing a turn. The covers had fallen from a bare shoulder, revealing the curve of her breast. The pose was one of innocence and sensuality, both the essence of Romaine, a woman utterly lacking in guile, a woman so sexually demanding that Decker had managed only four hours sleep last night.

Earlier that evening they had gone to dinner to celebrate her birthday, before returning to her apartment. That's when her husband Dorian had called, drunk, maudlin. Afraid that he might call again, Romaine had asked to be taken to Decker's place. There he had presented her with six origamis for her birthday. She watched with bright-eyed fascination as he selected sheets of colored paper and carefully folded them into stars, birds, flowers. Michi had patiently taught him the art of paper folding, encouraged him to learn to create the intricate patterns.

And then they had sat on the floor, drinking wine in front of his fireplace, talking and laughing, and after a while Romaine turned on the radio. When she found a Hispanic station, she stripped down to wispy lavender underwear and high heels and began dancing the *salsa* for him, as if it were the most natural thing to do. It was the sexiest dance he had ever seen and he couldn't take his eyes off her.

Romaine was a truly gifted dancer who loved the world but not the business of dancing. She loved the gypsies, the Broadway dancers who went from show to show and spent their lives in class. But she hated the discipline, auditions and rejection that were so much a part of show business. All she wanted to do was dance. In the few weeks of their affair she knew Decker only as a karate instructor, whose dojo was in the same Lincoln Center building as her dance studio.

Decker had kept his identity as a cop a secret and now it was almost too late to tell Romaine the truth. He feared rejection. A cop's world was insular and dangerous and few women were strong enough to be a part of it. Marla had tried and failed.

Romaine's dance had turned Decker on and she knew it. As the fire covered her with flickering shadows and orange light, she unhooked her bra, revealing full, swaying breasts. Before he could grab her, she laughed and leaped out of reach. Decker crawled after her, caught her ankles and pulled her down on top of him. He buried his face in her breasts, wetting the flesh with his tongue. Romaine took his earlobe between her teeth, then tongued the outer edges of his ear. Her tongue was fire, igniting a lust in him that he wondered could ever be satisfied.

"Let me," she whispered. She preferred to undress him, slowly and patiently. When they were both naked, she led him, as he straddled her, balancing on his hands and knees, and placed his penis between her breasts. She trembled, moaned and squeezed both breasts tight against his hot flesh. Decker moved back and forth, and each time his penis neared her mouth, she licked it hungrily.

The electric touch of her tongue, followed by seconds without it, was tantalizing to Decker, who suddenly found her hands cupping his buttocks, nails digging painfully into his flesh. She pulled him forward until his penis was in her mouth and then she rolled them both to the side, toward the heat of the fireplace, swallowing Decker so deeply that he could not stop himself from coming. She held him close, refused to let him withdraw, swallowing and moaning, the vibrations from her throat buzzing through his loins. Her tongue flicked across his swollen flesh and he died the delicious death that was the soul of all lovemaking.

He collapsed, drained. The fire crackled and warmed him and he knew he could not move if his life depended on it.

That was only the beginning. It was hours before they made their way to the bedroom, where Decker, caught up in her unselfish desire, brought her to orgasm more times than he had thought possible. But all things are possible with clean living and the power of prayer, he told himself.

Before dropping off to sleep she said, "I could love you, Manny. I really could. You make beautiful things and you make me laugh and that makes me feel you care. When I'm with you, I feel safe. I don't know why, I just do. And it's not because of your karate. I just feel safe with you and right now that means so much to me."

She touched his lips with her fingertips. "Don't be scared. I'm not asking you to love me. I'm just saying you don't even have to be kind. Just act kind, that's all I'm asking."

For Decker, it was the most uncomfortable moment of the night, a time when he was reminded that he was hiding, pretending to be something he wasn't. A part of him knew that one day he would be found out and the one who'd get hurt would be beautiful, trusting Romaine. He did not love her. He could, however, act kind.

It was dawn when he ran out of the park and down Central Park West through still-empty streets to the dojo on West Sixty-second. He let himself in with his keys, locked the door behind him and turned on all the lights. The dojo, once a small hat factory, was a large airy room with high ceilings, polished wooden floor, one mirrored wall and windows that looked out on Lincoln Center and Broadway. Now Decker was home.

In the instructors' changing room, he stripped, toweled himself down, then wrapped his right knee in elastic bandages. When he had changed into one of the two *gis* he kept in the dojo, he left the small room and walked to the center of the floor, knelt in a formal bow, weight on one heel, bad knee to one side.

He knelt in front of a large photograph of Gichin Funikoshi, a gray-haired Japanese man whose small face radiated dignity and strength. Funikoshi was the founder of modern karate, the man who had systematized the ancient fighting form and introduced it to Japan from his native Okinawa. Decker closed his eyes in meditation and sat silently for five minutes. When his mind was tranquil and clear, he opened his eyes, bowed to Funikoshi and rose.

He began with thirty minutes of stretching exercises, starting with neck rotation, then moving down his body, arms, spine, legs. Spreading his legs he slowly sank to the floor in a perfect split, and then held the position for a full minute. Next, he swung his legs forward, stretching the tendons and muscles in his calves and thighs and spine. On his feet he twisted his trunk left, then right, before stretching it by swinging his upper body in large circles. After shaking his wrists and ankles, he kicked high with both legs, forward, then left and right, and behind. He was warmed up.

For the next half hour he practiced *katas,* selecting *Ten No Kata Omote,* a sparring *kata,* or form, designed to be practiced alone. These techniques were aggressive and powerful in the Japanese style. Nothing evasive, nothing eventual. Power delivered to the opponent.

He began slowly, always with an imaginary opponent before him, one who wanted his life and would not compromise. He stepped forward with his right foot in a front stance, using his right hand to punch to the stomach. Drawing the foot back, he stepped forward on the left side, punching with the left hand. Next he stepped forward, punching right fist to the face, repeating to the left. Then he switched to reverse punch, left foot forward, punching right hand and doing the sequence to the other side. Blocking techniques followed, lower body, middle level and face. When he had done the sequence a second time, he started over again, faster, this time with a *kiai,* a yell, on every punch. He did the entire *kata* at top speed twice more, pushing himself to eliminate seconds from his reaction time, emitting a stronger *kiai,* drawing more spirit and commitment from himself. Punch, block, counterpunch.

Finished, he stretched lightly, then began basic kicks: front, side, back, roundhouse, always starting slowly, gracefully, and steadily gathering speed until his *gi* snapped with his power and sweat poured off him onto the floor. The sun rose, found its way into the dojo, first casting long, thin shadows, then laying down golden carpets and Decker, warm, intense, *committed,* felt the sun on him and met it, wrapped himself in its fire and continued training.

He moved to the mirrored wall on his right. Instead of hand techniques this morning he practiced *empi,* elbow strikes, attacking upward, forward, sideways, left elbow, then right, performing from different stances. He knew who the enemy was now; the enemy was inside him. It was fatigue, hunger, the desire to quit. And he knew he would defeat that enemy, as he had before.

He saw the beauty of his form and was pleased, pleased at its clean lines and purity and he committed himself more, pushing his body, mind and spirit until the salt from his own perspiration blinded him and his arms ached.

When the truth he lived by in the dojo told him he could do no more, he stopped. And walked around the empty dojo, warming down, getting his breath back, satisfied with what he had achieved and allowing his mind to return to reality.

The telephone rang.

Shocked, Decker stopped. The natural order of his life could not have been more disrupted than if someone had taken a shot at him.

It rang again and he stared at it. No one had ever telephoned him here. Not even the department. An angry Decker walked to the enclosure containing two desks, file cabinets, plaques, trophies, photographs and billboards. He never wanted to be called here.

The phone rang a third time. He picked up the receiver.

"Did I disturb you?"

LeClair. Shit.

Decker, chest rising and falling, didn't trust himself to speak. The heat of resentment almost blinded him. Finally, "Finishing up."

"Good. Eases my conscience somewhat. I understand a dojo's a sacred place. Don't want to interrupt a man who's reaching out for the Almighty. Couple of things I wanted to touch base with you on."

"LeClair, I'm due in court this morning. We're filing new charges against the pimp who attacked Kanai's son-in-law.

It's now murder. I'm supposed to be at the arraignment, since I'm the arresting officer."

"Heard about Mr. Tada. Shame. Alan Baksted. As they said of Quasimodo, does that name ring a bell?"

Decker untied his black belt and hung it on his shoulder. "Kanai says he's a partner in the Golden Horizon."

"*Was,* my man. Got blown away last night in Atlantic City. Someone left a half dozen torn fifty-dollar bills on or about his person."

Frowning, Decker chewed a corner of his lip. "Terminal case of sticky fingers. He took from the wrong people, looks like."

"It would appear, Mr. Manfred. It most certainly would appear. You and I must have words. For one thing, I'd like to know where Dorian Raymond was last night. That little action in Atlantic City has all the earmarks of a shooter who knows his business. Mr. Raymond, if you remember, is a man you're to keep an eye on. What time are you due in court?"

"Nine-thirty."

"Gives us two hours—"

"With all due respect, you're forgetting something. I'm not due to see you today and I do have other cases, not to mention a whole new set of forms to fill out on the late Mr. Tada."

LeClair hesitated. Decker knew the prosecutor was trying to decide how hard to push. "Well now, Mr. Manfred, answer me this, if you will. When can I expect word from you on Dorian Raymond's whereabouts last night?"

Survival.

And who gets thrown to the wolves? *Act kind.*

Decker closed his eyes. "I know where Dorian was last night."

LeClair waited.

"Atlantic City. Called his wife from there sometime between nine-thirty and ten P.M."

"*All right.* Yes, yes, yes. Love it. Now, let's squeeze from the other side. How about getting in touch with your boy Kanai and finding out if he's heard from Marybelle about coming up with the money for a share in Golden Horizon."

"Kanai's burying his son-in-law, so he's not going to be any help to us for a while. The burial involves certain rituals, ceremonies. The Japanese regard death as a sacred sorrow. If Baksted got whacked for the pigeon list—"

"Which seems more than likely—"

"—it makes more sense to wait a week or so before approaching Kanai."

"Kind of glad I went out on a limb for you, Decker, and made the department give you that attaché case. Cast your bread upon the waters, so to speak."

"Kanai's no fool. We'll have to give him something from time to time, just to keep the game going."

"Like what?"

LeClair wasn't the type to give up anything. His next unselfish thought would be his first.

"Information," said Decker. "He smells something's wrong with Marybelle. He knows when a cop starts asking questions, it's time to start counting the silverware. If we get proof that Marybelle is a Molise front, Kanai will want to know."

"Decker, I'll tell you something that really happened. My grandfather was a black Southern Baptist preacher. Had two sons. One, my uncle, was a hunchback. Now, he heard my grandfather preaching all the time about God does everything perfect, we live in a perfect world, shit like that. One day my uncle says, 'If God is perfect, how come I'm a hunchback?' My grandfather says, 'He made you a perfect hunchback.'

"So, Decker, it's obvious that some people are born to suffer and they might as well live with it. Before you start revealing any confidences to your boy Kanai, check with me first. Is that clear?"

"Clear."

"Hey, hey," said LeClair. "Lighten up, my man, lighten up. We've got a long way to go, you and I. We do it together, we get there in half the time. Incidentally, something you might find interesting about Major Trevor Sparrowhawk. CIA is stonewalling us on him. Won't tell us dick about what he did for them in Saigon. We knew he hired out to them as an independent, but nobody wants to say what he did. Typical of those fuckers."

"I can only tell you what I heard," said Decker. "I heard Sparrowhawk killed for them. So did Dorian Raymond."

"Doesn't come as a surprise. We know that in Saigon, Sparrowhawk and Raymond also had contact with a Japanese named George Chihara. He had a daughter, who I think you knew."

"Michi. We were going to be married. She's dead."

"Sad." LeClair waited a respectful three seconds, then began again. "Cong rocket attack on her home. Bodies found and accounted for. Sparrowhawk and Raymond saw the attack, I hear."

Decker began taking the bandages from his knee. "A third man was with them. Robbie Ambrose."

"Mr. Ambrose. Yes, yes. Says here he's also a karate man. Whole fucking world's gone chop socky. Okay. Now we get another player in the game. Paul Molise, Jr., known Mafioso who sees a chance to profit by the war and shows his face in Saigon. So we got mob, we got CIA, we got American military personnel and we got one Mr. Chihara, Japanese. Not to mention one Englishman, one Major Sparrowhawk. All huddled around the same campfire. Ponder that, if you will."

"What about me? I was there, too, remember? Same time. And I knew them all."

LeClair chuckled. "They hated your guts, Decker, and you know it. That's your saving grace. You were on one side and they were on the other. You were a marine guard, and if it wasn't for your relationship with Michi Chihara, you wouldn't have had any contact with these people. Except maybe Robbie Ambrose. He beat you twice, didn't he?"

"Yes."

"Decker, you say you only *heard* things in Saigon about our happy little bunch. What brought them together? What did you hear about that?"

"Money. Narcotics, graft on Vietnam construction projects, diamond smuggling, gold smuggling, gunrunning. Everything was an open secret in Saigon, especially during those last crazy days. Especially then. Here, it's classified. Over there, even the monkeys knew what was going on."

"Well, suppose I try the CIA again. End run this time. Use a little influence. Use what you got, to get what you want, they say. Your knee okay?"

"Can't kick."

"Jesus, too bad. Well now, tomorrow morning it is. My office, nine-thirty A.M. sharp. And be nice to Mrs. Raymond,

Decker. Try a little tenderness. Women go for that shit. Little bit of kindness goes a long way."

Decker hung up first.

That night in the dojo, Decker worked his advanced students hard because he wanted to cleanse himself, to block out what he was doing to Romaine. Dorian's phone call to her had pulled Romaine closer to LeClair's ambition than Decker wanted her to be, and there wasn't a thing he could do about it. Except throw himself deeper into karate.

The dojo, the Manhattan Karate Club, had five instructors, four Americans and one Japanese. Two of the Americans, Nick and Grace Harper, a husband and wife approaching sixty, owned the club. Both had struggled in the martial arts for years, teaching, demonstrating, losing money. In good years, they just managed to get by. Since the late seventies, the dojo had shown a profit, repaying twenty-five years of the Harpers' sacrifices and belief.

Other instructors were Luke, a thirty-year-old black schoolteacher, and eighteen-year-old Tommy, a Japanese black belt who had been practicing since he was nine. Decker was the best fighter, the best teacher. He accepted no fees for teaching; he did it because he liked Nick and Grace and because they left him alone. Their dojo, near Lincoln Center and just two blocks from Decker's apartment, was on the second floor of a building that had once been a small hat factory.

Tonight the class sparred slowly, getting the feel of fighting in combinations. Decker, Luke and Tommy circulated among the students, correcting, encouraging, maintaining a tight control over everyone. Fighting could easily get out of hand, especially when tempers flared. And the greatest danger came from beginners, who didn't know how much damage they could do.

As usual, there were visitors. Some came to watch with an eye toward joining. Others waited for wives, husbands, friends. They sat on benches near the exit, whispering or not talking at all.

Decker rarely paid attention to visitors, especially when he was teaching. But tonight he saw the spectators turn their attention to a woman who stood in the doorway. Decker stopped moving around the floor long enough to let his eyes follow theirs. The woman was Japanese, small, elegant, striking. She wore a Black Diamond mink coat, a fur hat to match. Boots that probably cost a month of Decker's salary. Reluctantly he turned from her and back to his class. There were more than fifty students on the floor, fifty sets of egos that needed stroking.

Decker squatted beside a nine-year-old girl and showed her how to form a proper karate fist. Fingertips tight into the base of the fingers, thumb pressed down on top of the first two fingers. Squeeze hard.

Still squatting, he looked again toward the door. For a second he imagined that the Japanese woman was staring at him. Hard to tell with those oversized dark glasses hiding much of her face. Decker rose, watched the nine-year-old throw a few punches and look to him for approval. Grinning, he rubbed her head and nodded. And then he was walking among his students again, stopping to correct a man's stance but positioning himself so that he could see the door. Interesting. The woman *had* been looking at him.

She removed her glasses for a clearer look at him and was now putting them back on when Decker stared at her. The half smile on her face intrigued him. But he told himself, let it go. Didn't look good for an instructor to abandon a class to hit on a visitor, no matter how beautiful she was. But there was something about her that drew him closer. He wanted to talk to her.

Then she tilted her head to the left, her gaze behind the dark glasses aimed squarely at Decker. Now he couldn't look away if he wanted to. Because something in that one motion, in the way she moved her head reminded him of . . .

But it couldn't be. He shook his head to clear his mind. Definitely could not be. But the more he said that to himself the stronger the idea grew . . .

Without thinking he tapped Luke on the shoulder and said, "Take over."

Luke glanced at the doorway. There was appreciation in his voice. "Oh yeah, I can dig it."

Decker walked past him to the Japanese woman, who smiled openly at him. No mistake about it now. Visitors on the wooden benches eyed both players, the mysterious lady and the *karateka.*

Decker's reason weakened. Which part of him, he wondered, was responsible for what he now saw? His eyes? His mind, which refused to let go of the past? Or was it his heart, which could not stop loving a dead woman?

He stepped forward to embrace the illusion.

And his world changed forever.

"Michi?"

"Manny." Her voice was a whisper. But the sound of it was a scalding jolt to his sanity.

She held out her arms to him, but Decker could only stand and weep.

It was Michi. And she was alive.

Two

Kai-Ken

In feudal Japan, a knife used by
women for self-defense

6

Two hours after leaving the dojo, Decker and Michi knelt in front of a *tokonoma,* an alcove in the sunken living room of her apartment on East End Avenue. Both wore black silk kimonos with *mons,* the Chihara family crest, on the back of each sleeve. The crest, in gold, silver and white, featured a medieval bowman aiming his last arrow at an eagle soaring high against the sun. It symbolized the Chiharas' descent from the Minamoto clan, feudal Japan's most skilled archers.

A scroll, hand-painted in gold, blue, green and white, hung from the alcove's bare wall. It, too, showed a bowman, this one sitting alone in meditation beside a tree-shaded stream. He was Yoshiiye of the Minamoto clan, the first prominent archer to appear in Japan's history books. His ability with the bow, and as a battle strategist, had won him the title *Hachiman Taro,* eldest son of the god of war.

On the narrow floor of the alcove were two bronze vases; in each was a display of *ikebana,* the Japanese flower arrangement created from the barest minimum of material. With only a handful of small yellow roses and evergreens, Michi had created a *shoka* design, the heaven-man-earth presentation first brought to sixth-century Japan by Buddhist priests from China. Decker noticed that in each vase she had deliberately torn a single petal on one rose.

Furyu.

A reminder of the imperfection in perfection. A reminder that nature, like all else, was transitory, and often painful.

In the dojo they had said little to each other. *Ma,* the Japanese called it. The ability to enjoy the company of friends and loved ones in silence. The talent for mastering the pauses and periods of quiet that occur in conversation when one dares not risk saying what he truly feels. At times *ma* is mere politeness. Or a protection, a layer of outer calm and self-control. It can be called timing, a mastery of unspoken rhythms.

In the taxi, Michi did say, "I love you, Manny. I have never stopped loving you. I, we, will say the rest in time."

And Decker, because he could not measure his happiness, because he set no conditions on her returning to his life, could ask for nothing more. Quickly—it surprised him just how quickly—he fell into her rhythm. But he did say that he had never stopped loving her.

"My mother and sister died in Saigon," said Michi, "but not my father. He fell into the hands of the North Vietnamese. For years I tried to free him. I had no choice."

Decker knew the rest. *Giri.* The Chihara family was imprisoned by the tradition of a rigid and demanding bloodline, one supported by a society that was just as inflexible. The Chihara bloodline, traceable back one thousand years, was that of samurai who had served emperors and shoguns, princes and clan leaders. Eventually, the samurai themselves had emerged as an elite.

The Chiharas had always been privileged members of Japan's ruling military. During World War II Michi's father, George Chihara, had been the ultimate samurai, a member of the *Jinrai Butai,* or Divine Thunderbolt Corps, the nickname given to the *Tokko-tai,* Special Attack Forces. Kamikaze pilots.

Bad weather had forced the cancellation of George Chihara's death flight in a small rocket plane, whose nose was armed with 2,800 pounds of explosives and whose target was to have been an American destroyer transport off Okinawa. Kamikazes were considered by many Japanese to be samurai of the skies. Decker had found Chihara threatening, someone who, though bound by samurai traditions of loyalty and honor, had still become enslaved by greed.

Saigon, 1974. It was Decker's first sight of George Chihara and he never forgot it. Squat and powerfully built, with a large head of toadlike ugliness, Chihara was about to kill. Not once, but many times.

Unknown to Chihara, his daughter and Decker watched from a window in his villa as he barked a command, and dozens of maimed, starving and vicious dogs collected from Saigon's streets were driven by cursing servants, with clubs and kicks, into a large pen surrounded by thick wooden fences six feet high.

Decker, Michi clinging to his arm, looked to the right. Chihara, hard eyed and unsmiling, stood on a platform overlooking the enclosure of howling, snarling animals. In one hand was a six-foot-long Japanese bow; a quiver of arrows was slung on his back. He was dressed in a bloodred kimono trimmed in gold, the family crest on the back and sleeves. He also wore a hachimaki, *a wide headband containing the characters for* Jinrai Butai *and the red circle that symbolized the rising sun. The wearing of a* hachimaki *was part of the preparation for a great physical and spiritual effort, for combat.*

Reaching over his shoulder Chihara took an arrow from the quiver, notched it to the bow and in the tradition of Oriental archers, held the bow and arrow overhead before bringing it down and sighting on a target. Bowstring and feathered end of the arrow were squeezed between index finger and bent thumb, allowing for a smooth release.

Chihara shot his first arrow. And hit a tawny-colored mongrel in the neck, lifting the animal from its feet and into the air. The dog fell to earth and disappeared in the milling pack. A second arrow passed through the bony, sore-encrusted body of one dog and lodged itself in the jaw of another. Another shaft pinned a small dog to the inside of the wooden pen. And now panic spread among them and they fought each other to escape, vainly leaping high against the wall.

Chihara the archer, the descendant of samurai, continued to slay them.

Michi looked away. "Once a month he does this. For hundreds of years archers practiced their skills this way."

Walk easy around this son of a bitch, thought Decker. Walk real fucking easy.

For a thousand years the Chihara family had been taught to choose *giri* over *ninjo*, human feelings, to preserve the group and the institution over the individual. *Giri* was duty, loyalty, social responsibility. *Ninjo* was chaos and disorder, tragedy and unrest. For Michi to fall in love with Decker had taken great courage and he loved her all the more for it. Still, she could never completely extricate herself from the burden of those thousand years and he knew that. But in the nightmare of Vietnam, love was all he had. And he would not give it up.

Love had brought them together. In Saigon, they had met on *Tanabata,* the Japanese festival honoring two lovers—a pair of stars called Vega and Altair, who legend said were to meet once a year in July, providing it did not rain. Offering food to the heavenly lovers, crowds gathered to watch the sky and pray for good weather. They wrote poems on strips of colored paper and hung them on bamboo cuttings planted in gardens. When he met Michi on a Saigon street, amid festival crowds, twenty-four-year-old Decker, having neither garden nor bamboo cuttings, had been carrying his poem in his pocket. The twenty-two-year-old Japanese girl had been shocked to find an American aware of the custom, let alone sensitive enough to believe in it.

"The worse it gets over here," said Decker, "the more I find myself hoping. Just writing the poem made me feel better. Don't know what I'm going to do with it, though."

Michi, eyes on his face, held out her hand. Sakaye, her older sister, who had accompanied her to the festival, watched, brown eyes darting from the slim, beautiful Michi to the young American. She saw him give Michi his poem, saw their hands touch and linger there before withdrawing. Thinking of their father, Sakaye knew that what she had just witnessed presented as much danger as the NVA, the North Vietnamese army, now advancing closer to Saigon each day.

Even before meeting her, Decker knew of Michi's father, one of Southeast Asia's most prosperous Japanese businessmen. George Chihara owned two airlines, real estate in South Vietnam, Laos and Macao, a construction company, and he manufactured children's toys. And because the CIA occupied three floors of the six-story American embassy in Saigon, Decker knew that Chihara was a CIA front man, who used that connection to deal in narcotics and smuggle gold and diamonds.

Chihara's other questionable connection was with the American Mafia, the Molise family in New York. In Saigon, the Thing, as the mob called itself, had gotten rich in U.S. military construction, and in gold and narcotics. Nor had the

Thing failed to get its share of the millions connected with American base clubs scattered throughout South Vietnam. Chihara's appeal to American organized crime had been his expensive arrangements with corrupt Vietnamese politicians and certain American generals.

Chihara had been the leading *kuromaku* among Saigon's Japanese. Named for a black curtain used in the Kabuki theater, a *kuromaku* was a power broker in the dark world of Japanese business. With his steely gaze and questionable ethics, Chihara had been called "the Snake" for the speed with which he went after business rivals. The CIA needed Chihara. And because he knew too much, it also feared him.

In her huge Manhattan duplex overlooking the East River, Michi and Decker stripped, then washed before soaking in a large bath, whose walls were murals of snowcapped mountains, cloudless blue skies and ancient temples. The colors were beige and gray, black and gold, with sections of floors alternately covered in tatami and shag rugs. There was taped music—*koto,* the thirteen-string Japanese harp, and wooden flutes and the *samisen,* a Japanese balalaika with a parchment-covered sound box.

In the sunken living room, a skylight looked down on a fireplace, and telephone tie lines to Tokyo, cable television and a telex were hidden behind a black and red lacquered screen. The money for all of this came from diamonds. Michi headed the New York office of Pantheon Diamonds of Tokyo and was one of her country's highest-paid executives.

Decker told her of his work and of being a field associate, something he had kept from his family.

Michi said, "It sounds dangerous. No one likes being betrayed."

"I'm careful."

"And you are pleased to live with the tension of being a field associate."

"Like always, you read me loud and clear. Having anyone else know that much about me would be uncomfortable. You, I can accept it from."

"Because I accept you as you are. Always."

"In Saigon, I made you a promise. I said that I would

come to you, to take you with me on one of the last flights out. I did come, Michi. Believe me, I did."

"I know. I was told that you had kept your promise."

Decker closed his eyes. "Too late. Too goddamn late. The house was destroyed. Viet Cong rockets. Killed your family. Killed you, I thought."

"A friend, Kiye, you met her once, she was in the house that day and it was her corpse that was mistaken for mine. You said Major Sparrowhawk told you I was dead."

"Him. And Dorian Raymond and Robbie Ambrose. They said they saw the house get wasted. CIA confirmed their story. Christ, for a long time I hated Sparrowhawk. Hated Dorian, hated Robbie."

Michi looked at him for long seconds before asking, "Why?"

"Thought maybe they could have saved you. Never got along with them anyway. Bumped heads with those bastards a couple of times."

In Saigon, Decker and another Marine had escorted a CIA agent to a payoff with Vietnamese agents working with Sparrowhawk, who, as a soldier of fortune, had hired himself out to the CIA for good money. At the payoff site, something had gone wrong; two people had been killed. Badly wounded, the CIA agent had given the payoff money, $50,000, to Decker. Sparrowhawk, however, had insisted that it be turned over to him, to dispose of as he saw fit. Decker refused. It had ended up with Decker aiming an M-16 at Sparrowhawk's gut, ordering him to call off Robbie and Dorian.

And just before the fall of Saigon, the wife of an ambassador's aide and the Marine who was her driver had been kidnapped by several ARVN; the South Vietnamese army officers planned to hold them in exchange for a flight out of the country. Decker had learned where the Americans were being held captive and rescued them, killing three ARVN. The dead officers had been associates of Sparrowhawk's, who was enraged at what he called their needless slaughter.

Decker knew damn well that the Englishman had come up with this scheme to ensure the officers' escape from the advancing Communists and get them a seat on a plane. But there was no proof of Sparrowhawk's involvement; in any case, the CIA ordered the affair closed. No one at the embassy, especially the CIA, wanted to believe that Sparrowhawk was less than untainted, at least as long as he worked for them. And no one wanted to give the South Vietnamese, already panicky and demoralized, any more ideas about saving their skins at American expense.

"That last day," said Decker, "I tried everything I knew of to get to you. But damn, things just kept going wrong. I was ordered to pick up several officers and get them to the embassy and on to a helicopter. I had to chase around after American civilians. Never been so goddamn busy in my life. If I didn't know better, I'd have sworn somebody fixed things to keep us apart."

He did not see Michi blink. When he did turn to her she was staring down at the water in the tub. She was even more beautiful than he remembered, with ivory skin and eyes as bright as dark jewels. Her hair was shorter, but she was as slim, as alluring as she had been in his dreams. There were moments with her tonight when he was almost certain they had never been apart.

Leaving the bath, they dried themselves and put on kimonos. After kneeling quietly in front of the *tokonoma,* they rose and went into the kitchen, where Michi made tea and Decker told her that he was investigating Sparrowhawk and Dorian Raymond. Oddly enough, he sensed that she was not surprised; but he decided that she was merely showing self-control. When she said she had been in New York since September, he asked her why she had not contacted him sooner.

She poured tea for them. "I must ask this of you, Manny, that we have between us *keiyaku.* Please?"

Decker nodded. *Keiyaku* was a contract, an understanding, with room for modification of that agreement as circumstances dictated.

Michi said, "Please when we are in public, call me Michelle. I am Michelle Asama, of Eurasian descent."

He waited for her to explain.

She sipped tea, holding the cup in two delicate hands, each of which had a jade ring on the forefinger.

"My father, as you know, had dealings in Saigon that were not always moral and truthful. That part of him I wish to cut away from myself. I do not wish the attention of American authorities or the CIA or anyone else who might associate me with him and that time. I have a new life now."

"You do not wish me to ruin it for you. Is that why you came to me tonight in the dojo?"

"I would not have come if I did not still love you and you know the truth of this. But yes, I did not wish to be embarrassed by an unplanned meeting and so I did come to you. But there is no second word with me. Sometimes we children of samurai are allowed *hoben no uso,* the truth of convenience. What you call 'white lies.' But I am not telling you that."

"I believe you. Michelle. Pretty name. French."

She poured tea for him. "The French are still in Indochina years after their defeat. I suppose the same will happen with the Americans. So it is agreed between us, then. I am Michelle. In public."

"You knew I would agree before you asked."

"Yes."

He looked at her again. She was stronger, yes. More determined. At twenty-eight, she looked ten years younger. For some reason he suspected she already knew quite a bit about him, and that was why she was not asking those questions one asks after a separation of six years. Decker pushed the thought aside. Nothing must come between him and Michi. Nothing.

"Your father," he said.

"He was sold to the Viet Cong. They had a price on his head. Someone decided to collect. Do not ask me who. In time, Manny. In time."

She left him to return to the alcove, where she stood as though gaining strength from her ancient ancestors. Decker joined her. For the second time that night, he wept. And when she reached over and took his hand, he remembered another promise they had made to each other, in another time, in another sacred place.

Tokyo. They had flown there on separate planes, to temporarily escape the war and her father. Here, they had climbed the short hill to Yasukuni Shrine, one of Japan's most famous religious centers. The grounds and all of the buildings were dedicated to the souls of soldiers who had fought and died for the nation. Michi and Decker walked among cherry blossom trees, gazed at stone lanterns hundreds of years old and took water from a little trough to purify their lips before entering some of the sacred buildings. In front of the Main Worship Hall they tossed coins in a box, clapped their hands to awaken the sleeping gods inside, then folded their hands, bowed their heads and made a wish.

Michi said, "Even if we die separately, we shall meet again and bloom in the garden here, which is a haven for all flowers."

"We will meet here after death, Michi. I promise."

In front of the alcove she said, "Do you understand that my obligation to my family, to my father comes before all else. Even before you?"

"I understand." He didn't like it, but there was nothing he could do.

From the alcove she led him to the small room where she slept. In Japanese fashion, Michi slept on the floor, on *futon*, quilted bedding sweetened by pine scent. Both slipped out of their kimonos and Decker stared at her lovely, small-breasted body, remembering, wishing. It wasn't necessary to make love to her. Not yet.

To hold her was enough. They lay side by side under a pale lavender quilt. But more questions floated to the surface of Decker's mind. He said nothing. Instead, he fought against sleep. Jesus, he didn't want to close his eyes and have it end, to awake and find Michi, Michelle, gone. And him alone in his own apartment, still pained by her loss.

But Michi stroked his face, fingertips brushing the scar over his nose, her lips on his eyes, and she told him that she would be beside him in the morning. He gave up the fight and fell asleep in her arms.

Michi held him, stroked his hair.

Waited.

And when his breathing grew deeper and his grip on her relaxed, she knew that she could leave. Easing off the bed, she knelt, hands folded, and stared at him. He didn't move. She knew he wouldn't, for she had drugged his tea.

Slipped the tablet in his cup.

A tear formed in a corner of Michi's eye and slowly made its way down her cheek. *Where there is love, there is pain.*

She pressed her temples with both fists. To reason about love was to lose one's reason.

Manny, my dearest love, forgive me.

She walked from the room, leaving him alone with his ghosts, his dreams.

In the kitchen, she emptied Manny's teacup and washed it. He was clever; she had seen the unspoken questions on his face tonight. Sooner or later those questions would have to be answered. Michi would have to be careful around him, which meant a constant awareness of small things.

Teacups, for example.

Next she dressed hurriedly, pants, boots, sweater, and walked to a small study, where she sat down at a desk to await an expected telephone call. *Small things.* She pulled the phone toward her, lifted it and turned off the bell that would sound when the phone rang. After a few seconds she reached under the desk blotter and removed a photograph she had hidden there. The photograph could mean Michi's death.

Taken six years ago in a nightclub on Saigon's Le Loi Boulevard, it was a black-and-white shot of five men sitting around a table; behind them stood Vietnamese and Thai hostesses, thin-shouldered women each in *ao dai,* the sensuous tuniclike dress. Michi's father was the center figure. On his right was the hawk-faced Paul Molise, Jr., and Dorian Raymond; to the left was Robbie Ambrose and Trevor Sparrowhawk. As if convinced of their betrayal, none of the five men was smiling.

Treachery did occur. Michi's father, mother and sister had been destroyed by the four Americans. As the sole survivor, she was obligated to avenge her dead. Repay injury with justice, said Confucius. Dishonor, said samurai tradition, was a scar on a tree, growing greater with time. After six years it was now time for Michi to kill the four Americans.

From a desk drawer she removed a *sambo,* a white wooden tray on which rested a *kai-ken* wrapped in tissue paper. Wound tightly around the knife's black and gold handle were interwoven gold and silver threads. Its polished nine-inch blade was razor edged and spotless. Taking the knife in one hand, Michi slowly sliced the throats of the Americans in the photograph. Her hand was steady; her eyes never blinked.

Finished, she returned the knife and tray to the drawer and

locked it. Then, taking the photograph, she walked to the living room, found a table lighter and stepped to the fireplace, where she dropped the mutilated picture on an empty grate. She opened the damper, then thumbed the lighter's tiny wheel, firing the corners of the photograph. It burned quickly, edges curling, blackening and then all of it disintegrated, floating up into the chimney in wispy bits.

Back in her study she had only a minute to wait before the small red light near the telephone dial began blinking. Michi brought the receiver to her ear, then spoke.

"I can come to you now."

She hung up and walked to the entrance of the room where Decker slept. Did he love her enough to forgive once he learned what she had done? Where one pardons, one could also condemn.

She went to a closet, found her fur coat and seconds later was in the hall, walking toward the elevator.

7

Dorian Raymond's apartment on Manhattan's Amsterdam Avenue and 110th Street faced the largest Gothic cathedral in the world, the Cathedral of St. John the Divine. Over the years it had become known as St. John the Unfinished, with only two-thirds of the church having been completed since stonemasons began wielding trowel and mortar in 1892. Dorian's apartment was equally unfinished, not that he gave a shit. After his separation from Romaine, a cop he knew had stumbled upon the dead and decaying bodies of twin seventy-five-year-old sisters in the apartment. They had died of natural causes, one of a heart attack, the other of starvation. It coincided with Dorian's needs at the moment. He was on the phone to the landlord while the bodies of the dead sisters were being wheeled down the hall. Why not?

Take care of numero uno.

All the interior decoration Dorian needed came from the police property clerk: a cheap bed, black and white television set, sagging couch, fridge, card table, a pair of folding chairs. On the bad side, the apartment was a little too close to Harlem to suit him, but at least he could handle the rent.

Tonight he blow-dried his hair in front of the bathroom mirror and reminded himself why he disliked the truth: once you knew it, you had to do something about it. Today he had made phone calls, told lies, spent a few bucks and come up with an educated guess about Robbie Ambrose. Which was that our Rob was a stone killer, a rapist-murderer who had trashed a few broads with his hands. And cock.

Problem: what to do with this bit of news. Give up Robbie? Or use the information to benefit Dorian Raymond in some way. True, a stronger case would have to be made before Robbie could legally be charged. No prosecutor would risk his reputation on the little that Dorian knew so far. But instinct and experience told him he was right. When it came to women, Robbie Ambrose was a headcase.

A homicidal looneytune.

Go back to Nam. There, Dorian learned that he hadn't known Robbie all that well after all. Take those occasions when Robbie went on missions alone, or with someone other than Dorian or Sparrowhawk. That's when Dorian heard the stories about Robbie being a *double veteran,* a soldier who had sex with a Vietnamese woman before killing her. More than a few of them did it. Not Dorian. Shit, you drew the line somewhere.

He asked Robbie about it one day. The two of them were getting bombed on *bami-bam,* beer, and joints laced with opium. That made answers to questions a long time in coming. "Hey, man, what the fuck can I tell you," said Robbie finally. "All *fugazi* over here. All fucked up. Number ten. The worst. Don't matter what goes down in this asshole country, know what I mean? Hey, papa-san, don't believe everything you hear, okay?"

Trouble was, Dorian had heard it from people who knew what they were talking about. Some of them, god, they weren't even women; they were ten-year-old girls and they had been fucked, then killed with rifle butts, with wire tightened around their throats until they were practically beheaded, by C-4 plastique explosive attached to their thighs and vaginas, by being driven at bayonet point into mine fields. As laughing Americans watched.

Women killed after sex. Deliberately. By fresh-faced boys from the good ol' U.S. of A.

But what the hell, Jack, it was Nam. *Fugazi.* Fucked up. Don't even think about it. *The only way to go was home.* Think about that.

And then there was today, just hours after Dorian had put Alan Baksted out of the casino business. After a hit, he always checked newspapers and television newscasts. Curiosity. And some small sense of pride. This morning, at an out-of-town newsstand near Times Square, he checked Atlantic City, Philadelphia and the main Jersey papers for news about the late Alan B.

Made it. Front page in most, no less than page three in the rest. In New York the best he could do was page four in the *Daily News,* but he did pick up a paragraph in the New York *Times,* a first. Not bad.

Now came the hair in the butter, the turd in the punch bowl. It was a paragraph at the end of the Baksted story, a few lines with an Ocean City dateline. A woman had been raped and murdered. She had been a clerk in an Atlantic City gift shop, also moonlighting as a part-time hooker. Dorian frowned. Fucking unreal. In seconds his mind began to collect bits and pieces and shuffle them around.

Before returning to the precinct, he threw away the out-of-town newspapers and purchased copies of every karate or martial arts magazine he could find. Christ, it seemed that everybody and his brother was into this shit. Women as well. Old Rob had made all of the magazines. Dorian was impressed.

Robbie was ranked the number-one light-heavyweight title contender in something called full-contact karate, which Dorian assumed meant nobody pulls their punches. He was on the cover of three magazines, was the subject of stories in all of them and his matches seemed to draw the biggest crowds. A fucking superstar. Almost thirty knockouts.

Stories covering several months of tournaments told of Robbie's fighting in Dallas, Minneapolis, Atlanta, Oklahoma

City. All victories by knockouts, nothing past the fifth round. There were other stories: Robbie's favorite fighting techniques; his plans to enter some world tournament next January; his challenge to the full-contact world champion in his division, who seemed to be ducking him. And why not, thought Dorian. You'd need a grenade in each hand to stop Robbie.

Back at his desk in the back of a crowded, frantic squad room, Dorian listed the dates of Robbie's most recent four fights. Then the detective reached for the telephone. In less than twenty minutes he had his answers. According to police departments in four cities, a woman had been raped and killed within twenty-four hours of the day on which Robbie fought in those cities. And while a weapon might have been involved, it was believed in most cases the woman had been murdered by someone who knew how to use his hands.

Karate? Boxing?

Either one.

In those conversations with the four police departments, Robbie's name never came up. Nor did Dorian mention why he wanted the information. The people he talked to didn't give a shit. They had other things to worry about.

Dorian saved New York for last. Bingo. Two weeks ago a woman who worked as a story editor for a film company had been raped and murdered in her Fifth Avenue office. That information came from the green sheet. Since none of the martial arts magazines had any news on this month's karate matches, Dorian phoned the biggest magazine at its California office and learned that there had been a major match in Madison Square Garden the night the film lady had gotten wasted.

Main event: Robbie Ambrose vs. Canada's light-heavyweight champion.

Robbie Ambrose the winner by a knockout in the second round.

At that point, Dorian left the squad room to walk outside in eighteen-degree cold and he didn't stop walking until he found a bar, where he swallowed two doubles. Scotch, with beer chasers.

Five very dead ladies.

All disposed of by someone who could use his hands and it

came up Robbie every time. Lord, tell me what I do next. Sparrowhawk. Dorian rested an elbow on the bar and covered his eyes. The Englishman would go bananas when he learned what Robbie had been up to in his spare time. He loved that bastard as if he were his own son. What's more, he wouldn't take kindly to Dorian harming him. Sparrowhawk was no one to have for an enemy.

Handle this one carefully, Dorian. Get smart, for once. Learn more about Robbie and his peculiar little ways, then figure out what's best for you.

Dorian looked at himself in the mirror behind the bar. He had a scary thought. Had Robbie killed before *each* fight? Oh, God, if he had it meant he had murdered *thirty women.*

Dorian bowed his head. Unreal. And dangerous information for any man to have, should Robbie ever find out about it.

In the bathroom of his apartment, Dorian turned off the blow dryer. He needed a drink. Then the downstairs buzzer rang and he grinned, raising his eyebrows in mock lasciviousness. Party time. He patted his hair, took a swig of mouthwash, spat it out. And checked his hair again. Then he trotted to the kitchen to buzz downstairs.

When the door to his apartment buzzed, he patted his hair once more. Jesus, why wouldn't it grow back? The money he had spent on treatments, salves, blow dryers, creams, clinics, pills. Just wasn't fair. On the way to the door, he turned down the lights, the better to hide his hair.

He opened the front door and smiled. "Well, all right, all right, all right."

She stepped inside and he closed the door behind her. Locked it. Looked at her again. Fucking beautiful. Different. Class.

She stepped into his arms and he drew her into him. Mouths, tongues met. His hand squeezed her buttocks. He got hard in record time. She helped. She found his penis, squeezed and Dorian was seconds away from coming in her hand. Her teeth nipped at his tongue.

He picked up Michi and carried her into the bedroom.

It had been easy to maneuver him into boasting. Sex, then flattery. Vanity was his weakness, drugs and liquor his vices.

Michi sipped from one glass, constantly refilling his, avoiding the drugs. She sat up in bed, sheet drawn close to her, head cocked to one side.

Listening.

Dorian, on his back, drew on a joint, held the smoke in his lungs before exhaling. "Everybody's fascinated by the mob. Ever since *The Godfather,* all you ever hear is the mob, the mob, the mob. Bunch of comedians. Mob guy I know is scared somebody's trying to kill him, so every morning he sends his wife out to start the car. If she don't get blown up, that sucker comes out and drives off. Fucking sweetheart. When I was new on the force I listened to some wiretaps on which you had the Mafia listening to opera. I asked somebody why. I mean the people in crime, by and large, ain't brain surgeons. I mean they get caught, right? Anyway, guy tells me the only language some wise guys speak is Italian. That's why they listen to opera. It's the only music they can understand."

He giggled. "You Jap women sure can fuck. I mean that as a compliment."

Michi stroked his thigh. "Tell me about the smart one, about Paul Molise."

Women. Turned on by crime, by hoods, by cops. Always. Dorian giggled, remembering the woman who insisted that he shove four bullets up her ass one by one before allowing him to fuck her.

"Paulie," he said. "Yeah, Paulie. Paulie the Beak, they call him, though he doesn't like to hear that. Has this big schnozz, this long nose. Doesn't mind being called Hawk, but otherwise don't get cute about his nose.

"Paulie's got smarts. I mean, who else figures out that by owning half the flea markets in New York, you got a great outlet for stolen goods. Paulie did. People go to flea markets all the time these days and they buy stolen shit and don't even know it. Stolen securities, ripping off union pension funds, defaulting on bank loans, discount stores, storing toxic wastes. Plus the usual shit. Porn, drugs, hijacking. Christ, this joint's had it."

Michi said, "I'll make another one for you." She did, licking the ends slowly, performing before Dorian's glazed eyes.

He grinned, remembering.

She lit the joint for him. "You said that Paul Molise is a legitimate businessman."

"Said he thinks he is." He took a deep toke on the joint. "Thinks he is. Park Avenue office, English secretary, computer, telex. Keeps regular hours, nine to five. Like clockwork. Doesn't even cheat on his wife. Can you imagine that shit? Goes home to Westchester like some kind of stockbroker."

"Does he not have men with guns in his office to protect him?"

Dorian snorted. "See, that's what I mean. Movie shit. Paulie's a businessman and he deals with other businessmen, legit guys, and you can't have shooters hanging around when that happens. Scares people. Attracts attention. He's got a chauffeur acts as a bodyguard, but the guy doesn't follow him around the whole time. Chauffeur's probably packing."

"Packing?"

"Gun." He aimed a forefinger and cocked thumb at her.

"Oh."

"How's your security system working?"

She bowed her head and smiled. "*Dōmo arigato gozai mashite*. Thank you very much."

A few weeks ago, Dorian had received a telephone call at the precinct: could he perform a security survey at Pantheon Diamonds on Madison Avenue. He had been recommended by businessmen who had met the detective at Gracie Mansion and been impressed by him. Dorian, like many cops, had an eye on the future. That's why a smart cop made as many contacts in the business world as possible, for the day when he wasn't on the force anymore.

He showed up at Pantheon Diamonds and made recommendations: a steel door instead of the glass-paned one they had at the entrance; new safes, with combinations to be changed frequently; deadbolt locks on the front door, locks at least two feet apart. Check with Management Systems Consultants for burglar alarms and security guards.

Michi, he knew her as Michelle Asama, was there. Nice. First-class stuff. Reminded him of Saigon, of the few good things about being over there. She was the kind of woman seen in that city's excellent French restaurants, on the arm of a Vietnamese general or French businessman. Expensive. Too expensive for most Americans, though Dorian had found ways to come into money while in Nam. A lot of money.

After the survey, Michi had phoned the precinct to thank him. Dorian had nothing to lose. He invited her for a drink. She accepted.

Dorian drew on the joint. He was getting sleepy, close to nodding out. "Met a few Japs in Saigon. Man, your people are fucking strange. Never invite you to their homes. We never saw this guy's family, this guy we had some dealings with." He hesitated. "Never saw them until the end."

Michi leaned forward. "The end?"

His eyes were on the ceiling. He spoke reluctantly, not wanting to remember. "Fall of Saigon. Just before the Communists took over."

Just before you betrayed them, thought Michi.

He touched her. She flinched. He didn't notice.

"Never in the fucking home," he said. "Like you."

"We are private people. We live within ourselves. The explanation of everything is within yourself."

"If you say so." He finished his drink. Michi refilled the glass.

Dorian said, "Within, huh? Only within I like is getting within you."

He became drowsier, slurring his words, spilling liquor on himself and the bed. She could have killed him easily, swiftly, with her bare hands. She was skilled enough. But she needed him, needed the information he could give her about the other three. Dorian Raymond was the weak link, the man who could more easily be used than the others.

"You almost fell asleep," she said.

He giggled. "Almost. That's my father's nickname for me. 'The Almost Man.' Almost became a lawyer. Quit college after a year. Bored out of my bird. Baseball tryout with the Mets. Almost made it. They almost signed me to one of their farm clubs but what the hell. Couldn't hit curves and breaking balls. Almost made it. No fucking patience for college or law school or hanging around the minors for five years. Too much in a hurry, my father says. 'The Almost Man' is always in a hurry."

He sighed. "Almost stayed married. Almost. Nice people, my old lady. Ain't got diddley squat to give her and I wish I did. She deserves the best. Just a sweet, sweet lady. Think she's got something going for her, though. Another guy. I just feel it."

He fell asleep.

Michi took the remainder of the joint from his fingers and angrily screwed it into an ashtray. He would die when it was right for him to die.

She dressed, and thought how pleased she would be to kill him.

Dawn. Decker's internal clock had trouble functioning this morning, but eventually one eye opened, then the other. It had been one of the deepest, most relaxing sleeps he'd had in some time. *And it hadn't been a dream.* Michi lay beside him on the floor, her face gentle and vulnerable in sleep. He leaned over, smelled her, closed his eyes with pleasure. In sleep she reached for him, her small fist closing around his thumb as a child might do. He smiled, kissed her hair and lay back down beside her.

When she opened her eyes, they made love.

And made promises.

8

Incensed and running out of patience, Trevor Sparrowhawk walked to a window and opened it with vehemence. Chilled night air rushed into the cramped, humid room. The silver-haired Englishman filled his lungs. He was close to stalking out of the hastily called meeting. Let Paul bloody Molise handle the problem himself. Then we would see who knew more about security matters: a professional soldier or a spaghetti eater.

They were on Long Island, in attendance at the opening night of a new auditorium, a circular, futuristic design of white marble, tinted glass and steel. Through a series of dummy corporations and front men, it was the latest legitimate business venture of the Molise family.

Through the open window, Sparrowhawk heard the clamor from a sold-out house of over twelve thousand people. With the exception of invited dignitaries, all had paid outrageous prices to see the hottest pop star of the moment, a tubercular thin English youth in green eyeshadow and lipstick and rolled socks stuffed down the front of his skin-tight trousers.

Back in his chair, Sparrowhawk lit a Turkish cigarette, crossed his legs and looked at the five men clustered around the one desk in the office. Paul Molise was the central figure, dark skinned, tall and long nosed; in his impeccably tailored three-piece suit he looked more like a high-priced surgeon than a merciless thug. Closest to him, and openly enjoying Sparrowhawk's discomfort, was the hairy and smirking Constantine Pangalos. Then there was Lloyd Shaper, bearded, portly, an accounting genius, and Livingston Quarrels, blond and blue-eyed, a Jew passing himself off as a Connecticut WASP. Quarrels, an attorney, headed one of Molise's dummy corporations and was one of three front men nominally in charge of the new auditorium.

Because the auditorium was important for Long Island, opening night had drawn New York's lieutenant governor, Senator Terry Dent, three borough presidents, along with other political and civic notables. Celebrities included sports figures from New York's professional teams, plus Broadway, film and television stars. Press coverage was extensive. Which is why Sparrowhawk demanded that security be perfect, an idea that had brought him into conflict with Paul Molise. And Molise's foul temper.

What they had clashed over was tonight's skim, money taken from admissions and concessions to avoid paying taxes.

Constantine Pangalos had devised the idea of listing the auditorium's official capacity as twelve thousand three hundred and thirty-two, some five hundred short of the actual total. Income from these *invisible* seats went directly to the Molise family, and since they controlled concessions for food, drink, T-shirts and programs, they skimmed from these receipts as well. Tonight's total skim came to almost seventy thousand dollars. Molise wanted that money carried to Manhattan and placed in a safe at Management Systems Consultants' office, where it would be picked up within hours and taken to the Golden Horizon in Atlantic City. Now. No excuses.

Intelligent men always make the same mistake, thought Sparrowhawk: we refuse to believe that the world is as stupid as it really is.

Tonight, Molise had brought only his bodyguard-chauffeur with him. Others associated with the family, particularly known hoodlums, had been told to keep away from the auditorium on opening night. Too much press, too many police on hand. Molise himself had entered the auditorium office unobserved and would remain there until it was possible to leave the same way.

Without men of his own to do his bidding, the next best thing was to order Sparrowhawk's men around, something the Englishman opposed.

"Cut the shit, Trevor," said Molise. "I said get four of your men in here now and I mean it. I want this money out of here before anybody starts poking around. I'm talking about tax people. Federal, state, local, whatever."

"And I tell you, I don't have four men to spare. I need every man I can get. We're fighting gate crashers, not to mention groups of drugged cretins trying to get in without paying. Barely holding our own against them. We're dealing with scalpers, counterfeit tickets, screwed-up seating arrangements and, God help us, backstage security. And that little twerp entertaining the throngs out front keeps mentioning John Lennon, so we have no choice but to assign a dozen guards to him."

"Fuck him."

"You're both consenting male adults and from what I understand, he might even enjoy it. Be that as it may, it's in his contract that we supply sufficient security."

Molise slammed a hand down on the desk. "Trevor, you're not in the army now. Somebody else gives the orders. You take them."

The Englishman's permanent squint hardened and he stared at Molise. Angry. His voice was a soft monotone. "We've had incidents tonight in the parking lot. Tire slashings, dope dealings, fights. As I said, we've managed to contain the situation so far, just barely. When the concert's over, we'll still need every man and the local police. Dignitaries must be escorted to the party two and a half miles away. We do want them to get there, don't we? Don't want them stabbed in the parking lot or urinated upon as they bend over to unlock their car doors, do we? Don't want them to rush the stage and kill our star performer, do we? Don't want to have the fans being trampled to death, do we? We've had emergencies tonight and on balance, my men are acquitting themselves quite well. However, there isn't an extra man to spare right now. You could put this entire auditorium venture at risk by insisting I try and supervise this opening shorthanded."

Pangalos used a pinky finger to dig wax from his ear. "*Now* is a very small word, not hard to understand. Paulie says now. I mean, what's to understand?"

Sparrowhawk eyed him coldly. "Tell me, please: does *Paulie* wipe his arse north to south or east to west. If anyone here knows, besides *Paulie,* I imagine it would be you."

Someone in the room snickered, someone else coughed. The Greek lawyer froze, finger still in his ear. His nostrils flared. He forced a smile, shook his head. One of these days, Birdman, one of these days. All Pangalos had to do was wait. And remember.

Asinine, thought Sparrowhawk. All of it. All of them. He stood up. "Paul, a single negative incident tonight and you've undone months of work. The press will see to that and the press is something we haven't bought and paid for just yet. If we let it be known that we cannot provide adequate security, all future bookings will disappear faster than a Jew's foreskin."

Livingston Quarrels laughed the loudest.

Paul Molise leaned back in his chair, listening.

"One night, Paul. One night makes or breaks this auditorium. I need every man I have. Can't spare one. Well, perhaps one. Robbie. If the money has to go now, let him take it. He's licensed to carry a gun and you know how good he is."

Molise inhaled. He was coming around. "Cash-flow problem at the Golden Horizon. Right now I need every dime I can get my hands on. Can't reach that fucking Jap Kanai. Still dragging his ass over his dead son."

"Son-in-law."

"Whatever. And even if I do get him to pop for ten percent I'll need more money for renovations, twice as much as I'd planned on. Look, Robbie's fine, but one man. Shit, that worries me. Two, okay, but one. Don't like it."

Sparrowhawk had won. At last. "Two men sounds bloody good. And I have just the second man. Dorian. He's here tonight with a rather smashing Japanese girl. Michelle Asama. She's one of our clients."

The men in the room knew who she was. And approved. Was Sparrowhawk the only one who found the idea of her and Dorian Raymond an extremely odd coupling? She was intelligent, cultured, capable of running a business; not the sort of woman one normally expected to find in the company of Dorian Raymond.

Sparrowhawk had met Michelle Asama a few times, first at her Madison Avenue office, where he had personally checked the installed burglar alarms, new safe, new door and introduced her to the security guards who would be protecting Pantheon Diamonds. And he'd met her on a few occasions with Dorian Raymond. She had clung to formality with him, always calling him *mister*, saying as few words as possible. While it may have been the Japanese way, Miss Asama still seemed more formal than called for.

Was it his imagination or did he detect in her a hostility toward him? Not to worry. She was a client, paid her bills on time and one should never mix business with pleasure in any case. Let her be as glacial as the Antarctic. Sparrowhawk was devoted to his wife Unity and after more than twenty years of marriage still preferred her company to that of other women.

Molise was talking to Sparrowhawk, agreeing to the idea of using Dorian and Robbie. But the Englishman only half listened. Something about Michelle Asama that Sparrowhawk had encountered tonight danced on the edge of his subconscious.

Backstage earlier, she and Dorian had been among the crowd sipping champagne, mixing with politicians and celebrities all happily posing for cameras. Not Miss Asama. She had been adamant about not being photographed. Shades of Jacqueline Onassis, thought Sparrowhawk. Or was she part

American Indian and terrified that the camera would steal her soul?

He had managed to engage her in a brief conversation, first complimenting her on the lovely black and white Halston she wore, with a white gold and black diamond pin on her heart. As usual, Miss Asama had seemed less than enthralled by his presence. Somehow the matter of education had come up, which led to a few words on French literature. Sparrowhawk had made a reference to the published works of Baudelaire.

Holding a champagne glass in front of her beautiful mouth and looking elsewhere, Michelle Asama said, "Baudelaire did not publish works, major. He published one single volume of poetry, *Les Fleurs du Mal.* If you are interested in *works* by French poets of that period, *symbolistes* they were called, I suggest you read Verlaine, Rimbaud and Mallarmé."

She turned away, leaving him more irked than angry. He knew his literature as well as any man, but she was right. Baudelaire had debauched himself into an early grave and hadn't lived long enough to turn out *works.* Still, Sparrowhawk didn't like the way she had made him feel like a schoolboy who had just been paddled across his backside.

Sitting in the office with Molise, Pangalos and the rest, Sparrowhawk suddenly remembered.

Major. Michelle Asama had called him major for the first time. She had never done that before. What's more, he doubted if she'd ever heard Dorian use the term. In the nauseating informality of all Americans, Dorian too often insisted on calling him *Birdman* or *Tweety Pie,* a vile habit acquired in Vietnam. He did use the name Trevor on occasion, but never major. Even if he had mentioned it to Miss Asama, he would have said it once in passing and not repeated it. Why would she associate that rank with him? Even Molise never called him major. Sparrowhawk himself no longer used the term. Only Robbie still accorded him that honor.

Molise said, "Let's go with Dorian and Robbie before I change my mind. Dorian's got a car, if I remember. How much should we give him?"

Sparrowhawk said, "Sorry. Would you repeat the question?"

"Dorian. How much?"

"Thousand should be sufficient. Bugger's only driving from here to Manhattan. Doesn't have to know how much he's carrying, either. He does have that Japanese girl with him."

Molise shrugged. "She can tag along with him. Looks normal, having a woman along. Dorian's a cop. He can give her a song and dance about having to return to the city on cop business. Tell me something: how does a schmuck like Dorian end up with a class act like her?"

Pangalos said, "Her side lost the war, so she's got to pay."

"Glaucoma," said Quarrels. "Check her eyesight. You'll find she has glaucoma. She thinks Dorian's Clint Eastwood."

Molise said, "A dipshit like Dorian getting into her pants. Go figure."

Had Michi made a mistake? Part of her said what happened had been unavoidable. The rest of her issued a warning: leave the auditorium as soon as possible, before questions were asked.

She waited in a narrow hallway before a closed door and a uniformed guard. Dorian was on the other side of that door, summoned by Sparrowhawk and Paul Molise. Were they discussing her? Had she somehow slipped up and betrayed herself? *Did they know about the incident in the ladies' room just minutes ago?*

She forced herself to stay calm, to tune out the uproar from the auditorium behind her. There must be no fear in her; fear weakened and robbed the mind of its powers.

The office door opened and she saw the four of them together—Molise, Ambrose, Dorian and Sparrowhawk. She turned away before the hatred on her face could betray her. Then Dorian had his arm around her shoulders. "Okay, babe. Time to roll." He carried an attaché case.

"Cop business," said a grinning Dorian. "Got to get back to Manhattan right away."

He was lying, but she didn't care. They were not onto her after all. She offered a prayer of thanks to the gods and to her ancestors. Before she finished, all four of them would be dead. She let him take her elbow and guide her out of the building and toward the parking lot.

* * *

Interrogation was an art at which Sparrowhawk excelled. In the course of his military career, he had interrogated men and women in Africa, Asia, Ireland, Europe, the Middle East. He had broken some, killed others and left his mark on the rest. But tonight at the auditorium he faced an interrogation session that was a first: he was about to question three American teenage girls about an incident that occurred minutes ago in a ladies' room. It could be that the incident was part of the opening hysteria. Or it could be something more. Sparrowhawk and two uniformed guards were in a barely furnished office with the three girls, who appeared to regret having come forward with their story. Recognizing this, the Englishman began working to put them at their ease. Softly, softly catchee monkey.

"Ladies, first let me say how grateful I am that you have voluntarily chosen to help us with our inquiries. Our security can only be better for it, thanks to such good people as yourselves. And I stress again that this is not a police matter. Your story will be held in strictest confidence. This need not concern your families, unless you wish it to."

The girls shook their heads *no*.

Sparrowhawk clapped his hands together. "Good. To begin. Oh, incidentally, anyone who entered the ladies' room to indulge in forbidden activity"—he paused, winked—"such as milk and cookies, well, all is forgiven."

Nervous giggles.

"There will be no search of your purse or person. Simply repeat to me what you told the guards. I want your account of what occurred as you saw it."

Reaching into a desk drawer he turned on a hidden tape recorder., Smiling, he leaned back in his chair. "Now let's see. I suppose we can start with the pretty one first."

Blushes. Smiles. Giggles. And two of the little dears began talking at once.

Michi was in the ladies' room to get away from Dorian, away from the pandemonium in the auditorium, away from the cloud of marijuana floating over the audience. Instead, she had walked into more sickly sweet air. More marijuana.

The smell reminded her of Dorian and their lovemaking. She hated it all the more.

This time it was three teenage American girls, leaning against washbasins and smoking dope and drinking from a pint bottle of vodka. The oldest could not have been older than eighteen, but all three were indulging in public behavior that Michi found distasteful and shocking. Why did American women cheapen and degrade themselves in front of others? Japanese women would never do such a thing, nor would Japanese society allow them to.

She washed and dried her hands and prepared to leave. The door flew open and two muscular young men, high school football players, entered. They were drunk and stoned on drugs. One carried a bagged bottle. A horrified Michi noticed that his fly was open and his penis, flaccid and pink, now dangled from his trousers. She looked away in disgust and shame.

"Hey, you guys," yelled one of the girls, "this is a ladies' room. Get the fuck outta here before I call a security guard."

The youth who wore a professional hockey team jacket spat at her. "Stupid cunt. Open your mouth and I'll shove my dick in it. Christ, man, nothing but pigs in here."

"Ain't all pigs," said the other, who held a bagged bottle and wore a football jersey. "Ain't all pigs, my man."

Michi decided to leave.

One of the American girls left the washbasin and walked up to the pair. But before she could say a word the youth in the jersey shoved her against a stall and leaned on her, his glazed eyes just inches from hers. "Hey, if I told you you had a nice body, would you hold it against me."

Michi walked toward the door. But the larger of the two, the one in the hockey jacket, blocked her way. "Hey, hey. Lady from the Far East. What's shakin', lady from the Far East? You want some 'ludes, man? Reds? Uppers? Downers? Shit, I got the world here in my pocket. Got drugs that won't quit."

"Let me pass, please."

"Say pretty please."

Michi bowed her head. "Pretty please."

He looked at his companion. "Shit, man, this one's mine.

She's fuckin' pretty. She can sit on my face any time. Ain't never had no Far Eastern lady."

His arm went around Michi's waist, drawing her to him. They were hip to hip. He was strong and reeked of liquor. "You and me, little mama. You pop one of these 'ludes and you gonna love me like I love you." His other hand came out of his pocket with the Quāāludes.

Michi lifted her knee and brought her foot down, driving a boot heel into his instep.

"Shit!" Tight lipped with pain, he backed off. But he was still between her and the door.

Behind Michi, the jerseyed youth said, "Ho, ho. Wasn't nice. Wasn't nice at all."

He loped forward, red eyed and half smiling. Dangerous.

Michi heard him. Looking over her shoulder, she saw him reach for her with both hands. She did it all in one motion. Crouched, sank below his arms, drove her elbow back into his stomach. He stopped in place, his eyes all white, arms clutching his middle. Still he staggered forward, left hand clawing the air after her. She caught his wrist in her small hands. Her right hand found his pinky finger. Gripping it tightly she bent it back with all her strength. Quickly. Broke it.

He squealed, clutched the damaged hand to his chest and lurched sideways, scattering the mesmerized teenage girls before crashing into the washbasins and falling to the floor. On his back, he rolled from side to side, moaning, left hand squeezed between his thighs.

"Oh, wow," said one of the girls, shaking her head.

Michi turned to see the first youth hobbling toward her. He favored his injured foot, dragging it behind him. His face was tight with hatred.

Kihaku. *Spirit. There was nothing more essential to victory. And it was manifested in* kiai, *the yell.*

The kiai *from Michi was not merely a sound from her throat. It was a warrior's cry from deep within her, a sound torn from her blood and nerves, from a thousand years of being samurai, and its eerie pitch was terrifying, hypnotic. The sound filled the room, bouncing from wall to wall, from floor to ceiling. In front of her, the youth froze, stunned.*

He stared into Michi's eyes and what he saw there frightened him. Blinking, he took one step backward and then another. He frowned, chewed his bottom lip, reached down to stroke his hurt foot.

Michi picked her purse from the floor and walked past him, never looking back.

Sparrowhawk said, "I see. And you're all in agreement on what happened?"

The three girls looked at one another, then nodded. Said the girl who had emerged as the leader, "She was terrific. Like Wonder Woman, you know?"

Sparrowhawk winced. "Ladies, I thank you. And may I invite the three of you to be my guest for our Christmas show. Each of you may bring someone if you like."

Squeals and shrieks of delight. Another rock star had booked for Christmas Day at the auditorium; he was almost as well known as the one onstage and, in Sparrowhawk's opinion, equally as odious.

When the girls had been dismissed, he said to his guards, "Check the infirmary. See if any young men have reported injuries. We're looking for a broken finger, a damaged foot. Should you locate these lucky lads, kindly inform me via radio. I'd like to talk to them in private."

"What if they give us a hard time?" said one guard. "Like maybe they won't cooperate. Or maybe they threaten to sue."

Sparrowhawk aimed his jaw at the guard. "Dear boy, the gentlemen in question will do exactly as I say. For starters, I plan to threaten them with jail. As in attempted rape. Or assault. Or drug dealing. After they have signed a release, I intend to question them at length. And they will talk, I can assure you."

"What about Wonder Woman?"

"You leave her to me. Just locate Laurel and Hardy, if you would be so kind. Off with you."

Alone, Sparrowhawk removed a small notebook from his inside jacket pocket and using a gold pen carefully printed the name *Michelle Asama* on one blank page. Under it, he printed the word *major*. Then he wrote the word *fighter*, but crossed it out. Instead he printed *warrior*. Seemed more appropriate.

He thought of the last Japanese warrior he had met. It was in Saigon, and the warrior's name was George Chihara.

9

Decker's partner was thirty-three-year-old Ellen Spiceland, a light-skinned black woman with high cheekbones, reddish brown hair and a tough attractiveness in spite of a permanently flattened nose. Her nose had been crushed at thirteen, when she had resisted a rape attempt by a Harlem minister. She was married to her third husband, a Haitian artist who was just beginning to make inroads into New York's art world. Since she was the stronger of the two and both feared loneliness more than subjugation, the marriage was a success.

In one of their first cases in a two-year partnership, Decker and Ellen Spiceland—the precinct called them "Black and Decker"—had tracked down the rapist of an eighteen-month-old baby girl. He was a Cuban who had entered America with the Cuban "Freedom Flotilla," many of whom were criminals Castro had wanted to be rid of. The detectives had knocked on the rapist's apartment door and were told to enter. They did. And found themselves staring at a thirteen-round Browning automatic. A shot was fired. Decker, expecting to die, tensed to receive the bullet.

But the shot hadn't come from the Cuban: Spiceland had a habit of always entering certain bars, apartments, after-hours clubs with one hand in her purse. Today it had paid off. She fired through her cloth bag, briefly setting it aflame, scattering coins and keys on the floor and putting a .38 caliber slug one inch above the Cuban's belt buckle. It took him thirty-six hours to die a very painful death. The killing was Spiceland's first; she celebrated with a thirty-five-dollar bottle of Dom Perignon.

Outside of her immediate family, only Decker knew of the

champagne. She said to him, "Twenty years I've been wanting to waste somebody like him. Twenty years."

She waited for his reaction. There was none.

But on her desk the next day was a gift-wrapped parcel with a signed card from him. Inside was a lovely new bag from Henri Bendel. The precinct picked up on it; before the week was out Spiceland received eleven new bags, some of them gag gifts, others from good shops and all with a signed card from fellow officers. She had passed the test that made her a good cop, a dependable partner for anybody.

Six months later it was Decker's turn to back her up when she said, "The Broom's playing cop, badge and all, and I don't know how to handle it."

Every precinct had a broom, a janitor. Many were buffs, fans of real cops, who didn't hesitate to pass themselves off as actual police officers.

Decker said, "You sure?"

"Kotlowitz told me. He's afraid to talk to anyone else. The Broom scares the shit out of him."

Kotlowitz, owner of a nearby clothing store, was new to the precinct. He was also something of an art collector; in addition to buying paintings by Spiceland's husband he had also introduced the Haitian to gallery owners, some of whom had shown an interest in his work. As for fearing the Broom, Kotlowitz had good reason. The Broom weighed almost three hundred pounds and had moments of belligerence. Behind his back he was called Pork Butt.

Ellen said, "He's getting free shirts, underwear, jackets, whatever he can from Kotlowitz, who doesn't know any better. He thinks the Broom is for real."

"Weird. The Broom can't even fit into any of that shit. What's he want it for?"

"Sells it, what else. Point is, it makes the precinct look bad and what do I do about it? I bitch to the captain and I'm a snitch. Manny, I can't handle that. I mean it's tough enough being black and a woman. Do I get tagged as a snitch, too?"

He looked at her carefully. "Just can't let it pass, huh?"

There was no hesitation. "No, Manny, I can't. I don't think that's what being a cop is all about. Maybe if I'd been around here for ten years or so, I could get away with dumping on 'the Broom.' But I can't because I'm still the new girl on the block and, in a way, I'm still on trial. You were the only one around here who would have me as a partner, remember? I mean, I'm kind of accepted now, but shit, man, it's still hard sometimes.

"Truth is, Manny, I don't like the Broom. I don't think he belongs here. He's a bully, when he thinks nobody's looking. Always throwing his weight around, which in his case is a lot. I've seen what he gets away with in the neighborhood. Never around cops, though. He picks out his targets very carefully. Neighborhood people. And nasty stuff that may not be criminal, but is still shitty. And the precinct knows it. Don't tell me they don't know. They goof on the man. They like keeping him around like he's some kind of overstuffed toy. They get their kicks laughing at him and he loves it, so long as it's cops who are laughing. Christ, what the hell do I do? Kotlowitz is a nice man. He didn't survive Auschwitz to have to put up with assholes like the Broom. Besides, he's been so nice to Henri and me."

There were tears in her eyes.

Decker said, "I know somebody at the precinct who can handle it."

"Who?"

"You don't want to know."

"You're right. I don't want to know. I just want 'the Broom' gone, that's all."

He was gone less than twenty-four hours later. Decker, as a field associate, made a call to Ron at headquarters and Internal Affairs took over.

Later Ellen said, "Manny, you're beautiful. And you're right. I don't want to know the somebody round here who's keeping an eye on all God's children. When you see him, kiss him four times for me, once for each cheek. But I never want to know who he is."

With Michi back in his life, Decker wished he could dismiss Charles LeClair as easily as Ellen Spiceland had dismissed her unknown benefactor. LeClair made it impossible to stop seeing Romaine; the prosecutor wanted to make cases against Senator Terry Dent and Constantine Pangalos and Management Systems Consultants, because like many federal prosecutors he wanted to see his own name in the paper, because he loved power and because, Decker learned, LeClair was one of several men being considered for the post of deputy attorney general, under the U.S. attorney general in the Justice Department.

LeClair also had feelers from a Wall Street law firm that wanted to hire a black attorney capable of becoming a partner in less than two years.

LeClair had an explanation for the hard time he was giving Decker. "Necessity doesn't leave a man a choice. They say the two worst things in this world are not getting what you want and getting it. I've had the *not* part. Now I want to see what the other part's like. Don't let Mrs. Raymond slip out of your life just yet, my man."

For almost a week, since Michi's return, the detective had given Romaine excuses for not seeing her. Now he began to resent her.

He saw Michi when she was free, when she was not involved with Pantheon Diamonds, which seemed to be most of the time. Two-thirds of the company was owned by a Tokyo conglomerate, with Michi controlling the remaining third. Like male Japanese executives, she put in long hours; she also gave business seminars to American corporations interested in Japanese managerial practices. The Wall Street *Journal*, *Newsweek*, the New York *Times* and three women's magazines had all scheduled stories on her.

It was LeClair who suddenly made him more protective of her. Whenever the prosecutor telephoned Decker at the dojo, as he did tonight, it was a signal that he wanted to emphasize his control over him, an attitude many U.S. attorneys had toward cops and agents assigned to them. A call at the dojo also indicated LeClair's desire for immediate information. LeClair was a black man in a world composed of WASP attorneys culled from prestigious Wall Street law firms. He wanted to do more than excel in that world; he wanted to rule it.

"Just want to remind you of the meeting tomorrow morning," LeClair said. "Looking forward to seeing you." Decker had seen him two days ago. And spoken to him yesterday. LeClair, obviously, felt pressured. "Heard anything from your girl?"

"You mean Romaine."

"Far as I'm concerned, you only got one lady. Something else going on I should know about?"

"Nothing you should know about."

"Flying to Washington this weekend for a meeting with the attorney general. Actually, it's a dinner party he's throwing for some Brazilian police officers, but I call it a meeting. I'll be on trial to see just how I conduct myself among all those high-stepping folks. He's been inviting guys eligible for the deputy spot down to D.C., with our wives, to see how we check out in social situations. My turn this week. Sure would be nice to drop some hard news on him, so he can see how well the third world acquits itself when it comes to important cases. You heard about DeMain and Benitez."

"No." They were two New York City detectives assigned to the task force. Decker knew DeMain, an experienced cop getting close to retirement. Benitez he had met on the task force. He was a quiet man, a hard worker with aspirations of one day going to law school.

"They're off the task force," said LeClair. "Couldn't quite measure up."

"That's going to hurt their careers."

"Exactly what I told them. In fact, I made sure of it. Took one or two phone calls, but I can guarantee you that being dropped from my group is going to hurt their careers more than a little bit. Anyway, you reach out for Mrs. Raymond, who I hear is one foxy lady. Find out what she has to offer in the way of hard news. Later, my man."

And I'd better deliver, thought Decker. Because LeClair would not hesitate to hurt anybody. Including Michi. Chocolate Chuck, the Teutonic Fuck. You better believe it.

Decker dialed Romaine and was relieved when her service picked up. He wasn't due to see Michi tonight, but he didn't want to see Romaine, either. Not right now. Not until he had figured a way to use her without sleeping with her anymore. Which was not going to be easy. His heart was with Michi. *Hada to hada,* the Japanese called it. Skin to skin. The ability to communicate and, above all, a willingness for each to expose their sincerity. Only with Michi could he ever feel that way. He hoped that Romaine would not return his call.

But a half hour later, bubbling and happy, she called back at the dojo, and Decker made a date to meet her in two hours. All of this caused him to want to do something to LeClair. All of it reminded him of the time when his life was not his, when others had ruled him.

Manfred Freiherr Decker (named for Baron Manfred von Richtofen, the legendary Red Baron and World War One flying ace) was born in 1951, in Yorkville, Manhattan's oldest and largest German neighborhood. His father owned a restaurant amid the beer halls, cabarets and sausage shops of East Eighty-sixth Street. His mother sang at the restaurant and on a local radio show aimed at the city's German-Americans. When the Korean War broke out, his father, a lieutenant in World War II, was recalled and died near Pusan when a captured North Korean pulled the pin on a grenade, killing himself and the lieutenant. His mother then sold the restaurant and, leaving Manny with uncaring relatives, went to Hollywood to pursue a career in musicals.

At the age of twelve Manny was reunited with his mother. Years of abuse, neglect and bad food had left him weak and sickly, a quiet boy who had not known a day without fear. His mother, having risen no higher than bit player in Hollywood, had returned to New York to marry a talent agent. The agent, obsessed with his clients and his own career, had no interest in a stepson, seeing him as little more than a nuisance. "He's made it twelve years without me," said the agent. "No reason he can't do another twelve without me following him everywhere."

In his new Greenwich Village neighborhood, Manny, as he'd always done, kept to himself. And because he was a loner and a new face, because he was thin and physically weak, he became a target. There were fights with Italians, Irish, Puerto Ricans, with a frightened Manny the loser almost every time. Uptown blacks, prowling the Village on weekends in search of easy prey, found it in Manny. Money, a wristwatch, a winter coat, schoolbooks were taken from him by force. By the time he was fifteen, he had been knifed twice. A chest X ray for one slashing revealed that Manny had once contracted tuberculosis. Two small spots were found on his right lung; both were now calcified and apparently harmless. It explained his constant weakness, the fatigue that never seemed to leave him.

It also meant tests to determine whether or not his body had completely healed itself. While the tests proved it had, they also added to the fear that had weighed him down all his life.

"Christ, what do you want me to do?" his stepfather asked Manny's mother. "Can't nursemaid him and my clients twenty-four hours a day. Let him carry a knife himself. Lift weights. I'll pay for it. Send him down to the Y. If nothing else, maybe they'll teach him to run faster."

At the local YMCA, it wasn't weight lifting or running that caught the boy's attention. On the second floor he paused in front of an open doorway to watch a karate class. Empty-hand fighting. The instructor was an American, small and wiry, with a close-cropped military haircut and the quickest fighting moves Manny had ever seen. Not only were his moves deadly, they were *beautiful.* Manny couldn't take his eyes off him.

The class, men and women in *gis*, went through basic punches, blocks, kicks, then did light sparring and finished with *katas,* formal exercises featuring prearranged actions and corresponding correct responses. At the end of the class Ran Dobson, the instructor and a Marine sergeant stationed on recruiting duty in Manhattan, teamed with a handful of advanced students to rehearse a demonstration scheduled for a New York high school.

The advanced students, all bigger than Dobson, attacked him with full force, first one at a time, then two, three, four. Defending himself with ease, the small Marine exhibited a beauty and power that mesmerized Manny. The students attacked with clubs, a chair and each time Dobson triumphed. With his hands tied, he defeated three men.

Using a hunting knife, one student rushed Dobson, slashing at his face, knees, driving the long blade toward his stomach; always the little man defeated his attacker, sometimes adding comical touches to the fighting that brought laughter from Manny and the rest of the class.

When the demonstration rehearsal ended to applause, Manny, who rarely spoke to an adult, entered the room to speak to Ran Dobson. All thoughts of weight lifting were forgotten. Manny had found something better.

He studied Shotokan with Dobson for two years. The

thirty-two-year-old soft-spoken Marine, a native of Oklahoma, also held black belts in judo, kendo, jujitsu; he was self-educated and, via correspondence courses, was about to complete a third year of college. His sense of irreverence was to rub off on Decker, who idolized Dobson, his first *sensei,* teacher. Shotokan was demanding, an aggressive and strong Japanese style of karate, which Dobson executed with a precise and lethal grace. Manny practiced that same way: exact and with full speed, full power.

Karate, stressed Ran, was a training of both body and mind, a discipline to be applied to every facet of one's existence. It was a way of thinking, a plan for living and, above all, a way of developing morality. Lacking these goals, all training was in vain; no amount of fighting skill could ever compensate for a lack of character. "Put a load of books on a donkey's back and you still got yourself a jackass," said Dobson. "As for fighting, you do it when you can't run away, when you can't talk your way out of it, when you can't back down. You heard me. I said back down. When you can hurt a man and don't, then you're worthy of the skill you carry around. You can be trusted with it and that's your character, your strength."

Ran explained the need for power in karate techniques, for attacking precisely and with all of one's strength. Destroy the enemy with one punch, one kick. "If you hit him once and don't stop him, he's going to inflict on you what is called bodily harm. You will then come to resemble hammered shit, assuming you live to resemble anything at all. Put your heart and soul in it. Nobody ever got a medal for finishing second in a fight."

Manny became obsessed by karate, its techniques, history, philosophy. So determined and persistent was he that often he practiced with Ran Dobson before and after regular workouts. He read the books on the martial arts and Japan recommended by the Marine and he attended practice even when ill or injured.

"You seem to know the first rule," the Marine said. "Don't bother unless you want it bad. Real bad."

Manny did.

As Manny became stronger in body and mind, more confident and skilled than the other students, Ran worked him harder, a reminder that in karate, as in life, one never stopped learning. The training was sometimes done to exhaustion, with Manny being made to practice after the others had finished. Daily workouts, whether in the club or at home, were Dobson's orders, for he recognized that persistence was Manny's true talent. Having achieved something for the first time in his life and having eased the fear he'd always lived with, the boy gladly did as his teacher asked.

Outside of the dojo, there were encounters that could not be avoided. When a black youth threatened to crush his skull with a chunk of ice unless he handed over his boots, Manny broke three of his ribs with a single side kick. Two members of an Italian street gang, remembering how easily they had once beat him, attempted to rob him at knifepoint; Manny broke the knife wielder's elbow and knocked the other unconscious.

"You've sent out a message," said Ran. "I think it's been received."

The Marine was right; the incident with the gang members marked the last attack on Manny in his neighborhood.

On the day that Dobson awarded Manny his black belt he mentioned his own upcoming transfer back to Japan. A new club was opening in New York, however, to be headed by a sixth dan Shotokan instructor from Tokyo. "I've written him about you," said Ran, "and he expects you in class when he arrives. You're born to a dojo, so don't let go. It'll serve you in more ways than one. Gonna miss you, good buddy."

They embraced. Trying to hide the tears, Manny turned away. When he looked around again, Ran Dobson was gone. When Manny next saw his *sensei*, the Marine would be dead.

Recognizing Manny's dedication and ability, his new Japanese instructor worked him even harder than Ran had. By the age of nineteen, he had become one of the East Coast's top tournament fighters, consistently defeating older and more experienced opponents; there was no one in his age group who could compete against him. He won his *neidan*, his second dan, from the new instructor, who refused to award that rank to anyone but Manny for four years.

Training meant more to him than the liberal arts course he had signed up for at New York's City College; he'd only done that to avoid serving in Vietnam, having no real idea of what he wanted to do with the rest of his life. Except for karate. In his third year, he flunked out, to be drafted just before his twenty-second birthday. At the induction station, every fourth man was pulled out of line and assigned to the Marine Corps. Manny, remembering Ran Dobson, changed places with the man beside him and was soon on his way to Parris Island.

Karate training and discipline prepared him to survive a brutal boot camp; he emerged as one of the top in his class—his appearance was all creases, spit shines, jarhead haircuts—and was chosen for embassy guard training, assigned first to Okinawa, then in 1974 to Saigon. In Saigon, he worked out with South Korean soldiers, training in Tae Kwan Do for a year and improving his kicking and throwing techniques. The South Koreans, feared by the Viet Cong more than any other troops, were tough, often refraining from pulling punches even in practices. Tournaments were brutal and injuries were common; still, over a period of months Manny defeated seven of the South Koreans' best fighters without a loss. He was unbeatable. His confidence had never been higher.

And then he fought Robbie Ambrose, a SEAL and the only other American besides Manny to enter the tournament against South Koreans, Japanese, Chinese and Thai fighters. He had never heard of Ambrose, who had been stationed at other Vietnamese bases before being assigned to Saigon. Both Manny and Ambrose made it through eliminations to face each other in the final bout. Before one thousand onlookers, Ambrose gave Manny his first defeat in years, damaging his collarbone and loosening teeth. The injuries didn't upset Decker; losing did.

His confidence was shaken. The fear almost returned.

He would clash with Robbie in Vietnam again, this time when Ambrose was with the Englishman Sparrowhawk and another American SEAL, Dorian Raymond. On that occasion Decker would have an M-16, but it would not erase the memory of his defeat at the hands of Robbie Ambrose.

Not long after that match, someone at the embassy decided to pull a surprise inspection at the GR Point on a nearby base. This was the Graves Registration Point, where the processing, embalming and identification of dead soldiers took place. The surprise inspection was to check on a rumor that heroin was being smuggled back to America in the corpses of dead GIs. Decker, because of his karate and proven ability with weapons, was picked to head a three-man escort accompanying two officers on a trip to the base, located just outside Saigon.

At the GR Point he came across the body of Ran Dobson, resting in a reefer, a refrigerated container. The sight of the chilled corpse almost made Decker faint; in death the Oklahoman looked even smaller and surprisingly relaxed, as though he'd figured out the joke but was reluctant to explain it to anyone else. He had arrived in Vietnam yesterday morning and was dead by nightfall, the victim of "friendly fire."

"American gunship," said the quartermaster. "One of ours wasted him. Happens all the time. A mistake, is all."

Mistake. The whole fucking war was a mistake and Decker now hated it more than he had hated anything in his life. Had the grieving embassy guard not met Michi Chihara then, his hatred might have seriously corroded him.

But he lost her, too, and coming so soon after Ran Dobson's death, it closed his heart against all commitment. Life was faded flowers and the taste of bitter wine, a series of disillusionments one after another.

Back in "the world," in New York, he drifted into an outsider's occupation, into police work, where it was well within the rules to get close to no one and to use everyone. And to show that Ran Dobson's life had not been a waste, despite the manner of his death, Decker trained as hard as he ever had in his life. He also drifted into marriage with a woman whom he did not love; on his part the marriage had been an act of generosity, originating in polite indifference. Sex, the thing that had attracted him to her, was not enough to hold them together for long.

When he was ready, when he once more felt himself unbeatable, he yielded to pressure to again fight Robbie Ambrose. Robbie, a native Californian, had now settled in New York, taking a job with Sparrowhawk and the giant security firm Management Systems Consultants. For Ambrose, who had become an outstanding fighter, this was to be his last point match before switching to full-contact karate, something which had never interested Decker. The match took place in Madison Square Garden before a sellout crowd. Decker had never been better. He could not lose.

He did. And was almost crippled for life.

The fight was action from start to finish, with each man trying to be the first to score three points, theoretically three killing blows. When time ran out, a referee and four judges had the match even, two points apiece. Both men then fought two overtimes; it was in the final overtime that Robbie dropped Decker to the mat with a vicious sweep, taking both legs out from under him, before connecting with a stomach punch, then *accidentally* falling on Decker's right knee. *And breaking it.*

Victory to Robbie. And agony for Decker, who heard and felt the ligaments and tendons rip in his knee and screamed before passing out from the pain. At the hospital, two doctors told him he would never run again. He would always walk with a limp. Karate, or any sport for that matter, was out of the question. Forever.

The fear returned.

And then he thought of Ran Dobson. *First and only rule: Don't bother unless you want it bad. Real bad.* Ain't the size of the dog in the fight, it's the size of the fight in the dog.

In his hospital bed, a drugged Decker, his right leg in traction, slowly punched the air in front of him. When he had done that twenty times, he lifted his left leg in short, slow kicking motions. Training again, Ran. Dog's fighting back.

It was eleven months before he returned to Nick and Grace Harper's West Side dojo. By then he had strengthened his knee with weights, therapy, running. In weeks he was training hard. He learned to dodge and shift faster, using lateral movements rather than putting pressure on his knee by moving back to evade attacks. He improved his timing, increasing his speed so that he could get the jump on opponents without having to move much. His hand speed was now the best it had ever been.

He ran daily, jumped rope, lifted weights to keep the knee strong. But it would never be as strong as it had been before the *accident*. Still, there were those who thought he was better than the old Manny Decker.

Robbie Ambrose had deliberately broken his knee and Decker knew it. Robbie hadn't forgotten their last encounter in Saigon, when Decker, at gunpoint, had prevented him, Sparrowhawk and Dorian Raymond from walking off with fifty thousand dollars of CIA money. Everyone else saw the broken knee as an accident. Decker, however, knew better.

To retain his newly regained confidence, he pushed all thoughts of Robbie Ambrose into his subconscious. And in time, Decker almost forgot that he still feared him.

Fear. Because of it Decker made love to Romaine in darkness, afraid to see her face and not wanting her to see his. By allowing her to love him, he had become responsible for her. Sex had drawn him to Romaine; her need for love had complicated the arrangement. Who was tonight's mercy fuck really for? Romaine? Michi? Decker's career?

Romaine wanted Decker. But the one thing he had to give, himself, was no longer his to give. It belonged to another.

In the darkness she said, "Let's go away this weekend. I've got the money."

"Can't," he lied. "Have a tournament coming up. I'm refereeing and putting on a demonstration."

"Oh. Well, maybe some other weekend."

"Maybe. How'd you get so rich, all of a sudden?"

"Dorian. He gave me almost a thousand dollars."

"Still getting lucky at Atlantic City?"

"No. We had lunch. He wants to get back together again and he told me he's working on some kind of deal that's going to make him rich for life."

Decker held her hand, hating himself. "What kind of a deal makes a man rich for life?"

"He wouldn't say. He likes to brag, but he kept quiet for a change. He did tell me about some new opening last night he'd gone to. Some auditorium or arena out on Long Island. Lots of celebrities, big names."

She sat up in bed. "You're not going to believe this, but you know what he said? He said the auditorium doesn't have the right number of seats. Some lawyer for the auditorium, some Greek guy, came up with some scheme to cut down on the number of seats but nobody's supposed to know about it. Dorian thinks it's real smart what the Greek guy did. He likes those kind of flashy people, Dorian. Me, I think you can be too clever sometimes."

Decker said, "I'll go along with that. Sly little devils, these lawyers. And you say this one's Greek?"

10

Trevor Sparrowhawk felt exhilarated, as he always did when the hunt was on. This morning he stepped from a chauffeured limousine and, whistling a bit of Haydn's "The Seasons," walked into a Wall Street office building near the Federal Reserve Bank. Minutes from now he would know a bit more about his quarry, the physically adept Michelle Asama.

In the lobby he headed toward a private elevator being held for him by an attendant in a beige and yellow uniform. The elevator serviced only Management Systems Consultants, located on the top four floors of the forty-four-story building. The lobby directory, however, did not list the security firms or the names of any of its officers. An MSC guard, dressed as an elevator attendant, prevented anyone without the necessary coded identification from boarding the elevator.

In the early days of the firm's existence there had been some discussion as to whether or not the elevator guard should be armed. Was it good or bad public relations? Would potential clients be alarmed or somehow reassured to know that the finger that pressed the starter button could in seconds wrap itself about a trigger?

Sparrowhawk claimed the last word. "Violence, dear friends, is the rhetoric of our day, unfortunately. As for those of you who feel that an armed guard in the lobby is extreme, let me join William Blake in noting that the road of excess leads to the palace of wisdom. I say there is nothing wrong if potential clients view an armed guard as a symbol of distrust on our part. Distrust, gentlemen, is our only protection against treachery."

Thus the attendant/guard, who greeted Sparrowhawk before closing the elevator doors behind him, wore under his knee-length coat an Ingram M-11, a machine pistol that weighed less than four pounds and fired fourteen shots per second. As an added security precaution the guard, via a hidden beeper and using a code changed daily, checked in hourly with an upstairs supervisor.

On the forty-fourth floor Sparrowhawk stepped from the elevator still whistling Haydn, but faster now. A wave of the hand to the uniformed guards on either side of the elevator and then he was in the reception area of his office. "Mrs. Rosebery," he said in crisp greeting to his secretary. Twenty minutes ago she had reached him on the car phone to report the arrival of the information he had requested on Michelle Asama.

Damned efficient, Mrs. Rosebery. Sixtyish, a long-faced Yorkshire widow in tweed suits and sensible shoes and with an unwavering belief that the world had slipped into darkness with the death of beloved King Edward VII in 1910. She claimed to be a descendant of Spencer Perceval, the only British prime minister ever to be assassinated. She herself had toiled for two prime ministers and had turned down a salary of twenty-five thousand pounds a year from a banker in the City to follow Sparrowhawk to America.

Sparrowhawk, after telling Mrs. Rosebery to hold all calls and messages, closed the door to his private office, a comfortable room of paneled walls, shelves of hand-bound books, copies of impressionist paintings and for a desk, a Louis XV commode veneered in tulipwood and kingwood and mounted in ormolu. He opened the drapes. Magnificent Manhattan lay at his feet as London never had. The view was heart stopping. Cloudless blue sky over the Hudson River; tugboats towing ships into West Side piers; thousands of skyscraper windows on fire with fiery sunlight; and on the street below, slow-moving specks that were people, cars, buses. Invigorating, all of it.

He clapped his hands. To work.

Behind his desk, bifocals resting on the tip of his long nose, he read about Michelle Asama.

The source of his information: Management Systems Consultants, its worldwide investigative connections and computers. The cream of former law enforcement personnel made up the company's board of directors, its roster of officers, its chief investigators. CIA, FBI, the Justice Department Strike Force, New York Police Department, Israel's Mossad, Interpol, New Scotland Yard, U.S. State Department, the French Sûreté, Royal Canadian Mounted Police, the security division of top American multinational corporations. Men who had once worked in these organizations now worked for MSC because it paid the highest salaries in the private intelligence field.

Money, naturally, was a factor in luring top talent; Sparrowhawk received $750,000 a year, plus bonuses and expenses. But pulling down three times the average law enforcement salary wasn't the only reason that former policemen, spies and investigators brought valuable files, expertise and contacts to MSC. Those who came here or to other private security companies were *players*, men hooked on the game, who could not live without intrigue or dirty tricks or investigations.

Sparrowhawk had assembled a formidable staff, one quite capable of relieving Michelle Asama and anyone else of the burden of their secrets.

On to Miss Asama.

Early records missing. Sparrowhawk frowned. Convenient. The absence of verifiable fact always allowed speculation to run rampant. Born in Saigon, but information on much of her life destroyed or lost in Communist takeover in 1975. Spent time in Tokyo, where available records claim she entered the world on August 29, 1953. Father was Japanese shipowner, mother the daughter of French importer. Parents died in Singapore hotel fire when she was fourteen. Thereafter she divided her time between Saigon and father's relatives in Tokyo.

Educated in Tokyo and Paris, with business courses in America (UCLA). Unmarried, no children, no criminal record. No available hospital records, indicating no major illnesses. She owned one-third of Pantheon Diamonds, money having been left to her by her father. A Japanese conglomerate, whose name Sparrowhawk recognized, owned the other two-thirds. So far, nothing out of the ordinary about the lady. Clean as the proverbial hound's tooth.

Sparrowhawk sipped tea and continued reading. Pantheon dealt primarily in gems, rarely buying industrial diamonds. Miss Asama was known to the Diamond Trading Company, an organization that handled sales for the world's principal diamond producers. Ten times a year the DTC invited buyers to sales, known as sights, held in London, Lucerne, Johannesburg, Antwerp, Tel Aviv. Only 230 customers a year qualified to attend the sights, no easy matter since South African syndicates, which controlled the diamond trade, had to approve each name. Miss Asama had qualified with ease.

Pantheon sold to the best-known jewelry designers in the world, as well as to exclusive shops in a dozen countries. The three-year-old company was a profit maker and apparently Miss Asama was the reason; her grasp of the business ranged from a knowledge of marketing to the cutting and polishing of stones. She was highly paid and was no figurehead. She actually ran the company.

Sparrowhawk paused to light a Turkish cigarette. Rare that a woman, and a young woman at that, rose so fast and so high in the Japanese business world, a totally male preserve. The Englishman used his gold pen to make a check mark on the report. Either the lady was setting records for efficiency, or she had friends in high places. She would not be the first woman to trade her favors for a boost up the corporate ladder.

And this too caught his eye: Michelle Asama had no personal credit cards. Not one. Company credit cards and a company expense account, but zero in the way of personal credit cards. Personal purchases apparently paid for in cash. Another check here.

Neither Sparrowhawk nor his wife Unity had personal credit cards. It was a protection against prying eyes, a way of keeping out of the computers of credit bureaus and banks, who too easily turned over information to anyone who asked for it.

MSC clients paid in cash, too. Along with oral agreements,

this was a safety measure to keep information on security matters from falling into the wrong hands. Cash, for the most part, was untraceable. That made it a protection, one more brick in the wall of secrecy around Sparrowhawk and the people who hired him to guard their lives and property. Did this mean that Michelle Asama had something to hide?

Records indicated she had no trouble with U.S. Immigration, taxes, police or their Japanese counterparts. And yet . . .

Major. One word. How much of life had turned on just one word.

Nor could Sparrowhawk erase from his mind eyewitness accounts of her disposal of those two American halfwits a few days ago.

"A woman against two men?" Robbie had said. "No doubt about it, the lady's good."

"When you say good, how many years of practice are we talking about?"

"Well, major, I'd say at least five years. That's how long it takes to learn basic karate techniques. And that's if you practice three times a week minimum. You get your confidence from experience, no other way, and that lady sure sounds confident to me. I mean from what you tell me she could have killed those clowns, really done a number on them. But she did just enough, know what I mean? Now that's cool. That's really being in charge."

He paused. Then, "If what those three girls told you is true, especially the part about the *kiai,* the lady, whoever she is, is really into karate."

Sparrowhawk said, "Not to put too fine a point on it, but would you say that her *kiai,* as you call it, indicates a deep commitment to this karate business? Does it make her special in any way?"

"I don't follow you."

"Would it make her some sort of samurai? Remember, she could have seriously harmed those louts, but didn't. From what I can gather, samurai have some sort of higher calling in the martial arts. Or are supposed to have."

"Hey, anything's possible. I mean you're right, she could be a samurai or related to one, I suppose. In the old days Japan had a lot of women samurai. They killed, too. Just like men. Sometimes they were better. They could get close to a man where another man couldn't, know what I mean?"

"Quite."

"Yes, sir. Tough ladies, those Japanese."

Yes, thought Sparrowhawk, remembering how the Chihara women had died when he, Robbie and Dorian had come for them. In a lifetime of soldiering he had never seen anyone, man or woman, die with more courage. A mother and her two daughters. Ready to meet death. Death always came too early or too late. That's how it had been with Sparrowhawk's family and that's how it had been in his life as a soldier. It came sooner or later, but it always came, this door of darkness, this great unknown, this tragic last act.

It always came.

11

Northern England is a harsh and rugged region split north to south by the mountains. To the west lie the high peaks of the Cumbrians, and to the east the windy and desolate North York moors. The natural barriers of mountains and moors form obstacles to communication and exchange; they foster provincialism and a fierce loyalty to one's own town or village. In the north one finds a robust national patriotism, one stronger than any existing elsewhere in the British Isles.

Northern people have always been fighters. They took up swords against the Vikings and the Scots and in the War of the Roses, the long struggle between the great families of York and Lancaster for the throne of England. The Industrial Revolution began here, with children working nineteen-hour days for a penny a week in "dark, satanic mills." Class wars between factory owner and worker found gritty and unyielding northerners on both sides, refusing to bend or compromise.

Trevor Wells Sparrowhawk was born in northern England's key city of Manchester, in a row of cheap terrace houses darkened by smoke from steel and textile mills. His father, a schoolteacher, named him after a grandfather who was a nineteenth-century trade unionist and H. G. Wells. His mother was a seamstress and a socialist, forever opposing the capitalists who sweated northerners in unsafe foundries and factories.

While Trevor's father gave him a lifelong love of literature, it was his mother who taught him that law and justice did not exist, that the world was governed by might or mercy.

In the north, a boy became a man at an early age. By fifteen Sparrowhawk was in his third year in the steel mills, a stocky, strong lad determined to survive. Those who didn't survive were his relatives, friends and neighbors, dead from mine explosions, consumption, starvation, black lung. Strikes, hunger marches and massive rallies failed to prevent more dying. When Britain went to war with Germany for the second time, the dying only increased. A 1941 Luftwaffe bombing raid, aimed at Manchester's factories, killed Sparrowhawk's parents and two sisters, leaving him with no reason to remain in a city that had brought so much death into his life.

Lying about his age, he enlisted in the army. "Not to worry, lad," a cheery lance corporal said to him. "It's war and the devil knows it. He'll make room in hell for the likes of you and me. Besides, if you're the right sort you'll come to love war, especially if you're winnin'. 'Tis the excitement what matters, nothin' else. Neither the good nor bad of it. Just the excitement."

Sparrowhawk was never to hear a better reason for war's appeal to him. For the first time in his life power, *a gun*, lay in his hand. The pleasure was as exquisite as reading Shelley alone by a quiet lake.

He took to soldiering with enthusiasm, excelling during training and showing a particular combination of discipline and independence that brought him to the attention of the Special Air Services Brigade, a newly formed commando unit. It was a secret and elite corps, specializing in hit-and-run raids and in pinpointing targets behind enemy lines for

RAF bombers. More choosy about its recruits than any other branch of service, the SAS trained in four-man teams for the most dangerous operations of the war. Sparrowhawk's SAS unit was shipped to North Africa, where it teamed with the Long Range Desert Group to destroy hundreds of Luftwaffe aircraft on the ground. The commandos also demolished tons of badly needed German war supplies.

Next, the SAS was sent to Sicily, France and Holland. So effective were they that Hitler ordered them hunted down and disposed of at all cost. Ensuring that SAS men who fell into German hands would face torture and certain execution. In a Normandy village a French double agent betrayed Sparrowhawk's four-man team to the Gestapo, who cut out the tongue of one commando and broke his spine with iron bars. A second was set afire in the courtyard in front of Sparrowhawk's cell.

But before Sparrowhawk and the remaining team member could be disposed of, a British bombing raid inflicted heavy damage on the village, flattening buildings, including the jail, and freeing the pair.

"Toddle on ahead, mate," Sparrowhawk said to his friend. "A matter to dispose of first, then I'll catch up to you."

"We'll both dispose of it," the commando said.

Lacking the papers and weapons, they hid until midnight, then made their way to the edge of town, to the small farm where the treacherous double agent lived. Moving from shadow to shadow they slipped into the barn to wait. They knew the traitor's routine. Dinner, followed by Camembert cheese and apple brandy, then a trip to the barn to tend cows and a pair of horses. Hungry, filthy, red eyed from lack of sleep, the commandos looked around for weapons.

An hour later the traitor, relaxed and smoking a long clay pipe, strolled into the barn. Sparrowhawk, wielding a sickle taken from behind the door, beheaded him and stuck his head on a pitchfork. The grisly trophy was left standing in a stall and facing a mare about to foal.

"Nietzsche's Gentlemen," the SAS's detractors called it. A private undisciplined collection of thugs and psychopaths quick to do the dirty work in the name of king or queen. Sparrowhawk, who stayed on with the regiment after the war, knew better. There was no more disciplined group of soldiers in the world than the SAS; its standards were so high that troopers with years of experience in other regiments failed to qualify for the SAS no matter how hard they tried.

Snobbery was another reason for the criticism; the SAS had little respect for rank, an attitude unacceptable to regular army officers in a class-ridden society. SAS officers were respected only on the basis of performance, not commission. The unit's secrecy also lent credence to much of the criticism leveled at it. But secrecy was necessary, for the quiet wars now being fought against communism were delicate exercises in edged diplomacy and killing.

Quiet wars protected oil rights, gold mines, shipping lanes, friendly leaders. With cold efficiency, Sparrowhawk and the SAS plied their trade in Malaya, Borneo, Africa, South Arabia. It was an exciting and dangerous time and Sparrowhawk was never happier. He had found his Holy Grail, the beige SAS beret and cloth badge bearing the well-known winged dagger.

When he was thirty-five he met and married Unity Palethorpe, the sister of an SAS trooper, a shy woman one foot taller. From the beginning they loved each other deeply. She was intelligent, reserved and devoted, seeing him as heroic and sensitive. They shared a love of books, animals, Haydn and a reverence for the monarchy. "We married and lived happily ever after," Sparrowhawk said of her, quoting Churchill's description of his own marriage.

They had one child, a daughter Valerie, who, with her golden hair and fair skin, Sparrowhawk called his piece of the sun. He loved them both, the tall, plain woman and the little girl who delighted in wearing the decorations awarded to her father in secret and unpublicized SAS ceremonies. It pleased him that among his daughter's first words were *"Free beer,"* the SAS recall code that drew the men back to base to pick up uniforms and equipment for a mission. But her mother stopped the child from saying *"Double tap,"* the SAS code for two shots in the head.

For Sparrowhawk the only release he needed from his work was time with Unity, the two strolling arm in arm through the woods or along a country road while he told her of the intrigues, betrayals and assassinations concocted in

Whitehall's corridors of power, to be dealt with by "Nietzsche's Gentlemen," often at the cost of their lives.

"You've got clowns in Whitehall," he told her, "who paint their damned faces red with our blood."

That's when he spoke to her of those who had failed "to beat the clock," who had been killed and their names inscribed on the SAS regimental clock tower in Hereford.

Sparrowhawk said to his wife, "I'm beginning to believe that all of life is a preparation for death. Can't say as I like the idea. Makes God out to be a witless ass if he can't think of a more clever ending than that."

In his forties, Sparrowhawk, now a major, was relieved from active duty and assigned to administrative duties at SAS headquarters. Restless and ill at ease behind a desk, he soon tired of working with recruits and greeting members of Parliament on inspection tours. He was a soldier; he craved the excitement of combat. But combat was a young man's job. Sparrowhawk endured desk duty as long as he could, for less than a year. Then he resigned to work for a London security firm composed of ex-SAS men like himself. The firm, however, went bankrupt and Sparrowhawk, with a family to support, was forced to work as little more than a hired muscle.

He served as bodyguard to arms dealers, Arab sheiks, visiting American film stars, the children of wealthy industrialists. A few British businessmen consulted him on security measures for themselves and their companies and once he served as go-between in a Rome kidnapping. He was getting older, but not richer.

To pay for private medical care for Unity, Sparrowhawk turned thief. He stole industrial secrets and church antiques coveted by a private collector and love letters being used by a New Scotland Yard detective to blackmail a homosexual member of Parliament. It was with relief that he returned to soldiering late in 1974, accepting a job with South African forces to help track down black guerrillas on the country's northern border. The contract lasted a month, paid little and was notable only in that Sparrowhawk killed a Russian woman.

A pair of Russians were in the South African bush to gauge the amounts of black military resistance to that country's white regime; they were serving as temporary advisers to the guerrillas when all fell into an ambush set by Sparrowhawk. One of the two Russians could have escaped, but stayed behind to help his wounded comrade. When it was apparent that neither could get away, the one who had not been wounded fought with a ferocity that stunned Sparrowhawk.

It was Sparrowhawk who finally killed him, only to learn that the determined fighter had been a heavyset woman with the slant eyes of her Tartar forebears; the comrade she had refused to leave was her husband. When she saw that he was mortally wounded, she had fought to the death rather than surrender. Sparrowhawk was impressed and disturbed by her bravery. Anyone who seemed fearless in the face of death left him uneasy.

On his return to Johannesburg he was offered five thousand pounds to escort a diamond dealer to Saigon, where the dealer was to purchase gems owned by a South Vietnamese general. The Vietnam War, which in truth had begun in 1946 with France opposing Ho Chi Minh, was winding down. American troops, per the Paris cease-fire agreement of January 1973, had been withdrawing from Southeast Asia for the past two years. A small number of military advisers remained, along with the American embassy personnel in Saigon. However, it was only a matter of weeks before the NVA, the North Vietnamese Army, would move south and take Saigon.

The general that Sparrowhawk and the diamond dealer came to South Vietnam to meet was planning to leave, but not empty-handed. Diamonds, like gold, were an inflation-proof currency.

When the diamond deal was concluded Sparrowhawk was offered more work in Saigon. With the CIA.

Ruttencutter, the slim, icy New Yorker who proposed that Sparrowhawk work for "the Company," said, "We've little choice. The Paris treaty planted an international commission in this city and its people are watching us like hawks. The feeling is it's best not to bring any more of our own people here. So we're forced to use independents, free-lancers like yourself. You come highly recommended."

"Terribly kind of you." In the humid monsoon weather, in

sticky heat, Ruttencutter never perspired. He talked out of the side of his mouth, which Sparrowhawk found amusing.

"Means you keep a low profile," said Ruttencutter. "Poles, French, Hungarians are hot to hang truce violations on us. Bastards spend most of their time with the bar girls. I hope they get a dose of the clap that won't quit."

"Not to veer off on too sharp a tangent, but what do I do in a war which appears to be nearing its end?"

"This and that. One thing and another. Specifically? Let's say you act as a courier between here and Hong Kong, Singapore, Thailand, Laos. Make a little trip to Cambodia. Ride shotgun on certain flights on a certain airline in which we have an interest. Join some of our people on little trips outside of Saigon."

Sparrowhawk's eyes narrowed. "Sounds quite scenic, actually. You're leaving out something."

"Which is?"

"You neglected to mention killing for you."

Ruttencutter looked away. "Whatever will be, will be, as they say." He turned back to Sparrowhawk. "Ten thousand dollars a month. Interested?"

Sparrowhawk gave him a concentrated look, then said: "When do we commence our association?"

Special jobs. One involved taking part in the interrogation of Viet Cong prisoners kidnapped from villages at the CIA's request by Robbie Ambrose and Dorian Raymond, two American SEALs who did the odd task now and again for the frozen Ruttencutter. Sparrowhawk and the SEALs formed an attachment of sorts, though neither GI struck him as a giant intellect. Robbie, however, had an appealing politeness that hid the most extraordinary capacity for violence. An amazing hand-to-hand fighter. Dorian was somewhat dimmer, with infantile dreams of sudden wealth and a taste for dissipation.

Being involved with the CIA brought all three into contact with George Chihara, an influential Japanese businessman and one of Saigon's prime movers and shakers. Chihara was also a CIA front; the airline ostensibly owned by him was actually CIA backed and used to transport opium grown by northern tribesmen to Saigon, to fatten the bank accounts of South Vietnamese politicians and generals. Aiding the opium traffic was the price America seemed willing to pay for allies in the fight against communism.

Sparrowhawk found Chihara more than slightly reptilian in appearance. Chihara also had the Japanese reserve with strangers, and kept his home and family apart from his business dealings. From the beginning, Sparrowhawk doubted Chihara could be trusted. His airline flew CIA agents to and from the north; the roads and surrounding countryside were almost entirely in the hands of the North Vietnamese and air travel was not merely the safest way of travel. It was the only way.

Chihara also arranged for CIA agents to receive the high black-market rate for dollars, and used his considerable influence with Saigon politicians, when asked by the Americans. All of this, plus Chihara's legitimate business had made him rich. He was to grow even richer from his association with Paul Molise, an American Mafioso who had come to Saigon for opium. Chihara saw that he got all he needed.

Robbie knew quite a bit about Paul Molise, a lean, intense man who insisted on wearing three-piece suits at all times and actually had a university education, something Sparrowhawk would never have associated with the son of a wog thug.

"Paulie's different," said Robbie. "Smooth. Like spit on a doorknob. College, computers. Got smarts up the ass. Father heads the biggest 'family' in New York. *Capo di tutti capi.* Boss of bosses. Paulie's king shit. He's got generals on his payroll. American generals, man. Has gooks bought and paid for, too. Politicians, generals. That's how he gets all the dope he needs."

Sparrowhawk, like most Brits, found American criminals fascinating. "I thought the Mafia was getting its heroin out of Turkey and Marseilles."

"No more. American and French cops put a stop to that. Busted people in the States, France, Sicily. Plus the Turks aren't letting their people grow opium anymore. You got brown heroin and pink heroin coming out of Mexico. But addicts like white. Best white around is over here. Fry your brains, that shit. Get it right from 'the Golden Triangle.' Burma, Thailand, Laos. Figure a way to get it to the States and, man, you're in business. Molise has a few other things going for him, too."

"Such as?"

"Well, major, it's like this. Construction. Somebody's got to build bases, roads, airfields, movie theaters, bowling alleys, ice cream parlors. I mean you got to have those things, right? Army figures Americans can do it better than the gooks, so they hire Americans. Lot of money changes hands, but what the hell. Enough left over for everybody. Then there's slot machines for the soldiers' clubs, liquor, food, jukeboxes, furniture, kitchen equipment. You name it. See, you got to have these things, else GIs go crazy. I bet Molise is copping a fortune out of this war. Far as he's concerned the war can goddamn go on forever."

Sparrowhawk's nose wrinkled in disgust. Not at the profit being made. God knows he was not that naive. What he found disgraceful was the pampering of field soldiers. No wonder America was losing the war. The Viet Cong went all day on a handful of uncooked rice and ditch water. No comparison.

He said, "I gather Mr. Chihara isn't exactly destitute himself."

"If you mean he's getting his out of this war, you're right. Gold, dope, his businesses. Ol' George—"

"You said gold."

"Seen it myself, me and Dorian. We had to go into Cambodia. Bring back an agent before they wasted his ass. Gook agent. Should have left him there, but that's beside the point. Used one of Chihara's planes. Made a stop in some fuckin' town, can't remember the name, but it was gold bars we picked up. Seen it myself, me and Dorian. See, major, you got to remember right now paper money ain't worth diddley squat. Gold, diamonds, dope. That's worth something. If you want to leave this armpit of a country and have something to show for it, you go for something hard like that."

"Gold, diamonds, dope."

"There you go."

Robbie lowered his voice. "Tell you something else. Ol' George is buying all the gold and diamonds he can get his hands on. Buying it from all over the place, here, up north, Thailand, Laos. All over the place. Sends them planes of his out and they come back nice and heavy. Be willing to bet that ol' George has a pile of shit hidden somewhere."

"How do you know he hasn't sent it all out of the country?"

"Some of it, sure. Not all of it. He's got it coming in every week. Couldn't possibly have sent it all out."

April 1975. Paul Molise took his time stubbing out a cigarette. "How many days you figure before this city falls to the Cong?"

Sparrowhawk said, "Hours. Days. For certain, within the week. There'll be the usual bloodbath, phony trials, the customary purge. A lot of people will die and their deaths won't be easy. Communists are puritanical and puritans are among the most sadistic bastards on God's green earth. I've seen what they've done in other countries. I don't expect it to be any different here."

"I invited you and Robbie here for a reason." Molise poured scotch into two glasses. Robbie had previously shook his head in refusal. The three men were in Molise's suite in a hotel on Nguyen Hue Boulevard. Three stories below in the street an overturned jeep still burned where looters had left the vehicle and its dead driver. Smoke from midnight fires floated from the U.S. embassy, the presidential palace and a handful of government buildings, where documents were being burned to keep them out of Communist hands. Power and peace of mind now belonged only to those able to buy their way out of the doomed city.

Molise said, "I want to talk about George Chihara."

Sparrowhawk looked at Robbie. Dear God, we pay for everything in this life. Molise had promised Sparrowhawk the job of a lifetime, the presidency of a private intelligence firm in New York at a salary larger than anything Sparrowhawk had ever dreamed of. Tonight that promise had given Molise the right to drag Sparrowhawk and Robbie out into Saigon's dangerous streets for a little chat. After curfew, no less.

Sparrowhawk was already a part-time employee of Paul Molise. With CIA permission the Englishman occasionally served as his bodyguard, particularly when the American was carrying large amounts of cash around Saigon to pay for heroin or morphine base. Molise, Chihara, Ruttencutter, the French underworld and South Vietnam's leading politicians all knew one another. Narcotics, Sparrowhawk observed, had a way of bringing people together.

"Before I get into Chihara," said Molise, "I'd like to start by saying I want you"—he pointed to Sparrowhawk—"to delay your departure from Saigon."

"You must be mad. I'm booked on a helicopter leaving this cesspool in forty-eight hours."

"Call it a favor. To me."

Has me by the balls, thought Sparrowhawk, and all because of that New York job. Having taken the bugger's bread, I must now sing his song. On the other hand, what good is the promise of lucrative employment to a dead man?

"I have no wish to rot in a Viet Cong jail cell," Sparrowhawk said.

"Five hundred thousand dollars for twenty-four hours of your time," said Molise. "The money will be waiting for you when you arrive in New York. Or I can put it in a bank of your choice anywhere in the world."

Sparrowhawk's eyes narrowed.

Molise finished his scotch and poured another. "I was to go back to my father with the biggest heroin deal since we first started dealing with these assholes. But I can't do that now, thanks to Mr. Chihara."

Sparrowhawk knew why. Two days ago Saigon customs officials had received a tip that someone planned to smuggle 100 kilos of heroin out of the country. Ordinarily the officials would have been bribed and the heroin allowed to continue on its way, in this case to Canada, then down to New York. All of Saigon knew the heroin, purchased at a cost of several million, belonged to Paul Molise. And the city knew that someone he trusted had betrayed him.

"Chihara fucked me," Molise said. "Don't ask me how I know. I know, that's all. The people who told me are very reliable. Chihara and everybody else want to get out of Saigon with all the money they can. He's got people in his pocket I can't touch and I'm talking about the presidential palace, which is as high as you can go in this town. It's a crazy time over here now. All of us, we're playing a game without rules. Saigon's going down the toilet and nobody gives a rat's ass. So nobody keeps their word anymore."

Molise shook his head. Down on the street there was the

whack of a single pistol shot. None of the men moved. In Saigon gunshots were as common as motorbikes.

"My money, my heroin and I can't do shit about it. Chihara arranges a deal for me, then screws me and I'm supposed to walk away and keep quiet." He said something softly, in Italian, eyes glazed with hatred. Sparrowhawk didn't understand the word, but the meaning was clear.

Vengeance.

Sparrowhawk ignored his drink. He had a feeling his life was going to change forever. Best keep a clear head for the next few minutes.

Molise said, "Fucking Chihara got a third of what the Buddha-heads took from me. They had me set up all the time. Anyway, couple days from now Chihara's moving one last load of gold and diamonds out of Saigon. Along with his share of my heroin. Cong's overrun the airfield at Bien Hoa, so there goes Chihara's planes. He's made arrangements to get out by ship, which is tied up right now in the Saigon River."

Molise leaned forward and aimed his drink at Sparrowhawk. "I want you to bring Chihara's ass to me. Bring that bastard to me, along with his diamonds and gold and my heroin. No way I can face my father again until I've dealt with this fucking business and believe me, I'm going to, one way or another. You lose respect, you lose everything and, mister, no way am I going to lose respect. I don't have my own people here. I've got an accountant who's down the hall in his room with the runs and I've got one construction man meeting with some people tonight to get whatever he can for the equipment I'm forced to leave behind. But no shooters. I don't have shooters. Anyway, I don't want Chihara dead. Dead isn't good enough. Want him to bleed. Want him to wake up every morning and know that what's happening to him is because of me."

Chihara has planted thorns, thought Sparrowhawk. Therefore he can hardly expect to gather roses.

Molise said, "I'm turning him over to the Cong. They have a price on his head and they'll be glad to see him. When they finish with Mr. Chihara the bastard will wish he was dead a hundred times over."

"He's got a wife and two daughters," Sparrowhawk said.

"They go, too. But you do a job on them. Something special before you kill them. Use your imagination. I want Chihara to suffer and I want him to know I did it."

Sparrowhawk took his first sip of scotch. Well, that would certainly settle Mr. Chihara's account. Sparrowhawk, however, could see no reason to do anything special to a man's wife and daughters. Should he agree to handle this dirty business the women would be treated respectfully. A double tap for each and that's the end of it.

"I think you can bring Dorian in on this, too," Molise said. "Where is he anyway?"

"Fucking his brains out over on Tu Do Street," Robbie said. "Whores are practically giving it away. Some of the girls figure if they're nice to Dorian maybe he'll help them to get out before the Cong takes over."

Molise said, "I've got a rundown on Chihara's villa. Guards, servants, all the information you'll need. He'll move the gold and diamonds out on a truck. Seven guards armed with automatic weapons. You'll have to take them out."

Robbie shrugged. "No problem."

Using a thumbnail, a thoughtful Sparrowhawk stroked a waxed end of his mustache. Robbie, lad, there was a problem.

Behind a narrowed gaze the Englishman leaned toward Molise and said coldly, "Now let's have the real story."

The Italian stared at him for a long time, then looked away. "I'm paying you—"

Sparrowhawk was on his feet, punctuating his words with a clenched fist. "You're not bloody well paying me enough to get myself killed. No more games, sir. *If. You. Please.* Chihara's a CIA agent. You're too close to Ruttencutter to do this on your own. You had to have clearance first, which means someone has concocted an altogether different brew from the one you're describing to me. Before you remove a country's agents from the face of this earth you get permission."

Molise rubbed his unshaven chin. "It's been cleared. Believe me, it's been cleared."

"Oh, I do believe you. And since this concerns my life and Robbie's, I'd prefer you keep me fully informed. Why do Ruttencutter and the CIA want to destroy George Chihara, a man who, until now, has served 'the Company' well and true?"

Molise stared at the ceiling, where a small lizard crawled from behind a slowly revolving wooden fan to begin a long trek across the ceiling and toward the front door. "Two reasons. Actually, one. They want to trade him for one of their guys the Cong's had for over a year. An American."

"Why Chihara? Why not some other poor unfortunate?"

"Like I said, it's all part of the same big picture. The CIA plans to leave agents behind here in Saigon when it moves out. Locals. Vietnamese. Something it's been working on for weeks."

"I'm aware of the plan."

"Supposed to be a secret. Anyway, a few days ago a couple of very important Vietnamese approach the CIA and threaten to blow the plan sky high unless the CIA pays what is called a 'tax.' They threatened to give a list of those agents to the Cong."

"Unless the CIA paid up."

Molise nodded. "That wasn't all. There was also talk about the South Vietnamese setting up mortars and rockets on rooftops near the American embassy, attacking the embassy and the helicopters taking people out to the American carriers offshore. Unless the CIA paid the tax." Molise sighed. "Ten million."

"Jesus." Sparrowhawk took his first sip of scotch.

Robbie whistled. For a while the room remained silent. Outside, rockets and artillery could be heard in the distance. The Viet Cong was inching closer with each second.

Molise said, "This 'tax' shit came from the Vietnamese but Chihara was behind it. He gave them the list of agents and he came up with the idea of putting on the squeeze while everybody's in a panic to quit this fucking place. For which I don't blame them in the least."

Sparrowhawk gazed at Molise from the corner of his eye. "And with that, Mr. Chihara was living on borrowed time, expendable to both you and Mr. Ruttencutter."

Molise's smile was wire thin and glacial. "Sometimes you just get lucky in life. Seems me and Ruttencutter wanted the same thing at the same time."

"Not so lucky for Mr. Chihara, I'm afraid."

"Lucky for you, though." Molise looked down into his drink. "Still want that job in New York?"

New York
November 1981

In his office at Management Systems Consultants, Sparrowhawk finished reading the last page of the report on Michelle Asama, made his final check mark, then tossed his gold pen on the desk. He brought his tea to his mouth, sipped and recoiled. Cold. He set the cup aside, but decided against asking Mrs. Rosebery to make him another cup. He wanted to be alone for a while longer, to think about Saigon, about what he had done there on that final night, rather than return to Manchester and be poor again.

Chihara's villa. The smell of tea, fish, cinnamon on the humid night air. Inside the sprawling, whitewashed building George Chihara lay facedown on the tatami that covered his living room floor. Robbie, knee on the back of Chihara's neck, grinned. He knew what was coming next.

Sparrowhawk pressed Chihara's right wrist into the mat and aimed a Colt .45 automatic at the back of the Japanese's hand and as Robbie giggled, the Englishman pulled the trigger.

No shot. No sound. No bullet.

Chihara, neverthless, felt a horrible pain.

The .45, a CIA weapon, had been converted to fire darts that tore into the body with the force of a bullet and killed without making a sound.

The dart ripped into Chihara's hand, driving through bone, tendons, ligaments, pinning the hand to the floor. Somehow he managed not to cry out, but stiffened and gritted his teeth; the veins in his temple pressed hard against his perspiring skin.

Minutes ago, Sparrowhawk, Robbie and Dorian had killed the seven guards in front of the villa, catching them unawares while they loaded the truck with flat wooden packing cases. Then the Englishman and the two Americans had rushed into the villa, killing three more guards and two servants. Chihara was their prisoner. But before they had reached him he had yelled something in Japanese. A command? A warning? Sparrowhawk didn't know. He did know that three women at the top of the winding staircase had turned and run toward a room behind them, locking themselves inside.

At the same time a car nearing the villa had suddenly pulled away.

Questions, calling for immediate answers.

Sparrowhawk tapped Chihara's bleeding hand with the barrel of the .45. "Once more. Who was in the car that just left here? What did you yell out to them?"

Chihara's breathing was raspy, ugly. He said nothing.

Sparrowhawk stepped over his prone body. The chunky Japanese tried to throw Robbie off and failed. Attempting to quiet him Robbie dug the point of a k-bar into his ear. Still Chihara struggled. He knew that Sparrowhawk was about to work on his other hand and so he shifted, attempting to hide his left arm under his body. Robbie, however, punched the Japanese in the left bicep with vicious force. Chihara went limp. His arm was stunned, pained.

Without a word Sparrowhawk pulled the arm away from the body, stepped on the wrist, fired a dart into the hand. The steel-tipped projectile tore off the pinky and ring fingers. Blood spurted onto the tatami and Chihara, crazed with pain, almost succeeded in throwing off Robbie.

Sparrowhawk said, "Who was in that car? What did you say to them?"

"Servant," Chihara whispered. "Told him to escape."

The Englishman looked at Robbie, then at Dorian, who held an M-16 on several quiet Vietnamese servants. Eyes on the group, Dorian said, "Hey, Birdman, suppose the fucker's lying. Suppose whoever was out there has gone to bring back help."

"That's occurred to me. Which is why we'll be moving on. But first, we have three women upstairs." He looked down at Chihara. "Are they armed?"

Silence.

"Robbie, be so kind as to turn the gentleman over and don't be too nice about it."

Robbie wasn't.

Chihara's hands bled profusely. His round face was beaded with perspiration. His nostrils flared as he fought against the pain. But his eyes, hot with hatred, never left Sparrowhawk.

The Englishman touched Chihara's scrotum with the .45. "I shan't ask you again."

Chihara quickly said, "They have no guns."

"Observe, Robbie, how threatening to remove a man's penis tends to concentrate his mind. Dorian, keep an eye on things down here. Robbie and I are going upstairs to see to the ladies."

There was a light in Robbie's eyes. "Hey, major, Paulie said something special. Like do a number on them."

"I know what Paulie said, but we'll do things my way, if you don't mind. We only have Mr. Chihara's word that his warning was issued to a servant and no one else. I'd hate to be caught here by some of Mr. Chihara's more violent associates. Besides, there's no need to drag things out. Dispose of the women as quickly as possible and that will be the end of it."

"You're the boss."

On the second floor the two men thumbed the safety off their M-16s and cautiously made their way from door to door, trying each knob, holding their breath. The last room on the right, its door locked, made them stop.

Sparrowhawk nodded at Robbie, who held the butt of his M-16 tight against his hip, aimed at the lock and jerked the trigger. The lock disappeared, ripped from the door along with chunks of wood. Robbie kicked the door open and the two rushed in, crouched, eyes and rifles sweeping the room in front of them. Silence. A clock ticked on an end table and warm night air came through an opened barred window to mingle with the smell of perfume.

Robbie saw them first. He pointed, a forefinger aimed at a four-poster bed.

Sparrowhawk took a step forward, then stopped. On the bed two Japanese women lay side by side, their blood-covered bodies limp in death. One was small, her dark hair mixed with gray; the other was young, in her early twenties. A bloodstained knife lay near a pillow, while a second knife had slipped from one dead woman's hand to fall to the floor. A third woman, also in her twenties, sat in a stuffed chair facing a dressing table. Her bloodied corpse stared unseeing into a large oval mirror. Each woman had her ankles tied together.

Ritual deaths. Sparrowhawk knew it. And yet he knew nothing. There had to be a reason for these three deaths, an important reason.

"Killed themselves," he whispered. "Took their own lives. Bloody fools."

He had to know why. A heat that reminded him of the oppressive air in a Manchester steel mill suddenly seemed to fill his brain, leaving him weak and uneasy.

Robbie said, "Seppuku. Read about it, but never seen it before." He was detached, unaffected, totally at ease with what was around him.

Sparrowhawk looked at him. "Hara-kiri, you mean."

Robbie shook his head. "Wrong term. Hara-kiri's the term, but even that's only used by people outside of Japan. Seppuku's the word. Means stomach cutting. Samurai and high-class people kill themselves this way as a matter of honor. It's like death is your own business. You pick the time, the place. You cheat your enemy, stop him from doing what he wants with you. You escape, you might say. Avoid disgrace. Most of the time only important people were allowed to kill themselves this way. Never saw it done before. Read about it, but never saw it."

"Is it part of that karate business you practice all the time?"

Robbie shook his head. "No way. Belongs to old-time samurai. Stab yourself in the stomach. Knife goes in low on the left side, then you drag it across and up. A guy stands behind you with a sword, they call him a kaishaku, sort of a friendly executioner, and when he thinks the pain is too much for you he swings that sword and wham, there goes your head. I mean like your guts are sliding out onto the floor and the pain has to be something, so this kaishaku, he's doing you a favor by killing you."

Robbie moved closer. "See? Notice something. These women didn't cut themselves in the stomach. Look here. Cut themselves in the neck. That's how women are supposed to commit seppuku. Find that artery and you dig in. Those *knives are called* kai-ken. *Special weapons for women. Like they use them on themselves or you or whatever."*

Sparrowhawk shivered. "Dear God, where did they find the courage? Where?"

Downstairs Chihara sat on the floor, bleeding hands resting on his thighs. Blood dripped from his ear where Robbie had cut him with the k-bar. The Japanese looked up at Sparrowhawk with contempt and defiance. The Englishman felt uneasy. Something told him it would be wiser to kill this man and be done with it.

"It is easy to die unwillingly," Chihara said. "The difficult thing is to die submissively."

Sparrowhawk ached to kill him. But that's not what Paul Molise wanted.

He said to Chihara. "They're dead. Doesn't that bother you?"

Slowly, a small smile on his wide face, the Japanese shook his head.

"You're lying."

Chihara looked away.

"I said you're lying. Tell me you're lying or I'll kill you here and now."

"You won't kill me. And the women have escaped from you. We have won. A samurai does not fear shi."

Sparrowhawk looked at Robbie, who said, "Shi *means death."*

The women. Now Sparrowhawk knew what he felt when he saw them; he felt afraid and he felt cheated, as if they had put something over on him, as if, yes, they had won.

Chihara said something in Japanese. Robbie smiled and shook his head. "No way, José. Never happen." He looked at Sparrowhawk. "Man says even if we kill him, says he's going to kill us all. You, me, Dorian, Molise. Says there's no way we can stop him. Something about reaching past death to get all four of us."

"Why were their ankles tied together like that?"

"Part of the ritual. When women commit seppuku *they tie their ankles together to protect their modesty. Don't want their legs to be getting twitchy in death and flying all over the place and letting guys have a cheap thrill looking up their dresses. Japanese are polite all the goddamn time."*

Dorian, rifle still on the cowering servants, caught Sparrowhawk's eye. "Hey, Birdman, how about it?"

Sparrowhawk nodded. It was not true that God alone could finish. Robbie, as always, was alert and needed no prompting. Safeties came off and without a word the three fired into the servants. Doomed Vietnamese men and women screamed, pleaded, attempted to flee. Round after round of bullets tore plaster from the wall, shattered windows, shredded furniture and lifted hysterical servants from the floor to slam them into the chairs and tables. Shell casings popped from the rifles to bounce around on the tatami like brass insects.

Sparrowhawk held up a hand and the shooting stopped. Blue smoke rose from the heated weapons. In front of the three men lay mutilated and mangled human beings covered with plaster dust, furniture chunks and broken glass from windows and French doors, their bodies appearing little more than bloodied rags. Do and have done, thought Sparrowhawk.

He spun on his heel. "Bring the little Jap and let's get out of here."

In the truck, Robbie drove while Sparrowhawk sat beside him. Dorian and a bound Chihara were in back, hidden by packing cases, luggage and household items. Sparrowhawk could hear Dorian tearing at the suitcases. Looting, as usual. A witless ass, Dorian, and greedy to boot. Sparrowhawk had negotiated one hundred thousand dollars apiece from Molise for him and Robbie, payment for their services tonight. And still Dorian played the role of the vulture.

The Englishman did not dwell too long on Dorian's shortcomings. There was something else to do in connection with Chihara's villa.

A half mile from the village the truck pulled over to the side of the road where Sparrowhawk, via a hand radio, called down a rocket attack on Chihara's tastefully appointed home. The attack, plus keeping Manny Decker occupied elsewhere for the past forty-eight hours, indicated that Ruttencutter, on rare occasions, could be a man of his word.

In the warm night and to the thunder of distant artillery, the truck moved along wide boulevards lined with tamarind trees, avoiding crowds and traffic where possible, carefully eyeing cyclo drivers, child beggars, old men in the conical hats of Viet peasants, teenage whores and others who might be a stalking horse for bands of armed looters. Safeties off, Sparrowhawk ordered. Grenades to be near at hand.

No more thoughts of shi *and George Chihara. Instead Sparrowhawk put his mind on the five hundred thousand American dollars to be deposited in his name in a Liechtenstein bank, and on the job of a lifetime waiting for him in New York; and he told himself that the deaths of three Japanese women held no meaning for him.*

Sparrowhawk would build a new life on the corpses of George Chihara and his wife and daughters. As for reaching out from beyond the grave, the thought was a rather featherheaded notion, the prattling of a simpleton. Shi, *Mr. Chihara, was the end of all things, a silence.*

New York
November 1981

A second reading of the Michelle Asama report pushed Sparrowhawk into making a telephone call to Belgium. Using an unlisted phone kept in a locked bottom drawer of his desk he dialed Nial Hinds, a British arms dealer with warehouses in Brussels and Liège. Liège was where Hinds spent most of his time; the French-speaking Belgian city was the center of the European arms trade, and had been since the Middle Ages. An arms fair was held here each week, drawing hundreds who moved among displays of rifles, pistols, grenades, tanks, missiles as though strolling through a vegetable market. Hinds, like all arms dealers, welcomed cash customers of any ideological persuasion.

Red faced and portly, Hinds was also a classical organist of some accomplishment and one of the dealers trading in American arms captured by the Viet Cong. He was the man to ask about George Chihara.

"Do my best, old sock," Hinds said over a scratchy transatlantic connection. "Take a day or two, you know. Bloody Cong have so many revolutionary committees and party chairmen to go through. Swine don't return your calls half the time."

"Quickly as possible, Nial. Handle it yourself. Don't want this to get about. Private inquiry, call it."

"Get back to you. And you owe me one, old fruit."

"I'll remember."

"Won't let you forget."

Hinds's call from Belgium came two days later. This time the connection was worse; the wire was riddled with echoes, crossed conversations, unexplained silences. Sparrowhawk could hardly hear the arms dealer and it annoyed him. Leaving his desk, he carried the phone to the window and looked down on Manhattan. The November days were getting shorter, darker.

"Nial, speak up. I can hardly hear you."

". . . said a woman tried to free your Chihara. He's dead."

"When did he die?"

"Woman . . ."

"Woman? Nial, you said woman. Who was she? Was she related to Chihara? Can you describe her?"

"Hello, Trevor? Trevor? Are you there? Damn this thing. Can't hear you . . . Trevor, I'm leaving for Zimbabwe."

"Nial, the woman—"

Silence. The line was dead.

Enraged, Sparrowhawk, telephone in one hand, receiver in the other, beat against the window. No one came back from the dead. No one. *Shi* was the end of all things.

"Mr Sparrowhawk, are you all right? I heard banging—" Mrs. Rosebery rushed to him. "Good Lord, your hands."

They were bleeding. As George Chihara's hands had bled that last night in Saigon.

Three

Bassai

Karate *kata,* or form, involving repeated switching of blocking arms, indicating changing from disadvantageous to advantageous position. In performing this *kata* one aims for a will similar to that required to smash into an enemy's fortress.

12

Coming to Las Vegas was as dangerous as anything Dorian Raymond had ever done in his life.

He was in the city where, in the next few hours, Robbie would probably rape and kill a woman before stepping into a downtown hotel arena to fight the light-heavyweight champion of Mexico. Too nervous to sleep, Dorian got out of bed shortly before noon. He showered and shaved, then did a little cocaine for courage, pouring the white powder onto a small hand mirror and using a razor blade to shape the powder into a pair of thin lines before inhaling it through a rolled one-hundred-dollar bill. He dressed in a black sports shirt, beige summer suit, looped two thin gold chains around his neck and left his hotel room. At the front desk he handed his room key to the clerk, a round-faced Hopi Indian girl, who mechanically suggested he have a nice day and ignored his bold gaze at her breasts swelling under a beaded vest.

For a few minutes Dorian hung around the lobby staring at two million in silver dollars on display. The money, which always drew a crowd, was stacked on a raised platform and flanked by sunburned, crew-cut security guards wearing black uniforms, mirrored sunglasses and nickel-plated revolvers on one hip. Dorian had seen their kind in Nam, rawboned Southerners who collected ears from dead Vietnamese, strung them into a necklace and wore it long after the ears turned brown and stinking. Hardasses who could drive a nail into your forehead with one blow of their fist.

A new ruling in Dorian's precinct had forced him to make the trip to Las Vegas. All long-distance calls now had to be accounted for. Blame it on a budget squeeze coming out of the mayor's office. Long distance had to be official business only, which left Robbie out. He wasn't official business, not until Dorian had explored the benefits of turning Robbie in. Or not.

Nor would telephoning from home work at the moment, not if Dorian wanted to get close to Robbie before the murder went down. How could you say, "Sergeant, I'm telephoning about a whacko who's about to rape and murder a woman in your town. Sure I know who he is, but right now I'd like to keep that to myself. Tell you this, though: our boy is a karate freak. He'll waste this broad, then go out and half kill some other karate guy. I think there's a connection there. Anyway, soon as the killing's over, call me at home, not at the precinct. Sorry, no questions about how I know all this. It's our little secret, you and me. Have a nice day."

Impossible to run that by anybody and not have it blow up in your own face. No, Dorian had to find a city where Robbie was scheduled to fight, and then stay out of sight while Robbie played his little game. After that, Dorian would know for certain that Robbie had a tendency toward unsavory acts.

Las Vegas was Dorian's favorite city. Around-the-clock action. Gambling, women, good food, tennis at three in the morning and a glittering style that Atlantic City and Caribbean casinos couldn't match. There was the Circus-Circus casino, where gamblers could look up and see a full circus performing high overhead, complete with the sideshow and brass band; there was year-round jai alai, the world's fastest sport, at the MGM Grand; a lake in the lobby of Caesars Palace, with a live band playing on a floating barge; a slot machine at the Union Plaza, where the grand prize was an airplane. People who put down Vegas wouldn't know a good thing if it fell from heaven and bit them on the ass.

Outside his hotel, Dorian closed his eyes while waiting for a taxi, letting the mild desert air wash over him. The weather here was a thousand times better than New York, where the snow and ice came up to his balls. He had gone directly to the hotel from McCarran Airport and had tried to nap, but couldn't. Too antsy. Too worried about Robbie.

He told the driver to take him to police headquarters and when the driver asked him what was wrong Dorian flashed his badge and said he was a New York cop paying a courtesy call, nothing more. The badge nailed the driver's mouth shut, which suited Dorian just fine.

Time to make this tfip had come from Dorian's personals, the three days off New York cops received each year to deal with personal affairs, no questions asked. Now that he was in Las Vegas, he suddenly felt as though his dick was hanging over the fence and Robbie had the knife.

Stepping into the police station cheered him up. Cops were cops all over the world; they took care of their own. The Vegas cops could not have been friendlier, treating Dorian, a New York City detective, like a visiting celebrity. Kojak, Columbo and Dirty Harry rolled into one. He wasn't alone anymore. Somebody found a bottle of Wild Turkey and a package of paper cups. Two drinks later Dorian, his jacket off, was laughing.

Still, he did not forget why he had come here. He wanted the cops in this town to know who he was when he contacted them again. Meanwhile it was let's hold hands and get acquainted.

"Fewer tourists is right," the duty sergeant said. "Hotels here have lost a little to Atlantic City. Gasoline prices have hurt us, too. Too expensive to drive, so we aren't getting the numbers anymore from California, Arizona, Utah, New Mexico. Worst thing, one pit boss tells me, is there aren't that many high rollers anymore, the guys who pop for three million a night and don't know it's gone. If you've got a good pigeon list on you I know two hotels who'll give you at least two and a half million for it."

Dorian said, "I'll remember that. Still got the world's most beautiful hookers here?"

A lieutenant said, "You expect a married man to answer that?"

Everybody laughed.

"The whores won't ever go away," the lieutenant said. "I know pros been working here for years. Christ, since the Korean War almost. And you got showgirls and cocktail waitresses peddling their hips for a few bucks and college girls flying in from Los Angeles for a weekend, sucking a few cocks, then going home with enough money for a new car. We get the runaways, too, just like you do in New York and just like in New York they get chewed up by pimps."

Dorian lit a cigarette. "Whores mean sex crimes."

"Tell me about it. Always one john who freaks out and it's

the girl who pays and I'm not talking about money. Other day a guy from Houston tied a broad to a bed, then did a number on her with a straight razor. Paid her five hundred bucks to let him shave her fuzzy, then got carried away. Stuffed a towel in her mouth and cut her up something fierce, then just walked away and left her there. When we found her she looked like chopped meat."

It took a few more drinks before Dorian learned there hadn't been a rape-murder in Las Vegas for a month and a half. Robbie had a clear field. The most recent incident involving a female had occurred yesterday, when a naked woman had been arrested in front of a wedding chapel on the Las Vegas strip. Naked, except for boots and mustard smeared over her body, the woman had been talking about Jesus to anyone who would listen. Dorian laughed.

Time to leave. Slightly drunk, Dorian felt sad at leaving his new friends. He was on his own again. It was him and Robbie now. One on one and no margin for error.

Two cops drove him back to his hotel, telling him to keep in touch while he was in town. Don't hesitate to call us hick law enforcement officers if you need anything. The rest of the guys would be told that Dorian was in Vegas and to keep an eye out for him. Perfect. I'm on a roll, thought Dorian.

At the cashier's window he purchased some silver dollars and found a slot machine that took five silver dollars at a time. Ten times he inserted the five, and ten times he lost. On the eleventh time he hit the jackpot, winning two thousand dollars. Bells went off, lights flashed and the machine played "The Battle Hymn of the Republic." A security guard with a canvas sack helped Dorian collect his prize money and exchange it at the cashier's window for hundred-dollar bills.

Winning revived his appetite. At the hotel dining room he ate a late lunch of steak, chicken, ribs, baked potato, chocolate cake washed down with champagne. Winning brought him company, too. A cocktail waitress who sold him cigarettes congratulated him on hitting the jackpot and looked at him long enough to let Dorian know she meant it. And she had a friend for just one hundred dollars more.

An hour later all three were in Dorian's room. Something special, he said. It's been a good day and I know it can only get better. Paying for sex never bothered him. Sometimes it was a lot cheaper than getting it for free.

It began with the friend, a showgirl, licking cocaine from Dorian's cock, while the waitress used her tongue on his anus. Fuck Robbie. Dorian lay on his back while the waitress sucked his toes and the showgirl straddled him, grinding and writhing. Then the two girls put on a show, licking and sucking each other and using a vibrator, giving him another hard-on and then he was pushing one on her back and forcing himself into her; he didn't know who it was and he didn't care.

More cocaine. And then they were in the bathroom, with the laughing girls gently pushing Dorian into an empty tub. Giggling, he lay on his back, long legs dangling over the side and one of the girls got into the tub, crouched over him, rubbed her body against his and slowly pissed on him, warming him with her urine and her smile and exciting him so quickly that his cock shot straight up and poked her in the stomach. The other girl joined her, pissing on Dorian's chest, arms, thighs. A golden shower. Dorian came twice. Las Vegas was some kind of town.

When the girls had gone, Dorian, feeling loose and feeling good, cleaned himself, then went into the bedroom and turned on the television set. A pitchman was offering a free shotgun or Magnum rifle to anyone buying a mobile home. Dorian walked over to the dresser, knelt down, removed the empty bottom drawer and turned it over. Still there. Untouched and waiting. His future and Romaine's. Five typewritten pages he had taped under the drawer. Five pages containing the names of 200 of the wealthiest men in the world. It was a copy of the pigeon list he had killed Alan Baksted for.

Where I go, it goes, thought Dorian, who had been uncomfortable at the thought of leaving it behind in New York. If you've got a good pigeon list on you I know two hotels who'll give you at least two and a half million for it.

Dorian was going to find a way to turn these pages into a lot more than two and a half million. Just as he was going to find a way to make what he knew about Robbie Ambrose pay off.

* * *

Robbie was losing the fight, surprising Dorian, who had expected better from him.

In front of Dorian, who stood in the rear of the packed hotel arena, a cheering, beer-drinking group of Mexicans waved red, white and green flags and yelled themselves hoarse as Hector Quintero drove Robbie Ambrose into the ropes with a series of vicious kicks. Quintero, with eagles and haloed crosses tattooed on his shaven chest, was long armed and tall, with an unblinking gaze and dark beard. He had a quick, stinging left jab and long legs, which he used well. His strategy was to press Robbie at all times. Attack from a distance. Use the jab and kicks to keep Robbie away and outside. The Mexican's kicks were awesome. He switched stances frequently, left leg forward, then right, kicking with his front leg, then the rear one, tireless in his assault. Now he had Robbie on the ropes. Quintero hooked two punches to Robbie's stomach, then spun around and caught him high on the cheek with a spinning backfist that dropped the former SEAL to one knee. The Mexicans leaped from their seats, spilling beer on each other and screaming, *"Quin-tero! Quin-tero!"*

Robbie sprang up immediately. The referee, however, made him take a standing eight count.

The bell rang, ending round four. Quintero's round for sure, thought a disappointed Dorian. By his count the Mex had won two rounds, Robbie one, with one even. Maybe there was something to eating refried beans after all. For the first time Dorian began to have doubts about Robbie and the killings. A quick call before fight time to the Las Vegas police had revealed no reported rape-murders.

Had he been wasting his time? So much depended on Robbie killing a woman here. Dorian wanted something on Robbie and maybe, just maybe, that would lead to something on Sparrowhawk. And all of it would be to Dorian's advantage. The more the detective thought about it, the more pissed he got at the thought that Robbie might not be a killer.

Fuck you, Golden Boy. Dorian decided to join the Mexicans and root for Quintero.

Round five.

Robbie, in yellow satin *gi* pants, black belt around his waist, shuffled forward slower than he had in previous rounds. To Dorian he seemed gun-shy, anxious not to get too close to Quintero. Quintero, on the other hand, came out smoking, throwing kicks, jabs, wild uppercuts that would have hurt Robbie, had they landed. Somehow they didn't.

Robbie ducked, sidestepped, evaded, effectively staying out of reach. He made no attempt, however, to counterattack. Quintero's reaction was to become even more aggressive, to throw wilder punches and kicks. A sold-out arena, over five thousand, cheered the Mexican, urging him on to victory. His padded feet and hands brushed Robbie's face and stomach, not connecting, but coming close.

For all of the support that Quintero was receiving, he had not hurt Robbie this round. Hadn't touched him.

And then the two fighters clinched. Contemptuously, Quintero shoved Robbie away without waiting for the referee. Then the Mexican gestured with his hands for Robbie to come forward and fight. Boos from the crowd. Whistles of derision were aimed at Robbie, along with the chant, "*Ambrose sucks, Ambrose sucks.*" Dorian heard someone say, "Fucking East Coast hype, that's all he is. Dude's got no balls, man. No fucking balls."

This wasn't the Robbie Dorian remembered. The Mexican was kicking his butt. At least until now.

The detective stepped to his right for a better view. Thirty dollars for standing room. Hottest fight in Vegas since last summer's heavyweight championship bout at Caesars Palace. Right now in the ring, it appeared that Quintero had things all his way, taking his time as he deliberately tracked Robbie from one corner to another, shuffling forward with that demonic stare, trying to get closer to land that one knockout punch or kick.

It happened midway through the round.

Dorian would never forget what he saw. One minute Robbie was backpedaling and getting booed. The whistling, jeers, catcalls. And then—

Robbie lifted his right knee to his chest, a preparation for a front kick. Quintero, hands low, stopped; he leaned back, keeping away from the expected kick. But no kick came. Instead, Robbie kept his right knee up and lunged forward like a fencer, landing a strong right jab in Quintero's face.

A quick left cross from Robbie followed, ripping into Quintero's right temple. So powerful was the blow that it spun the Mexican around, leaving him glassy eyed and staggering. And vulnerable. Robbie drove a savage left hook into Quintero's kidney, bringing him up on his toes. The Mexican stumbled forward, then turned to face Robbie in time to take a spinning back kick to the stomach that folded him in half. Two uppercuts, so fast that Dorian barely saw them, dropped Quintero to the canvas.

In front of Dorian the Mexicans fell silent. Not the rest of the arena. They were out of their seats and cheering the unbelievable turnaround.

The referee's arm rose and fell with the count. Quintero's handlers leaped into the ring and dragged him back to his corner. Someone broke a capsule under his nose and the Mexican stirred. His left foot began twitching involuntarily.

Robbie, arms held high in victory, faced two television cameras ringside as the crowd picked up the chant.

"Rob-bie."

"Rob-bie."

"Rob-bie."

Something about the scene around Dorian frightened him. The crowd, the chanting, Robbie's sudden annihilation of Hector Quintero. Robbie had killed someone in Las Vegas. Dorian didn't know who or when, but it happened. The fight here convinced him of that. Robbie had been faking in the ring, all along being in control, leading the Mexican on until he found his weakness. Sly son of a bitch. Hiding himself in front of five thousand people. Golden Boy, you are definitely something else.

Dorian left the hotel quickly, anxious to get away before Robbie saw him. He was also in need of a drink and a telephone. Where is she, Golden Boy? Where is that lady you killed, whose blood gave you the strength to do what you just did to Hector Quintero? Gonna find out, Golden Boy, and when I do, I'll own you.

Lake Mead, the resort thirty miles east of Las Vegas on the Arizona-Nevada border. In a two-room cabin near a clump of pine trees, Christina Cholles put the finishing touches on a painting of the beautiful sandstone cliffs, which met the water's edge on the Arizona side of the lake. She lightened the blue of the lake by adding white, then took a smaller brush from between her teeth and darkened her version of the cruise ship that toured the lake three times a day. The actual lake was more spectacular than any painting. It was 115 miles long, a man-made wonder created by the incredible Hoover Dam, and Christina never tired of it.

Rain had been falling steadily since early morning. She'd had to close the cabin door and windows and could not see the lake itself. No matter. An hour or two more and the painting would be finished. Meanwhile rain was coming through a leak in the roof and dripping onto her bed. William would have to fix that.

Closer to the lake were stores, buildings, the cruise ship, tourists. All the company you wanted if you wanted it. Their cabin was more isolated, within walking distance of one of the canyons in the area that was popular with hikers, backpackers and campers. After working all year in a San Francisco bank Christina preferred the quiet. An hour ago she and William had gone to the store to buy food, then to the post office to pick up mail. He had taken the car and driven to Las Vegas for a dental appointment, leaving her alone with Vivaldi, her painting and her Christmas tree. The tree, small and plastic, was kept lit all year round in her San Francisco apartment. As usual, she had taken it with her on vacation; it cheered her and reminded her of happier times, when her family had been together. Now, her mother was dead from lymph cancer and an older brother had been blown apart by a claymore mine near Da Nang. She rarely saw or heard from a second brother, currently working for an aerospace company in Texas. As for her father, he was old and embittered by a recent leg amputation for diabetes, and too unpleasant to be around.

Christina Cholles was twenty-seven, a thin-faced redhead whose blue eyes were her best feature and who attracted men through a sense of humor and a knack of appearing to listen intently to their every word while her mind was elsewhere. She and William both worked in a San Francisco bank and both liked the quiet of Nevada and Arizona. This was their second vacation together, and, while they enjoyed each other's company, Christina found herself disliking her job more and more.

She was an assistant manager and had gone as far as she

could. On vacation together this year, she and William would have a chance to talk about their future and about another job for Christina.

This morning at the post office she had received two pieces of mail from the bank. One was a note reminding her that her painting for the bank's art show was due the first week in December, not that it would be any great masterpiece. She painted because she enjoyed it. The second bit of mail, also from the bank, was a reminder that she was to enroll in an advanced computer program for junior executives. She threw both notes away in the post office trash can and wondered what the bank would say if they knew she planned on leaving early next year even if she didn't have a new position to go to.

William wanted her to stay at the bank with him; she knew it even though he would not come out and say so. He had a future there and would go far. But if she was to be happy she could not be too concerned with him. It was a thought that upset her.

There was a knock on her cabin door. At first she thought it was William, back early from Las Vegas. "William?"

"No, ma'am. Police."

She froze, paintbrush held near her ear. "Police? Is anything wrong?" Had something happened to William?

"No, ma'am. I've flown down from San Francisco to ask you some questions about a man you work with."

She sighed with relief. William was all right, thank God. As for the bank, all she could think of was: not again. Three times during the past few years shortages had appeared and always it had to do with computers.

She opened the cabin door. Poor man. He was soaked, his topcoat dark, his hat dripping. Both hands were in his pockets. He smiled and showed her his gold badge. Christina instantly decided that he was friendly, seemed embarrassed.

He stood and waited until she invited him in.

They grinned at each other. "Somebody in your bank's been at it with computers again," he said. "Couple million this time. With that kind of money you can only end up in Vegas. I mean, where else can you have big fun twenty-four hours a day?"

It suddenly occurred to her: was he talking about William?

The detective removed a hand from his pocket and took

off his hat. As his hand came out of his pocket a folded piece of paper fell to the floor. Christina bent down and picked it up. She started to hand it back to him, then stopped. It looked familiar. And it was creased, as though someone had crumpled it before throwing it away.

Good Lord, it was the note sent to her by the bank concerning the new computer program. Now why had the detective taken that from the trash, where she'd dumped it? Had he been following her?

She looked from the crumpled note to him. He gave her that boyish grin again and fingered a golden stud in his right ear. He wore gloves.

When he kicked the cabin door shut behind him she flinched. It was seconds before she found her voice. "I . . . I don't understand."

He took one step closer. "Doesn't matter. It really doesn't matter."

13

There was a time when Robbie Ambrose had not been *bushi,* when he had not been a warrior and invincible. Then he had been weak and women had tried to destroy him. But in the end he had escaped their tyranny.

His Westwood, Los Angeles, home had been ruled by women: his mother, two aunts, a sister. Robbie and his father, a timid history professor at UCLA, were the only males, often at the mercy of the women. For the first ten years of his life Robbie, a blond and pretty child, was made to wear girl's clothing by a mother who openly spoke of her preference for her second daughter, and made it known that there would be no more children; childbirth was painful and sex repulsive. From then on his mother never again slept with his father. And she and her unmarried sisters made no secret of their preference for a house without men. In the words of one aunt, Robbie was an unwanted mistake.

At twelve, Robbie, urged on by his fourteen-year-old sister, entered into an incestuous relationship with her. Guilt and fear outweighed the pleasure; his sister mocked his fumbling efforts yet forced him to continue by threatening to tell their mother. When an aunt discovered them having sex, Robbie was beaten by the three older women so savagely that he could not get out of bed for weeks. Traumatized, he did not speak for over a year.

Robbie was then sent to a strict boarding school, where even a slight infraction of rules brought down swift punishment from the staff. Pleas from his father allowed Robbie entrance into the house only on holidays and for a limited time during the summer. He was forced to sleep alone, in a room with the door open and a small night-light on. The women had to know what he was doing at all times and the sister had to be protected.

At fifteen he visited his father on the UCLA campus, where the two attended a Japanese historical and cultural exhibition. Here, a spellbound Robbie watched his first karate demonstration. Such men, the *karateka*s, appeared to him as gods. What power they must enjoy from possessing such a skill. Robbie would have given years of his life to be one of them.

With his father's help he found books on karate, other martial arts and on Japan and studied them avidly. At school he practiced alone for hours, devouring page after page of instruction. When an older boy tried to take the books from him Robbie kicked him in the jaw. A staff member confiscated the books and Robbie set fire to his office to retrieve them. It took four staff members to physically overcome the enraged youngster, but not before he hurt two of them seriously enough to put them in the hospital. The next day Robbie's family was ordered to remove him from the school.

At home there was a shift in relationships. Robbie was now bigger, stronger, more sure of himself. A new hand was on the whip. The women soon learned to fear him, to know that there was no way they could control him. School was of little importance to Robbie; he lived for the martial arts, for karate, judo, kendo, stick fighting. He trained in Little Tokyo dojos and in clubs in downtown Los Angeles, and when he was not in a dojo he was in a gym, honing his body with weights, running, swimming.

At seventeen he made black belt, fighting in tournaments with a ferocity and savagery that terrified older and more experienced opponents. He was frequently disqualified for unnecessary roughness and lack of control.

But he was rarely defeated. And he was able to protect his father from the women.

When his mother, in a fit of anger, tossed one of his father's carefully prepared history papers out the window, Robbie slapped her hard enough to drive her jaw out of line. An aunt caught prowling around Robbie's room had her arm broken. His sister proved more difficult to deal with. When she returned home from college she looked at Robbie not as a brother but as a man. An attractive man. In her eyes he saw the memory of that time and knew that she remembered, too. He saw it in the way she baited him with a word, with the way she cupped her breasts, the way she touched his hard-muscled arms, the way she brushed against him. It was in her knowing smile.

It happened just after his twentieth birthday. His sister waited until the house was empty. Then she came to Robbie's room, bringing him *Imagawayaki*, the Japanese waffle filled with sweet bean paste, one of his favorite foods. She also brought him drugs and wine. He never remembered how it happened, but happen it did. Both naked, both wanting each other, the guilt and fear rushing back to claim him once more and, above all, the pleasure.

Then she sat up in bed and began to mock him, laughing and threatening as she had done long ago. This time it would be rape and she would swear to it. No boarding school for Robbie. He was going to *prison*. The women—his mother, aunts, his sister—had worked out this plan to rid themselves of Robbie permanently, to once more take control of the house, and there was nothing he could do to stop them. Robbie, in a haze of drugs and wine and feeling the fear again, sprang up in bed, cupped his sister's chin in his right hand, placed his left hand behind her ear, and savagely turned her head as though it were a steering wheel, snapping her neck.

There was no hesitation about what to do next. Taking her in his arms he carried her limp, nude body down the hall to the bathroom, sat it in the tub and turned on the water. Then he hurried to her room, got a robe and slippers and returned to the bathroom, placing them near the tub. After soaping and washing her body, he let the water run out but did not clean the tub. Lifting her up, he sat her on the floor, back against the tub. Then, cupping her wet head in his hands, he pulled it toward him and smashed it into the edge of the tub with all his strength.

Her death was ruled accidental, the result of a fall while stepping from the tub. Traces of drugs and alcohol found in her body supported the verdict. Still, Robbie thought it best to leave California, to get as far away from the women as he could. Vietnam was the obvious answer and so was the navy, with its Black Berets, the Sea, Air, Land guerrilla force known as SEAL. Out of 250 men, Robbie was one of 6 to qualify for SEAL training.

In Vietnam he killed on orders. He and his SEAL team worked with the CIA, assassinating Cong leaders, capturing weapons and records and destroying supply caches. There were even times when killing was fun. Once, to prove that a certain Cong leader had actually been assassinated, Robbie's team brought back both of his feet, encasing the grisly trophies in wet clay.

Like others, he took drugs before going out on a mission. The drugs did what you wanted them to. They made you alert or happy and killed any feeling that might weaken you. Robbie smoked grass laced with opium, swallowed amphetamines and Dexedrine. He did cocaine. Sometimes he shot up with the morphine worn around his neck, ordinarily to be used if he were wounded. Being wired on drugs gave Robbie a thousand eyes. Wired meant hearing the footfall of an ant.

He had taken drugs on the day he raped a Vietnamese woman and, still in her body, sliced her throat with the nine-inch blade of his k-bar. He never forgot that day, for seven members of his SEAL team were killed in a Cong ambush. Only Robbie survived. That night his drug-induced dreams were not of his dead comrades but of himself and *Hachiman Dai-Bosatsu,* god of war. The dream changed Robbie's life forever.

"Give me a woman in sacrifice," said the god of war, "and you shall never be bested in any combat. You will live forever and be *bushi.* You will be invincible."

Other SEALs said Robbie wept in his sleep that night. Only Robbie knew that the weeping had been in gratitude to *Hachiman Dai-Bosatsu*—not for the seven who had died.

The truth of the dream could not be denied. By killing his sister and terrorizing the women in his family he had survived. And he had avoided prison. And he had come to Vietnam, where he had met Major Sparrowhawk, the Englishman who was the strong father Robbie would like to have had. Everything good in Robbie's life had come from dominating and destroying women.

Even after leaving Vietnam and going to New York with the major, Robbie continued to hear the voice of the god of war. Drugs helped. They led him back to *Hachiman,* back to strength and victory. To know and act are one and the same. Knowledge, true knowledge, came only from *Hachiman.*

Robbie believed. And to believe meant living according to that belief. He did not hate the women he killed. He needed them. Together they were united in *Chi-matsuri,* the rite of blood demanded by *Hachiman.* Because of them Robbie could defeat anyone.

Robbie knelt beside Christina Cholles's dead body and kissed her still-warm lips, then stood, fixed his clothes and put on his wet coat and hat before going back out into the rain. He grew stronger with each step; his ki, *his energy began to expand.*

And then he heard it. He stopped. His senses were so sharp he could hear raindrops falling into the lake almost a mile away.

But he heard other sounds, too, sounds that could only reach the ears of a true bushi. *Eagles shrieked inside his skull and bared their talons as they attacked from out of a blood-red sky, to swoop down upon a brown, smoking earth. He heard the hiss of metal upon metal as* Hachiman *unsheathed his sword and moonlight reflected on that great weapon, a light so piercing that only a true warrior could look upon it with the naked eye.*

In the heavy rain, Robbie stood and gazed upon that wondrous light.

14

Manny Decker turned right onto the huge parking lot and braked the dark blue Mercedes to a halt just inside the entrance. After slipping the keys into his overcoat pocket, he took a pair of wool-lined leather gloves from the seat and left the car without locking the door. Several feet away from the Mercedes he stopped in ankle-deep snow to stare at the new Long Island arena built by Paul Molise. Very impressive.

Three gigantic ovals of off-white marble and green-tinted glass stacked one on top of the other rested on thirty feet of marble and steel columns. Winding staircases and stainless steel escalators led inside. Between the columns were fountains, miniature pools and flower gardens. Modern and distinctive.

Icy winds from the freezing waters of nearby Long Island Sound sliced into Decker's back and neck. To prevent his hat from being blown away he pulled it down until it almost hid his eyes. His one wish was to see Charles LeClair naked in these freezing waters, his black ass going down for the third time. LeClair, who had ordered Decker to drive out here in twenty-two-degree cold.

"Listen good," the prosecutor had said. His forefinger was an inch from Decker's mustache. "I want me a copy of that jiveass seating plan, the one your girl friend says was put together by a certain Greek lawyer. When I have that particular document, I have Mr. Constantine Pangalos."

LeClair turned his back. "I'll answer your unspoken questions. No, I can't have it mailed to me. No, I don't trust local town officials out there or the police either, no offense. Why? Because, Mr. Manfred, the construction industry in New York is rotten from top to bottom. Everybody pays off. Everybody has his hand out. Everybody breaks the rules. So you can bet your pension that Molise and his front men have done their share of paying off. That new arena is good business for the town. The people out there are going to protect it. The minute they get wind of the fact that a federal prosecutor is interested in that phony seating plan, it's going to disappear in a puff of smoke."

Decker said, "Or somebody makes changes in it."

LeClair smiled, looking like a wolf pulling his lips back from his teeth. The gesture belonged to the hunt. It had nothing to do with social graces.

"You're playing the game the way I like to see it played, Mr. Manfred. What other thoughts are flitting across your crafty mind at the moment?"

"That somebody out there knows the plan is phony. Somebody in the department of building records, somebody on the zoning commission, maybe even in the mayor's office. You don't spend thirty million dollars without drawing a crowd. I'd say—I'm guessing now—but I'd say the local city hall was on top of this project from the beginning and got its share under the table and knows about the phony plan. In other words, I stand to get my chops busted by going out there to pick it up."

"Decker, Decker. Trust me."

In God we trust, thought the detective. All others pay cash.

"Soon as you arrive out there," LeClair said, "get on the horn. A minute later, a federal judge will telephone building records. I guarantee it. What's so funny?"

A smiling Decker said, "I was just thinking of the three greatest lies. No offense, but your saying 'I guarantee it' sort of set things off in my mind."

"Oh? What are the three greatest lies?"

"You really want to know?"

LeClair waited.

Decker said, " 'Your check's in the mail.' 'I won't come in your mouth.' 'Black is beautiful.' "

LeClair howled. "Jesus, that's funny. Got to remember those." He repeated them quickly, half to himself, half out loud, then said, "Okay, back to business. You'll be covered out there. I do guarantee it. Hey, man, don't laugh, I mean it. The phone call from the judge will happen. All you have to do is pick up the plan and toddle on back into Manhattan. Don't need a platoon for that. One plan, one man."

LeClair, in his high-back leather chair, began a gentle swing left to right. "Fact: that seating plan, as it now stands, constitutes fraud, a crime punishable by imprisonment. Talking about tax fraud, stock fraud. Fact: the IRS and the state tax people aren't the only ones in the dark about those five hundred missing seats. Bet you the banks who went for part of the building costs don't know. Bet you the entertainers booked in there on a piece of the gross don't know. More fraud. Mr. Manfred, you get me that seating plan and I've got Constantine Pangalos in a tight grip about the scrotum. And I have lapsed Hebrew Mr. Livingston Quarrels as well."

LeClair leaned forward, hands folded on a desk totally cleared of papers, topped by a spotless blotter. It was, Decker knew, a sign of an organized and exact mind. The old Prussian heritage.

"As Molise's attorneys of record," said LeClair, "our boys will have to take the weight. Oh, they'll have a choice: they can spend time in a federal penitentiary, which as you know is hard time indeed. Or they can give me Paul Molise and Management Systems Consultants. What we have here, Mr. Manfred, are dominos stacked neatly in a row. Knock down one, they all fall. And Senator Terry Dent? Icing on the cake."

In the three days since LeClair had learned about the suspect seating plan he had also learned that Dent had paved the way for the building of the arena. Permits, the elimination of red tape, bank loans at favorable interest rates. The senator's influence had smoothed the way, and LeClair guessed that when the task force dug deep enough they would find that Dent was probably a silent partner in one of the companies fronting for Molise and had points in the auditorium. Dent was known to be greedy.

Decker had told LeClair about the false seating plan before the prosecutor had gone to Washington for a special weekend with the attorney general. By the time LeClair passed the information on, it had become the biggest breakthrough to date in the government's case against Management Systems Consultants. LeClair's chances for the deputy-attorney spot had never been better.

On his own, Decker had learned what LeClair did to those he considered less than helpful to his career, such as DeMain and Benitez, the two cops who had been dropped from the task force.

DeMain, in his forties, had been forced into an early retirement. Budget cutbacks, he had been told. Early retirement meant only a partial pension for a cop who had been wounded six times and had more citations for bravery than he could count. Benitez, who had hoped to become one of the few Puerto Rican lieutenants in the NYPD, learned that his name had slipped from the top of the list of those eligible for the lieutenant's examination to the bottom. He had been an outstanding officer until assigned to LeClair's task force. Now, it would be at least three years before he could hope to move back up the list.

It did not pay to run afoul of Chocolate Chuck.

LeClair said to Decker, "Tomorrow when you go out to Long Island, you'll be prepared. Warrants, papers, whatever I think you need. If the judge does his stuff you probably won't need to use them. Seems to me we can draw blood with this one. We're doing it right, the three of us. You, me, Mrs. Raymond. Mr. Manfred, you make sure you give that woman what she needs."

LeClair leered.

"And she still doesn't know you're a cop?" he continued.

Decker closed his eyes. "No."

"Mr. Manfred, you are one silver-tongued devil." LeClair leaned back in his chair, his steely gaze taking in all of the detective. "You're good at hiding yourself from people. Yes, sir, that is one thing you are good at."

Before driving out to Long Island, Decker had spent the night with Michi at her apartment. Yes, he had hidden a part of himself from her, the part that was Romaine. Blame that on LeClair. Tonight Decker was going to be happy no matter what the cost, no matter how hard the effort. Nothing was going to spoil this evening with Michi.

She cooked *soba*, buckwheat noodles, and they ate them the Japanese way, noisily drawing them in through the mouth and laughing. There was *unagi*, eel filleted and cut into strips, then dipped in sauce, charcoal broiled and served on vinegared rice balls. Since a Japanese cook was judged by her ability to make soup—Japanese soup was considered an art—Decker made a point of praising Michi's clear soup of trefoil, chicken balls and lemon peel shaped as oak leaves. Rice was served in *meoto-jawan,* matching bowls which were part of the concept of paired items—chopsticks, bedding, teacups—to be used by husband and wife. It was a custom Decker and Michi had shared in Saigon, where she had brought matching teacups for the two of them. Decker still had the cups at home.

The meal took an exciting turn with the serving of *fugu,* a puffed-up black fish, hideously ugly and potentially fatal. Eaten raw, its glands contain a powerful poison, so the utmost care has to be exercised in removing it from the meat. But *fugu* is delicious; its meat has a pearly white color and tonight Michi had sliced it extra thin and arranged it in a beautiful arabesque on blue and white porcelain plates, all set on a red and black lacquered tray. The entire presentation was so beautiful that Decker was reluctant to touch it.

In Japan the appeal of *fugu* lay in its danger. One who had eaten it became a member of a mysterious and exotic cult. Lists were kept of the famous who had died while dining on *fugu.*

It occurred to Decker that Michi might be testing him, to see if he would step deeper into her world.

Michi, kneeling on the floor to Decker's left, took a piece of the fish and, with her eyes on the detective, slowly ate it. Decker reached for a paper-thin slice, hesitated a second, then put it in his mouth. Salty. But delicious. His heart was pounding, but he chewed and swallowed. Michi ate a second piece. Decker, trusting her, loving her, did the same. Without knowing what the test was, he knew he had passed it because Michi took his hand and smiled so sweetly at him that he wanted to take her in his arms and hold her forever.

He sipped Suntory, the smoky Japanese whiskey. "After this," he said, "tomorrow won't seem so dangerous."

"Tomorrow?"

He told her about Paul Molise's new arena and its phony seating plan.

"You will arrest Molise?" she said.

"First we grab his lawyers—they put the plan together—and we hold their feet to the fire. That's LeClair's job and he's good at it. Lawyers live soft lives. They don't want to go to prison. Hey, one day in jail's enough. Sometimes when we want to make a suspect talk, we pop him on a Friday—"

"Pop?"

"Arrest."

"I see."

"We arrest him on a Friday, late on a Friday, then he'll have to stay in jail for the weekend. Courts are closed on the weekend, so bail can't be set. Now that's just two days and three nights, and you know by Monday our suspect's ready to tell us anything we want to know. That's how bad jail can be."

Michi held her cup while Decker poured sake for her. She said, "Paul Molise has managed to avoid your American jails. And even if he is judged to be a criminal, he has powerful friends. You told me of Senator Dent and I know of the American military and intelligence people who were his friends in Saigon. Do you honestly believe anything bad will happen to him?"

Decker sighed. "We can only try. Can't do any more than that." He put down his whiskey, took her hand in his and kissed the palm. "I tried the *fugu* tonight because of you."

"I know." She seemed pleased.

And he noticed that she almost, *almost* said more. Was she going to tell him about the six years she had spent apart from him? She turned away and her eyes glazed over, as if looking back, remembering.

Decker said, "I've made a lot of mistakes in my life, but it was no mistake to have loved you. Please tell me: am I fooling myself?"

She looked at him. There was a sadness in her face, but the smile came and she said, "No. From my heart I tell you this."

Her eyes shimmered behind tears and she took his hand and placed it on her breast, over her heart. *"Shinju,"* she whispered.

Shinju: if the heart were to be cut open, only her love and devotion for him would be found there. The word also referred to a double suicide by lovers, who sometimes used a red cord to tie themselves together at the waist before leaping into the sea.

Michi, however, was not speaking of death. She was telling Decker that he was truly loved.

"*Shinju,*" she repeated. He leaned over and kissed her tears and then her mouth before she could say more.

On Long Island, Decker had followed LeClair's plan exactly. He arrived in the town around lunchtime, giving him fewer clerks to deal with. Then he called LeClair and waited ten minutes before appearing at the building that housed seating plans and similar records. Inside, almost everyone was out to lunch. The clerk in charge was sufficiently intimidated by a telephone call from a federal judge to hand the plan over to Decker without a fuss. The detective put it in a brown manila envelope, folded it twice and placed it inside his overcoat.

A chunky woman in sequin-studded eyeglasses and a floor-length sheared beaver coat entered the office as Decker was leaving. The clerk rushed to her, clutching one of her ample arms, and with one eye on the departing Decker, began whispering in the woman's ear.

The chunky woman chewed her thin bottom lip and fingered her gaudy eyeglasses while impatiently waiting for the phone to ring at the other end. She gripped the receiver with a meaty hand. Ring, goddamn it. Dimitrios was a schmuck to have handed over that seating plan, detective or no detective. There would be hell to pay over at the arena. She knew that for sure.

"Hello, who is this?"

"Livingston Quarrels."

"Thank God. Just the man I want to talk to. This is Mrs. Kuhn over at building records. Something you should know about."

Minutes later Quarrels dialed Constantine Pangalos in Manhattan.

"I don't believe it," the ex-prosecutor said. "What a bunch of dipshits you got out there. That plan can put us all in the toilet, you know that, don't you?"

Quarrels left his desk in the arena office, walked to the window and looked out at the parking lot. "Connie, I didn't—"

"Yeah, yeah. You didn't, I didn't, nobody did it. The fucking elves in the fucking forest fucking did it. Jesus."

"Connie—"

"Moskowitz, do me a favor and stop whining. I'm trying to think."

Moskowitz. Pangalos only called Quarrels by his old name when he was pissed.

At the window Quarrels said, "Hey, wait a minute. There's a guy out there in the parking lot. He's looking up at the building." The lawyer stepped to the side and out of sight. Gripping the receiver with both hands he whispered, "You think it's him, the guy who took the seating plan?"

"Jesus you're there and I'm here. What am I, a goddamn psychic? What's the guy look like?"

Quarrels peered out again. "Hard to tell. Hat pulled down low. Hey, the wind just blew his hat off and he's chasing it. Got a mustache, slim—"

"Seven to five it's Decker. Phone call from a federal judge, and a New York detective shows up flashing warrants. That's task force clout and a task force detective sergeant with a mustache means Decker. Shit, we can't let him walk away with that seating plan. Look, is Buscaglia still around?"

"Yes. He's been here since early this morning with the new security guards from MSC. He's showing them around the arena. Also he and I have to work out the guards' pension deal."

"Let Buscaglia figure out how much he's going to steal from the pension fund and the union dues some other time. Right now that ginzo's going to earn his money. Get him to the phone. I want that goddamn plan back."

There was sweat on Quarrels's upper lip. "Connie, the guy out in the parking lot is a cop. We can't—"

"Moskowitz, shut the fuck up before I piss on the phone and it runs into your mouth. You want to do time in a federal pen for fraud?"

In the parking lot Decker finally caught up to his hat, brushed snow from it, then jammed it back on his head and held it there with one hand. Time to leave before the wind blew the Mercedes away. The car, less than two years old and containing a mobile phone, had been confiscated from a

Colombian cocaine dealer by federal narcotics agents. Any vehicle used to transport illicit drugs—car, private plane, yacht, motorbike, even skateboards and roller skates—became the property of the federal government.

In the Mercedes, Decker turned on the heater and blew into his gloved hands. When the car felt warmer he switched on the ignition and heard the powerful motor rumble, but before he could back out of his parking spot two cars sped out of nowhere to block his way.

Doors opened, men sped toward Decker. Two had guns.

One, in a red cap and sheepskin jacket, tapped on Decker's window with the butt of a .357 Magnum. "Fingers on the head," he said. "You do anything else and I'll fire one warning shot through your stupid forehead."

Decker looked to his right. The second gun carrier, bearded, stocky, knelt down and held a .22 in a two-handed grip. He was aiming at Decker's right ear.

"Hey, asshole," said Red Cap. "I said outta there."

"I'm a cop. My badge is in my inside jacket pocket. I have federal warrants—"

"You got trouble is what you got." He leveled the Magnum at Decker's left temple.

The detective used one hand. Opened the door slowly, gently easing the door the rest of the way with one foot. Decker got out, hands on his head.

Red Cap stepped back, gun still aimed at Decker's head. "Get his piece."

A third man, in a blue down vest and a checkered hunting cap, walked up to Decker, yanked his overcoat and his suit jacket open, popping all the buttons, and removed the detective's .38 Smith & Wesson. He pocketed it and stepped back.

Red Cap stuffed the Magnum into his jeans. "Let's have it, numb nuts, and you can make it as hard on yourself as you want."

Decker, hands crushing the hat on his head, saw no reason to play dumb. He had been spotted back at the records building; the four goons breathing steam in his face knew what they were looking for.

"Right hand overcoat pocket," he said.

Red Cap curled his lips. He had planned on dealing with a liar, not someone who gave in so easily and spoiled the fun.

But they'd get around to the fun in a minute or two. He stepped forward, found the envelope, stepped back. A peek told him the seating plan was inside. Satisfied, he folded the envelope in haphazard fashion and jammed it into a jacket pocket. From another pocket Red Cap moved a hand radio, extended the antenna and flicked the *on* switch. He turned toward the arena.

Static. Then, "Frank here. Got him. Over."

"Good." A male voice through the static. "The package?"

Frank tapped his jacket pocket. "Safe and sound. Over."

Through the crackling the voice came back hard, detached, strictly business. "You know what to do. Make it look good."

"Gotcha. Over and out."

Frank pushed the antenna down and tucked the radio back in his pocket. When he stepped closer to Decker, the other three followed, tightening the semicircle in front of the detective, whose back was to the Mercedes. Frank's hand went up in a stop signal, and the four halted. "Put away the gun, Richie. Man said make it look good, not crazy. Let's not draw any more attention to this thing than we have to."

The gun, of course, had made all the difference. Still, the expression on Decker's face never changed when it disappeared. He took a deep breath, held it for a count of three, then exhaled slowly through his nose.

Ready.

Frank the Red Cap pulled a pair of black leather gloves from a back pocket of his jeans and put them on, taking time to admire one clenched fist. "Shame on you, detective sergeant who-gives-a-shit. Getting yourself mugged in a quiet little town like we got here. Sad. Somebody steals your gun, badge, wallet, car. Leaves you lying here in the parking lot. We were in the arena the whole time it happened. Got witnesses. We seen the guys who did it, though. Crazy teenagers. By the time we run over here to help, shit, it was too late. The kids had split. Worst thing is we can't make no positive ID of the perpetrators. You know how it is. People will get hot and bothered over this for two minutes, then they won't think about it no more. I mean it's sad, but what the fuck can you do?"

A smirking Frank turned to look at his team and then back at Decker, who, hands still on his head, kicked him in the balls with casual contempt, his foot, knee and thigh muscle driving deep into the soft place, leaving Frank popeyed and doubled over in pain.

In one motion Decker whipped off his hat and backhanded it into the face of one bearded man, temporarily stopping him, then stepped behind the open door of the Mercedes and slammed it into the man in the hunting cap, who had charged him. Hunting Cap crashed into the Mercedes and slumped to the ground with a broken wrist and four broken fingers. Of the two remaining attackers, both bearded, the larger one rushed Decker, slipped in the snow, but reached out to catch the detective in a bear hug and pin his arms to his sides. There was the smell of beer and peppermint about the attacker. "Cocksucker. Your ass, now."

Decker kneed him low, and when the man released his grip Decker grabbed his head with both hands and pulled it down on his raised knee, shattering nose, teeth, jaw. His beard bright with his own blood, the man fell to the ground, writhing and groaning.

One more. A second bearded man. He tapped his gloved palm with a tire iron and circled to his right, eyes on Decker. The detective slowly eased out of his overcoat, his gaze fixed on the last man.

The bearded man stopped. His eyes flicked to the three on the ground; the one with damaged hands sat up, his back against the Mercedes, hands resting on his thighs. Red Cap attempted to crawl. A third lay still. Tire Iron hadn't made up his mind yet. Go for it. Or run. Decker inched forward, mindful of the snow. *Zanshin*. Concentration. Decker's eyes bore into the man with the tire iron.

Decker tossed his overcoat at him. It landed, covering the man's head and shoulders and he cried out under it, his arms flailing.

Decker was on him. *Kiai*. Decker's yell echoed across the empty parking lot, across water white with floating chunks of ice, across a blue and cloudless sky. As he yelled he attacked the lump under the coat that was Tire Iron's head. Two punches, left-right, arms extended, straight bone driving into the skull, as Decker struck from a crouch, gloved fists clenched to a white-knuckle tightness, ankles and thighs squeezed in a granitelike stance.

Absolute concentration.

All mental, emotional and physical resources collected and delivered to the point of impact.

The result was maximum force.

Tire Iron dropped backward, arms flung wide, head and shoulders still wrapped in Decker's overcoat. He lay inert, a foot drawn up close to his groin and one hand near Red Cap Frank's rear.

Decker, alert, calm, looked around. Four men down, no one else coming out of the arena. Fighting outside of a dojo or tournament rarely gave him satisfaction. Certainly Decker would have preferred to talk his way out of fighting. Given the chance, he would have even backed down. There was no glory in fighting untrained men.

But having no choice, he had fought to win. Decker wanted to talk to Red Cap Frank, who seemed to be the leader. Frank, who still lay on the ground with damaged balls and a face blue from a lack of oxygen.

In studying the martial arts Decker had also learned *kappo*, the system of resuscitation. Hundreds of years ago these methods of emergency first aid had been one of the most guarded secrets in the martial arts, never to be handed down from master to pupil without the master's permission. Now they were known by instructors and senior black belts the world over.

He went down on one knee behind Frank, sat him up, then with hands under his armpits lifted him inches from the snow before gently dropping him on his buttocks. He repeated this several times before using the bottom of his fist to gently tap Frank's back, from his shoulders to the base of his spine. Next, he removed Frank's shoes, and again using the bottom of his fist pounded the heel of each foot several times.

Normal color gradually returned to Frank's face. His breathing became less labored. Removing the red cap, Decker used it to wipe cold sweat from Frank's face, then said, "Head down. That's it. Now take deep breaths, hold it for a count of five, then let it out slowly. Good. Can you stand?"

"I'll give it a shot. Jesus, where did you learn to kick ass like that?"

Decker pulled the Magnum from Frank's belt, retrieved the envelope and his own .38 and took the .22 from the bearded man he had kneed in the face. "Jump up and down a couple of times," he said to Frank, now on his feet. "Come down flat-footed."

Frank did, nodding his head to indicate that he felt as well as possible under the circumstances.

Decker said, "It bounces your testicles out. Brings them down where they used to be."

"Glad to hear. Jesus, I'd like to have died when you kicked me."

Decker flashed his badge. "Detective Sergeant Decker and I'm with a federal task force." He jerked his head toward the arena. "Who sent you after me?"

A chastened Frank cupped his sore scrotum. "Guess we all got our ass in a sling now. Buscaglia. He's probably watching us through the window up there. Son of a bitch should have come out here himself."

"Did he say why he wanted this envelope so badly?"

"He don't want it. Lawyer named Pangalos wants it. He's really pissed, Pangalos, about you having the envelope."

"Frank, do me a favor. Get Buscaglia on that radio of yours."

Frank took out his radio, got it working and called for Buscaglia.

No answer. Frank looked betrayed.

Decker, with exaggerated politeness, held out his hand. "May I?"

Gripping the radio, the detective walked over to the Mercedes and stared across its hood at the arena. He brought the radio to his mouth. "Buscaglia, this is Detective Sergeant Decker. You have thirty seconds to get your ass out here."

No answer.

Decker flicked the sending switch. "Sal, I want you outside. *Now.* If you don't come out, I'm coming in after you. You don't have enough security guards to stop me. Let's put it this way: they don't get paid enough to try. Now make nice and tippy-toe on out here."

Decker flicked the receiving switch. Still no answer.

Decker was about to turn and pick up his overcoat when he saw a lone figure walk slowly down a winding marble staircase and stop on the bottom step. The balding man in sunglasses and an expensive camel's hair coat held a hand radio to his mouth.

"So I'm out. So what?"

"Start walking."

Sal Buscaglia didn't move.

A grinning Decker looked back at Frank, then to Buscaglia again. This was the fun part of being a cop. Controlling people's lives. Buscaglia had come this far. Who did he think he was kidding?

The union leader stepped from the staircase and headed toward the parking lot. Decker never looked at Frank. But his voice spelled control. "Frank, get my coat and hat for me, will you? I want to look good when Sal arrives."

Mind games. Cops played them all the time. Anything to keep the perpetrator off balance. And to let him know you're in charge.

A docile Frank held Decker's hat and coat out to him. "Frank, I think your friend, the one sitting by my car, can walk. Looks like his hands are damaged. Please move him away from the car, if you will. And don't forget to have your men taken care of. I think Sal ought to pop for any medical bills involved. Ah, here he is, our boy Sal. *Suede shoes? In snow?* Oh, Sal, you are something. Came downstairs so fast you forgot your rubbers, I bet."

At the Mercedes, a sullen Salvatore Buscaglia stopped by the car trunk. Decker couldn't stop grinning. Sal, in his time, had probably stuffed a few people in car trunks. Did he think the same thing was going to happen to him?"

"Charge me. You gotta charge me. If I'm under arrest, what's the charge?"

Decker jerked his head toward the Mercedes. "Get in, Sal."

Buscaglia shook his head.

A smiling Decker got into the car and slammed the door. Both he and Sal knew how the game was played. Sal had to look good in front of his men. And whoever was watching from the arena. But he had come this far. Who was he kidding?

Buscaglia dragged his steps and got in on the passenger's

side. Twice he looked back at the arena as though expecting help. During the return trip to Manhattan he never said a word, which didn't surprise Decker. That's how the game was played.

15

In his Park Avenue office Ushiro Kanai put down a newspaper clipping he had been reading and swiveled around in his chair to stare at a painting on the wall behind him. The painting covered the space between two windows facing the Waldorf-Astoria Hotel across the street. Measuring seven feet by seven feet, the painting was an example of *yohaku,* the artistic use of empty space. *Yohaku* literally meant white space and reflected the Japanese way of achieving balance by pairing incompatible objects. A mass of thick, shapeless red brush strokes filled the top right-hand corner of the painting. A vaguely triangular pattern of gold and yellow took up two square feet of space in the bottom left-hand corner. And in the center was a blob of black streaked in bright red. The rest of the painting had been left blank. Color and *yohaku,* white space. Tint and emptiness combining to create an off-balance elegance, a sense of restfulness.

The painting, a favorite of Kanai's, had been done by Yoshi Tada, the son-in-law murdered a month ago.

Yoshi, a skilled accountant, had also been a promising artist. His work hung in Tokyo's principal museums—Tokyo Metropolitan Art Museum, Bridgestone Gallery and the National Museum of Modern Art in Kitanomaru Park, beside the Imperial Palace. Two paintings hung in the permanent collection of Osaka's Municipal Art Museum, and there had been talk of Yoshi having his own exhibition in Kyoto's Prefectural Gallery.

Kanai's fingertips traced the yellow and gold, then moved

up to the white emptiness and he wondered if he had not killed his son-in-law by killing the young man's dream.

Murakami Electronics was Ushiro Kanai's entire life. Loyalty to the company came before family, friendships and confused dreamers like Yoshi. In the end this self-interest, masquerading as virtue, destroyed the unhappy young Yoshi Tada. Over the past few weeks grief and guilt had driven Kanai into deep reflection, and he now saw the role both he and his daughter had played in Yoshi's sad life.

Yoko, Kanai's daughter, was spoiled and self-centered. She hated New York and lived only for the day when she could return to Japan. A woman of stronger character would have complained less and tried to be more supportive of her husband. This was Kanai's fault. She was his only child and he loved her dearly; it had always been difficult to be harsh with Yoko.

A word from Kanai and she and Yoshi could have returned to Japan together, saving the marriage, saving Yoshi's life.

But instead the industrialist had kept his son-in-law in New York, where his accounting skills were needed. Murakami's American investments—the takeover of the electronics company in California, real estate purchases in Texas and Arizona, the new hotel in Hawaii, the prospective investment in the Golden Horizon hotel casino in Atlantic City—all called for an accountant with above-average ability. Yoshi was hardworking and exact, conscientious and resourceful. Assign him a task and he stayed with it until completion, no matter what the obstacles.

Murakami needed Yoshi. And so did Kanai. Yoshi, however, had needs that could no longer be satisfied working for Murakami. To be truly happy he needed to devote himself to art.

This conflict between *giri* and *ninjo*, personal human feelings, was invariably brought to a head in New York. Here, Japanese businessmen stuck together, spoke only Japanese, worked sixty-hour weeks and drank sake toasts to the day when their three- to five-year company assignment in America would come to an end and they could return to Japan.

Yoshi the artist, however, found something attractive about New York. He loved its freedom and energy.

It had taken all of Yoshi's courage to speak to Kanai about these conflicts. But from the beginning Kanai gave him no hope. "By chasing shadows one loses substance. A life as an artist can never bring the power and esteem to be found working for Murakami. You are my son-in-law. You are guaranteed success here, great success."

Yoshi said, "For me, business does not offer the passion to be found in art. I wish to work with passion in everything I do. I wish to work in something that demands my best every minute of my life. I do not feel that way . . ." He stopped.

"You do not feel that way about your work at Murakami. Yes, I know. But feelings are to be forgotten. Strength comes from ignoring feelings and choosing duty. Duty and loyalty. Loyalty to Japan, to the family, to the group and yes, to Murakami. Duty and loyalty mean strength. Yoshi, you have a duty to me, to Murakami, to my daughter. Turn your back on illusion. *Giri* is the path. There can be no deviation from it."

Yoshi did not answer. Kanai, however, saw an answer in the young man's troubled face. *Take away my illusions and you kill me.* A few weeks later, Yoshi was dead.

Kanai turned his back on the *yohaku* painting. Sorrow for the dead was always accompanied by guilt. On his desk was a framed wedding photograph of a smiling Yoko and Yoshi, their eyes bright with tomorrow's promise.

Kanai removed his glasses and rubbed his eyes, as though to blot out the sight of his beloved daughter Yoko, now sick with grief. He remembered her in Tokyo at the *otsuya,* the vigil before the funeral, greeting Yoshi's family at the door and weeping with them. During the Shinto ceremony, when prayers were offered for Yoshi's soul, she had to be supported by relatives as she approached the altar to receive the traditional *tamagushi* branch from the *sakaki* tree, which was to be placed on a special table, its stem pointing to the altar. Afterward she was to step back, bow and clap her hands four times. But Yoko could not go on. She bowed, clapped once, then fainted and had to be carried from the shrine.

Since then she had remained *mo-chu,* in mourning, spending her days in a Shinto shrine, offering prayers, incense and *tamagushi* branches for Yoshi's soul. We both should have loved him more in life, thought Kanai.

It was time for Kanai to do his duty and leave all else to the gods. He buzzed his secretary and ordered her to get Detective Decker on the phone. Then the Japanese industrialist returned to the pile of press clippings on the murder of Alan Baksted. He knew he could not avoid telephone calls from the Marybelle Corporation and its attorney, Constantine Pangalos, forever.

Sooner or later, Marybelle and Pangalos would want an answer about buying into the Golden Horizon. But there would be no two-million-dollar Atlantic City investments made by Murakami until Kanai had spoken to Decker about Alan Baksted's murder. Japanese businessmen who made two-million-dollar mistakes did not become presidents of multinational corporations.

Kanai's secretary buzzed him. "Sir, I have the police station, but Detective Decker is not there. A woman, Detective Spiceland, has answered. She says she's his partner."

Kanai closed his eyes in disappointment. He needed to talk to Decker-san as soon as possible. But perhaps the woman could be of some help. He remembered her, a light-skinned black, with dark red hair and a harsh but sensuous face. She and Decker-san had come to his office the day after Yoshi had been stabbed.

"I will talk to the woman."

Kanai, the receiver to his ear, bowed politely. "Detective Spiceland, I am Kanai."

"Oh, yes. I'm sorry about Mr. Tada. I understand you were in Japan."

"Yes. The funeral, you understand. And business for my company, yes."

He fingered the press clips on Baksted's murder. "I ask your kindness in helping me to reach Decker-san. I do not wish to intrude on the work you must do, but I must contact him."

"I wish I could help you, but he was out on Long Island for most of the day. This task force business. He's not due to come into the office. He had a little trouble out there and he brought some guy back with him, so they'll probably be downtown at Federal Plaza till quitting time. I could try to locate him, but it won't be easy."

Again disappointment. Kanai's eyes moved over the clips and caught something he had ignored earlier. A small paragraph with the dateline reading Ocean City told of a woman who had been raped and murdered the same night Baksted was shot to death.

Something about the woman's death seemed familiar. Death by a blunt instrument or possibly by the blows of a very strong man. *Hai.* Last month on Fifth Avenue a woman had died in the same way. And these deaths resembled those of a woman in San Francisco and one in Dallas, each having occurred while Kanai had been in those cities on business. Was he the only one to have observed the similarities in these killings?

"Mr. Kanai?"

"Please to forgive. I was reading something of interest. I apologize for allowing my mind to wander."

"Hey, I just remembered. My husband's an artist and he's having his first New York exhibition tonight. Manny's supposed to try and make it to the show. We're expecting critics from a couple of newspapers to be there. This is the only thing's been on my mind all day, that show of his."

Kanai thought of Yoshi. "You sound very proud of your husband."

"Proud? I'm 'bout to burst, let me tell you. That man's suffered so much to get to this night. He's had his heart broken so many times by the art world, I don't know how he kept going on. Friend of ours, Mr. Kotlowitz, he got Henri next to the gallery people and they liked his work and next thing you know, wham, we got the show. Look, if Manny doesn't call in, I still might see him at the show. Damn, it's almost five-thirty and I should be at the gallery by six-thirty."

She was happy and reached out to include him in that happiness. "Mr. Kanai, I hope you won't think me pushy or anything, but would you like to attend Henri's exhibition? Frankly, we need all the bodies we can get, 'cause he's not known, not yet anyway. It's at the Cleveland Gallery on East Fifty-seventh Street. You might run into Manny over there. Besides, if I say so myself, my husband's a damn good artist."

Kanai thought of Yoshi, of what he might have become.

The Japanese said softly, "Your husband is a most fortunate man to have someone who believes in him as you do. I would be most honored to attend."

"Hey, all right." She laughed. "Be an invitation for you at the door. Looking forward to seeing you there."

After hanging up, Kanai again looked at the wedding photograph of Yoko and Yoshi. An impulse, of course, his attending the woman's show. He should have shown this sort of kindness to Yoshi. Let this expiate some of his guilt. Let it be seen by Yoshi's spirit as a humble offering begging forgiveness from a prisoner of his *karma,* fate.

There was another reason for attending the show: to find the effect of Decker-san, Baksted's murder and Marybelle Corporation on Murakami. Kanai had his duty and Decker had a role to play in it.

Decker-san the *karateka. Hai.* He would be able to put himself into the mind of the madman committing these ritual murders, the madman who himself was a *karateka.* Kanai knew that the murders were the work of one man. A severe beating, followed by rape, followed by what appeared to be a single killing blow.

Hai. The death of one woman in a city would not indicate a pattern and obviously the killer knew this, for why would he move from one city to another. Two women killed this way in the same city would also be difficult to connect. Perhaps impossible.

Kanai had given the killer a name. *Kaishaku.* A very special executioner. Decker-san would understand. But would he act? Could he get others to act before more women were brutalized? Kanai, like all Japanese, was appalled at the high incidence of crime in America. Yoko's death at the hands of someone like the *kaishaku* would have destroyed him.

The Japanese picked out three Baksted murder clippings with the Ocean City murder tagged onto the end and placed them inside his suit jacket. Kanai wondered if Decker or any one man could deal with this killer.

16

As Ushiro Kanai prepared to leave his office for the Cleveland Gallery, Paul Molise used an attaché case to push against the revolving door of his Park Avenue office building and outside into the frozen December darkness. Pausing, he placed a copy of the Wall Street *Journal* under one arm, then used the free hand to turn up his coat collar. Shoulders hunched, he joined the crowds moving toward the corner. An extended working day and the lack of any food since a quick lunchtime sandwich only aggravated his anger at what had happened today at the arena. Connie Pangalos. Sal Buscaglia. Assholes, both of them.

Aldo, Molise's chauffeur-bodyguard, left the warmth of the limousine to hurry around the car and open a back door. He didn't have to be told that Molise was in a shitty mood; you could see that from the way he walked. Wisely, Aldo decided to say nothing, drive carefully and pray that he didn't get a ticket on the way to New Jersey.

As he walked toward the car, Molise slapped his thigh with his folded newspaper. That business out on Long Island today with the task force cop and Buscaglia's security guards wasn't just wrong; it was dumb. Hadn't been Buscaglia's idea, that's for sure. He did what he was told, no more, no less. Give him money to blow at the track or on some blonde with tits like dirigibles and he was happy.

As for Livingston Quarrels, the closet Jew's biggest fight was trying to get his wife into the Junior League and his daughter to be satisfied with owning two jumping horses instead of three. Today's trouble on Long Island had been caused by Constantine Pangalos, who had come unglued at the thought of making license plates in some federal prison. Schmuck. Of all people, Pangalos should have known better.

So Decker gets the seating plan. So what. There were ways of dealing with that. That's why Sparrowhawk and Management Systems Consultants were around, to find out who in law enforcement wanted a fat-paying job in private security after retirement.

People like Manny Decker had to be finessed. You let him think he's winning, then you show him that all along he had only been spinning his wheels in place. You do this by using money, brains, connections. Instead, Pangalos fucked up and the seating plan, along with Buscaglia, was down at Federal Plaza in the hands of the ambitious Charles LeClair.

The trouble out at the arena had resulted in a quick meeting in the back of a Mulberry Street social club in Little Italy among Molise, his father the don, and Giovanni Gran Sasso, Johnny Sass, the *consigliere,* the adviser. A very nervous Constantine Pangalos was there too, forced to sit in the bare room and remain silent while the three Sicilians spoke in Italian and made decisions about the rest of his life.

After the Italians had deliberated among themselves they told Pangalos that he had acted stupidly, and from now on was to do nothing until they told him to. Buscaglia knew better than to open his mouth. The four security guards, each of whom had been hurt, would file countercharges against Decker, causing any charge against Buscaglia to eventually be dropped.

"When you sleep, you sleep for you," Johnny Sass told Pangalos. "But when you work, you work for us. Teeth placed before the tongue gives good advice. That's an Italian saying. It means you shut your mouth, you never make a mistake."

As for who would take the blame for the phony seating plans, that would be Pangalos and Quarrels, the Greek and the Jew. If arrested, they would have the best lawyers and the don guaranteed that the case would appear before the correct judge. Files would be stolen, destroyed or doctored to help their case. Leave that to Sparrowhawk and MSC.

With the old don watching, Johnny Sass had placed his face nose to nose with Pangalos and told him not to make any more trouble. The Greek, looking as if he'd just eaten a dead rat, had looked away. He had been sentenced and he knew death was not far away. Johnny Sass had never liked

Pangalos. As a prosecutor he had sentenced some of the *consigliere*'s friends and hounded others.

At the corner near Molise's limousine a Santa Claus rang a bell to encourage people to drop money inside a black kettle suspended from a wooden tripod. In his other hand he held a tape recorder playing tinny Christmas carols. Molise felt like pissing in the kettle. First week in December and Santa's already on the street with his hand in your pocket. Before you knew it there would be carols in July.

He stepped inside the car, and Aldo slammed the door behind him and then walked out into the street to enter the car on the driver's side. Molise wondered if it might not be better to skip dinner and meet his wife at his daughter's school, where she was to perform in a dance recital; at least he could catch part of it. He wondered if Tricia might grow up to become a professional ballerina. Now that would be something.

These thoughts relaxed him. Eyes closed, he leaned back in his seat. And never saw Aldo die.

A slim figure in dark clothing, face hidden by floppy hat, dark glasses and a scarf, hands in the sleeves of a fur coat, detached itself from the crowd crossing the street in front of the parked limousine and walked up to the open window on the driver's side. After looking to make sure no one was watching, the figure removed one hand from a sleeve, reached through the open window and slit Aldo's throat with a knife. A *kai-ken.*

A quick shove and the dying chauffeur-bodyguard was down on the front seat and out of sight.

Hark the herald angels sing. Glory to the newborn king.

The figure withdrew both hands from inside the limousine, pocketed the wet knife and looked around. No one was watching.

Molise, eyes closed, felt a rush of cold air as the door opened and someone slipped into the back beside him. *What the fuck.* He frowned. Aldo should have been more alert.

Michi removed her scarf, letting him see her face. Then she removed the floppy hat she wore and Molise saw the *hachimaki,* the headband with the characters for *Jinrai Butai* and a red circle that symbolized the rising sun, the headband that had belonged to her father.

Molise said, "Look, I'm in a hurry to get home. What do you want? Did Dorian send you here? Is that it?"

Michi said, "*Kataki-uchi.*"

"Lady, I haven't the slightest idea what you're talking about. *Kataki* what?"

"Measure for measure. Retaliation."

Molise leaned toward the front. "Hey, Aldo, get rid of this crazy bitch, will you? I really don't have the time—"

Michi, seated to Molise's left, drove the edge of a booted foot into his ankle, causing him to cry out and lean down toward the pain. As he did, Michi bent over him, arm extended overhead, fist clenched, then brought her elbow straight down, striking Molise behind the ear and driving him to the car floor.

The pain split his skull and he wondered what the fuck she had hit him with. He fought to stay conscious, tried to rise, to grab the seat and pull himself into a sitting position, but he couldn't. The Jap woman was sitting on his chest, her knees pressing down on his biceps. Crazy bitch. What had he ever done to her?

God and sinners reconciled.

No one passing by the parked limousine stopped to look through the tinted windows. In any case, Michi and Molise were out of sight, on the floor and in the darkness of the back seat.

Kataki-uchi. Justice. Revenge. And by her hand. Manny's American justice would not satisfy Michi's ancestors.

Reaching down to her boot top, Michi pulled out a steel needle, four and a half inches long, its point sharp enough to draw blood by the merest touch, and, squeezing it with both fists, placed the point under Molise's jaw, hesitated only for a second, then drove the needle through his jaw, tongue and into the roof of his mouth. He shivered, groaned, tried to throw her off and failed.

God, the pain. He struggled, but she was more than a match for him now. The blow behind the ear had weakened him and the pain in his mouth and head terrified him. *The needle.* One sound and he would rip his tongue in half.

There was another needle in her hand and she held it close to his face so that he could see it. Then she shoved it through his right eye and into his brain and he made a sound, sending blood pouring from his mouth. He had to throw her off, but it was getting dark and he had no strength. His mouth was filled with his own blood and he wanted to swallow but that meant more pain because of the needle piercing his tongue.

He never saw the third needle, but he felt it.

In his left eye, into his brain. He groaned, stiffened and relaxed.

And died.

Michi removed the blood-wet needles, placed them in the pocket of her fur coat and sat back on the seat, eyes on Paul Molise. She whispered their names—her father, mother, sister, closed her eyes, bowed her head and remembered that you could never live under the same sky with someone who had done you a wrong. *Ren-chi-shin,* the sense of shame, could only be removed when those who had committed the wrong had been removed from under that sky. Blood must be washed with blood.

She put on her hat, covered her face once more, stepped from the limousine on the traffic side and in seconds was swallowed up by the crowd.

17

Decker blew gently on a *shakuhachi,* a wooden flute given to him by Michi, who clung to his arm as they stood in the Japanese Garden, part of the fifty-acre Brooklyn Botanic Gardens. The two were in front of the Cascades, five waterfalls over echo caverns designed to intensify the sound of falling water. Surrounding the waterfalls and miniaturized landscape were forest-sized pine trees, hills and a lake narrowed and shaped to reflect shadows and the beauty of the *niwa,* the Japanese landscape garden.

Designed in 1914 by famed Japanese landscape architect Takeo Shiota, the Japanese Garden offered an escape into a "mirror of nature." Decker came here often, and he wanted to share the beauty and tranquillity with Michi, who was leaving tomorrow on a business trip to London, Amsterdam and Paris. She would purchase diamonds, meet prospective buyers and return to New York in approximately ten days. Decker had already begun to miss her.

From the echoing waterfalls they walked in silence to Drum Bridge, gracefully curved and casting a reflection in water so that, combined with the bridge itself, it formed a circular, drumlike image. Steppingstones had been placed in the water to trace the flight of wild geese. When the couple stopped again it was at the *torii,* two logs placed horizontally on top of two pillars to form an archway marking the presence of a nearby Shinto shrine. The shrine was located in a pine wood on a hill behind the *torii* and was made of redwood and held together by wooden pins instead of nails. Decker had never gone inside. He had visited similar shrines in Tokyo with Michi and knew that the inside would be plain and empty, in keeping with Shinto's simplicity.

He stopped playing the flute and looked at Michi. Her eyes were on the shrine and he knew she was thinking of the old religion. Shinto was nature worship. Its *kami,* gods, were not only men, ancestors, emperors, but animals, rocks, trees, rivers, birds, mountains. Shinto was also purification by wind and water. The mouth and hands had to be rinsed before entering a shrine, a symbolic reminder of the days when one could not be admitted to the shrine without being immersed in a river or the sea.

Decker was about to play the flute again when he decided that it would intrude on Michi's thoughts. She obviously wanted to meditate on the shrine a little longer, so Decker pocketed the flute and stood beside her in respectful silence. Let her pray for her dead in peace.

What was it Kanai had said to him a few nights ago at the Cleveland Gallery?

"You here in the West fear that your god will find you guilty of your sins. We Japanese concern ourselves with avoiding shame. This means we must live up to the expectations of others. We cannot live merely for ourselves. This is why we work so hard in business, to avoid shame."

To avoid shame.

Decker thought of that when Kanai said, "According to your newspapers the killing of Alan Baksted remains unsolved."

"Seems to be the work of a professional hit man. Unfortunately, if police fail to solve a homicide within seventy-two hours, it usually remains an open case. Means we don't have witnesses, motives, clues and probably won't get them."

"There were torn fifty-dollar bills found on the body of Mr. Baksted."

"I guess he took something that didn't belong to him."

"I have received letters and telephone calls from representatives of the Marybelle Corporation. I am told I can now see its private lists of gamblers, what you call its 'pigeon list.' "

Decker's turn.

In the crowded gallery the two men stood side by side in front of a framed watercolor by Ellen Spiceland's husband. LeClair had ordered Decker to say nothing to the Japanese about Baksted, the Golden Horizon or the murder of Paul Molise junior. Decker didn't have to tell Kanai of Molise's connection to Marybelle and the Golden Horizon; the subject had already come up over dinner in the Fûrin a month ago.

Kanai was waiting to hear the effect, if any, of those two murders on any investment he might make in the Golden Horizon. How did Decker tell Kanai what he wasn't supposed to tell him?

The detective sipped warm champagne from a plastic glass, then said, "Officially, I cannot comment on this case, Kanai-san. Please understand."

"*Hai.* Duty, Decker-san. Please excuse my lack of understanding in expecting you to reveal what must remain a confidence between you and your superiors. Tell your secrets to the wind and the wind will tell them to the trees."

For the Japanese nothing was what it appeared to be. Kanai was either being considerate or was shrewdly challenging Decker to find a way to pass on information without breaking the rules. The detective was undecided about playing the game and then he remembered what LeClair had done to Benitez and DeMain and he remembered LeClair's way of despising those he had dumped on. He shrugged. And decided to play.

He said, "Kanai-san, are you going to buy one of Mr. Juriot's paintings?"

"He has talent, yes. A strong sense of color, perhaps too strong for my taste. But I understand that Caribbean artists tend to emphasize color. One or two works have impressed me. I would buy to encourage him, yes."

The detective looked at Kanai. "These days people buy art as an investment. A hedge against inflation. They also buy collectibles. But you see, you have to be careful with certain collectibles."

He sipped from his glass. "Myself, I'd hesitate if a collectible involved, say, two million or more."

He cocked his head for a final evaluation. *"Takai desu. Hai, takai desu."* Too expensive.

Decker looked back at Kanai in time to see the Japanese bow almost imperceptibly. But the detective noticed it.

"Domo arigato gozai mashite, Decker-san."

The detective returned the bow, his gesture just as contained and controlled. What Decker had just done for Kanai was no small service and both knew it. The detective would be in a position to collect on this favor in the future. And Kanai's sense of honor would compel him to repay.

In front of the *torii* at the Japanese Garden, Michi, eyes closed, bowed from the waist, then opened her eyes and smiled at Decker. He kissed her lips lightly, and they began walking once more, enjoying the crisp day and the clear, cold air. When they stopped to view the *Waiting House,* the tiny house where guests traditionally waited before being greeted by the host for the Japanese tea ceremony, she said, "I prayed for my father, my mother, my sister."

"Missed my chance," Decker said. "Should have offered a prayer of my own, a prayer that you'll come back to me from Europe."

She squeezed his arm. "You do not have to pray for that. I shall come back to you, I promise."

"Let me know when your flight lands. I'll try to meet you if I can. By the way, which god did you pray to, or is that a secret?"

She laughed. "No, it is not a secret. I prayed to the local *kami,* to whichever god lives in that shrine behind us. Every village, every town has its own god, so I asked the god of Brooklyn—"

Decker grinned. "You what?"

Michi continued in all sincerity. "I asked the god of Brooklyn for his protection and that I might endeavor in all things, that I might persevere and never retreat from my duty. I asked for strength to serve the divine will and, of course, I praised him, as is our custom."

Decker looked upward. "The god of Brooklyn. Five boroughs we got in this city. Does that mean each one has its own god?"

She nodded, still serious. "And each town in those boroughs, each neighborhood, each village, they have their own gods, many of them."

"I'll take your word for it."

"Something else I prayed for. I prayed for you, that you will be safe in your job, that you do not get hurt."

He drew her close to him. "All I want from the god of Brooklyn is that he give you two safe flights, one going, one coming. The rest of it I'll handle myself."

She looked down. "With Paul Molise dead, is it not easier for you?"

He shook his head as they began walking again. "Wish it was. Unfortunately, it's still hairy. Same bunch of players, except that one, Molise, is going to be replaced by someone we don't know, someone whose habits are a damn mystery, who we'll have to learn about pretty fast if we want to have a chance against him. I mean in one sense, it's starting over. The Molise family's still in business and so is Management Systems Consultants. With one player gone, a substitute comes in for him and the game goes on.

"See, Michi, we were getting close to Molise. Pangalos could have helped us squeeze him, but with Molise dead, Pangalos, at the very least is going to hang tough. Just makes it harder on us, is all. We needed Molise alive, not dead. And I still can't afford to make a mistake with LeClair."

LeClair was now in Washington for a quick conference with the Justice Department on whether or not Molise's death would spark an outbreak of gang war among organized crime. LeClair didn't know the answer. And neither did

Decker. If Paul junior's death was a mob hit, all hell was going to break loose among New York's five crime families.

Molise's bodyguard had had his throat cut. No mystery about how he died. Molise, however, was another story. Cause of death had been some sort of metallic object, something long, thin, sharp. Stabbed under the jaw, slicing the tongue in two and causing a wound in the roof of the mouth. Wounds in both eyes as well, but the coroner wasn't sure if the jaw and mouth wounds and eye wounds had been caused by the same weapons. Whatever the weapons, the killing had been brazen and deliberate.

Had Molise been killed as a warning to someone else? Had he been punished by someone in the underworld? His father had vowed to kill the person or persons who had murdered his beloved son. Decker didn't want to be the man who had iced Paulie. In the pre-Castro days, Paul senior had sliced off the ear of a man who had betrayed him, then tied the man to a rope and trolled him behind a fishing boat off the Cuban coast and watched as sharks, drawn by the blood, tore the shrieking man apart.

In the Japanese Garden, Decker and Michi stopped to look at a tall *Kasuga* lantern. Shaped out of stone into a miniature pagoda, the lantern bore signs of the zodiac. This was no place to be thinking of violence, and yet it was hard not to. At the Cleveland Gallery, Kanai had mentioned the *kaishaku* to Decker and Ellen Spiceland. A *karateka* who raped and murdered. Ellen had listened attentively, her mind storing up facts. Decker saw it in her face; she was going to do some checking on the *kaishaku*.

Meanwhile, Decker had enough to keep him busy. LeClair. The task force. Cases with Ellen, ranging from child abuse to burglaries, from rapes to violence in local schools. And there was his role as a field associate.

Kaishaku.

On the way to the Instruction Building of the Brooklyn Botanic Garden, Decker mentioned the *kaishaku* to Michi. As she listened she clutched his arm tighter. "It sounds like something your soldiers did in Vietnam."

Decker stopped. "Jesus, you're right. *Double veterans,* they called them. But isn't the *kaishaku* different?"

They resumed walking. "Yes," she said. "He is what you

call a second to the one who is to commit *seppuku.* To the samurai *seppuku* is a most honorable death. It is a form of self-punishment and only someone of great respect is allowed to perform it. He must have a *kaishaku,* a friend who was a swordsman, and stays close to him, to put him out of his misery if the pain was too much. You know how *seppuku* is done."

"Yes. The knife goes in deep on the left side and then is drawn across the stomach and up on the right side a little bit."

"Much pain," she said softly. "You can understand that someone might lose his nerve and cannot do what must be done to save his honor. Or they try to escape. To save them from pain and disgrace, it is the *kaishaku* who uses his sword to behead them. To us it is a merciful act to assist in *seppuku.* Women commit *seppuku* in a different manner."

"How?"

She stopped and turned to face the shrine on the hill behind him. The words came with great difficulty. "An artery here." She touched the side of her neck.

She turned to face Decker with tears in her eyes. "It is an honorable death for honorable people. When you do not want to be disgraced by your enemies—"

She couldn't go on. Decker took her in his arms. Children like Michi and her sister grew up knowing about *seppuku;* it held little horror for them.

What role had it played in Michi's life during the last six years? Decker wanted to know more. But he simply held her and said nothing.

Even though Kanai's daughter was now in Japan, Kanai still wanted to see the *kaishaku* captured. "I am one of the backers of the *suibin* tournament in Paris next January," he said.

"I didn't know that," said Decker. "Should be quite a show."

"*Hai.* But it would be most shameful if this *kaishaku* is among the contestants. I greatly fear he could be. He is a skilled fighter, one who might respond to the challenge provided by such a tournament."

"Don't see how you can keep him out. I mean, how can

you check the background of every single entrant? You're going to have hundreds of fighters from all over the world."

"It would be a service to the martial arts if he were to be apprehended or"—he drew a deep breath—"disposed of prior to the tournament. It would not be easy to stop him, but it could be done."

Not by me, thought Decker. I've got my problems with LeClair.

Inside the Instruction Department of the Botanic Garden, Decker and Michi walked past rooms where classes were being given in Oriental brush painting, photography, orchid growing, flower arrangement and origami wildlife.

After some urging on his part, Michi agreed to make paper animals. As the instructor and the small class watched, she calmly folded sheets of yellow, blue, pink and orange paper into tiny deer, birds, a bear, an eagle. She worked fast, as though she were alone and time had stood still. Magic.

Only when Michi finished did she look up, embarrassed by the attention. The instructor, a gray-haired woman wearing thick glasses and leaning on a cane, picked up a tiny deer. There were tears in her eyes when she said, "I have never seen anything so lovely."

Leaning forward, she kissed Michi and the class applauded.

The instructor held the deer in the palm of her hand as though the paper animal were alive. "May I please keep this, miss?"

Michi looked at Decker. "Asama. Michelle Asama."

"Miss Asama."

"Yes, of course."

The class moved closer, holding their hands out for the remainder of the paper animals. Decker was so proud of her, so very proud. He took several sheets of colored paper and placed them in the pocket of Michi's fur coat. He was going to have her teach him to make paper animals.

They drove back to Manhattan in the Mercedes that was on loan to Decker from the task force, taking the Brooklyn Battery Tunnel to the southern tip of Manhattan and stopping off for dinner in Greenwich Village, in an Italian restaurant where the waiters sang opera and the owner's pregnant dog wandered from table to table silently begging. A waiter dropped to one knee in front of Michi and sang an aria from

La Bohème and kissed her hand and she seemed so happy; Decker decided that this was not the time to ask her who in her family had committed *seppuku*. Nothing must spoil this night together.

At her apartment she made love with an energy that almost intimidated Decker. It seemed more like combat than love, almost like what had gone through her mind at the mention of *seppuku*. But then he was caught up in it and he couldn't think anymore. He *felt*. He *experienced*.

They made love in the bath. She soaked his body in almost scalding water, purification, she said. Shinto. And then, after they had soaped each other from head to toe in yellow lather, she guided him to the floor, to a mat beside the sunken tub and she gave him a massage. She lay on top of him, rubbing her lathered body back and forth on his, slowly, and though Decker became totally aroused, she refused to let him make love to her. "Wait," she whispered. "Wait."

She stood on his shoulders and walked down his body, down his spine and onto his buttocks and calves, then walked backward until she reached his shoulders. On her knees she made the same journey, down and back. The pleasure was sharp, on the edge of pain. Decker groaned. The sweetest pain he had ever known.

Using one lathered knee she rubbed his buttocks, then slid down to rub her lathered breasts against his buttocks. To hell with it. Decker couldn't hold back any longer. He stiffened, rubbed himself against the soaped mat and came. Michi continued. Sitting on his soaped calves, her bare buttocks sliding around on his flesh, she picked up one of his feet and rubbed it against her breast and moaned. Decker felt himself getting hard again.

Michi signaled for him to turn over. When he did she began to slide and writhe against him, her eyes closed with pleasure. Sitting up she began to pound his body with the edge of her hand, then with the bottom of her fist, working her way from shoulder to thigh, hurting and yet at the same time exciting him. Did he come again or imagine it? At this point, how could he know?

She led him to the water and they slipped into the tub together. When the soap was washed off, they changed the water and sat down in it once more and made love, with

Michi mounting Decker, clutching him, rocking gently back and forth on his thighs, the music of the thirteen-stringed *koto* coming from a speaker high on the wall; and Decker was so in love, so fucking happy, so completely her captive.

He was drowsy. Ready for sleep. Through his semiconsciousness he felt her lick blood from his mouth that was drawn by her teeth, and then his tongue met hers and there was the taste of blood mingled with the sweet softness of her mouth. He knew that so long as Michi loved him he would submit to anything she asked. His surrender was complete.

"You," he whispered, and in that single word was all that he was, and all of it he offered to her.

18

Ellen Spiceland entered her apartment on tiptoe and closed the door softly behind her. After hanging a leather overcoat, hand-knitted sweater and cloche hat in a hall closet she removed her boots, bent down to rub feeling into icy toes, then padded into the kitchen, boots in hand. Her holstered .38 Smith & Wesson remained clipped to an alligator belt with a Haitian mahogany buckle, a recent anniversary present from Henri. The gun would stay on her hip until she entered the bedroom to look in on her sleeping husband. There she would hide it in a slipper on her side of the bed, within easy reach if she needed it during the night.

Their home was a two-bedroom apartment in upper Manhattan's hilly Washington Heights, with streets that twisted and dipped sharply and a view across the Henry Hudson River of the New Jersey Palisades, purple cliffs rising above abandoned factories.

Before Henri, Ellen had never gone to a museum in her life. Art, culture, literature were all white people's pastimes.

Life, she learned early on, was a struggle. To win that

struggle she left home and Harlem at eighteen to go downtown, and worked three jobs to support herself and graduate from City College. Then she got hit with the racism and sex discrimination of the Police Department. And somewhere in all of this survived two bad marriages and a miscarriage that hospitalized her for over a month, bringing with it the news that she could never have children. So she was a survivor.

In gentle Henri, a slight, handsome Haitian twenty years her senior, she found the right man to be strong for, one who needed her to protect him from the world.

Yet, Henri, in his own way, did the same for her. His intelligence, sensitivity and talent were a comfort to her after a working day of danger and abuse, and often hostile public, all exacerbated by the helplessness she felt in the face of the misery around her. How did a cop survive? Detachment, humor, alcohol, drugs helped.

In the kitchen she moved around on stockinged feet. She lit the oven and placed her wet boots on its open door to dry. After rubbing her hands in the oven heat she turned around and let the heat warm her ass. She thought of how confused this *kaishaku* business had left her. How could she get that killer off the street? Manny was too busy with the task force to help her and the rest of the guys were uninterested.

Kanai, who had bought three of Henri's paintings, bless him, had said the murders were the work of one man, though Ellen wondered how he could be so sure. But he was Japanese and karate *was* Japanese fighting. The problem, as Ellen saw it, was that the *kaishaku* moved from city to city. Pinning down someone like that was like trying to nail custard to the wall. She had to talk to Manny, a karate man himself.

The telephone on the kitchen wall rang and Ellen grabbed it immediately. Didn't want to wake up Henri. The man needed his sleep.

"Hello?"

"Ellen? Manny."

"Just the man I want to speak to. How's it going down there?"

"Busting my chops with these phony assault charges by Buscaglia's guards. LeClair doesn't want me wasting my time in court with these things, so what it's going to come down to is both sides are going to drop the charges. What counts is that seating plan. We can use it against Pangalos and Quarrels. Their names are on it."

Ellen squeezed the receiver between her jaw and shoulder and moved around the kitchen assembling what she needed for a fresh cup of coffee. "Anything new on who got Molise?"

"Zilch. Street has nothing about a war, nothing about anybody coming in from out of town to perform a hit, nothing about trouble inside the Molise family. Beginning to look like some crazy just decided to kill the first people he found parked in a limo on a Manhattan street. Maybe Molise and his bodyguard just happened to be in the wrong place at the wrong time."

Ellen spooned coffee beans from a tin and into a grinder. "Who's taking Paulie's place?"

"Don't know. For now Gran Sasso, Johnny Sass, is calling the shots. Paul senior's too broken up. Whoever takes over, his first job will be to learn who did Paulie. What's with Raoul and his lady?"

Raoul was the Dominican pimp who had stabbed Yoshi Tada to death. That day Ellen was in court for preliminary hearings concerning bail and charges.

"They're talking manslaughter two," Ellen said.

"A joke. That's all it is. Why do we even bother arresting these clowns. Asshole judges."

"How's this for a joke? Bambi, Raoul's lady of the evening, had at least two venereal diseases. If Tada had lived he'd have come down with syphilis or herpes at least."

"You're kidding." Manny chuckled.

"Thought your warped mind would find that amusing."

"We chuckle and guffaw and somehow make it through a most trying day."

"I know. And love makes the world go down and all that. Look, Manny, be serious for a minute. This *kaishaku* thing—"

He groaned. "I knew it, I knew it."

"I can't let it go."

"I know. Okay, let's hear it."

She shrugged. "Tell me how to go about getting him."

"Holy shit. Is that all you want to know? How to grab

some sicko who goes around the country raping and beating women to death with his bare hands? Look, suppose Kanai's all wrong about this. Suppose it's not one guy, but a series of coincidences?"

She finished grinding the beans, switched the receiver to another ear and poured the ground beans into a filter resting over a bone china cup. As she added boiling water she said, "Manny, stop jerking me around, okay? We both know Kanai did not get to where he is by being stupid. So let's just start by saying he knows."

"If you say so. Actually you're right. Kanai's no dummy. Hey, all I called about was to see how it went in court today, that's all. Stop sticking your finger in my eye."

She stirred her coffee.

"Please, Manny."

He sighed. "Go."

"How do I pin this guy down? Where do I start? I mean he's all over the place. I spoke to the captain about it and he says the only reason he's letting me make a few calls on this thing is *A*, because a woman was killed in New York and *B*, because I'm a woman and he doesn't want me yelling discrimination or sexism or shit like that."

"Blackmail."

She sipped coffee. "Screw him. Anyway, I can't get away with blackmailing him forever. If I don't come up with something in a hurry, it's bye-bye *kaishaku* and back to the real world."

"Kanai says he's a *karateka,* our boy, and he moves around. Could be a traveling salesman, maybe, but Kanai says the man's good, and very skilled, so that's out."

"Why?"

Decker said, "Wouldn't leave him time to train. If he's that good he trains all the time. Only way to stay in shape. He could be some kind of worker, whose job takes him from city to city. Okay, so here's what you do. Work with those cities Kanai told you about—"

She set the cup of coffee down, went to the wall where a metal writing pad hung beside the phone and reached for a magnetized pen.

She said, "New York, Atlantic City, Dallas, San Francisco. Wait, it wasn't Atlantic City, it was some town outside of Atlantic City. Real small town. I forget what it is but I have it written down at the office."

"No problem. Hey, yesterday a friend reminded me about *double veterans,* GIs who raped and killed women in Vietnam."

"Hooray for our side."

"I know. The worst. Anyway, get lists of all dojos in those cities. Karate clubs. Get the membership lists of those clubs, if you can; but it won't be easy and it means a ton of names. We have one hundred twenty people in our club."

"Oh, God."

She stopped writing. "Manny, you said karate clubs. What about judo?"

"Judo is throwing techniques, not striking. This guy's a fighter. Uses his hands. Hey, hey, hey—"

"What's wrong?"

"Nothing. I just remembered what Kanai said. He said he didn't want this guy in his tournament, that this *kaishaku* was a skilled fighter and might enter the tournament. Tournament. Jesus, why didn't I see that before?"

"See what?"

"Fighter who moves around. Tournament. Competition. Matches. *That's* where you start."

There was a light in Ellen's eyes. "Manny, you are one beautiful man. Sounds good. Real good. I don't know anything about this stuff except that you wear your pajamas when you do it."

"That's *gi,* wiseass."

"Whatever you say. So our boy goes from city to city fighting, you think?"

He cautioned her. "Stay cool. Don't get your hopes up. Just a theory, that's all."

"Hey, man, what the hell do we do every day of our lives except make educated guesses, right?"

"What can I tell you. Now what I want you to do is find out if there was a tournament in any of these cities around the time a woman was killed. Call the martial arts publications."

He gave her eight names of publications, three of which were in Los Angeles.

"List of fighters at each tournament," said Ellen, writing as she talked.

"Who said minorities are dumb."

"You're a kind person—the kind I'd like to kick. I do like the tournament idea, though."

"Now you've got *me* interested. When you get the names let me have a look at them. Who knows? Maybe I'll get an idea just by running them through the old mental computer."

"Manny, I don't care what they say about you, I like you anyway. By the way, everything all right with you?"

He had told her about Michi. Not everything, not even most of it. Only that there was now someone special in his life, someone he had met a long time ago and had run into again. And they were taking it slow. And hoping.

"It's cool," he said. "She's away on a business trip. She promised to come back."

"She better. If she hurts you I'll kick the white off her behind."

"She's Japanese."

"Whatever. Manny, thanks. I mean that."

"Don't bother thanking me. You're right. This shit, whoever he is, deserves to die. Maybe we can get lucky and at least get him off the streets."

Ellen said, "Could happen to any of us, Manny. Me. Even your lady, whoever she is."

Decker said nothing.

Then, "Yeah, even her. But you know something? If that ever happened, I'd kill him. I swear to God I'd kill him. Doesn't matter who he is or where they hid him or how long it took me, I'd find him and I'd kill him."

19

Trevor Sparrowhawk watched with pleasure through the window of his Connecticut home as a lean, spotted doe, trailed by a spindly-legged fawn, stepped from a clump of maple trees and cautiously picked its way across snow to sniff timidly at a cardboard box of spinach, hay and cabbage.

Between nibbles of food the doe lifted her head to glance around for enemies, real and imagined. Sipping tea and milk from a Wedgwood china cup, Sparrowhawk reminded himself that to fear anything was to give it power over you. How much power had he given Giovanni Gran Sasso and Alphonse Giulia, Don Molise's nephew?

Several days ago, after young Paul Molise had been laid to eternal rest in a Long Island cemetery, a meeting had taken place with Gran Sasso and Giulia in the spacious back seat of a stretch limousine returning to Manhattan. Sparrowhawk had been the only other person present. Until now the Englishman had dealt solely with young Paul, who, despite a certain stubbornness, could at least be reasoned with—unlike the more hardened members of the Molise crime family. It now appeared that the old order was to yield to the new; and the new, Sparrowhawk feared, would be more difficult to manage.

Gran Sasso and Giulia were a demanding pair not given to compromise. Gran Sasso, Johnny Sass, was in his late sixties, a rumpled, white-haired man with an intense admiration for Mussolini, food stains on his tie and a deceptive way of putting people at ease before destroying them with his keen intelligence. He specialized in corruption, and in the bribery of judges, court officials, politicians and police. The one Molise family member whom Sparrowhawk felt was his intellectual equal—and perhaps superior—the *consigliere* was the one he feared most.

Alphonse Giulia, called Allie Boy, was fortyish, muscular and balding with a greased widow's peak and a face partially discolored by explosives used years ago in a labor dispute. He handled the Molise narcotics interests, expertly walking a tightrope between Colombians, who controlled New York's cocaine trade; Harlem blacks, who needed the Italians' overseas narcotics connections; and the "Westies," Manhattan's West Side Irish thugs, often used for contract killings and hijackings. The "Westies," in their Roaring Twenties slouch hats, striped suits and spats, were quick to torture and kill. Even the Italians were scared of them.

Sparrowhawk found Allie Boy to be a surly bugger, tactless in speech and manner and perennially suspicious. For tax purposes, he owned a bakery in Astoria, where he was said to keep over a half million dollars in cash stashed in the closet guarded by a vicious Doberman. An avowed miser, he saved string and tin foil and forced his wife to make her own dresses.

The wogs, never strong on diplomacy, made it clear that they were in charge. Sparrowhawk had better go along with it or he was out.

Gran Sasso looked out through a car window at Shea Stadium. "You got one thing to do for us and that's to help find out who killed Paulie. Don't bother telling me how you don't get involved in certain things, how you want to keep your hands clean. Forget your company's image. What you got to worry about is Paulie. He's dead."

"Paulie was a good kid," Allie Boy said in a high-pitched voice. "Nobody fuckin' breathes till we get the guy who burned him. Get out there and learn what you should learn, then turn it over to us. We'll make him wish he'd never been born."

Sparrowhawk smoothed the creases on his mourning suit. "I'm sure. You realize, of course, that there is absolutely nothing to go on. Not a clue."

Michelle Asama eased into his thoughts. It would, of course, be sheer madness to mention her to the wogs. They would want to know why they hadn't been alerted about her before. Given the present mood in the car this lapse on Sparrowhawk's part could well mean his own demise. Sparrowhawk had his suspicions about the lady, but they had to be verified first.

Suppose, for example, that Miss Asama was related to the late, unlamented George Chihara. Her presence in New York could thus bode ill for those responsible for Mr. Chihara's death. That would be Sparrowhawk, Robbie, Dorian. And Paul Molise. Could any woman be that dangerous?

The idea of losing his life did not exactly fill Sparrowhawk with great tranquillity. The elephantine Gran Sasso pressed a button on the armrest that elevated a plastic shield between them and the driver, and leaning forward, said casually, "You want somewhere to start, I give you somewhere. Saigon. Start in Saigon."

As he scratched his great stomach, Sparrowhawk felt the certainty of reaching old age grow dim.

Now Sparrowhawk watched the doe lift her head from the cardboard box, ears flat against her skull, nose pointed toward a clear sky. Listening. Then she nudged the fawn, pushing it away from the food, and the two animals galloped off into the forest. It was a full two minutes before the car appeared. Sparrowhawk was impressed. This was an early warning system to be reckoned with. Maybe he would need one. And very soon.

Sparrowhawk walked across his book-lined study and opened the door. "Unity, love, they're here. Bring the cheese and biscuits to my study. Coffee for Dorian. Robbie will have his usual."

"Straightaway, love."

The house Sparrowhawk lived in with his wife and daughter was a converted seventeenth-century English barn. A small fortune had been spent to make the house livable and, located now on property just outside of Waterbury, Connecticut, it included a swimming pool, guest house, tennis court and an outdoor patio.

Inside, the house had been made fit for a Victorian gentleman of the nineteenth century. There were paneled rooms and long hallways of dark, polished wood, and walls hung with tapestries. Persian rugs and medieval weapons, and elaborate stained glass windows. But Sparrowhawk's pride was his collection of rare books, first editions of Byron, Tennyson, Carlyle. They were all English. By choice. Sparrowhawk loved England and he vowed he would one day return there to live.

A wireless perimeter burglar alarm guarded these riches, with a backup battery power system in case of electrical failure, and a motion-detector alarm sensitive enough to signal the presence of an intruder. A telephone, with a prerecorded message of alarm, had been programed to automatically dial local police in case of a break-in. The phone also contained a "line seizure," sounding an alarm when the lines had been cut and opening the lines, even when busy, to incoming calls. Sparrowhawk's relationship with the local police was excellent, thanks to his generosity in finding well-paying security industry jobs for anyone leaving the force. If he was away from the house for any length of time police either telephoned his wife or looked in on the house twice a day.

Roaming the property were three trained Alsatian guard dogs. Of the loaded guns hidden in strategic locations throughout the house, the most devastating was the American 180 laser submachine gun, which fired thirty .22 caliber bullets per second, with enough firepower to knock holes in a brick wall or chop down a tree.

Should all else fail there was a safe room in the cellar, separated by a steel door. A security procedure that Sparrowhawk had recommended for many of his clients, this one-room stronghold contained food, two-way radios or a telephone, weapons, water. If necessary, a handful of people could survive in such a room for days.

At twenty-one, Sparrowhawk's daughter, Valerie, was a beautiful woman, intelligent and disciplined, with a sense of humor and a mind of her own. She was tall, though not as tall as her mother, with blonde hair, blue eyes and fair skin. She was ambidextrous, a brilliant scholar, and in her final year at Yale.

What pleased Sparrowhawk most was her lack of self-consciousness about her beauty. She expected from life only what she was capable of earning. To Sparrowhawk, there was no higher compliment.

"Daddy?"

She stood in the doorway of his study, barefoot in cutoff

jeans and a university sweat shirt, cradling an armful of schoolbooks. Boadicea, a pet spider monkey, rested on her shoulder. The monkey lived on cocoa, packets of bugs and orange slices and was not a favorite of Sparrowhawk's.

"Must study for midterms," Valerie said in a voice with only the remnants of a British accent after six years in America. "I'll leave you here with your cohorts to decide the fate of Western civilization."

She didn't care for Dorian or Robbie. To her, Dorian was a nerd. Of Robbie she said little, admitting only that she found him creepy but didn't exactly know why. Sparrowhawk had once hoped the two would come to love each other and perhaps marry, but Val would have none of it. Other than hello and good-bye, the two had nothing to say to each other. Unity had been the one to finally tell her husband, "She doesn't fancy him; she never will. Some women have a need to love that leads them into just any relationship; that's not Val. She'll love when she finds the man who deserves her and not before. Robbie's not that man, Trevor, and I think we both know it."

Unity was correct, of course. Not that Val lacked her share of suitors. There were a few local university boys with perfect teeth, overdeveloped bodies and underdeveloped brains; certain university professors had more than a scholarly regard for her; and the richest man in Waterbury, a codger in his seventies sporting a pacemaker, offered Val fifty acres of prime Connecticut real estate if she would marry him. But Sparrowhawk's daughter had no interest in any of them.

Now she fluttered her fingers at Sparrowhawk in farewell as she left the study. Shame Robbie's not the one, thought Sparrowhawk. Still, you couldn't force these things, especially with such an independent-minded young lady. Sparrowhawk wondered who the man would be. Because Valerie Lesley Judith Sparrowhawk was quite a young lady.

Sparrowhawk leaned against an English oak desk facing Dorian and Robbie, who sat on a black leather couch. "Our Italian friends have gone absolutely bonkers over Paul's murder, as you well know. What you don't know is that Gran Sasso and Alphonse, in their infinite wisdom, have decreed that MSC play a major role in locating the guilty party."

Dorian stopped sipping his coffee. "Dumb. I mean we're meeting here in your place because it's safe, because at the moment the cops and the task force are both sniffing around Molise's people, and anybody who goes near them. When they learn you're digging into Paulie's background, that's as good as saying MSC is mob."

Sparrowhawk took a pack of Turkish cigarettes from the pocket of his smoking jacket. "I couldn't agree with you more. It does negate what I've tried to do with MSC. But, short of demanding a recount and having myself elected head of the Molise crime family, there's little else I can do. Bear in mind that we are, all of us, most certainly being watched. The forces of law and order will want to know if young Paul's demise signals a takeover attempt of some sort. They'll want to know who's filling Paul's shoes. More than likely that information is already on the street."

"Alley Boy and Johnny Sass," Robbie said. He finished his mixture of spinach and carrot juice, then placed the empty glass on an end table. "That Allie Boy is really off the wall. Has a Cuban girl friend in Long Island City. Won't come to her place, won't take her to a motel. Afraid of being bugged or something. He's so paranoid about being under surveillance, he screws her in the back of a station wagon. Every time Allie Boy leaves his bakery in his station wagon instead of his Ford, whoever's watching knows he's off to get laid."

Sparrowhawk blew smoke at a desk lamp and stroked one end of his waxed mustache with a thumbnail. "Well, who said romance is dead? But anyway, Dorian's correct about surveillance for the rest of us. Still, I am to proceed with a probe of young Paul's Saigon days. Alphonse and Mr. Gran Sasso want a detailed picture of his dealings there."

Dorian shrugged. "Why not Saigon. Got to start somewhere, right? Any leads?"

Sparrowhawk watched him through a spiral of rising cigarette smoke. "Nothing specific at the moment. MSC's working on it. Saigon, Hong Kong, Macao, Cambodia, Thailand." He turned to screw his cigarette into an ashtray on the desk. "Tokyo."

He looked at Dorian. "The places where Paul did business, you see. And, of course, the people there with whom he did business."

"What about the Caymans?" Dorian asked. "Paul had companies registered there and in Delaware. New Jersey, too. You know, the straight people who were taking his money and probably thought he was nothing more than a greasy ginzo hood."

Sparrowhawk raised both eyebrows. "Point well taken, dear boy. By the way, we do have our own sources within the police department, but I would appreciate your keeping me informed of anything you hear, whether at your precinct or elsewhere."

"You got it, Birdman."

"Good. One more thing. The wogs believe that Pangalos and Quarrels will probably have to be given the chop. Sent to join Jimmy Hoffa, as it were."

"Double hit?" said Dorian.

Sparrowhawk poured himself more tea. "Gran Sasso feels neither man is willing to face prison. Certain truth in that, I suppose. Pangalos has already had two sessions with LeClair regarding the seating plan. I'm sure LeClair's threatened him good and proper. Either of you have any idea of what life behind bars would be like for a former prosecuting attorney, a federal one at that?"

The Englishman sipped his tea, then added more milk. "The inmates would tear him apart. Kill him, most likely. As for Quarrels, the man's a competent attorney but his spine is made of whipped cream. Paul's death, sad to say, has left both without a protector. Gran Sasso has never liked Pangalos. He only tolerated him because of Paul and Paul's influence with Don Molise. Quarrels is another write-off as well. And all because of that seating plan, I'm afraid."

Robbie said, "Blame Decker."

"Yes and no. Oh, he did snatch the plan. He most certainly did. But has it occurred to either of you to inquire how Decker came to know about it?"

Dorian and Robbie fell silent.

It was Dorian who finally said, "Plan or no plan, I don't think it's cool to go around blowing away people right now. Not with Paulie still in the news."

"Agreed. But you see, in this world might makes right. Gran Sasso and Alphonse must establish their authority in the absence of any other authority. What better way to do it than to see that our two attorneys turn up their toes. Paul would have handled it differently, but Paul is no longer with us."

Dorian snorted. "So we grease them."

"That seems to be the plan. I understand your reluctance, but that will have little effect on Tweedledum and Tweedledee. Simply stand ready to perform as ordered. I'll tell you when."

Dorian said, "Make sure the two of them are in the same place at the same time. I don't want to have to come back for seconds. Shit, I still don't think it's a smart thing to do."

Sparrowhawk held up a forefinger. "Forgot to mention. Another reason Gran Sasso is thinking about disposing of Pangalos and Quarrels is to protect the esteemed Senator Terence Dent. Mr. Sasso does not want our senator dragged into the mess over this seating plan—which could happen, since Dent does have a hidden financial interest in the project. Dent is important to Molise interests. After all, one doesn't get to own a United States senator every day."

Dorian pointed to Sparrowhawk. "You tell fucking Johnny Sass I want top dollar for this hit. He wants me to whack out these two guys, it's gonna cost him big bucks. Jesus, just thinking about it is eating away my stomach lining. Where's the john?"

"Where it's always been. End of the hall and to your left. And do try not to get soap on the mirror, will you please? That mirror cost me a bloody fortune and I'd prefer it to remain in its present condition, without any of your artistic additions."

When Dorian had left, Sparrowhawk closed the door behind him and stood near it facing Robbie. He held up a hand in warning.

"Robbie, lad, just listen. It could be that Dorian is as big a problem to us as Pangalos. I'm talking about that young Japanese lady of his, Miss Asama. She could well turn out to be tied in somehow with George Chihara. Perhaps even related to him, I'm not sure."

"No shit."

"Too much shit, if you ask me. Mention none of this to Dorian. Not a word, you understand?"

"Hey, major, you don't have to tell me that."

"Good. Now I'm having MSC look into her background, her diamond company, its backers, board of directors, the lot. I don't plan on turning that information over to the wogs. Not just yet. I'll get to why in a minute. There's no direct proof she's related to Chihara, only the possibility. Been unable to reach bloody Nial Hinds, who's been in Africa, then the Middle East and now supposedly in Argentina doing God knows what. Selling the guns dropped by your American army when they fled Vietnam, I expect. Hinds first put me on to a Japanese female who is said to have comforted George Chihara in his declining years—Miss Asama, *I* think."

Robbie scratched his throat. "Think she got Paulie? Class job, if she did. One woman against two men."

"You mean has she gone from bouncing moronic American boys off tile basins to slitting the throats of known Mafiosi? I wish I knew, dear boy. I wish I knew. If she has, it means she's here to do the dirty to—"

He pointed and whispered, "To thee and me. And Dorian as well."

Robbie let the information register, thought about it for a few seconds, then snorted. "If she's gonna bring it to me, she better bring it good."

Sparrowhawk put a hand on his shoulder and looked him in the eye. "When I tell you to and not before. Clear?"

"You're calling the shots, major. Think Dorian's with her against us?"

"No. He was with us when we took Chihara. If she's samurai, there'll be no pardon. Dorian will have to pay for his sins, as will we all. But, cheer up, this is assuming she is the avenging angel we suspect. Right now she's out of the country on business, so while she's abroad I'm going to have her New York flat gone over with the finest of fine-tooth combs. I'm also having her followed by our operatives abroad, who will look into her associates, friends and lovers over there. Anyone who is capable of sending Paul on to his reward in that fashion cannot be underestimated."

"Major, suppose it turns out that she did waste Paulie? What then? You going to turn her over to Johnny Sass? I mean, he's gonna make some kind of connection between her and us, and he's gonna want to know how come we waited so long to tell him. We worked with her father in Nam, remember?"

"I can hardly forget, dear boy." He looked over his shoulder at the study door, then back at Robbie. "I've thought of the possibility that Gran Sasso and Allie Boy just might feel there's a bit of collusion going on here. To avoid you and I having to undergo any suffering at their hands, I propose to turn Miss Asama over to them, along with Dorian as well."

"Major, I don't get it."

"He'll be back any minute, so listen up. Michelle Asama and Dorian are what you would call great and good friends."

"He's jumping her bones, you mean."

"This means, to all intents and purposes, he can be portrayed as her protector. Let's just say he knew of her plans in advance, that he aided her to some degree. Even prevented me from learning about her sooner. Get it? Dorian obstructed my investigation, and all for love. That leaves us in the clear for not having solved the mystery earlier."

Robbie shrugged. "Why not. But none of this makes sense if she's not the one we're looking for after all."

"Dear boy, years of hunting and being hunted have left me with an instinct about people. I feel rather strongly that Miss Asama is either the one we're looking for or knows who is. Everything about her smells of intrigue."

Sparrowhawk moved closer. "I have an alternative plan. It may be that we'll have to eliminate Miss Asama on our own, and it could be to our advantage to handle the whole thing quietly. I've not asked you to kill since you've come back, but I am alerting you now that I may call upon you to . . ."

Robbie grinned. He looked ten years younger. "Major, you want it, you got it. If you say she goes, she goes."

"Just this once, Robbie. After that, no more. I promise."

"Hey, I'm cool. She's gone." He snapped his fingers. "Like that."

The study door opened and Dorian reentered the room. "What the hell you two talking about? Know something, Birdman? That bathroom of yours looks like a damn cathouse. Mirrors trimmed in gold—"

"Gold paint."

"Rugs on the floor, paintings on the wall."

"Prints. The work of John Singer Sargent, an American portrait painter who lived in London."

"Hooray for him. I miss anything?"

Sparrowhawk said, "We were talking about Robbie's next fight. When is it, lad?"

"Week from now. Boston."

Sparrowhawk clapped Robbie on the shoulder. "Good for the firm to have Robbie fighting and winning like that. Excellent public relations. Impresses clients when they read that sort of thing."

Dorian crossed the room to a sideboard, opened a decanter and sniffed.

"Scotch," said Sparrowhawk.

Dorian poured some into his coffee cup. "What I'm looking forward to reading is the autopsy report on Paulie. All kinds of rumors going 'round. Like maybe he was killed as part of some weird religious ritual or maybe there's a Manson-type gang working New York or maybe Aldo the chauffeur was fucking the wrong broad and somebody cut up Paulie because he just happened to be in the wrong place at the wrong time."

With his back turned, Dorian did not see Robbie and Sparrowhawk exchange glances. Shortly after the killing, Robbie had told Sparrowhawk that Molise appeared to have been killed in *ninja* fashion. *Ninjas,* Robbie explained, were medieval Japanese assassins and spies who usually used steel needles, but were supposedly no longer in existence.

Would Michelle Asama know *ninja* techniques? There were men in Japan who could teach her, said Robbie.

Sparrowhawk watched Dorian pour himself a second cupful of scotch and wolf it down. Red faced with liquor, our Dorian, and less than immaculate in appearance. A bit thick in the head as well. But not a bad sort. Still, the thought of handing him and Miss Asama over to the wogs was a warming one. It would certainly help the Englishman get through the next few days.

Four

Yoin

The sound a bell makes after being struck;
an indelible memory

20

It was late afternoon. Decker stood in front of Michi's apartment and removed a set of her keys from his overcoat pocket. An unsealed envelope had been tucked in the doorjamb. Curiosity made Decker take a peek. A Christmas card. Signed by every doorman in the building, all ten of them. A reminder that this holiest of holidays was only a couple of weeks away and that Miss Asama's generosity would be remembered throughout the year. Ho, ho, ho and up your chimney, thought Decker.

He tried to insert keys into the top lock and finally, after three tries, found the right one. Two more tries and the bottom lock finally yielded.

Michi had asked him to collect her mail and water her plants while she was gone. Decker was surprised. But he saw the request as a sign of her growing trust, so had readily agreed. Was this a test to see if he would respect her privacy? He didn't think so. He had not pressed for answers about her past and didn't plan to. Treat time gently, said the Japanese, and it will treat you gently as well.

He was late getting to Michi's apartment and now would be late getting to his own precinct. He could blame LeClair, who had kept him down at Federal Plaza longer than usual. But Captain Agrest, Decker's precinct commander, could care less about the federal government's claim on Decker. He had a precinct to run and did not appreciate the growing pile of paperwork on the detective's desk.

To catch up at the precinct he'd have to put in some overtime. Decker could sneak in morning workouts at the dojo, but he'd have to get someone else to teach his evening classes for the next few days. Damn. He'd miss the teaching.

But LeClair smelled blood and wanted his services immediately. "Mr. Manfred, I do believe we have Mr. Pangalos and Mr. Quarrels by their gonads, thanks to you and that seating plan. Now, it behooves us to squeeze. Tax fraud, conspiracy, you name it. Quarrels is ready to deal. He's given us a sample of what he hopes will help him to avoid incarceration."

"Like what?"

"Like the names of those Delaware companies Paul Molise used to wash money he brought back into this country from the Caymans. Like information on the courier system used to get the money down to the Caymans and back. He's also let drop a word or two about the Marybelle Corporation."

LeClair buffed his fingernails against his chest, then looked at the shine. "Quarrels says your boy Kanai pulled out of the Golden Horizon."

Decker stared at him. "I gave you my word," said the detective, "and I kept it. Nothing about the casino or the people behind it or Baksted's murder. If you remember, Kanai had his doubts before Baksted got burned."

"So he did, so he did. Maybe Kanai gets visions in the night. And I hear Jesus lives."

"It be's that way sometimes."

"It do, oh, it do."

They both laughed.

"Before you leave us today," LeClair said, "I'd appreciate you dictating a report on just how you came to obtain the seating plan. Leave out the name of your informant. One of my girls is waiting next door to take your statement."

"Can't this wait? I've got to show up at the precinct."

"Mr. Manfred, day after tomorrow I'm due in Washington again. Your report figures prominently in my plans. It's going to help me implement phase two."

"Phase two?"

"To leave Terry Dent twisting slowly, slowly in the wind. I'm gonna catch me a United States senator. Gonna grab more media attention than anything since ABSCAM. But you see, the boys down at Justice want to make sure we're proceeding correctly. They don't want any more overturned convictions of congressmen, because that tends to make Congress pret-tee angry. The bottom line is, Congress has enough juice to hurt anybody who hurts it. Since ABSCAM, our senators and representatives have all been paranoid, not to mention downright nasty, to anybody coming after one of their own. Got to be sure, this time."

Decker said, "And Pangalos?"

"Mr. P.? He's always on my mind. Dude's hanging tough, but for sure I have a way of getting to him. I'll start by working Quarrels. Get a little bit from him, then let Pang know. So, the longer Pang waits to come on board, the more he'll have to give in order to become a player. He thinks he's having it all his way by gluing his lips together and going eyeball to eyeball with me. Shit. I'm gonna tie a knot in his dick that sucker will never be able to unravel. Either he does the right thing or he's on the street alone."

"Throw his ass in jail, why don't you."

"Because Mr. Manfred, as much as I want his ass in jail, I also want to get MSC, and Mr. P. can help me do that. But first I want Pangalos to suffer."

I believe it, thought Decker. You really want to show Pangalos who's the better man.

LeClair said, "He's been told that I just might dig into his clients' background. When his clients hear that, they'll drop Pang like a hot rock. Since he's been in my office enough, the street knows I'm getting closer, so maybe it's a wise thing to back off from Mr. P. for a while. I want him isolated, alone, with nowhere to go. I'm gonna cut his options. Leave him with nowhere to run except into my waiting arms."

On a hunch Decker said, "Has anybody ever done anything like that to you? Given you no choice, I mean."

LeClair looked down at his highly polished shoes. There was a long silence. Then, "Long time ago. I was a kid. Prelaw. Howard University down in D.C., where my father was on duty with the Pentagon. Bunch of us coming back from a basketball game in Baltimore. Kids. Maybe too much to drink, but not making any trouble. Some white cops grabbed us. Took us down to the station house."

He looked up. "Niggers in a white station house. Imagine that. Know what they did? Held a gun to our heads, each one of us, and said, 'Sing a chorus of "Old Man River" or get your brains pushed through your ears.' They all sang. Except me.

"I said pull that trigger, but I'm not singing a note. Well, of course I became the center of attention. Somebody checked me out, learned my father was a two-star general at the Pentagon and I was allowed to go. But not without a cracked cheekbone, and a couple punches to the kidneys to remember them by. Thoughtful bunch. But the rest of them had it worse.

"Taught me something," LeClair continued. "Taught me that power can save your ass, so I'd best get me some. Taught me, too, that cops can get carried away. Need to be controlled."

Fucked over is what you mean, thought Decker, remembering DeMain and Benitez.

"Anyway," said LeClair, "somebody gave me a choice. So now I'm giving Mr. Pangalos one. He can choose to work with me, or I can choose to send him to prison. I guess he doesn't realize that one of these days the Molise family isn't going to be so occupied with who killed Paulie. And then, when they turn their full attention to brother Pang, that's when he just might need a friend."

Decker said, "Talk is there's an open contract on whoever got Paulie. Quarter million for the person who gets the killer, no questions asked. You're probably right about Molise's people concentrating on it. Wouldn't surprise me if they didn't put MSC on it as well."

LeClair nodded in agreement. "Meanwhile, you truck on next door and ask for Rochelle. She's waiting to hang on your every word."

Decker rose from his chair and turned to leave the room. LeClair said, "One more thing, Mr. Manfred."

The detective stopped, back to the prosecutor. "Mrs. Raymond shouldn't be left alone too often, my man."

Decker never turned around. And he never answered. He simply began walking toward the door.

Fuck me, he thought. LeClair knows about Michi.

Decker turned the key, pushed the door open and stepped inside Michi's apartment. After closing the door behind him he switched on the light and walked to the edge of the sunken living room. The smell of cigar smoke was still fresh in the air. The silver ashtray was missing from the coffee table. Whoever was hiding in the master bedroom had taken the ashtray with him. The bedroom door, which Decker had closed yesterday, was *almost* closed today. Cracked just enough to allow someone to peek out.

Decker concentrated. Mail left on the coffee table yesterday was still there. A shoji screen was not where he remembered it and the two *ikebana* vases in the *tokonoma,* the alcove, were slightly closer together than they should be. Decker had surprised someone.

The detective tossed the mail onto the coffee table and took off his overcoat, folding it over his right arm. He unbuttoned his suit jacket and moved the folded overcoat to his front. Slowly, he crossed the sunken living room and moved toward the bedroom, which stood at the head of a narrow hallway leading to more rooms. Before he reached the bedroom the door swung open slowly and a man in a porkpie hat and knee-length leather coat eased out into the hall. Both hands were in his pockets.

Both hands came out slowly. One was empty, the other held a badge.

"Police. We'd like to see some identification."

"We?"

"My partner. Behind you."

Decker looked to his left and down the hall. A second man had stepped from a bathroom. He was young, not over thirty and powerfully built, with wide shoulders, a thick neck and drooping blond mustache. He wore jeans, boots and a heavy white woolen sweater. He approached Decker tapping the palm of one hand with a rubber-handled screwdriver. Decker smelled trouble.

He looked back at the eight-hundred-dollar leather coat. "Cop, you said. Like to see that badge again."

"I just showed you my badge, Mr. . . ."

"Decker's the name."

"Decker. We're here officially."

"Oh? Let's see your potsy."

Leather jacket turned an ear toward Decker as though he hadn't heard correctly.

"Potsy," he repeated, pulling his overcoat from the hand that held his .38. "Means shield. Badge. A cop would know that."

Decker took his badge and ID from an inside jacket pocket

and identified himself. With his gun hand he motioned the guy in the white sweater closer. "You guys are good. Two first-class locks on that door and you walked right through them. Probably didn't come in through the front lobby, either. What did you use, freight elevator? Basement garage?"

Leather Jacket filled his cheeks with air and blew it out through his mouth. "Whoo boy. My horoscope said be careful in meeting new people today."

Decker turned his head to the right and dodged the screwdriver hurled at his left temple—but not in time to avoid a painful blow to his cheekbone. In the same motion White Sweater dropped to the floor on his right side under Decker's gun hand, kicked up with his left foot. His boot heel smashed into the detective's right wrist. The gun went flying. White Sweater had reason to be confident. He had martial arts training and he was good.

The kick numbed Decker's right arm. Hot needles scraped at every nerve and fiber. But when he saw Leather Jacket, a few feet away, bending down, reaching for Decker's gun, his training said ignore the pain. Face sticky with his own blood, his right arm on fire, he leaped forward and kicked Leather Jacket in the ribs, once, twice, lifting him off the floor and sending him backward into the wall.

Decker turned to face the other guy just in time. He moved like a cat, his eyes never leaving Decker. Whoever had trained the son of a bitch had trained him well. He took one long step, then leaped sideways high in the air, feet drawn up close to his buttocks. In midair he lashed out with his right leg in a side-thrust kick, the leg stretched to its limit, boot heel reaching toward Decker's face.

Decker felt the rush of air as the leg passed within inches of his head, then whirled around to see the big man land out of range, on his feet, knees and ankles bent for excellent balance. And then he was facing Decker again, body sideways, inching forward, eyes locked with Decker's eyes, each man looking for an opening to exploit.

White Sweater aimed a kick at Decker's groin to bring the detective's hands down in defense, then quickly spun around, back to Decker, and threw a high kick at his head. Decker retreated, kneading his right arm.

He flexed his fingers, squeezed his fist, felt the feeling and strength returning. Then he kicked twice, aiming low, going for a knee, an ankle. The big man backed up, but not far. Just out of Decker's range. He wasn't running. This guy was a thinking fighter.

But he had overlooked his partner. Behind him, Leather Jacket struggled to get to his feet, wincing at the pain in his ribs and hugging himself with both arms. He was halfway off the floor, back against the wall before he said, "Fuck it," and slid down the wall back onto the floor, and into his partner, clipping him from behind at the ankles.

Off balance and arms flailing, White Sweater looked down at his partner, his back to the detective. This was Decker's chance. With his right foot he pushed hard behind the big man's knee, driving him to the floor. Now he had his man where he wanted him.

Moving quickly, Decker applied the choke. With his right arm around White Sweater's throat, right hand deep and thumb inside, left hand under the big man's left armpit and over the left shoulder, Decker threw himself backward to the floor, pulling White Sweater with him. Then the detective wrapped his legs around the big man's hips and thighs and, holding him in place, began choking him, pushing the edge of the left hand into his neck, pulling the right hand into the other side of the neck, across the throat, to cut off the brain's supply of oxygen.

Decker held his grip just long enough; didn't want to turn the guy into a vegetable. His victim fought, wriggled, clawed at Decker's arms. And then weakened. When Decker felt the man's muscles relax, Decker released his grip, pushed the now unconscious man to one side, and retrieved his gun. Then he bent down and patted Leather Jacket. No gun. But he was carrying a very interesting ID.

Leather Jacket's name was Jay Pearlman. Decker eyed him. "Both of you work for Management Systems Consultants?"

Pearlman, eyes closed, kept both hands on his right side. "Yeah."

"Where is he?" Decker asked.

"Where is who?" Pearlman said. "Shit, I think you broke something."

"The brains of this outfit. Muscles over there isn't the type to give orders. And you're not carrying cigars."

"What the fuck is that supposed to mean?"

"Want me to kick a hole in your other side? Don't play dumb. You weren't supposed to get caught at this, remember? I'm talking about the man who smokes those expensive Cuban cigars I smell. You don't and something tells me the man lying there with the twenty-eight-inch neck doesn't either. Now who smokes Cuban cigars and is the best wiretapper in Manhattan?"

Decker turned around to face the bedroom. "*Oye,* Felix, get your garlic-eating ass out here."

The bedroom door opened again and a small, smiling Cuban, cigar clenched between white teeth, stepped into the hall. He was well dressed, three-piece gray suit, tie, a Burberry topcoat over one arm. An attaché case was in the other hand. "Decker, my friend. *Como está?*"

"Felix."

They knew each other, the wiretapper and the detective, had even worked together. Felix Betancourt, fiftyish and patrician, nicknamed Elegante for his manners and bearing, was an electronics genius. He'd had a hand in the Bay of Pigs, Watergate and several other top political scandals. He had worked for the CIA, FBI, State Department, both major political parties and the biggest multinational corporations. He had also worked for Washington and New York newspapers, labor unions, New York police and organized crime. MSC had him on a six-figure annual retainer. At a time when information was the most valued of all currencies, Felix Betancourt was king.

For all his elegant ways, Felix was thoroughly amoral, always for sale to the highest bidder. But it didn't stop Decker from liking him.

"Like your tie, Felix."

The Cuban looked at it. "Two hundred dollars. Handmade. Special silk. They feed the worms oak leaves, nothing else. Gets you that nice brown color." He looked at the unconscious man in the white sweater. "I told him you were good, but he say bullshit. He say he can take you with his eyes closed."

"His eyes are closed now."

Felix grinned. "You're right about that, my friend. Toby

here say he trains with Robbie Ambrose, who is a champion. He tell me he was going to turn your asshole inside out."

"What's in the attaché case, Felix?"

The Cuban took the cigar from his small mouth and shrugged.

Decker said, "Empty it on the living room coffee table and when you're finished you and your friends here can take out all the bugs, taps and transmitters you planted. You better not miss one, because tomorrow I'm having one of your competitors come in here and sweep the place from top to bottom. And if he finds so much as a single strand of wire—"

Felix smiled. "Decker, my friend, I know when to cut my losses. We are professionals, you and I. I take out all the stuff, you see."

The man on the floor moaned, stirred.

The Cuban said, "I do not mean to pry, my friend, but you had the key to this place. Does that mean the lady is a friend of yours? If I had known that I would not have taken the job."

"Felix, you'd bug Christ's tomb if there was money in it. Go in the living room and open your case. And put that ashtray back where you found it."

Twenty minutes later Decker sat alone in Michi's apartment and tried to figure it all out. *Molise's people are going all out to nail the guy who killed Paul Molise. At the moment that's all they're doing. Wouldn't surprise me if they didn't put MSC on it as well.*

To protect Michi he had let Felix and his friends walk. No sense calling any more attention to her than was necessary. Felix had taken some of Michi's letters, personal papers, a passport and company files. Nothing a jury would convict him for, assuming he ever came to trial. Lawyers for Felix and MSC could delay the trial for two years or more and by that time the offense of snatching a handful of papers wouldn't exactly alarm a jury.

It had to be Sparrowhawk. He ran MSC. But he was supposed to be finding out who burned Paulie, nothing else. Did he and the Molise family think Michi had anything to do with that? Decker shuddered, threw his head back against the couch and closed his eyes. Could he keep Michi alive if Sparrowhawk and the mob wanted her dead?"

During the past six years Decker had hidden from the women in his life. And in time he began to be fooled by his own designs, as distanced from his feelings as the women he kept at arm's length. After all, eventually deception becomes self-deception. He had accepted it, every bit of it, and it hadn't mattered a rat's ass one way or another. Until Michi.

With her return, he had begun to live. He had become vulnerable. He had committed himself. With her, he had everything to hope for. And everything to lose.

He sat in the apartment until the early December darkness fell, his mind chasing shadows and fighting fear.

At 5:32 that evening Sparrowhawk and Robbie strode briskly across the crowded sidewalk to the limousine that would drop Robbie off in midtown and take Sparrowhawk home to Connecticut. Robbie was the first to notice the man standing beside the chauffeur.

Then Sparrowhawk looked up. God in heaven. Decker. A rather rude shock indeed.

Decker said, "Back off Michelle Asama. Don't bug her apartment, don't bird-dog her, don't open her mail, don't come near her."

Sparrowhawk's eyes became slits. "May I ask if this is official?"

"Ask."

"Is this official? I mean, she's not under arrest or in protective custody or—"

"It's not official."

"I didn't think so. By the way, heard you injured two of my men today. Aren't you getting a bit carried away with your prowess?"

"One of your men attempted to put out my eye with a screwdriver."

"Pity. And you didn't arrest them." Sparrowhawk looked at Robbie. "Imagine that. Someone tries to turn him into a Cyclops and he doesn't arrest them." He looked at Decker. "Now, let me get this straight. Any involvement with Miss

Asama is strictly unofficial, not part of your professional duties."

Decker shifted uneasily. He was beginning to regret having come down here.

Sparrowhawk sensed his uncertainty. "Since this is unofficial, detective sergeant—"

"Personal." The minute he'd said it, Decker knew it was a mistake.

Sparrowhawk raised both eyebrows. "Personal, is it? Ah, that puts an even different light on the subject matter. Personal, Robbie. Did you catch that?"

"Sure did, major."

"Tell me, detective sergeant, does this mean I don't have to take you seriously? After all, what do you and I have between us that could be called *personal*? Now, Robbie, he handles my personal confrontations, don't you, lad?"

"Anytime, major. Anytime. Me and Detective Sergeant Decker we met personal a couple of times."

Sparrowhawk rubbed his jaw and frowned in mock thought. "Ah yes, I seem to recall those two occasions. Yes, it's all coming back to me now."

Decker looked at Robbie. The one man who had shaken his confidence, who had driven him out of tournament fighting. Suddenly the wounds from those two defeats were bleeding again, the pain returning. And Decker now knew that the fear had never really gone away.

He forced himself to speak. "You heard me. Leave her alone."

Sparrowhawk said, "May I please be allowed to enter my car?"

Decker stepped aside and the chauffeur opened the back door. Sparrowhawk entered first. Robbie, close behind, put a foot in the car, stopped and, turning toward Decker, shook his head sadly, knowing that he didn't have to threaten Decker or challenge him.

Because Robbie was better. It was that simple.

He touched the golden stud in his ear and stepped into the limousine.

As the car pulled away Decker knew that he had made a terrible mistake. He had warned them. The possibility of taking them by surprise was no longer an option. He had told them he was coming. Dumb.

Sooner or later he would pay for that mistake. And so would Michi.

21

Giovanni Gran Sasso was not impressed by Atlantic City's ultramodern casinos. In fact, the *consigliere* did not gamble at all and disapproved of those who did.

What did please the hulking white-haired man was Atlantic City's proximity to the ocean. Smelling the salt air reminded the *consigliere* of when, as a young man, he had made a walking tour of coastal towns in his native Sicily, sleeping under the stars and living on bread, cheese, wine and fruit. He had never been happier in his life.

Tonight in Atlantic City Gran Sasso and Alphonse Giulia, heads close together in conversation, walked slowly along the empty and fog-shrouded boardwalk, trailed by two bodyguards. They had just emerged from a secret meeting with Senator Terry Dent, who had come up from Washington to discuss his future under the mob's new power structure. Dent had warned the Italians that they were being betrayed.

"LeClair's got a pipeline to your people," Dent said. "I don't mind telling you that it's making me goddamn uneasy. For one thing LeClair's pushing the Justice Department to make an official request to the Cayman government for your banking records."

"The Caymans won't cooperate," Gran Sasso said. "The minute they do, they lose a few billion dollars. Nobody would trust them after that."

"My gut instinct says you're right. But what really bothers me is that the Justice people knew what they were looking for. And requests have been made to Delaware for information on Marybelle, on Scarborough Realty, on the Edwards-Brewer Corporation."

"All ours," said Giulia.

"All yours. The news got around because a couple of Delaware congressmen bitched at being singled out for such a probe. And the Delaware people don't want to honor that request. Like you said, the minute you start passing out information like that you lose customers. When you're hiding money you don't take out a goddamn ad saying you're hiding it. You guys got a leak somewhere and that doesn't make me sleep any better at nights. If we're going to do business together you have to hold up your end. I know Pangalos claims he hasn't talked, but what about Quarrels?"

Gran Sasso poured more Chivas Regal for Dent. "You said something about the casino's license being in trouble."

"That's another thing. The New Jersey Gaming Commission's been approached by LeClair to give some thought to doing just that. Looks like you guys aren't the only ones who don't want to see the Golden Horizon close down. A Jersey congressman, who I won't name, got in touch with me, feeling me out about whether or not I and some of the New York congressmen will help him fight LeClair. Close the casino and a lot of tax money goes down the tubes. Not to mention jobs."

Gran Sasso agreed. It also meant losing a place to wash his money. Gambling was a cash business. Cash came in and out of the casino at all times. Legally. It would not do to have either the casino or MSC shut down.

Dent waggled a forefinger. "You better give some thought to LeClair's plans for the grand jury, when he starts parading his star witness or informant against you. He plans to have the jury masked. The jury, not the witness."

"Nigger's fucking crazy," Giulia said.

"Think so? I don't. You haven't the faintest idea what the move means."

Gran Sasso said, "It means he's making sure he gets a conviction or an indictment. It means he's telling the jury they shouldn't let this man see their faces if they value their lives. The black man's very clever. How did you hear about this?"

Dent looked angry. "LeClair's talked with the Justice Department about me and I don't like it. Don't like it one fucking bit. They want to make sure they don't violate my civil rights while trying to hang me. Other night I'm at a party in Georgetown and a guy from the FBI was there. Seems his daughter's moving to New York and needs a job. We got to talking and he told me about LeClair's mask idea."

Gran Sasso thought for a while, then reached over to touch Dent's wrist. "Senator, do us all a favor. You make sure this girl gets a job, a nice job. Something special, something her father will be real proud of. I want this FBI guy to owe you. You have trouble finding her something, you get in touch with me. I'll make sure something turns up. When she's got the job, make sure this guy knows you did it. But don't go back to him for any favors until I tell you to.

"Now, before we go any further, I understand there was something else you wanted our help on."

Dent exhaled. "Asa Arnstein."

"The department store guy," Giulia said. "Supposed to be some kind of strike against his stores. He's really loaded, this Arnstein."

"One of my biggest contributors," Dent said. "Nice fat checks. Doesn't miss a campaign and if I need a little extra, he's there, what can I tell you. If I say the party needs a check, no problem. I owe him. I wonder if you could put MSC on this thing. Have them check out the union leaders, half a dozen people. Fucking troublemakers, all of them. See if there's anything in their background that can be used against them. I'd like to pay Arnstein back. Would make me look like a big man. He can't afford a strike. Can't afford what the union's asking."

Gran Sasso and Giulia exchanged glances. Arnstein's money kept Dent in office.

"We'll take care of Arnstein," the *consigliere* said. "You want him to either win the strike or have it called off before it starts."

"That's right."

The *consigliere* turned his hands palms up. "It's done."

Dent smiled, pleased with his own power. "Much appreciated. By the way, before it slips my mind there's some mining stock that an Arizona senator assures me is certain to climb.

I was wondering, could you give me an advance on my percentage of the profits from the new auditorium?"

"How much?" asked Gran Sasso.

"Fifty thousand."

He knows we can't refuse him, thought the *consigliere*. "I'll have a package at your Washington office tomorrow. It will be addressed to you personally."

Trade-offs. Always necessary when one powerful man deals with another. It didn't matter why Dent needed the cash; he could not be denied it.

"Beginning to look like Pangalos or Quarrels may have talked," said Dent. "That seating plan. Christ, was that a body blow."

Gran Sasso poured anisette into his espresso. Some things should not be discussed in front of a United States senator. "Senator, don't concern yourself with Pangalos or Quarrels. Things will work themselves out. You will see."

On the boardwalk Giulia, head bent forward, hands in his pockets, said, "Wonder what Dent would have done if he'd known what we got planned for those two guys."

Gran Sasso said, "People put their hands over their eyes, then complain it's dark. He knows, but he doesn't want to know. Seventy-five thousand we're paying that cop to handle this business. He told Sparrowhawk he wouldn't do it for less."

"He's good, the cop. Didn't he say he wanted both of them in the same place, same time? That's not gonna be easy."

The *consigliere* said, "On the contrary, my friend. That is the easiest part of all."

Ironic, he thought. He was older than Pangalos and Quarrels, but he would outlive them. This time tomorrow both lawyers would be dead.

Constantine Pangalos sat up in bed, annoyed. He switched the telephone receiver to his left ear, away from his wife, who lay sleeping beside him. "Buscaglia, you know what time it is? Fucking quarter to twelve is what it is. That's midnight, not high noon."

"So I called you at midnight. Sue me. But wait till you

hear why I called. How'd you like to get out from under on this seating-plan shit?"

"You got me out of bed to ask me that? Come on, I don't have time for games. And I'll handle my own problems, okay?"

"Connie, you didn't hear me. I'm saying I can arrange for that seating plan to walk out of Federal Plaza. The one and only copy. The one piece of evidence they got against you and Quarrels."

Pangalos stood up and harshly whispered, "You giving it to me straight? Because if you're jerking me around—"

"Well, I sure as hell ain't doing it because I want to get into your pants. It's gonna cost you. Five for me, ten for the guy walking out with the file and no argument. Take it or leave it."

"Guess I've got no choice. Jesus, that could pull me out of a very big hole. If that plan disappeared I could tell LeClair to go fuck himself."

"I already spoke to Quarrels and he practically kissed my ring. He's ready to jump at the deal. Between the both of you I figure you'll have no problem raising the money."

"Money I got. It's that seating plan that Decker . . . who's your contact down at Federal Plaza?"

Buscaglia snorted. "You think I got bird shit for brains? That's my business. I tell you, then we both know. If you remember, Decker dragged me down there. I didn't exactly volunteer to go. Soon as I get there I meet this guy from my old days on the waterfront who ain't exactly a friend, but we know each other, and what happened on the waterfront between him and me is now water under the bridge. He was an investigator for a federal commission that gave me a lot of trouble. But like I say, that's past. Young guys coming up, blacks like LeClair taking over. Time for my friend to get out. He'd like to treat himself to a nice vacation, him and his wife."

Pangalos saw himself wriggling off the hook and giving the finger to LeClair. "I like it. You know I asked Sparrowhawk about MSC doing something for me with the task force. But he said it was impossible, that the guys down there were handpicked and couldn't be touched and that LeClair was too smart to leave his files unguarded."

Pangalos chuckled. "Fucking jungle bunny, that LeClair. I'm gonna beat him."

Buscaglia said, "That's why I'm coming to you instead of MSC. I tell them about my friend and they take him over. He becomes their contact, you know how they work. I tell them and I lose my piece of the action. It's their deal and I'm shit out of luck. I can always use a few bucks, you know that."

"Sal, you just saved my ass. And I'm not about to forget it. How soon can you set things up with your boy?"

"Soon. He's close to the files now, but LeClair don't take no chances. File guys are rotated, so my friend won't be there long. Hey, before I forget, you know we're talking cash. No checks."

"Okay, okay. Cash. Quarrels—"

"He's in, I told you. He says it's fifty-fifty. Seventy-five hundred apiece. For that you get the plan, plus a copy of your file, whatever LeClair's got on you guys. Show that seating plan to Johnny Sass and Allie Boy and you're home free."

"Jesus, I've seen stuff walk out of just about every kind of office. Never thought I'd end up hoping some stuff on *me* would up and disappear. How soon can we meet, me, Quarrels and your boy?"

"LeClair's taking him off files. Tomorrow's his last day. We finish this thing tomorrow night, if that's all right with you."

Twenty-two hours later, on a deserted block near Forty-eighth Street and Eleventh Avenue filled with deserted tenements, Pangalos stepped from a cab and waited until it pulled away before walking to a car parked in front of a boarded-up building across from an empty schoolyard.

Suddenly he felt nervous and quickened his step. He was carrying almost eight thousand in cash and wearing a gold watch worth five thousand, and didn't relish the prospect of being a good night's work for any passing junkie. He was so close to getting out from under. What a break that Decker had taken Buscaglia to Federal Plaza in Manhattan instead of booking him out on Long Island. Once Pangalos got his hand on that seating plan, his problems were over. Let LeClair stay up nights wondering how the plan got "lost" or "misfiled." Without the plan, he had no case.

At the car Pangalos looked around, saw another car coming toward him and hesitated. But the car passed him, reached the corner and turned left to head downtown on Eleventh Avenue. Pangalos waited until his heart stopped pounding, yanked open the front door, slid into the front seat beside Livingston Quarrels and pulled the door closed. He blew warm air into his gloved hands and looked around the car.

"You look like you just caught your wife going down on the delivery boy. Where's Buscaglia and his friend?"

Quarrels turned a tear-stained face to him. "Connie, I really don't understand what's going on. He made me come here and wait. I had to do what he said."

Pangalos frowned.

And behind him Dorian Raymond, hidden down on the floor of the back seat, sat upright, pressed the dark barrel of a silenced .22 against Pangalos's temple and pulled the trigger. There was a soft *pop*, the Greek's head flopped to one side and he quickly slumped in his seat.

Quarrels pulled away from the dead man in horror, looking wildly from the Greek to Dorian. "Dorian, I did it. Did what you asked. You said I'd be free to go. Please, I want to go home to my wife. Please."

Talking, Dorian knew, only made it worse. The best he could do for Quarrels was to make it quick. He fired twice, head shots, sending one bullet through Quarrels's right cheekbone and another through his eye. Quarrels sagged, his left arm tangled in the steering wheel, right arm resting on top of the driver's seat.

Closing his eyes, Dorian bowed his head. This one hurt. He'd known both of these guys for a couple of years and whacking them bothered him more than he thought it would. And he wasn't finished. Johnny Sass wanted a message left behind. Leaning over the front seat Dorian pushed the end of the silencer deep into Quarrels's mouth and pulled the trigger twice. Quarrels's head jerked with each shot. Dorian pushed Pangalos down on the seat, leaned forward and grabbed the Greek's hair, yanked his head back and fired twice into his mouth.

The message was that the two lawyers had talked too much.

Nerves screaming for a drink, Dorian unscrewed the long silencer from the .22's barrel, slipped it into an overcoat pocket and then put the .22 into his other pocket. He wasn't the brightest guy in the world but he didn't need to be told that maybe it was time to stop. Baksted, Quarrels, Pangalos. His friends. And he had killed them.

Get out. That's all there was to it. He had money. Seventy-five, plus another twenty or so in the bank. Almost one hundred thousand. And his copy of the pigeon list. He could turn that into millions, enough for him and Romaine to live comfortably for the rest of their lives.

Money would bring Romaine around. He knew it. She was the only woman he felt at ease with. He'd learned his lesson when she had walked out. All he needed was one more chance with her, just one. Let her see how well he could take care of her. Then she'd give it another shot.

Right now he was going to an Eighth Avenue bar, have a few drinks and think about how he was going to handle this Robbie situation. After Quarrels, he never again wanted to look into the face of a friend who was about to die.

In a bar on Eighth Avenue and Forty-ninth Street, he sat among faceless men in overcoats and dark hats, drinking scotch and swearing to himself that his past would never be his future. Take the money and run. Take Romaine with him and disappear into the sun.

He stayed in the bar for a long time, because the last thing he wanted was to go home and dream of the men he had just killed.

22

In Amsterdam's Rijksmuseum, Michi showed no sign that she knew she was being followed. She tagged behind a small group of tourists moving from one Rembrandt painting to another and when they stopped in front of *Night Watch* she stopped, too.

She looked at her guide book, then back at the painting. Minutes later she detached herself from the group and left the room, deliberately walking toward the man who had followed her from the Okura Hotel. He appeared to be deeply engrossed in Rembrandt's *Jewish Bride*. But his feigned concentration was too forced, an obvious performance. Michi neither slowed down nor acknowledged him in any way.

She left the museum. Outside, a cold wind made her cover the lower half of her face with a black scarf and draw her white fur tighter. It was Sunday and Amsterdam was quiet. She stood and looked around. No major traffic today.

Michi began walking. She welcomed the exercise and a chance to get away from the hard bargaining involved in diamond dealing. She passed tree-lined canals, the homes of Rembrandt and Anne Frank and walked along quiet side streets of narrow buildings and elegant mansions. She never once looked behind her.

When she came to the Albert Cuyp market she stopped and made her way through the rows of stalls selling antiques, old jewelry, wooden shoes and diamonds, finally stopping at a fish merchant's stall, where she ordered a plate of raw herring. As she ate the tender and tasty fish she casually glanced to her left. He was there among the crowds, a round-faced man in a dark green anorak, tinted square-shaped glasses and a hearing aid. He stood in front of an Indonesian food stall, hands outstretched and waiting for a dish of coconut and fried bananas. He gave the stall owner two guilders, pocketed the change, then, holding the dish to his face, began shoveling the fruit into his wide mouth.

Michi turned her back to him, threw the unfinished herring in a nearby cardboard box overflowing with trash and shouldered her way through the market crowds. She had also been followed during her two days in London. Before leaving her London hotel room one morning, she had deliberately placed a diamond on the floor near the door. While attractive, the stone was flawed. But to the untrained eye it appeared to be a valuable stone. She left the Do Not Disturb sign on the door.

On her return the room seemed untouched. Bed unmade, newspapers deliberately strewn over chairs and couch, towels on the bathroom floor, a tray of half-eaten food near the television set. Everything as she had left it. The diamond, however, was gone. Had the intruders not been greedy she might never have noticed they were there.

Since her run-in with the two American youths at the Long Island arena, Michi realized she had to be more careful. She must do nothing further to call attention to herself, nothing more to alert the men she had come to America to kill. Luckily, there had been nothing in the London hotel room that might have betrayed her. Fifteen thousand dollars in cash was in the hotel safe, along with a sealed envelope containing three passports, each issued under a different name.

After killing Paul Molise and his chauffeur she had hidden the *kai-ken* and certain papers, so anyone breaking into her New York apartment would find nothing that would reveal her real identity or true purpose in coming to America.

But she obviously had made a mistake at some point. How else to explain the search of her room, the man following her in Amsterdam? Why had those stupid American boys entered the ladies' room? But maybe it wasn't that; maybe something else had given her away. A word, perhaps. Or had she been recognized by someone?

When she returned to America she would tell Manny the truth. They loved each other, but she knew that love would find no peace until she had done her duty to her family. Michi had sworn to kill men involved in Manny's investigation. Was his love for her strong enough to make him understand why?

Leaving the market she headed back to her hotel on foot. But instead of going back to the hotel she stopped two blocks away at a small cafe, where she ordered a glass of Genever Dutch gin flavored with orange. From her table she could see the front door. No sign of the man in the dark green anorak. Which did not mean he had stopped following her.

Michi asked for the telephone and was directed downstairs. Here she took an address book and a handful of coins from her shoulder bag. After positioning herself to see the stairs, she dialed. For a long time the telephone rang at the other end and she was almost ready to hang up, when—

"Hello?"

"Manny, is that you?"

The voice, at first guarded, now relaxed. "Michi. Where are you calling from?"

"Amsterdam. How are you?"

"Fine. Just fine. I miss you. When are you coming back?"

"I still have business here, then I have to go on to Paris. Are you sure everything's all right? You sound tense."

He laughed. "I'm always that way whenever someone calls me this early in the morning, especially at the dojo. I like my workouts to stay private. But you can call me here anytime."

She smiled. "Thank you. I just wanted to say that when I get back you and I will talk. I will tell you everything. Everything. Do you understand?"

His voice was gentle. "Whatever you want me to know, that will be enough."

"I think I can trust you now."

"You mean because I haven't ripped off your apartment?"

"I just know, that's all. Tell me something: why are you in the dojo so early on a Sunday? I had a feeling you might be there, but it does seem strange that you would work out so early."

"Not so strange if you knew what was happening. We had two murders here yesterday. Couple lawyers. The guy I work for on the task force is pretty angry about it. He's dragging us downtown on Sunday for a nine o'clock meeting. We think we know who did it. Somebody you and I both know. Dorian Raymond."

The smile faded from Michi's face. "Will you arrest him?"

"No hard evidence. Just a theory. It's his kind of handiwork. Twenty-two caliber. Head shots. And he knew the victims. I think we'll probably bring him in for questioning and see if we can scare him into admitting something. The problem is, if he did it, he did it to keep them from testifying against Management Systems Consultants, Sparrowhawk and the Molise family. There went our only two sources of information. Smart thing now is to talk Dorian into testifying against these people. Make some kind of deal with him if we can. That's what today's meeting is all about."

Michi said, "So he will be in jail soon?"

"Who knows? Depends on whether or not we can shake him up. Throwing him in prison won't give us the people the task force wants. But we'll sure as hell try. Look, why are we talking about my damn job? Finish buying all those diamonds and get on back here."

She became flirtatious. "You mean the warrior is committed to something besides karate?"

"Come on back and I'll show you."

"There is so much I have to say to you."

"Do I get the feeling that this time you're going to tell me the whole story?"

She closed her eyes. "*Hai.* I will tell you what happened during the years we were apart. I will tell you what really happened to my family and why I came to America. Please do not let anything change between us. Promise me you won't."

"I promise. I think it will bring us closer, at least I hope so. Look, let's give it a try. Let's not let another six years go by without trying. I wish you were coming back on the next plane."

No sooner were the words out of his mouth when the idea flashed into her mind. *Hai.* Take the next plane to New York. And kill Dorian Raymond.

It would be dangerous. She would have to evade the man following her, then fly to New York and without being discovered by Manny or anyone else kill Dorian Raymond, then return to Europe. To do this would take all of her training, all of her cunning, all of her concentration. And all of the blessings from the gods and her ancestors.

"The next plane," she whispered.

"Don't I wish," Manny said.

She broke out of her reverie. "Thank you."

"For what?"

"For loving me. I cling to that. It is all I have. Love me, Manny." Her eyes filled with tears. "Please love me."

She hung up abruptly.

Thirty-five hundred miles away, Manny yelled, "I love you! I love you! I love you!"

He paused. "Michi? Michi? Hello? Hello?"

The sound of her name echoed throughout the empty dojo and there was only the long figure of Decker, the phone pressed to his ear and the red sun of a new dawn crossing the polished wooden floor to reach out for his sweat-stained body.

Twelve hours after speaking to Michi, Decker pressed the downstairs buzzer in Romaine's apartment building and waited to be buzzed inside. Romaine lived in a West Eighty-fourth Street brownstone, near Riverside Drive and within walking distance of the boat basin on the Henry Hudson River.

Romaine buzzed him in. He wasn't looking forward to seeing her, but he had no choice. LeClair was in a shitty mood, thanks to Pangalos and Livingston Quarrels being blown away. Even his staff wanted nothing to do with him. The double slaying had seriously damaged any case he had against MSC. Two dead mob lawyers had slowed down Charles LeClair's march to glory, and he did not take it lightly. Since the discovery of the bodies LeClair hadn't got off the phone with the Justice Department. And the press was having a field day with "The West Side Murders." Oddly enough, MSC's name had not been mentioned.

Dorian Raymond, however, had no such luck. At least not in LeClair's office.

"Bet your ass it was Dorian who did the hit," LeClair said. "Who the hell else could it be?"

Decker shrugged. "Wish I knew."

"Yeah, well I wish you knew, too. Tell you this for sure: you had better drop everything, and I mean everything, until we straighten this one out, until we can get some kind of handle on it that I can pass on to the Justice Department. From now on you stick to Dorian's wife. Don't even let me hear 'bout your eyes wandering elsewhere, you dig? I want to know where Dorian was last night. For that matter, where were you?"

"Hey, look, you blaming me for those two guys getting burned? Come on."

LeClair, in disgust, threw a pencil over his shoulder. "Words between you and me don't cut it no more. Hand me something, Mr. Manfred. Hand me something this time tomorrow."

He didn't bother to say *or else*. He didn't have to.

LeClair said, "So forget that Japanese lady. Because if I decide you ain't on the team, then, Jack, it's down to the short strokes and I start playing hardball and I don't stop until one of us is lying facedown in the dirt. And, as you might have guessed, I don't plan on being the one. MSC ain't gonna beat me. And I ain't about to lose that assistant attorney general's job."

He leaned back in his chair, removed his glasses and rubbed the bridge of his nose with a thumb and forefinger. "See, Decker, I look at how you treat your women and I'm goddamn sure I don't want you treating me like that. So just get the fuck out of here."

Below the belt, sure. And on target as well.

It hurt and it made Decker afraid that there was some truth there, that he might end up treating Michi the way he had treated the others. Good sex at the beginning. But then nothing more than hints about who the real Manny Decker was. At least he never made promises.

Today's phone call marked the first time Decker and Romaine had spoken in days. He wondered if she had heard from Dorian, who, since the murders, had dropped out of sight. He had called in sick at his precinct, but wasn't at his apartment. He hadn't been in the after-hours clubs he usually frequented, nor had he been in touch with his bookies. Word on the street was that he no longer owed money, unheard of for Dorian.

Decker wasn't looking forward to seeing Romaine, but LeClair hadn't given him a choice. Playing LeClair's game was the only way to keep him from Michi. Decker wondered how much the prosecutor already knew about her.

At Romaine's door Decker hesitated, shrugged, rang the bell. Get it over with. He heard someone near the door, heard a scraping near the peephole, then locks were being opened. Slowly, hesitantly.

Romaine had been crying. Her eyes were red, puffy. A tear clung to her chin like a drop of rain. She stepped aside without a word. No kiss, no gesture of welcome. Decker felt the chill. Inside she closed the door, dabbed at her eyes, then turned away from him. The frost was getting thicker. She said, "If you had trusted me you would have known that it didn't make any difference. All you had to do was tell me."

"Tell you what?" He knew. But he had played the role of deceiver too long to relinquish it that easily.

She turned. "You're a cop. You were never interested in me. You wanted to learn about Dorian, didn't you?"

From the moment he'd entered her apartment Decker knew what would happen. But he still wasn't prepared. He stepped toward her, arms out, but she stopped him with a shake of her head. "Dorian," she said. "That was it all along, wasn't it?"

His shoulders slumped. He looked down at the rug.

"We never had a chance," she said. "People like you never play fair."

The words of a child. Words of truth without guile. Right on target. And he remembered how it had felt when he believed himself to be unloved. A kind of death.

"I'm sorry," Decker said. "I did care for you, I really did. Hurting you wasn't part of the plan."

"I'll say this for you, Manny. You keep your promises. You promised me nothing and that's just what I got."

Manny locked eyes with Romaine once. Then, with a shrug, turned toward the door.

When he had gone she closed the door quietly behind him and leaned against it, her shoulders shaking. Then the bedroom door opened and Dorian entered. He walked over to his wife and took her in his arms.

"It's all right," he said. "It's all right. Me and you from now on. Like I told you, I'll have more money than we'll ever be able to spend. All I have to do is sell that list I showed you. Me and you, we're going where there's a lot of sun."

He kissed her hair, then began to stroke it. "Please give me another chance, babe. I'd go down on my knees, you know I would, if, shit, I don't know what to say. Never was all that good with words. I love you. Ain't no other way of saying it. I'd give every dime I got for another chance with you. Romaine, let's give it one more shot. Please."

Her arms went around his waist, gently at first, then tighter and she clung to him and for the first time in years Dorian wept. "We'll make it," he said. "I know we will."

"LeClair. Who's this?"

"Decker. I just left Romaine Raymond. I'm calling from a public booth not far from her apartment."

"Shit, sounds like she lost that loving feeling. What happened, hot breath? How did she find out you were two-timing her?"

"I've located Dorian Raymond."

"Now that's more like it. That's the kind of thing I expected when you came on board. Where?"

Decker looked up at the stars. "Last place you'd expect him to be. With his wife."

LeClair laughed. "Hey, man, you shittin' me? With his wife? Now ain't that a bitch. With his wife. And you there at the same time." LeClair laughed louder. And Decker hated him more than ever. "Mr. Manfred," said the prosecutor, "has anyone ever told you that you lead a goddamn interesting life?"

23

Sparrowhawk drew the only conclusion possible: Michelle Asama's very existence meant his life was in danger. Proof lay in the latest report on her that lay before him. Like it or not, he had become the hunter again. How else could he survive? He had to solve the mystery of this Japanese woman.

He used his gold pen to tap a page of the report resting in front of framed photographs of his wife and daughter. "Look here, Robbie. This page of names. Three Japanese gentlemen, each connected to our Miss Asama. Mr. Kneji Daigo, Mr. Noboru Abe, Mr. Shigeji Shina. Important men in Japan. The first two are bankers, respected, prosperous, powerful. The third, Mr. Shina, is a leading figure in Japanese military intelligence. Quite brilliant, I'm told. Now we move on to the next page, this one here. I give you Mr. Tettsuo Ishino. And how does Mr. Ishino earn his daily bread? By being one of Amsterdam's leading diamond merchants."

Sparrowhawk tossed the pen on the desk. "And what do these four Oriental gentlemen have in common? Each was a member of the *Jinrai Butai*, or the Divine Thunderbolt Corps."

Robbie said, "Kamikaze pilots."

"Right you are, lad. Kamikaze pilots who were denied the opportunity to die for their beloved country. I don't have to tell you about the *Jinrai Butai*. You're the martial arts expert around here. In the case of these gentlemen bad weather prevented their flights, or mechanical failure cropped up or the war ended. And there's another underlying factor. These gentlemen all served in the exact same suicide unit as George Chihara."

"Wow."

"Wow, indeed."

Robbie shook his head. "But major, it can't be. You're saying Michelle Asama's related to Chihara, maybe even to one of these other guys, and that she's out to get us for what we did to her family six years ago in Saigon. But you're forgetting one thing. Didn't we take care of everyone in the house that night?"

Sparrowhawk raised a forefinger. "Ah, but did we? Think back, lad. Remember a car approaching the villa, then suddenly speeding away? Remember our attempts to convince Mr. Chihara to tell us who was in that car?"

Robbie grinned. "I remember. You were going to shoot his balls off with that dart gun. I remember the car. Somebody shows, then splits. Never came inside. But didn't we find three women upstairs? One old broad and a couple of young ones?"

The Englishman put a hand on Robbie's shoulder. "We assumed, lad. We assumed that they were related to one another, that all were members of the Chihara family. But we never checked to make sure, did we?"

Robbie shook his head.

Sparrowhawk clapped his hands. "So what do we have? We have one old-boy network composed of kamikaze pilots who somehow managed to avoid the Grim Reaper and who today have money and power and who, I am quite willing to assume, stand ready to help the daughter or relative of an old comrade-in-arms. The bankers furnish the money, while the gentleman in intelligence furnishes what we know to be the most valuable commodity of all. Information."

"Hey, major, didn't Chihara send a lot of diamonds out of the country the last few months he was in Saigon?"

"I was coming to that. According to our investigators, it's on this page, the two bankers and Mr. Ishino were business associates of Chihara's while he was in southeast Asia. Ishino was doing diamond deals with Chihara the entire time. The bankers handled Chihara's cash, investments, loans, and I'm sure made a pretty penny doing it. Whatever other worries Miss Asama might have, money certainly isn't one of them."

"Major, how about checking out the guys over at Pantheon, her diamond company?"

"Done. Two members of the board of directors are related to now deceased members of the *Jinrai Butai.*"

Robbie chuckled. "I'll be dipped."

"None of the men is as dangerous as I believe Miss Asama to be. Everything points to the lady being out to even the score for what happened in Saigon. If she isn't a samurai she bloody well thinks like one."

Robbie touched the gold stud in his ear. "It's over. She'd be smart to leave it at that."

"But she can't, not with her background. And no one knows that better than you. She has a duty, an obligation. She'll fulfill it or die trying."

"Being willing to die for a thing doesn't make it right. Doesn't make you smart. Just makes you dead, is all."

Sparrowhawk reached for a Turkish cigarette. "I'm afraid it's not quite that simple, not with this crowd."

"Where's Michelle whatchamacallit now?"

"Amsterdam. Doing diamond deals with Mr. Ishino, I'm sure. We have her under a twenty-four-hour watch. I arranged for a Paris agency to keep tabs on her. They found nothing in London and so far there's no report of anything unusual happening in Amsterdam. She attends the diamond sights, buying primarily polished stones. Spent over a million dollars in only three days. Has an excellent eye, I'm told."

"Is she carrying around that kind of money?"

"Diamond business works on trust. You buy, then agree to pay on a certain date. If you don't, they blacken your name. Engage in fraud or go bankrupt and the diamond world knows it within hours. You're barred for life, or until you make good on your word. Even then you might be prevented from attending future sights. A very tightly run industry. One treads carefully in it or else."

Robbie said, "What's she do in her free time?"

"In London, nothing. In Amsterdam, she spends time with Mr. Ishino and his family. No unsavory acts, if that's what you're hinting at."

"And she's got both Decker and Dorian eating out of her hand."

Sparrowhawk patted his silver hair. "Now there's a situation which bears looking into. Michelle Asama and Detective Sergeant Manfred Decker. How did that come about and when? I can imagine her with Decker more easily than with Dorian."

He shook his head. "Speaking of Dorian, I had hoped the wogs would hesitate to give Pangalos and Quarrels the chop. Alas, it was not to be. I suppose the fuss over these deaths will cool down eventually. Meanwhile, the press is filled with tales of 'the West Side Murders,' as they're called. For the moment let's say nothing of this report on Michelle Asama. As far as Gran Sasso is concerned we're still working on Paul Molise's Saigon contacts. Nothing definite just yet."

"Major, back in Saigon, right after I beat Decker the first time, he took off for Japan like a bat out of hell. I remember thinking he's going there to work out with the top karate guys, maybe pick up some pointers and come back and kick my ass. I asked somebody about it and they said he was going to Tokyo to meet a girl. I got the idea she was Japanese. Just from what was said by other people about the places he planned to visit there. Somebody said she was from Saigon, but I never was that interested so I forgot about it."

"Did he usually go to Japan to meet girls?"

"You mean did he have girls come over from the States to meet him? Hey, if he did he'd probably have met her in Hawaii. That's what everybody else did."

"Unless she was Japanese."

"Unless she was Japanese."

Sparrowhawk said, "Something else to pour into the computer." He looked at his watch. "And speaking of computers, I'm late. Have to check out a new security system we're installing. By the way, congratulations on your Boston victory last night. First-round knockout, I hear."

Robbie grinned. "Wanted to make an early plane back to New York."

"Don't see how you do it. Practice hard every day, year in, year out. But it seems to have paid off. You just can't seem to lose."

"I do the right thing, major. Whatever has to be done before each fight, I do."

"Discipline, exercise, proper diet, moderation in all things. Sacrifice."

Robbie tossed him a playful military salute. "All the time, major. All the time."

24

LeClair drummed on his desk with the fingers of both hands. Dorian Raymond sat before him, a suspect in six unsolved mob-related murders.

"You're a cop," he said to Dorian, "and you know how the game is played. You stonewall me, play hard to get. Delays, postponements, appeals, plea bargaining. Maybe you get lucky. Maybe you walk."

LeClair leaned back in his chair, hands behind his head. "I want you. And I'm going to get you. No matter how long it takes, no matter what I have to do. You're going to do time, Mr. Raymond. That's a fact."

Dorian looked at the ceiling. "Mind reading the charges again?"

"Cute. Real cute." Dorian knew there were no formal charges. He was in the federal prosecutor's office for questioning, nothing more.

And Decker, sitting on a leather couch across the room, knew Dorian was smart enough to realize one thing. No charges meant no hard evidence. LeClair, however, was nobody's fool. Not even his own. He knew where to shove the knife.

"Found you with your wife," LeClair said sweetly. "Could it be that love is more wonderful the second time around?"

Dorian, who had been lighting a cigarette, stopped. His eyes went to LeClair, then to Decker, then back to the cigarette. He filled his lungs with smoke, exhaled twin jets from his nose and crossed his legs. But LeClair knew he'd gotten to him. Dorian was more alert now, more tense.

"I could jail your wife," LeClair said.

"Fuck you," said Dorian, putting out the cigarette after only two drags.

"No, Detective Raymond. Fuck her. Just thinking of a tasty little morsel like Romaine Raymond would make a bull dyke's day in the joint."

"No way you can touch her. No way. Whatever I'm supposed to have done doesn't concern her. She's a dancer, that's all she is."

"Aren't you forgetting something? We found you in her apartment. Once I pass that little bit of news around she can be dragged in here, strip searched and held for a day, two days, maybe longer.

"She'll be one messed-up little girl by the time that happens. A day in jail's more than enough to fuck up anybody's head. Just let a half dozen prisoners catch her alone in the shower and shove a flashlight—"

Dorian was out of his chair. "You cocksucker!"

Decker stood up, ready to interfere. Reluctantly. He would have enjoyed seeing Dorian punch LeClair out. LeClair, fingers steepled under his chin, used a forefinger to indicate Decker's presence to Dorian, who glanced at his fellow detective, then slowly sat down.

LeClair snorted. "Too bad. I was hoping to see Mr. Manfred here strut his stuff. I hear he's pretty good. Anyway, where were we? Ah yes, your wife. Something else I should tell you. I can have her held as an accessory and bail set so high that she can't possibly make it. And in case you're wondering what I've got on her that makes this a practical idea, she can place you in Atlantic City the night Alan Baksted got two in the head. Maybe she even helped set up the hit, who knows?"

"Doesn't mean shit and you know it."

LeClair grinned. "Yeah, but I'd get a real kick out of trying. Of course we could always work something out."

"Like what?"

"Like you telling me what you know about Management Systems Consultants. And what you know about Senator Terry Dent's connection with the Molise family. And what you know about the Molise family itself, who we both know ordered Pangalos and Quarrels to be killed."

Dorian looked away.

LeClair's voice softened. "It won't be easy, I know. You go against the wise guys, you spend the rest of your life hiding.

But it beats the shit out of federal prison. You won't last a month in Atlanta or Leavenworth and you know it. A cop is nothing but dead meat in the joint."

LeClair threw up his hands. "Hey, why am I going on like this? You might not even have anything worth listening to."

Dorian lit another cigarette. Decker noticed that most of the fight had gone out of his fellow officer. But Dorian was not completely beaten.

He said, "First, let me say I'm admitting nothing. If I had a statement to make I'd do it with an attorney present. Second, there is a deal I'd like to talk about and it has nothing to do with MSC or Molise. It has to do with a guy who's killed a lot of people. A lot."

LeClair said, "What's a lot?"

Dorian looked up. "Thirty. Maybe more. All women."

LeClair snorted and waved him away. "Okay, so you're too scared to give me Molise. All right. But, man, don't waste my time with this off-the-wall shit. Thirty women. Come on."

"I'm not shitting you. I said thirty and mean thirty. He rapes them and then he punches them out. Uses karate."

Decker cocked his head and listened more carefully.

LeClair said, "And you know who this karate killer is?"

Dorian nodded.

"Hey, Decker, you hearing this?"

"I hear it."

"Just want to make sure my ears aren't failing me in my old age. Now Sergeant Raymond, you say you know who this man is and yet you haven't come forward until now. Why?"

"What the fuck for? There wasn't anything in it for me until now. We got a deal or don't we?"

"Who is he?"

Dorian shook his head. "No way. First I want to make sure we got a deal. I want it spelled out. I give you this guy and you drop all charges against me. And my wife. I mean all charges. You grab this guy and you close a lot of cases in a lot of cities. Yeah, I know him all right. We were in Nam together. When I learned it was him, I flipped out."

The pieces spun around in Decker's brain in a whirl, then came together in one final *click*. He wanted to jump up in the air and scream. He was on his feet. "Excuse me. I'll be right back." He left without waiting for LeClair's reaction.

In the outer office he paused near the secretary's desk, then changed his mind. Better make the call outside. In the hall he waited impatiently for the elevator and when it came, squeezed himself into a crush of people. He could feel the energy of almost *knowing*, of almost being sure, and it made him almost unbearably restless. He pushed his way off the elevator, stepping on feet and ankles as he ran toward a bank of telephones.

He pulled out the change in his pocket. No dime. Shit. He did have a quarter. He used that and dialed his precinct with a shaky hand. Busy signal. Jesus.

He hung up, pressed the return button, got his quarter back and dialed again. *Don't let the line be busy*. His hand shook. The line rang. Come on, come on.

"Detective Spiceland. Manhattan West. May I help you?"

"Ellen, it's Decker. This *kaishaku* thing. What have you got? Quick. I'm due back upstairs."

"Manny, I'm on two phones."

"Let 'em wait. Tell 'em you'll call them back. It's important. Believe me."

"Okay, okay. Lighten up. I'll be right back."

She put Decker on hold. The detective began chewing a thumbnail. *Had to be. It had to be him.*

"Back the same day. Hello? Manny?"

"I'm here, I'm here."

"All right. Here's what I've done so far. Like you said, I contacted the martial arts publications. Got tournament dates, got the names of men competing in the tournament. Spent most of my time trying to find out if a woman was raped and killed the night the tournament was held. The answer is yes. Happened in the city or just outside in a suburb or something. Close enough to allow a man to get from the murder to the tournament in plenty of time. Times of death all seem to be before the tournament, though in a couple of cases the coroner wasn't too sure. But it's definite that the tournaments and the killings happened the same night."

"How many tournaments did you check out so far?"

"Nine. Also called nine police departments in those cities. Came up with nine female victims. No special type. Caucasian, black, Hispanic."

"Okay. Now listen carefully. You have those magazines there?"

"Sure. Right in front of me."

Decker closed his eyes. "Open them up to the tournaments you checked out. Only those tournaments."

"You mean get the names of the guys who competed?"

"Ellen, just do it, okay?"

"Don't scream. I get enough of that shit around here when you're gone. I'm looking. I'm looking."

"See how many times the name Robbie Ambrose crops up."

"Spell it."

"R-O-B-B-I-E A-M-B-R-O-S-E. Hurry, up, damn it."

"My, aren't we testy today. I'll be glad when your girl friend comes back from Europe. Ah, here we go. Denver, April this year. Winner by knockout, Robbie Ambrose. Check my list of murders. Woman raped and murdered in Denver same night. New magazine, turn the page. Dallas Challenge Pro-Am. Winner by knockout, one Mr. Ambrose. Woman raped and killed in Dallas that same night. Something called 'the Battle of Seattle.' Robbie Ambrose. Knockout third round. Woman raped and killed in Seattle approximately an hour prior to the tournament."

"Keep checking," Decker said.

Minutes later a subdued Ellen Spiceland whispered, "Holy shit. Manny, do you have any idea what this means?"

"It means we've found the *kaishaku*. It means we know the identity of somebody who may have raped and murdered at least thirty women. It means Robbie Ambrose is the *kaishaku*."

25

From the window of his apartment Dorian looked down on the Cathedral of St. John the Divine ten stories below. His fingernails scraped at the seal around the neck of a fifth of vodka.

Despite today's ball-busting session with LeClair, it had been a good day. He drank to that, bringing the vodka bottle to his mouth and taking a big swallow. He was under suspicion, but so what. There were no witnesses and it didn't look like LeClair had any evidence. Best of all, tonight he was moving back in with Romaine.

Dorian lifted the bottle in a toast to the cathedral. It's been divine, John. See you around.

He turned from the window to his television set and the Monday night football game. Today he'd laid five thousand on the Minnesota Vikings, who were ahead by twenty points and about to score again. If the Vikings hung on and won he would use the money to buy Romaine the sable coat she'd always wanted. Getting his hands on that pigeon list sure had changed his luck with Romaine.

He remembered how depressed he'd been after killing Pangalos and Quarrels. He'd gotten drunk and stayed drunk and with nothing to lose he'd dropped by to see Romaine. She had been down, too, way down, thanks to that prick Decker.

Dorian walked over to the television set, turned up the sound and placed the bottle of vodka on a folding chair. Then he walked into the bedroom, took folded shirts from the top of a dresser and dumped them into an open suitcase lying on the bed. One suitcase, that's it. Two framed photographs—one of his graduating class at the Police Academy, the other of him and Romaine on their wedding day. A Bible given to him by his mother to keep him alive in Vietnam, which he never read. Other than the clothes on his back, he was taking nothing else with him. He had all the money he needed.

He closed the suitcase, carried it into the living room and looked around for his shoes. He found them near the couch, shook a cockroach out of the left one and put them on. He leaned back on the couch and watched Minnesota kick a field goal to go up by thirty points. He shoved a clenched fist at the screen. Way to go, Vikings.

Cigarettes. Where the fuck were his cigarettes? He found what was left of a pack in a jacket pocket and made a mental note to stop off and buy more before going to Romaine's. At least there was still some grass left. He kept it hidden in the bathroom, taped behind the toilet. Grass made him horny. Might be too soon to put a move on Romaine, but he could try. You never know.

Robbie. Why the hell did he have to start thinking about Robbie now? Dorian reached behind the toilet, found his stash and took his rolling papers from the medicine cabinet. He rolled a fat joint, a farewell to his apartment, this neighborhood, this life.

Back to Robbie. At first LeClair hadn't been interested. "I want Management Systems Consultants," he said. "That's why you're here, in case you haven't figured it out."

Decker still had not returned when Dorian said, "This is your lucky day, Mr. Prosecutor, because the man we're talking about just happens to work for them."

LeClair took his time answering. "Sergeant, I'd appreciate it if you kept this between us. I don't want Sergeant Decker to know what you've just told me."

"Don't worry about it. Decker's not exactly one of my favorite people at the moment."

Dorian was no fool. LeClair had just done a 360-degree turn. Suddenly he was interested in Robbie Ambrose, very interested. And Dorian took advantage of it. He stood up. "You know where to find me. No sense me staying here, seeing as nobody's filing any charges. When you're ready we'll talk some more. One thing: any deal we cut means total immunity and I want it in writing. Romaine's part of that deal. If we do business you stay the fuck away from her. Or there won't be any deal."

In his apartment Dorian took a toke on the joint, held the sweet smoke in his lungs for a long time, eyes closed. Panama Red. The best. He exhaled.

The front-door buzzer sounded. Dorian shook his head to clear it.

"Yeah?"

The buzzer went off again.

"All right, all right." Whoever it was hadn't bothered to ring from downstairs. That was the trouble with this damn building. No doorman and the tenants were forever leaving the front door open or buzzing in people without asking who they were.

Buzzzzzz.

"Coming, goddamn it." He stood up. Woozy. He giggled. He planted his feet, squeezed his eyes shut and opened them, then started toward the door. At the door he took a few deep breaths, then looked through the peephole. Holy shit.

He opened the door.

Michi walked past him.

Grinning lasciviously, Dorian closed the door and flopped back against it. "Hey, Michelle. Well all right. When did you get back? Thought you was supposed to be gone ten days." Christ was he horny.

He started toward her, the joint pinched between a thumb and forefinger.

Michi said, "Are you alone?"

Dorian looked around. "I'd say so. Yeah, I would definitely say so."

Of course she wanted to party. Why else had she come. Dorian felt his hard-on. One for the road. Last time getting it on with Michelle. After tonight it would be just him and Romaine.

He said, "Let's go in the bedroom."

"Please turn out the lights."

"In the bedroom we can—"

"The lights. Please turn them out."

He frowned. Sounded like she had some kind of attitude. Okay, if it made the bitch happy he'd turn out the lights.

He saw Michi look toward the window facing the street. "Hey, momma, don't worry 'bout the neighbors. Nothin' out there but 'Big John.' Biggest goddamn John you ever saw."

He laughed at his own joke, switched off the light, then, as he turned to offer Michi a drink, he felt his jaw explode with pain.

Michi had smashed him under the chin with her right elbow, snapping his head back and forcing him to bite down on his tongue hard enough to sever the tip. When Dorian's hands came up to his mouth, Michi drove that same elbow deep into the pit of his stomach, knocking all the air out of him. And as his hands came down, the fingers of her left hand flicked out like a snake's tongue, stabbing at his eyes, blinding him.

He fought for air, tried to cry out and couldn't.

Michi attacked low, using her left foot to sweep Dorian at the ankles, taking both feet out from under him and dropping him heavily to the floor. He landed with a grunt, and before he could make another sound Michi shoved the sharp heel of her boot into his throat.

Dorian lay gagging on the floor, hands on his throat, his large body rolling from side to side. Michi turned from him and walked to the window. She peeked through the curtains down at the street below. Ten stories. *Hai*. She parted the curtains, unlocked the window and opened it. Cold air hit her face, tearing her eyes.

She walked back to Dorian, placed a gloved hand under each armpit and dragged him across the floor, past the flickering picture on the television set. Lifting his dead weight to the window was not easy, but she managed. Now he was half in, half out of the window and directly over a square-shaped, old-fashioned marquee leading to the building's entrance.

Michi bowed her head to the memory of her family, then took off the dark brown cap that hid her hair and the *hachimaki* she wore around her forehead and temples. Wrapping her arms around Dorian's thighs she pushed him out of the window, then leaned to the right where she could not be seen.

She left the window open.

Picking up her cap she walked across the room and looked out through the peephole to make sure the hallway was empty. Seconds later she was out of the apartment and walking down ten flights of stairs, fully expecting to find a crowd when she reached the ground floor. Instead the street was almost deserted. A bewildered Michi, scarf and dark glasses hiding her face, hesitated, then looked up. Dorian had landed on the marquee and no one had noticed.

Across from Michi the great doors of the cathedral swung open, sending light and sounds of medieval Christmas carols into the street. Throngs of people began to file out into the night. Michi hurried away from them.

Eight hours later Michi was awakened by an Air France stewardess. The flight was ahead of schedule. Because of strong tailwinds the plane would be landing at Charles de Gaulle Airport a half hour early. Michi, hungry and still tired, stretched and looked around the almost empty plane.

She found her boots, put them on, yawned. Through the early morning fog below she could see patches of green fields and scattered houses. The pilot came on the intercom to say that Paris was in the grip of a winter freeze. Michi smiled. Perfect.

The plane dropped lower, popping her ears. She worked her jaw until she could hear again. Her ears cleared in time to hear the screech as the wheels touched down, skidding slightly on the runway, and then the plane was on the ground. Michi's heart beat faster. The most dangerous part of her plan lay ahead.

The plane came to a halt and she was out of her seat instantly, in the aisle reaching for the overhead luggage rack and her shoulder bag. A stewardess politely but firmly requested that Michi sit down until the engines were off and the plane had come to a complete stop. Michi smiled. "I am very sorry. Yes, you are right." She had been too anxious. She must not be that careless again.

There was no delay at customs; she had nothing to declare and was waved through without an examination of her shoulder bag, her only luggage. There had been only a cursory examination of her false passport, the one listing her as an American. After making one telephone call she found a cab.

And on the way into Paris she reminded herself that she had only two more men to kill and then she would be free to be happy with Manny for the rest of her life.

She woke up when the taxi entered Place de la Concorde.

The sight of the magnificent square excited her. Just before reaching the rue du Faubourg St.-Honoré the driver slowed down. Michi took a ski mask from her lap and pulled it over her face.

"Froid," she said. Cold.

She wasn't the first woman the driver had seen wearing a ski mask in this weather.

The driver turned onto rue du Faubourg St.-Honoré, the street of the most elegant shops in Paris. Michi's destination was the Yves St. Laurent boutique.

But before her driver could get there, a second cab coming from the opposite direction reached the boutique first. Michi's driver hugged the curb of the narrow street and waited, his motor idling.

From the second cab a woman in a white fur coat, boots and a floppy black hat, her face covered by dark glasses and a black scarf, stepped out and entered the St. Laurent boutique. Michi paid her driver, and as she walked toward the boutique she saw the Renault. It slowed down behind the second cab and a man in a dark green anorak and square-shaped tinted eyeglasses stepped out, stopped long enough to touch the hearing aid in his left ear, then crossed the street. He entered an empty cafe where chairs were piled on tables and an Algerian mopped the floor.

Pulling a copy of *Paris-Match* from his pocket, the man in the anorak took a chair from one table, sat down and ordered cappuccino. He began to read.

Fifteen minutes later a woman wearing Michi's cloth coat, cap and ski mask left the boutique and entered a taxi that had just dropped off another customer. Michi, hidden from view, watched the cab pull away. Her heart was in her throat. But no one followed, not the man in the anorak, not the Renault. She bowed her head in gratitude to the gods. She had been successful.

Michi turned from the door and walked back into the shop, where she purchased skirts and a new pair of sunglasses. When she stepped onto the street she was once more wearing her white fur, floppy hat, dark glasses. The scarf was around her neck, not her face. No need to hide now.

She walked along the rue du Faubourg St.-Honoré, stopping to buy perfume and a sweater. An hour later she hailed a cab and asked to be taken to the Hotel Richelieu just off the Étoile at the head of the Champs Élysées. Here, in a suite with a balcony overlooking a courtyard, Michi soaked herself in a bath, then checked the room for signs of entry. She found none. After making several business calls, she left a wake-up call for three in the afternoon, then lay down to sleep.

At 4:15 that afternoon she was in front of the hotel being ushered into a taxi by the hotel doorman. When her cab pulled away from the hotel, the Renault, with a man in the anorak at the wheel, fell into line, taking care to keep two cars between himself and the cab.

26

The FBI agent walked to the door of the bedroom, pushed it open with his foot and looked inside. He shook his head in mild disgust at the mess, then turned away and walked back to the front window to stand beside Decker. Together the two looked down at Dorian Raymond's corpse, now lying on top of the apartment house marquee ten stories below. Several men standing around the corpse stepped aside to allow stretcher bearers to move away the body. Decker watched flashbulbs go off as last photographs were taken of the dead man.

Decker turned to the FBI agent, who was also a member of LeClair's task force. "What do you have?"

The agent pursed his lips and shook his head. "Zilch. No sign of forced entry. No indication of a struggle. Window wasn't broken. The fingerprints we're getting say he was the only one near that window. Neighbors didn't hear a thing, but then again nobody ever does. Tenants in two apartments were out at the Christmas pageant across the street. Other tenants on the floor went to bed at 8:30 and slept like a baby all night."

Decker said, "LeClair doesn't like it."

"LeClair doesn't like anything."

"Says it's one hell of a coincidence, Dorian going out the window like that."

The FBI agent turned around to watch someone dust the television set for prints. "We found empty liquor bottles and an opened fifth of vodka. Found a joint on the floor, some grass in the john, Quāāludes in the bedroom and a vial of cocaine in a suitcase on the bed. Maybe he got stoned and thought he was Superman."

"Doesn't the suitcase tell you something else? His wife says he was packing to move back in with her. Why kill himself now?"

"So he changed his mind. I hear tell he has got himself a foxy old lady." Decker looked at him to decide whether the agent was getting personal, then decided he wasn't and let the remark pass.

Upon hearing of Dorian's death, LeClair had ordered Decker and two more task force members to hustle over to the apartment and nose around. But a local West Side precinct was handling the investigation, so Decker and the task force guys were mere observers.

No one was ready with a quick opinion on Dorian's apparent suicide. It could be death by his own hand or it could be death with a little help from his friends. The final verdict would have to wait until the investigation was completed. Decker wondered if Molise's people hadn't been the ones. Or had Dorian really just gotten high and accidentally fallen out?

Decker walked aimlessly around the apartment. It was crowded. Cops, forensics, representatives from the coroner's office, the mayor's office, the police commissioner's office. The reporters were restricted to the hallway and downstairs in the lobby.

Suddenly the apartment door was opened and Decker saw them. Hand-held cameras, harsh lights carried by jeaned assistants, all decked out with clipboards, microphones and tape recorders. Decker felt the usual surge of disgust. Onlookers at the orgy. Ready to shape the truth to whatever half-assed theory would sell papers.

What the hell was he doing here? He was here because LeClair was furious that there was no way to work out a deal with Dorian Raymond. And where did this leave Romaine? Decker had to try and see her today. He owed her that much. He wondered if it were true that Dorian had been planning to move back in with her.

He strolled into the empty bedroom. The fingerprint boys, official police photographers and investigating detectives were through for the moment. Decker had the room to himself. As he glanced around the room, he couldn't help but feel that there was something sad about the way Dorian had lived. "The Almost Man," he had called himself. It had been that way at the end, too. He had almost gotten back with his wife, almost made a deal with LeClair to stay out of prison, almost lived to see his birthday a week away.

Decker, hands in his overcoat pocket, sat down on the bed. Either suicide or death by the Molise family. No matter what the reason it was never smart for the mob to kill a cop. It always brought down heat. Cops and professional criminals usually got along well with each other, both understanding the importance of sticking to the rules.

Decker was about to stand up when an object on the floor under an end table caught his eye. Someone had probably unknowingly knocked it down. Decker reached for it. And his heart almost stopped. He looked over his shoulder to make sure he was still alone, then looked at the object in his hand. It was a tiny reindeer, a beautiful example of origami wildlife.

He put it in his pocket, then stood up. He felt sick, warm, sweaty. He needed air. He hurried from the bedroom, crossed the living room, then opened the door and plunged into the crowd of reporters, shoving them aside until he reached the stairs. Yanking open the fire-exit door, he dashed through and stopped at the head of the stairs, both hands squeezing the iron railing.

Decker breathed deeply, sucking air in through his mouth, then slowly began walking down the stairs. In his overcoat pocket the tiny reindeer seemed to burn through to the skin like a red-hot coal. He continued walking down into darkness, neither knowing nor caring where he was going.

At the next staircase he stopped to throw up.

Five

Chanbara

Traditional Japanese drama involving sword play with its choice between *giri,* duty, and *ninjo,* feeling or inclination

27

Sparrowhawk listened to the call coming through his speakerphone with the intensity of a man whose life hung on every word.

He needed sleep. Fatigue had knotted his back muscles and brought back his migraine headaches. In the two days since Dorian's death he had slept a total of six hours. What kept him awake at night was the lie that Dorian Raymond had killed himself.

Sparrowhawk was confused, too. Michelle Asama had dug a pit, and he knew that if he didn't push her in he would be pushed in himself. Somewhere along the line she had overdone her deception. He had to find out where.

Now he sat at his desk at MSC, palms pressed together in front of his long nose, his unblinking gaze squarely on the speakerphone directly in front of him. Behind him, cooing pigeons on a window sill flapped their wings. Robbie sat to his left, legs outstretched and squeezing a rubber ball, first in one fist, then in the other. His eyes were on his pulsating fists, but his attention, like Sparrowhawk's, was riveted to the voice of the caller in Paris, who spoke with a German-Swiss accent.

"We followed her from the hotel in Amsterdam to Schipol Airport, where she boarded a private plane to Paris. The plane belongs to a Mr. Tetsuo Ishino. I believe that is how you pronounce it. He is a leading diamond dealer in the Netherlands, Mr. Ishino. Quite wealthy and a member of the Amsterdam Chamber of Commerce. Has a daughter married to an Anton Koestraat, a Dutchman who owns real estate—"

"Will you bloody well get on with it, man," snapped Sparrowhawk. "I don't give a tinker's damn about Mr. Ishino's daughter or the bugger she's married to. Stick to Michelle Asama."

"Yah, I understand. Well, we could not board her plane—"

Sparrowhawk rolled his eyes toward the ceiling.

"—so we have our people in Paris waiting for her when the plane lands at Charles de Gaulle Airport. She clears private customs, then she takes a private limousine to Paris."

Sparrowhawk massaged his tired eyes. "Thorough, Dieter, quite thorough."

"Yah. Anyway, she goes to the Hotel Richelieu, just off the Champs, checks into a top-floor suite."

"I take it since you've not mentioned it that you've not been able to get into the suite."

"You are right. We have not. She did not leave until yesterday and we thought maybe she come back quick. She was sick, so we think maybe she not stay out too long."

Sparrowhawk's fingers slid away from his eyes. "Sick?"

"Yah. She stay inside her room the whole time. Two nights, one day inside. She does not come out and we cannot go in. A hotel doctor comes up to see her and we learn from somebody that she is being treated for a cold. Yesterday is the first day she comes out. She goes shopping on rue du Faubourg St.-Honoré, first to Yves St. Laurent, then to other shops."

"And during her entire Paris stay she's been under surveillance?"

"Yah. We have men in the lobby around the clock. We know what she is doing in the hotel."

"Really? And what is Miss Asama doing?"

"Business. No telephone calls, but she writes letters."

Sparrowhawk leaned toward the speaker. "And to whom were these letters addressed?"

"I cannot say. They were dictated in the room, typed there and kept by Miss Asama. She mailed them yesterday when she went shopping. She kept the secretary's note pad as well."

Sparrowhawk slammed the palm of his hand down on his desk. "Bloody cheek. She's either a very careful businesswoman or she knows we're on to her. And you're quite certain she hasn't left Paris since her arrival?"

"Rest assured, sir, she has not. She is still here, conducting business outside the hotel now. Meeting diamond dealers, diamond cutters and people from whom she will probably make private purchases. She is reportedly interested in a necklace called 'Lagrimas Negras,' black tears. It is made of black diamonds from Brazil and belongs to an Italian countess, who claims it was Hitler's last gift to Eva Braun."

Robbie shifted the ball to his other hand. "Lady seems to have made one hell of a quick recovery from her cold."

Sparrowhawk gazed at him with red-rimmed eyes. He whispered, "So it would seem. Along with that we're asked to believe that Dorian Raymond, hardly the suicidal type, suddenly took it into his head to dive out of a window. The mind boggles at this mystifying series of events."

He said to the speaker, "And you actually saw her leave the hotel for the first time since arriving, and go directly to the St. Laurent shop."

"Yah. There were two of us in the car following. We both saw her. Same white fur coat, a rather grotesque hat that hung down over most of her face, dark glasses and a scarf across her mouth, I suppose, to prevent her from succumbing to more germs."

Robbie tossed the ball into the air and began to play catch with himself. "Who was that masked man?" he joked.

Sparrowhawk, annoyed and in no mood for levity, threw him a withering look. His headache was getting worse. Sparrowhawk was about to speak into the phone when he suddenly snapped his head toward Robbie. "What did you say?"

"Me?" said the German-Swiss voice three thousand five hundred miles away. "I said nothing."

"Not you. Robbie. Robbie, what did you just say?"

"I was only goofing on it, major. Sorry."

"Don't be sorry, lad. Repeat your words."

Robbie shrugged. "I said, 'Who was that masked man?' Like the way that lady was all covered up reminded me of the Lone Ranger."

Sparrowhawk flopped back in his chair and laughed. Bitterly. "Oh, she is a right clever little thing. A rather nasty piece of work. Definitely a crafty and cunning member of her species. In a strange way I admire the woman."

He looked at Robbie. "She did it, you know. She managed to be in two places at once."

Suddenly, Sparrowhawk remembered that Dieter wasn't supposed to know why he was following Michelle Asama.

He leaned forward toward the speaker. "Dieter, I owe you

an apology. You were telling me before about Mr. Ishino's family. Please continue and this time I shall listen most carefully."

"Well, he has three children. Two sons and a daughter."

Sparrowhawk looked at Robbie. "Tell me about the daughter."

"We have no pictures of her, but I can get one. I hear she is quite beautiful. Twenty-nine years of age. Two children, a boy and a girl."

Sparrowhawk swung his gold pen back and forth between his thumb and forefinger like a pendulum. "Twenty-nine, you say. Young. Approximately Miss Asama's age."

Robbie bounced the heel of his hand off his forehead, and mouthed the words, *oh wow*. He stopped playing with the ball.

Sparrowhawk kept his eyes on Robbie. "Dieter, you never actually followed her into the St. Laurent boutique, did you?"

"No, sir. It's all women in there. A man would attract too much attention. We wait outside. We see her go in, we see her come out."

Sparrowhawk dropped the gold pen on his desk, a dramatic punctuation to his conclusion. "You saw *somebody* go in, you saw *somebody* go out."

"I do not understand."

Sparrowhawk kneaded the back of his neck. "Amazing. Utterly amazing. That will be all, Dieter. Kindly bill me directly on this, if you please. Send the invoice with my name on it to my home. I don't want this to go through the accounting department."

"I understand."

"I'm sure you do. *Adieu*, and my regards to your family."

"Au revoir, monsieur."

Sparrowhawk pressed a button on top of the speaker and disconnected the line. "Robbie, remind me to see that this call is erased from the log of incoming calls. The private tape I have will be sufficient if I need to refer to it again."

He placed his folded hands on his desk. "She made the switch in Amsterdam. Ishino's daughter wore Michelle Asama's clothing, then got aboard her father's private plane and lured Dieter's men on a wild goose chase. Meanwhile Michelle Asama somehow returned unseen to New York, dispatched Dorian, then took herself off to Paris. There she simply switched clothes again, sent Miss Ishino or Mrs. Anton Koestraat on her way and it was back to the glittering world of diamonds."

Robbie said, "Dieter's men blew it. She knows she's being followed."

"To say the least. One thing's for sure: she's after the four of us. You, me, Dorian and Paul Molise. Dorian and Paul are dead. And then there were two. She's in full pursuit, lad, complete with horses, hounds and hunting horns."

"Decker. Think he's in on it with her?"

Sparrowhawk shook his head. "Negative."

"How can you be sure?"

"Simple. When Paul met his maker Decker was teaching a karate class on the West Side. More than forty witnesses place him there. When Dorian went out the window Sergeant Decker was at precinct headquarters attempting to catch up on paperwork. And finally, had Decker wanted to eliminate any of us he would probably have gotten around to it a lot sooner. Michelle Asama, for reasons known only to her, could not act before now. I would say that she and Decker have renewed an old friendship, one that undoubtedly began in Saigon."

"So you think she's related to George Chihara."

"Her recent actions indicate she is. If she hates us enough to kill us because of Mr. Chihara, then she is certainly a close blood relative of the man. Which brings me to a rather harsh truth. And that is, if we don't remove Miss Asama she will, in time, remove us."

Sparrowhawk and Robbie held each other's gaze. "I say this reluctantly, lad. You know I promised that I'd not ask you to soil your hands with this sort of business unless absolutely necessary. Unfortunately, it's become necessary. She is obviously the mystery individual who drove up to Chihara's villa six years ago and who was warned away in time. She may have taken six years to catch up to us, but I can assure you the lady has certainly thrown herself into her work ever since."

"We're not going to turn her over to Gran Sasso?"

"Dear boy, the mind of Paul Molise senior has become so addled by grieving over his dead son that he can no longer think rationally. He alternates between periods of deep mourning and a cry for blood. You saw how quickly Pangalos and Quarrels were disposed of. That, old chum, is the emotional climate surrounding the wogs these days."

The Englishman lit a Turkish cigarette. "If Michelle Asama talks to the Italians, my feeling is she'll hurt us, you and me. We're responsible for what happened to young Paul. Paul senior, in his present state of mind, might just draw that conclusion. So might Gran Sasso. So might Alphonse Giulia. And when it's learned that Miss Asama had help from certain Japanese gentlemen, I wouldn't be surprised if the wogs didn't decide that getting rid of us isn't the best way to avoid trouble with these men in the future."

He exhaled blue smoke. "No, lad, it's better if *we* dispose of Miss Asama."

Robbie held the black ball in an iron grip. "When do I leave for Paris?"

"Immediately."

Sparrowhawk stood up. "You'll need some sort of cover. I'll prepare documents for you to carry to Dieter's agency in Paris. You'll simply be on a normal courier run for MSC, just as you've done in the past. Pay attention. It's important that you deliver the documents to Dieter after you finish with Miss Asama. Let it appear that Dieter's agency is your one and only stop in Paris. Incidentally, would you like to spend a few days in Paris, a short holiday of sorts?"

Robbie shook his head. "Thanks anyway, major, but I have to get back here. Got a couple of fights coming up, then I'll be concentrating on the *suibin* tournament for January. That's when I'll spend time in Paris."

"As you wish. Decker's not interested in that, is he?"

Robbie snorted. "Are you kidding? Hasn't got the balls."

"Pity. Like to see that man get taken down a peg or two. Well, off with you now. And do be careful. Remember, she's killed three men that we know of. With her hands. Don't be careless or overconfident." Ridiculous on the surface of it, he thought. To be afraid of one woman. Michelle Asama, however, was no ordinary woman.

Robbie tossed the ball from hand to hand. "I'm not overconfident, major. Just sure. About as sure as you can get. The lady is definitely gone."

28

At 7:00 P.M. in Paris, a weary and reflective Michi stepped out onto the balcony of her hotel suite and looked across courtyard rooftops at the Eiffel Tower. Just before entering the hotel, Michi had stopped a few blocks away to watch a different light, a rekindling of the Eternal Flame on the tomb of France's Unknown Soldier, a ceremony performed at 6:30 P.M. daily under the Arch of Triumph. The honoring of the dead reminded her of her own family. There were times, she thought, when to remember was to suffer twice.

On the balcony Michi felt falling snowflakes brush her face. Tears of regret sprang to her eyes. More than anything Michi regretted the time she and Manny did not have together, time lost forever.

She stepped back into the warmth of her suite, closed the delicate glass doors behind her and pulled the drapes. She shook her head to clear it of snow, shivering as flakes landed on her neck and bare throat. Michi found the hotel menu, then telephoned room service and ordered filet mignon, a carafe of red wine, *pommes frites*, asparagus and a small salad, with a chestnut pâté for dessert.

Michi went into her bedroom, stripped nude, then showered. When she had changed into a gray silk kimono and clogs, she tied her hair back and went into the living room to sit at a desk and make out her agenda for tomorrow. Appointments with two diamond cutters and a dealer from Antwerp; a scheduled visit to a chic jewelry shop on Place Vendôme; lunch on Île St.-Louis with Countess Gautier, owner of the "Lagrimas Negras" necklace, which Michi, if she bought it, planned to have broken down into smaller, more lucrative pieces. Tomorrow was a full day. It would be wise to go to bed early.

There was a knock on her door. Room service, she thought, then decided no. She had phoned down her order only moments ago. Hotel room service in Paris was as slow as it was expensive.

She stood up. "Who is there, please?"

"Manny."

Michi dropped one hand to her heart. She rose and in her excitement knocked over her chair. She could not have wished for a more joyous surprise. Happily she rushed to the door, opened it and threw herself into his arms. She clung to him, buried her face in his shoulder, felt the snow on his coat collar against her ear and the pleasant roughness of his unshaven cheek against her skin. Manny was here, with her. She tightened her grip on him and attempted to lose herself in him.

It was a shock to her to realize that he was withdrawn, that he was pulling away from her. Michi glanced at his face. Manny refused to look her in the eye. He appeared tired, haggard, emotionally drained. Something was bothering him.

"Inside," he said, sounding very much like a policeman.

Michi backed up and Manny entered the room, closing the door behind him.

She said, "What is wrong? Please tell me."

He looked at her a long time before removing a hand from his overcoat pocket. Michi's eyes went to the lavender paper reindeer he held out to her.

"I found it in Dorian Raymond's apartment," he said. "He's dead, by the way."

Decker gently placed the paper reindeer on a coffee table and removed his hat. He looked at the tiny wet spots on the brim that were melted snow. "Happened night before last. Out the window and down ten floors."

His eyes went to her and she saw the sadness there. She saw fatigue and she saw his fear of impending betrayal. But he would not leave until he had learned the truth.

He said, "Did you sleep with him?"

Michi hugged herself and looked down at the floor.

When Decker spoke his voice was hoarse with hurt. "Think I'll sit down on the couch. Knee's bothering me. Does that in damp weather."

Michi kept her eyes averted. "Have you come to arrest me?"

He looked at the reindeer. "Don't know. Shit, I don't know. I came here for answers, I know that much. I've already gotten one. I was hoping it wouldn't be true." He closed his eyes. "Jesus. Why did you come back into my life if you didn't love me?"

Her tears blurred Michi's vision. "I do love you. I have never stopped loving you. I never will. If you walk from this room and never see me again I shall love only you. Only you."

"Maybe I'm not as sophisticated as I should be, but if you love me what the fuck were you doing spreading your legs for Dorian?"

His words were meant to hurt and they did. "Please, Manny. He meant nothing to me. Don't—"

"Don't what? Don't bleed when somebody stabs me in the back?"

"I used Dorian. That is all he was to me."

He waved her away. "Makes two of us you were using."

Michi said, "You did not come here just to ask me about my relationship with Dorian."

"Word is," said Decker, "that the only thing Sparrowhawk's been told to concern himself with these days is finding Paul Molise's killer. While you were gone some men from MSC broke into your apartment. I couldn't help but wonder if there wasn't some connection. Autopsy report on Molise says he was killed by needlelike weapons or possibly something thin and metallic like a surgeon's scalpel."

For the first time in minutes he looked at her. "Coroner's office has nothing definite on the weapon. Nobody asked me so I didn't tell them that it really could be a long needle, the kind of thing someone might be taught to use in *ninja* training. Lot of secret services use *ninja* techniques these days. CIA, KGB, MI 6, SAS, the SEALs and Green Berets are using them as well. And, of course, the Japanese secret service."

He waited for her to say something and when she didn't he continued. "The Cong captured your father just about the time he was winding down his business relationship in Saigon with Molise and Sparrowhawk. And from what I remember,

Ruttencutter of the CIA was a part of that crowd as well. So, it might not be too wild a guess to say there was some kind of falling out and your father ended up in a Cong work camp. You told me that much. What you didn't tell me and what I think happened is that his American and English business associates put him there."

Decker began massaging his bad knee with both hands. "If anybody can peg you as being George Chihara's daughter it's Sparrowhawk. He's a very intelligent and ruthless man. If he sets his mind to it he'll learn all there is to know about you. After that it's only a matter of time until . . ."

He continued to massage his knee. Michi said, "Until what?"

"Until he uses what he finds out against you."

"I didn't use you."

"Right. I tell you we're about to arrest Dorian and two hot minutes after our conversation Dorian's dead. There's evidence you were in his apartment, his bedroom, to be precise, and I think we both know that you had reason to want him dead. That's the way of the samurai, isn't it?"

"I have never lied to you. I may have kept things from you, but I did not lie."

He stood up, hands jammed in his overcoat pockets. "Just as soon as someone explains the difference between those two things to me, maybe I'll understand."

"And you," she said, "you have told the people in your life everything about yourself?"

She caught him off guard. He drew his head back and looked at her from eyes that were almost closed.

"Yes, Manny," she said. "You do hide things."

"You said you haven't lied to me. In that case let's go with this one: did you kill Paul Molise and Dorian Raymond?"

She turned her back to him, hugged herself and after a while she nodded and said, "Yes."

She turned and saw him almost shrink from despair. "It was my duty to kill them," she said. "I am samurai."

He waved her away. "Oh, Christ."

She drew herself up. "I shall kill Sparrowhawk and Robbie Ambrose as well."

He stood up, walked away from her, stopped, then turned around, a forefinger aimed at her head. "And what am I supposed to do while you're whacking these guys, sit outside in a car with the motor running? Make a chalk mark on the wall for every poor bastard you heave out of a window? I'm a cop, remember? And you've got me involved—"

"You're not involved. You have your duty, I have mine. No two people see the same world."

"Great. Fucking great. Can't wait to tell that to my precinct commander or Internal Affairs or to the guys in the squad room. Meanwhile, if the New York Police Department doesn't give us both trouble, there's always the Molise family, Sparrowhawk, Robbie and quite possibly a federal task force."

"They cannot kill me."

"Oh, no? Well, let me tell you something. They are damn sure going to try."

She took a step closer to him and when she spoke the words were delivered softly, but with more power than anything she had said to him. "I am already dead. The way of the samurai is death."

Decker watched her, eyes on her face, seeing her and trying to see more.

Michi walked to the couch, sat, then stared straight ahead and spoke as though in a trance. "For samurai, it is important that we die well. We must think of death every day. Only this way can we be strong enough to do our duty. I can live only when I face death, when I am truly willing and ready to die."

She looked at him. "I see how you in the West practice the martial arts. For you it is playing with the idea of death without dying. For me it is much more."

Decker said, "You can't come back to America. Even if I don't turn you in, your life is in danger. I stopped Sparrowhawk's men from taking anything out of your apartment. But they'll try again. And one day Paul Molise will learn what you did to his son. He'll kill you for sure. He'll take his time doing it, but he'll do it. God knows what LeClair will do to you, especially if he ever gets anything on you. And don't forget Sparrowhawk. He and Robbie know or soon will know you're after them. Go back to Japan, Michi. Leave now, tonight."

She shook her head.

"Goddamn it," Decker said, "all I can do for you is look the other way while you run."

The words were no sooner out than he regretted having said them. Her face said she had expected him to do more.

"I am committed to my family," she said. "One has to be true to something."

Her words made him angrier. She also knew that he was jealous of Dorian and wanted to hurt her for that. "Goddamn it," Decker said, "*giri* or no *giri,* it's not worth it. Your father's dead. You can't help him now."

"According to what I believe, I can help. I can help him, my mother and my sister. I can bring them justice. I can bring their souls peace. I said I would tell you everything."

She told him of the night in Saigon, when Sparrowhawk, Robbie and Dorian, on Paul Molise's orders, had come to the Chihara villa and forced Michi's mother, sister and best friend to commit *seppuku.* A CIA agent named Ruttencutter had also been involved. Decker remembered him from the Saigon embassy.

Michi said, "Ruttencutter and Paul Molise took my father's gold and diamonds and narcotics, then turned him over to the Viet Cong. My father was samurai. To be captured, then degraded by enemies is worse than death. Much worse. For three years I tried to free him. I spent money, I begged and pleaded with powerful men. I slept with those men whom I thought could free my father. It was my duty.

"My father was a special prisoner, a corrupt tool of the imperialists, the Viet Cong said. They wanted him alive, to parade him from town to town. He was an example of communism triumphing over capitalism. They kept him in work camps and once when I went to visit him at one, I managed to slip him a knife so that he could commit *seppuku.*

"The knife was found before he could use it. To teach him a lesson, the Cong cut off one of my father's hands. After that I refused to give him any more weapons. I was also searched very carefully after that. By men." *To remember was to suffer twice.* She looked away in agony.

She said, "Duty is never easy. Still, it must be done. For three years the Viet Cong led me to believe that one day my father might be freed. And then, the last visit. They made me watch." She blinked tears from her eyes. "A samurai fears only two kinds of death. Beheading and crucifixion. They knew this. The animals who held him prisoner knew this. So they made me watch while they beheaded him. They knew it would mean pain for him in the next world as well. But still they did it. Tell me, Manny, who is to pay for the filthy and obscene way my father died?"

He said, "I don't know."

"I know. And my father's friends in the *Jinrai Butai,* they knew as well. They were not fanatics, as you Americans tried to make them out to be. They were patriots, with a love for Japan that was so strong that they were willing to die for her. When your people sacrifice their lives for America, they are called heroes. When my people do it for our country, we are called insane."

Decker said, "No two people see the same world."

Her smile was bitter. "Thank you. Now let me finish telling you about my father's friends. They are men of strong loyalty, honor, men with a clear idea of duty. They are committed to one another. They are true to the highest ideals of justice and bravery, words which are meaningless in your society, which ignores them in favor of a freedom that has made your people slaves to everything that can destroy you.

"My father's friends did not force me to do anything. They simply reminded me that I was samurai. I had never forgotten it. They guided my life. They did not take it over, they simply guided it. They saw that my father's money came to me, money from banks in Tokyo, Hong Kong, Macao, Switzerland. Money and diamonds. I was rich and would never have to work again if I did not want to. But I would always have to live with myself and when I died I would have to face my mother and father and sister with my actions.

"The men of the *Jinrai Butai* had been frightened when they first joined the squadron in 1945. They did not know what to expect. It was my father who gave them courage, lifted their spirits, made them work hard in order to forget their fears. He led them in daily practice of the martial arts. He wrote songs for them and led the singing. He made them write letters home to their parents and he saw to it that the parents of those who had died received personal effects and a final letter from the commander or my father praising the dead boy. Those who survived and those who died well both owed him much."

Michi rose from the couch. "And they paid that debt by helping me. For three years they supervised my training. I learned to fight. And I learned to face death. I trained in secret dojos. I learned that it was my hand that must reach out for justice to my family, not theirs. It was my duty, not theirs.

"There were nights when I practiced karate in front of tombs. We believe that the spirits of the dead will come out of the tomb, enter our bodies and make us strong." She touched her thigh. "I strengthened my legs and my arms by training in water. It is good for the legs."

She began pacing. "Three years training my body and my mind. And then there were other preparations. A business had to be set up, one that I understood and could function in. One that allowed me to travel, to handle large amounts of money. Money is my protection. It allows me to be alone. This year, when I was ready, when enough information had been collected on the men who had turned my father over to the Viet Cong, I went to America to seek justice. Not revenge, Manny. Justice."

He said, "You tried to draw me closer. The *fugu*, the poisoned fish. You had me watch your apartment. You wanted me to become a part of what you were doing."

"My father's friends did not approve of my loving you. But I told them I had to see you, that I must see you. We could not, you and I, live in the same city without sooner or later meeting."

"*Giri* versus *ninjo*. Duty versus feeling."

"Yes. I sometimes found it confusing. Can you understand?"

"I don't know if I want to. Understanding means closing my eyes to the fact that you've killed two men and plan to kill two more. Three, if you ever get around to Ruttencutter. A cop's duty is to prevent that kind of thing. I'll tell you this: stay the hell away from Robbie Ambrose. We're checking him out now. He's a mass murderer, a head case who's raped and murdered thirty women. Don't tell me about your training. When it comes to Robbie you're fighting an animal, a very sick animal."

"Fear will not prevent me from facing him."

She saw his nose flare with anger. "That's another thing," he said. "That remark about being true to something. I know it was goddamn well aimed at me and I didn't like it. I'm committed to karate, to being a good cop, to . . ."

She waited for him to say committed to her, but he didn't.

"You are very good at karate, Manny. I have told you so many times. But your fear of one man—"

"I don't want to hear it. Just lay off that, okay?"

"Robbie Ambrose is not better than you. He uses your fear against you. If you—"

He slapped her face, snapping her head to the right and marking her skin with the imprint of his palm. He whispered, "Karate's all I have in this fucking world. Don't you ever tell me I'm afraid of Robbie Ambrose. I don't want to hear it."

Michi, her hands on the spot where Decker had struck her, said, "Please forgive me. I did not know that you would be so hurt by Dorian. I did not know how much you loved me. Oh, Manny." She wept and held her arms out to him, but he backed away.

She saw it in his face. The guilt and shame he felt for striking her overwhelmed him. "I've got to get some air," he said. "Walk around. Get my head straight. I'm sorry, really sorry. Didn't mean to do that."

He turned and hurried to the door.

He left before Michi could tell him that the blow did not matter, that she had endured infinitely worse over the past six years, that it was she who had hurt him, a hurt she now regretted more than anything she had ever done.

29

Michi stood in the doorway of her suite and willed Manny to return. But the elevator doors closed behind him and she heard the old car make its creaking way down to the lobby. She watched the elevator's indicator light show that he had reached the lobby. Had his love for her now turned to hate? For the first time she realized that being true to herself inevitably meant being false to Manny.

Suddenly the elevator light blinked and shifted right. The elevator was returning. Michi's heart began to pound so fast that she found it difficult to breathe. Manny. He was coming back to her. *He did love her.* The indicator light stopped at her floor and the elevator doors slid open.

Two Vietnamese waiters, boyish and slim in white jackets, stepped from the elevator with Michi's dinner order. One pushed a room-service trolley laden with covered food tins, clean plates, gleaming cutlery and a single yellow rose in a miniature blue Limoges vase. The other cradled an ice bucket containing a bottle of champagne in one arm and carried a carafe of red wine in his free hand. When they reached Michi both waiters nodded. "*Bon soir, madame.*"

Bitterly disappointed, Michi kept her eyes on the elevator. "*Bon soir.*" She stepped aside to allow them to enter her suite.

When the waiters had gone she sat alone at a wall table under a copy of the famed tapestry *The Lady and the Unicorn,* and read the card that had come with the champagne. It was a French diamond dealer, who had enclosed his home telephone number and his best wishes for an enjoyable stay in Paris. When Michi's eyes, hot with tears, could no longer focus she shoved the ice bucket to the floor, sending crushed ice flying across the rug and the opened bottle of champagne rolling to a stop near a stuffed chair. She tore the card into shreds and threw it aside, then swept the food, dishes and cutlery from the table.

Tired of being alone, of being afraid, of having to live with being a samurai and frightened that she had lost Manny forever, Michi dropped her head to the bare table and wept. Which was worse: the pain of love or having missed that pain? She had no answer.

Decker walked along the dark, deserted rue de Rivoli, the nineteenth-century arcade street of cafes, bookshops and deluxe hotels. Michi's hotel was more than two miles behind him. He had walked down the broad, lovely Champs Élysées and past Rond-Point park, where Parisians traditionally romped with their children. He stopped to watch the night changing of the guard at the Palais de l'Élysée, official residence of the president of France. But Decker had no idea where he was heading. Didn't care. He was calmer now, thank God. And feeling like shit for having struck Michi.

On the other side of the street night watchmen in battered kepis and baggy uniforms slammed and locked the tall, gilded gates to the Tuileries.

Now he stopped in front of a corner cafe that was closing for the night. Inside, a rotund, red-faced Frenchwoman, with raisins for eyes, mopped the floor, while outside a coal black Senegalese stacked wicker chairs on top of tables.

Without waiting for Decker to speak, the Frenchwoman stopped mopping to point to a sign hanging on the door. *Fermé*. Closed.

He turned and looked back in the direction he had just come from. He was wrong. Michi was right. No two people see the same world. She had her duty, her truth, and Decker had no business forcing his view on her. She hadn't forced hers on him. She had told the truth about herself, then given him a choice. Somehow he sensed that he had made the wrong one. Or perhaps hadn't chosen at all, which was just as bad. He had to make it up to her. Now. Tonight. Being apart six years was long enough.

Sure, he was jealous of Dorian. No getting around it. But Michi had said she never loved Dorian, and whatever else she was Michi was not a liar. Besides, she had killed Dorian.

Decker grinned in spite of himself. Throwing somebody out the window was one hell of a way to show you loved him. Decker loved Michi, plain and simple. And he would despise anybody who threatened that love. No wonder he had blown his cool. No wonder he had hit her. Jesus, he wished he hadn't.

He had two choices. Turn her in. Or leave her alone. His mind considered a third choice. Join her. Could he do that? Did he love her enough to become an accessory to murder? He didn't know. But first, he had to go back to the hotel and apologize. Talk some more. Work it out.

He was sure of one thing: he wouldn't turn Michi in. He'd take his chances on being an accessory after the fact. Whoever caught him would have to prove he knew about her plans in advance, and proving anything these days was tough. Look how hard it was to prove that Robbie Ambrose was a murderer.

Before coming to Paris Decker had said to LeClair, "Robbie Ambrose. That's the name Dorian was about to give you before he died."

"You sure?"

"That's why I ran out of here the day Dorian mentioned it. My partner and I are working on making a case against him. As you know, the three of us were in Vietnam at the same time. Dorian, Robbie and me. Over there the word was that Robbie was a *double veteran,* one of those guys who raped Vietnamese women, then killed them right afterward. Sick bastards, obviously. My partner's doing most of the work on this thing. We've got something started, but it's not enough to go into court with."

"I see. Well, well. And you're sure about the name?"

"I'm sure."

LeClair said, "This little vacation, where are you taking yourself off to?"

"No place special." Let word on the trip to Paris come out later. Decker wasn't going to advertise. He braced himself for LeClair's refusal. It never came.

"Bon voyage, my man. Touch base with you when you return."

Decker was shocked. He was almost shocked enough to

thank LeClair. Instead he lifted a hand in farewell and left the office.

Now Decker stepped from the arcades on rue de Rivoli and flagged down a taxi. He was going back to the hotel. Back to Michi. *Giri.* Can't live without it. Sooner or later everybody's got to stand up and be counted. He remembered her face, her disappointment when he had not committed himself to her.

He felt sick with guilt, but he'd see her and make it right. She would be pleased when he told her he would stand by her no matter what. Time for Decker to be true to the only woman he had ever loved.

In the cab he told the driver, "Hotel Richelieu," and added, "hit it. I'm in a hurry."

The driver stared at Decker uncomprehendingly, then turned back to the wheel.

Apparently he'd understood some of what Decker had said. The car took off, jumping a red light and rushing Manny back to Michi.

At the Hotel Richelieu, Robbie Ambrose stepped from an elevator with a folded newspaper under one arm and an attaché case in his other hand. The case contained two manila envelopes for Dieter, along with Robbie's passport and a copy of the rules for the January *suibin* tournament. The *suibin* meant point fighting again, but there would probably be some contact and Robbie wanted to know just how far he could go without getting disqualified. Full contact was a lot more popular in America and the Far East than anywhere else.

Still, winning the *suibin* trophy would mark Robbie as the best fighting man in the world and that's what he wanted. To win.

Tonight he wore an expensive leather jacket belted at the waist and a cap and gloves made of gray suede. He wore dark glasses and there was cotton in his cheeks to alter the shape of his face. Not that anyone even noticed him. A maid clutching a pillow and blanket knocked on a hotel-room door, ignoring Robbie as he walked behind her. When the door opened and the maid stepped inside, Robbie sprinted to a fire exit, through the door and down two flights to the floor where Michelle Asama had booked a suite. Dieter's information had better be good. If this was the wrong room it was going to be Dieter's ass.

On Michelle Asama's floor he dropped the newspaper, cracked the fire-exit door and watched two Vietnamese waiters walk past him toward the elevator. Robbie closed the door and leaned his back against it. He brought the heel of one gloved hand to his lips, peeled back the glove, letting the amphetamines drop into his mouth. He swallowed. And began to feel one with the god of war.

Turning, he cracked the door once more. His breathing had slowed down and his senses were exquisitely sharp. Strength filled his every muscle and power poured into his every nerve. After six years he was about to catch himself a ghost. A ghost who endangered his friend Sparrowhawk.

Music and the sound of a woman laughing filtered out of the room directly opposite the fire exit. Robbie closed his eyes, hearing the sensual laugh again and shivering as though he had just been kissed on the back of his neck. The drugs were taking effect.

Time to take care of business. Go for it.

He eased into the hall, looked both ways, saw no one. Soundlessly he approached Michelle Asama's door. *Give no warning. Wait for the opening and seize it.*

At the door he brought the attaché case up to cover his face. *Hachiman Dai-Bosatsu.* Great Bodhisatva, god of war. Sword forged by the four elements—metal and water, wood and fire.

Robbie knocked on the door. Gently.

He was ready to lie, to say that he was delivering flowers or something. But Robbie was surprised. He didn't have to lie at all.

He heard footsteps running toward the door. His instincts, sharpened by drugs and the power of *Hachiman,* said the door would open without question.

It did. It opened wide.

A tearful, smiling Michi said, "Manny—"

Robbie tossed the attaché case in her face and kicked her in the stomach, driving her back into the room. Inside, he slammed the door behind him and charged, giving Michi no chance to recover. Michi, doubled over and in pain and fighting for air, fought back bravely. When Robbie was almost on her she kicked low, aiming for his ankles with her clogs.

He was quick. He stopped, then sidestepped in the same motion. Her kick scraped his ankle, removing a little skin. The pain was slight, no more. It never even slowed him down.

Gasping for breath and dizzy, Michi held her stomach and backed away from her attacker. A bright-eyed and intense Robbie stalked her. With his right hand he faked a backfist to her head and when her right hand came up in defense, her right rib cage was exposed. Robbie aimed a roundhouse kick there with his left leg. A weakened Michi acted instinctively. Her right hand dropped down to block the kick, but she had little strength and wearing clogs left her off balance. Her block was feeble and ineffective.

Robbie's kick, strong, vicious, went through her block and his foot smashed into her rib cage, knocking Michi to the floor and knotting her face with pain. He was a split second away from kicking her in the face when he remembered. Her face had to be unmarked. Instead, Robbie kicked the fallen woman in the stomach twice, folding her in half. She made a tiny sound and her mouth was as wide as it could get, but the fight was gone from her. She clawed at the rug with the nails of one hand and tried to move. She was sweating, barely conscious and no more danger to him now.

He picked Michi up in his arms, smelled her perfume and felt her warmth against his chest and was happy. He carried her to the bedroom, laid her down on the bed as gently as possible, then returned to the living room. There was scattered food over half the room and dark spots on the rug that were melted ice and spilled champagne. Robbie had hoped to find a letter opener. Instead he found something better. A steak knife.

Back in the bedroom he lay the steak knife on an end table, then carefully opened Michi's kimono and looked at her naked body. Beautiful. This one was special. She had gotten away from him six years ago, driven away into the night. She moaned, opened her eyes and with all of the strength she had left tried to lift her head from the pillow. Robbie had rarely been as sexually aroused as he was now.

Michi knew she was going to die. But she willed herself to fight, not to fall back and close her eyes. Not yet.

Robbie was in love with her. He loved them all, each of the women he had held in his arms and then killed. But this one was special, she had been a fighter, someone worthy of respect and of all the love he had. Robbie bent down to kiss her.

Michi fought to lift her shoulders from the bed. The pain filled her insides; it expanded, retracted, then expanded once more, all but blinding her in its intensity. She moved closer to her murderer, aware of what he wanted to do. When his lips touched hers Michi returned his kiss, first licking his lips with her tongue, tantalizing him, drawing him near. Robbie relaxed, knowing now that she loved him as much as he loved her. Her tongue gently probed the inside of his mouth, darting between his teeth and lips and he gladly gave himself, opening his mouth, seeking her tongue, her soul.

The pain so shocked Robbie, who was leaning over Michi's body, that he kicked out with one leg and knocked the end table to the floor. Bitch. Fucking bitch.

Michi had bitten down hard, sending her teeth deep into the flesh of the bottom lip and tongue. With the nails of her right hand she raked the left side of his face, leaving blood-red streaks from cheekbone to jaw. She clung to his flesh with her waning energy. She tasted his blood in her mouth. And rejoiced.

Robbie punched her in the breast twice, snapping, whiplike blows and Michi fell back on the bed. There was blood on her mouth, jaw, teeth and her chest rapidly rose and fell with her tortured attempts to breathe. Her eyes were on fire with hatred for him. Of all the women he had killed, this one was the first to show no fear.

Robbie quickly reached down, pulled a handful of tissues from a box on the floor and pressed them to his bleeding mouth. He looked down at his jacket. There was blood there, too, but it was leather and could be wiped off in seconds. Using his free hand he took more tissues from the box and used them to wipe his blood from Michi's mouth. She tried to push him away, but was too weak.

He forced his fingers between her lips and as best he could wiped his blood from her teeth. When she tried to bite him

Robbie simply pinched her nostrils shut, cutting off what little air she was able to take in. She opened her mouth wider to breathe and then he was able to wipe her teeth.

After placing the tissues used on Michi in his jacket pocket, Robbie, a wad of tissues still pressed against his mouth, took more tissues from the box and pressed them against the scratches on his face. They stung. If she had scarred his face she deserved to die.

He walked into the living room, shifted the tissues from his cheek to the sodden lump in front of his mouth and picked up the champagne bottle from the floor. He held it up to the light. A third of the bottle left. Robbie returned to the bedroom, where he leaned over Michi and poured the rest of the champagne into her mouth. That should wash out the rest of his blood.

He laid the bottle down on the floor, and then he stood up and unbuckled his pants. He hadn't planned to fuck her. But she had bitten him, scratched him. Nothing on earth could prevent him from taking her now.

It was quick. He could hardly hold himself back. It was over in seconds and during that time he had kept the tissues pressed against his pained mouth. Once, he had almost dropped them. The pleasure he had found in her had been so keen the tissues had almost slipped from his hand.

Finished, he rose, zipped up his pants and then, because he could only use one hand, awkwardly put the kimono back on the semiconscious Michi. Oh, he did love this one.

Michi opened her eyes. "Manny . . . Manny."

Robbie shook his head. Not Manny. He took Michi's right hand, wrapped it around the steak knife, then placed the cutting edge against the left side of her throat. *Hachiman*. Robbie cut the artery. Michi stiffened. Blood spurted onto her kimono and the white bedspread beneath her. Robbie dropped her hand. Now her prints were on the knife.

The rest was easy. Robbie placed the blade against the right side of her throat and cut deeply. Michi whimpered, tried to rise. Robbie placed a gloved fist on her chest and kept her in place on her back. For a minute or so he watched the blood flow from both sides of her neck. Then he dropped the knife beside the bed and changed tissues before walking to Michi's closet. Here he removed a belt from her closet, returned to the bed and looped the belt around her ankles.

When Robbie had smoothed out her kimono he looked down at the dying woman, relieved. Nothing to be afraid of anymore.

He walked from the bedroom, careful to avoid stepping on plates and glasses. It never occurred to him to question why they were on the floor. Such thoughts were a deviation from his purpose, a lessening of his concentration. At the front door he cracked it, saw an empty hallway, then stepped outside, closing the door behind him.

He heard the elevator. Danger. Robbie ran toward the fire exit, pulled open the door and leaped into the dark stairwell. He closed the door behind him, but not all the way. Peeking through the crack he saw, well, what do you know. Decker.

The detective walked by Robbie, stopped in front of Michelle Asama's door and knocked. Robbie grinned. His mouth hurt, but he had to grin because everything had worked out so well and again he had come out on top against Decker. Turning, Robbie tiptoed gracefully down the stairs, tissues pressed against his mouth and feeling damn good.

30

At Kennedy International Airport Ellen Spiceland showed her badge and ID to a uniformed security guard, who signaled with a nod of his head that she could pass him and continue on to the customs clearance area. She hated airports.

The only reason she was out here this afternoon, when she should be Christmas shopping, was to warn Manny.

On the passenger side of the customs area Ellen showed her badge and ID again, this time to a uniformed black woman.

There were three lines of passengers waiting to be examined by customs inspectors. Ellen walked toward them. Shit, her feet hurt.

She thought about how much Manny had suffered since his girl friend's death ten days ago. Ellen stood on tiptoe, bobbed and weaved and saw him in the crowd. She waved. He didn't notice her. She called his name and after the third time he looked up. The sight of him made Ellen cover her mouth in horror. Manny looked dreadful.

She went to the head of his line and waited. He had lost weight and there were dark circles under his bloodshot eyes. He seemed to be in a stupor. His luggage, a single suitcase, was examined and his customs declaration slip stamped. When he closed the suitcase she rushed to him. He put an arm around her shoulders.

Ellen leaned back to wipe tears from her eyes with a gloved forefinger. "Boy, do you look awful. Oh, Manny." She hugged him again, then, taking his arm, she guided him out of the almost empty terminal and out onto the sidewalk. She buttoned his overcoat, adjusted his hat, then tenderly touched his unshaven cheek. "Didn't they feed you in Japan?"

He tried to smile, then abandoned the effort. "They fed me. Took real good care of me."

"Doesn't look it."

A red-capped dispatcher signaled a cab to stop in front of them. Ellen took Decker's elbow, guided him into the cab and watched the driver put the suitcase into the trunk. As the cab pulled away from the terminal she took his hand and squeezed it.

"Don't have to talk if you don't want to. Something I came out here to tell you, because I didn't want you getting hit in the face with it at the precinct."

He looked at her. And waited. Ellen fought back the tears. "LeClair's dropped you from the task force."

Decker grunted. He didn't seem surprised.

Ellen said, "It gets worse. All the information we had on this *kaishaku* thing? LeClair ordered us to turn it over to him. List of tournaments, dates of murders, background on Robbie Ambrose. LeClair's got it now."

She steeled herself for Decker's reaction. There was none. She waited a few seconds longer.

"Heard about it in Tokyo," Decker said. "Guy named Shigeji Shina told me. He's in Japanese military intelligence."

"Friend of yours?" Ellen was impressed.

"Friend of Michi's. Served with her father in World War Two. In Tokyo he kind of took me over. I stayed with him. He took me to the Shinto temple for the burial ceremony, explained the ritual to me, introduced me to people."

"And he knew about LeClair, about what he had done to you?"

"Mr. Shina knows a lot of things. He's a very smart man."

There was something odd about Manny. On one hand he looked like hell with the lid off. On the other hand he seemed completely in control. It was very *strange*.

Ellen said, "You should take some time off. Rest. Eat. Get yourself together. You've got vacation time coming."

"I'll be taking some time off next month. I understand Michi's death made the papers here."

"Yes. The press called her Michelle Asama." She hesitated before saying, "They claimed she might have committed suicide because she was grieving over Dorian Raymond."

Decker looked out the window to his left. "Doesn't matter what they say. Maybe it's better this way. What they don't know can't hurt her. Did you check on Robbie Ambrose like I asked?"

"Did more than that. I just happened to mention to a couple of the guys that I needed help, that you needed a favor. I wanted to know about Robbie Ambrose. Whether or not he was out of the country last week, whether or not he had scratches on his face. The guys know LeClair's a bastard and that he was probably fucking you over when he dropped you from the task force. They came through for us. And it wasn't easy. They all put themselves on the line with this one because of what LeClair said."

Decker looked at her.

Ellen said, "LeClair's left word that you and me and everybody else are to stay away from Robbie Ambrose. From now on Mr. Ambrose belongs to Mr. Charles LeClair, to do with as he pleases."

"Means LeClair's working him or plans to. He's going to hold the murders over Robbie's head to get him to turn informant on MSC and Dent and that crowd."

"It's shitty, if you ask me. Letting a guy who's killed thirty women walk around loose because he can help your career."

"It's been done before. You know that. I can't count the times I've looked away as a D.A. or a prosecutor has made deals with killers for information."

Ellen shook her head. "Still, Robbie Ambrose is one man I'd like to see in his grave."

Decker scratched the stubble on his chin. "You said the guys helped out."

"Did they ever. And on their own time, knowing that LeClair would kill them if he ever found out. First we checked with Interpol and U.S. Customs. Robbie Ambrose went to Paris last week, supposedly as an MSC courier. He made a delivery to a private security agency there run by a man named Dieter Rainer, ex-Swiss army officer. Day after the delivery Mr. Ambrose returned to New York. Very next day he flew down to New Orleans for a karate match. Won, as usual. So far there's been no record of a woman raped and murdered down there then, but we're still checking."

As the cab slowed down in front of a toll booth Ellen looked at Decker. For the first time since she had picked him up at the airport she saw a flicker of emotion cross his face. His jaw tightened and he began to take deep breaths. When he spoke his voice was harsh. "He didn't have to kill anybody in New Orleans. He was covered for this fight before he arrived. Any marks on him?"

She smiled. "That was my department. When he flew back from New Orleans I was waiting for him at Kennedy. From a safe distance, of course. The man's got marks, all right. Scratches on his left cheek and something wrong with his mouth, stitches in the lip or something. The stitches could have come from the fight, but the scratches didn't. Those guys wear gloves."

"Stitches didn't come from the fight," said Decker. "French pathologists listed Michi as a suicide. They found traces of alcohol in her system. Not a lot, but some. Food scattered all over the living room as though she had lost her temper and had a fit of some kind. Evidence of recent sexual intercourse indicated she might have killed herself after a lovers' quarrel. They had no explanation for her internal injuries. Someone said maybe she had hurt herself throwing all that food around."

Ellen said, "And that was it? They didn't push it any further than that?"

Decker shoved his hands in his overcoat pockets and leaned back in the seat. "This Shigeji Shina I mentioned. Smart guy. Some kind of brain. He has this friend, guy named Ishino, who's a diamond dealer in Amsterdam. Both Shina and Ishino served with Michi's father in the war."

"You keep calling her Michi. The papers called her Michelle. Is Michi short for Michelle?"

Decker shrugged. "It's not important. Anyway, this Ishino, he has a private plane. He and Shina talked the French into giving us Michi's body and we flew her back to Tokyo on Ishino's plane. In Tokyo Shina came up with his own pathologist. And this guy came up with a lot more information on Michi's death than the French pathologist did. For one thing, Michi's injuries weren't caused by a fall. They were karate injuries. The Japanese were quick to see that. For another thing, I knew that Michi was in no frame of mind to make love to anybody. She was raped."

Ellen whispered, "Robbie Ambrose. Shit, Manny, I'm so sorry."

Decker said, "Whoever kicked her in the stomach and ribs hurt her very badly. Probably caught her off guard. He was strong, very strong. My guess is she opened the door thinking it was me and he just wiped her out. And there's more." He continued in a monotone. "Shina's pathologist found bits of human skin between Michi's teeth and under her fingernails. Also found blood samples under her nails that weren't Michi's blood type." He looked at Ellen. "She fought him, fought him until she died."

Ellen touched Decker's thigh. "Manny, we've got him. If his blood type matches the blood found under Michi's nails, if his skin matches the skin found in her mouth, then we have that son of a bitch."

"LeClair will protect him."

"No."

"He will."

Ellen shifted in her seat to face Decker. "Manny, we are

talking about an animal, somebody who kills women because he enjoys it."

"We're talking about the real world, about law enforcement as it is. You don't make cases without informants and LeClair's only after one case right now and that's MSC and Dent. Sending Robbie to prison won't bring LeClair the glory he's after. That's why he dumped me from the task force. He doesn't want me anywhere near Robbie. Robbie's not going to prison until LeClair's finished with him, if he goes at all."

"Wait a minute. Wait a minute. Your friend Shina. We can get that report from his pathologist."

Decker shook his head. "No. Shina won't release it."

Ellen couldn't believe his ears. "He what?"

"Won't release it. No one in this country knows about it, except you and me, and I don't want you to say anything."

"I can't believe what I'm hearing. You've got a chance to stop Robbie Ambrose and—"

"What do you think LeClair would do with that report?"

Ellen waited.

"He'd sit on it," Decker said. "He'd claim his investigation of MSC and Dent came first."

There were tears in Ellen's eyes. "It's not right. It's just not right. I know it's the real world, but it sucks. It goddamn sucks."

Decker took her hand. "I want you to do a few things for me. You listening?"

"Yeah, I'm listening."

"Okay. We've got one stop to make before we get to my place. We've got to stop at Kanai's office. I've got a form here, which I want you to give him. He's expecting it. Tell him I'll get the check to him as soon as possible."

"Form?"

"It's for a karate tournament to be held in Paris next month."

She withdrew from him. "Are you out of your mind? You need time to rest, to get yourself together."

"I know what I'm doing. Just give the form to Kanai. Shina said Kanai can process it overnight because he's one of the organizers. It's all right, Ellen, believe me."

As the taxi rolled onto the Triborough Bridge, Manhattan's skyline loomed closer.

And Manny turned to Ellen with tears in his eyes. In a choked voice, he struggled to get the words out.

"We argued. I walked out. Shit, Ellen. If only I'd been there, if . . ."

He stopped, swallowed, struggled to regain control. Then, "She said you had to be true to something. She was. To her family and as much as she could be, she was true to me."

He brushed tears from his eyes with gloved fingertips. "Too late for me to take it back. What I said, what I did. I want your word. Nothing about the report. Nothing. Please."

She nodded. But she still did not really understand.

Decker said, "Michi said you have to be ready to die, then it's all right. You're safe then. I understand now what she meant. If I'd been in the room when he came . . ."

He sighed. "We'll both be in Paris next month. The two of us."

"Who? Who's the two of us?"

"Robbie Ambrose and me."

He reached inside his jacket and brought out what seemed to Ellen to be a folded handkerchief. He unfolded it and spread it across his knees.

"What's that?" she asked.

"A *hachimaki*. Japanese headband. Used to belong to Michi's father. He passed it on to her. Shina gave it to me. You only wear it on special occasions."

"What special occasions?"

"When you're going to war."

Ellen drew back in fear as Decker gave a small, cold smile. In his eyes, she saw death.

His head flopped back on the seat. "Got to be true to something in this world." Seconds later he was asleep.

31

Charles LeClair dropped a pile of newspapers on a card table, then sat down on a metal folding chair. He sighed and looked around the plain and mostly unfurnished apartment in a West Sixty-fourth Street Manhattan hotel, an apartment his office used as a safe house. He linked his fingers across a growing paunch, a gesture of smug satisfaction.

The two FBI agents who had accompanied him to this secret meeting were less joyous. They stood with their backs against the front door and wondered if the rumor about the smell outside in the hall was true. A Haitian couple in a nearby apartment had supposedly kept a dead son laid out in their living room for a month, while they attempted to bring him back to life with nightly voodoo ceremonies. The stench now permeated the entire floor.

But no smell could possibly spoil this day for LeClair, who placed the flat of one hand on the newspaper and said, "Today's afternoons. Big follow-up in tomorrow morning's papers. Still breaking big on all three television networks three days after the press conference."

He pushed the pile of newspapers toward Robbie Ambrose, sitting across from him. "Go on. Take a look."

Robbie never looked up from what he was doing. He continued to clip his nails and trim his cuticles, as though he were alone in the room.

LeClair said, "Yes. Well, let's see what we have." He took a paper from the pile. "Some more stuff about the task force charging Dent with accepting mob payoffs and rumors about Dent being asked to resign. I think I have a few quotes in this one somewhere. I know my picture's in the carry-over, middle of the paper."

He dropped that paper and picked up two more. " 'Dent

Declares His Innocence.' Chuckle-lacious, as my grandmother used to say. 'Dent says he will not resign. Vows smear tactics will not work.' " LeClair tossed the papers onto the table. "Innocent. Shit. Dent would steal sand from the beach if he thought nobody was looking. Caught him with his hand in the cookie jar this time. Old congressmen never die, they just steal away."

One FBI agent snickered. The other grinned. Robbie, eye on his thumbnail, filed it a bit more before using the tip of the file to push back the cuticle. "If you're finished, Mr. Prosecutor, I'd like to get out of here. Place stinks. Like to get in some running before reporting back to work."

LeClair drummed on the newspaper with his fingertips. "Couple things I'd like to touch base with you on first. I mean that's what a relationship is. Give and take on both sides."

Robbie put away his nail clippers. "Come on. Save that shit for somebody else. You want to throw my ass in jail, be my guest. Truth is, you ain't got that much of a case against me and you know it. No witnesses, no motive. Okay, so I talked to you guys some. I only did that to get you off my back, is all."

A grinning LeClair shrugged. "What can I say. You're right. When you're right, you're right. Nothing but circumstantial evidence and not too much of that." He leaned forward. "Just enough of it to hold you for questioning in a dozen cities. That's a lot of harassment, Robbie, my boy. Could last, oh, a few years."

Robbie returned the grin. "Man, you don't scare me. None of you clowns scare me. You think I didn't learn nothing working for MSC and Major Sparrowhawk all these years? Information. That's what matters. You want certain information from me more than you want to nail me for maybe, *maybe* killing a bunch of women. Hey, look, how come I'm not up on charges or anything? I mean cut the shit. Go play your games with somebody else."

LeClair leaned back in his chair. Shrewd. The lady killer may not be an intellectual, but he's definitely shrewd. He had something LeClair wanted and the prosecutor had to pay, that's all there was to it. In law enforcement you were only as successful as your informants.

Three days ago a Manhattan press conference announcing that formal charges were being brought against Senator Terry Dent had drawn the largest crowd of reporters since ABSCAM. Justice Department officials had flown in from Washington to pat LeClair on the back and hang around long enough to get their share of the publicity before flying back. LeClair, however, had been the Justice Department spokesman. He had been interviewed by the New York *Times, Time* magazine and three television networks. Thanks to Robbie Ambrose, LeClair had found the path to the top of the mountain.

And thanks, too, to Decker and his partner for putting together what little case there was on Mr. Robbie. LeClair had taken the case away from them, done it behind Decker's back, but rank did have its privileges. For the moment Robbie's alleged killings were on hold. First, Mr. Robbie had some work to do for the task force.

Was the security guard guilty? LeClair thought, probably. Mr. Robbie was not quite right in the head, for one thing. And for another there was no problem placing him in a city where a woman had been killed by someone who knew how to use his hands real well. It took a cop like Decker, LeClair had to admit, someone familiar with karate, to get this far in the case.

And speaking of Decker, LeClair had expected to receive more in the way of protests from him after being dropped from the task force and having the case snatched from under his nose. But so far there hadn't been a peep out of Mr. Manfred. Still grieving over the death of his lady in Paris. Some kind of a mess, thought LeClair.

LeClair would wait a while, give Decker time to get over his girl friend's death, then find a way to punish him. Make him look bad for having been dropped from the task force. It was always a good idea to leave your mark on the people you left behind; punishing a man made him, not you, appear to be the guilty party. A cop accused was a cop convicted.

LeClair watched Robbie touch the fresh scars on the side of his face, then move his fingertips to a lip wound. When the two men had first met just days ago the lip wound had contained several stitches. The stitches were gone now.

LeClair said, "I think we'd better talk about your future.

You still believe nobody at MSC knows you're working with us?"

"Not unless you told them. You grabbed me in the middle of the night at my apartment, dragged me over here and gave me some shit about having killed women I don't even know."

"Don't have to know them to kill them."

"Then you threaten me with prison or a nut house unless I cooperate with you."

"And you did cooperate, Robbie."

"Just to get you off my back, is all. Doesn't mean I'm guilty."

"Means you're still on the street, out here practicing your karate chops or whatever they're called. But it's the future I'm concerned with. Your future is with us, as a full-time informant under our protection."

Robbie leaped up, knocking the card table and newspapers to the floor. One of the FBI agents hurriedly began to unbutton his overcoat to get at his gun. "That's it," yelled a wild-eyed Robbie. "I'm getting the fuck outta here and if your friends over there try to stop me, they're gonna get hurt. You think I'm scared of guns?"

He pointed to the agent with his hand inside his overcoat. "I'll pull his head through the door before he can fucking blink. Want to see me do it?"

A calm LeClair said, "I believe you, Robbie." The prosecutor turned in his chair. "Lighten up," he said to the agents. "No problem. Robbie and I understand each other." He looked back at the security guard. "Robbie, just this one favor. Listen to this tape, that's all I ask. Do this for me, please."

A space cadet, thought LeClair. The man needs to be stroked and stroked and stroked. He won't give his candy to anyone but daddy and daddy is me. LeClair snapped his fingers. "Dominic?"

The agent who had been holding an attaché case walked over to the card table, set it upright and laid the case on top. Thumbing open the locks, he removed a small tape recorder, laid that on the table, then backed away.

LeClair said, "Have a seat, Robbie. This won't take long. One of the things you gave us was the location of three public telephone booths Sparrowhawk uses to talk to Molise's people. We've got taps on all three, same as we did with LoCicero. Remember that time last month when you were down in the Caymans and Decker took the call?"

Robbie frowned. "Yeah, but I didn't tell you nothing bad about the major and I ain't about to, either."

A smiling LeClair touched a finger to his lips, signaling for quiet. Then he pressed a button on the tape recorder, turned up the volume and leaned back in his chair, hands behind his head. The smile remained in place.

Clicks signaling the dialing of a phone. Three rings. Hang up. Dime returns. Dime dropped into pay phone. Clicks. Dialing. Phone picked up on first ring.

Gran Sasso said, "Yeah?"

"Sparrowhawk here. Received your message. What's the problem?"

"We've been talking, Alphonse and myself. And we have decided something."

"Which is?"

"Which is we very carefully looked over the charges against the senator. Took all the newspaper stories apart, listened to all the rumors, got some information from some of our people and we came to the conclusion that somebody we all knew gave up the senator. Somebody at this high-class organization you're supposed to be running for us."

"Preposterous. That's the same as accusing me and I don't like it."

"We thought about you, but we couldn't come up with a good motive. One reason we're talking like this instead of meeting face to face is that we're not too sure you don't have people watching you. Or somebody in your office reporting your moves to the feds."

Sparrowhawk was indignant. "Would you mind explaining yourself?"

"The Englishman wants explanations. Okay, Mr. Englishman. Somebody knew about Dent getting cash recently to buy that stock, the deal the Arizona senator's pushing. Somebody knew he's got points in the auditorium out on the island. Somebody knew that we put money in the senator's campaign through Delaware holding companies, through real estate companies. All of these things that somebody knew have to

do with how we move our money around. There's a big financial columnist on a certain New York paper, who we're paying to boost a certain stock for us. His name's being linked with the senator's."

"I don't see—"

"That's the point. You don't. And you should. We got two things here. The senator, who's important to us, he's in trouble. And too much is known about what we do with our money. How we change it over, who we give it to. See, Mr. Sparrowhawk, you're too close to this problem to give it the kind of attention it deserves. Me, I'm an old Italian who likes to sit and think about problems. Work them out in my head. So I'm saying that it looks to me like somebody very close to you gave up the senator. That's what I'm saying."

Sparrowhawk's voice was shrill. "Are you saying that my secretary—"

"You stupid man." Gran Sasso's tone was lethal. "You insult me. You talk to me like I'm some schoolboy who can be given a shiny rock and told it is a ruby and who will believe it. Do not ever treat me with such disrespect again, do you understand?"

"I understand."

"I am talking about your young friend, this Robbie fellow. He was the courier for certain things we did with our money. You chose him. He carried the stock money to the senator down in Washington and he carried the money to the newspaperman. He knew about the money going from the Caymans to the Delaware holding companies. Your young friend I'm talking about."

Sparrowhawk pleaded. "That boy's like a son to me. Don't ask me to harm him. I can't. I just can't."

"We got a problem here and it won't go away by itself. What I want from you is that you should help us make the problem go away."

"How?"

"Your young friend trusts you. You are the way to help us approach him."

Silence.

Then Sparrowhawk said, "Not approach. Kill. You want me to help you kill him."

"You got a nice house, nice job, nice family. I give you a

choice. You can have all those things or you can have nothing. Either you help us to deal with your young friend or we get somebody else to do your job. And we see you don't work in America no more. We see you don't stay in America. You come here with nothing, you leave with nothing."

Sparrowhawk's voice broke. "Don't ask me to do this. Don't. I beg you."

"You brought him to us. That makes you part of the problem. Now you become part of the solution or we solve it without you. And that means we don't need you for anything. *Let me tell you something. You think I don't have people at your office watching you?"*

"Spying on me? How dare you?"

"I know you. I know you better than you think I do. I know you sent your young friend to Paris and while he is there a woman dies."

Sparrowhawk spat the word out. "Bastard. You've bugged my office. Have you bugged my home as well?"

Silence. The tape whirled.

Then Gran Sasso said, "If you ever talk like that to me again I have you killed before the sun sets. Before the sun sets."

Silence.

Gran Sasso. "Maybe this all has something to do with Paulie, I don't know. But I find out. Believe me when I tell you I find out. Paulie is the one thing I ask you to do and I do not get any answer. I wonder why. I ask you to do that."

"It's not easy," said a chastened Sparrowhawk. "We're working on it."

"Working on it. For now you work on your young friend. Will you help us, yes or no?"

Robbie leaped from his chair, grabbed the tape recorder and hurled it across the room. An FBI agent took one step toward him, thought better of it and stopped.

LeClair, still in his seat, didn't look up. "The answer was yes."

Robbie began to sob. LeClair rose and patted him on the back. "Don't think too badly of him, Robbie. He's got a tough choice. The man tried. He didn't want to do it. But—" LeClair dropped his hand. "He's got a family to look after, a wife and daughter. Got to watch out for your women in this world."

Robbie gave the prosecutor a look that made him instinctively lean away. But LeClair recovered and continued stroking.

"I won't lie to you," the prosecutor said. "I need you. I've done a lot better with you than without you, that's for sure. You've got the power, dude, and I don't want to see you hurt."

LeClair touched his heart. An FBI agent looked down at the floor and shook his head. "Talking about in here," the prosecutor said. "In here where it really counts. I've been straight with you. No arrest, no public hearing, no incarceration. Guy like you has to be free."

Robbie sighed. "Free."

"Guy like you has to run outdoors, work out, be his own man. But to do that you have to stay alive. You should be in protective custody."

Like a petulant child, Robbie shook his head. "No way. I've seen what happens to guys in the federal witness program. They go crazy, or they end up with some shit life in some shit town or the mob finally catches up to them."

"Robbie, I'm on your side. I'm your friend, maybe your only friend. You heard the tape."

"Yeah, I heard the tape, but no custody and no prison. Especially no prison. Kill me now, but I ain't about to be cooped up. I got to fight. Got to go to Paris in January for the *suibin* tournament."

"Robbie, let's work this out. Custody's not what you think it is. Suppose, just suppose we were to set you up with your own dojo, your own karate club in another city. New name, all the money you need. No prison. How's that sound?"

"I want to fight in Paris. You let me do that and I'll cooperate with you all you want. I want to win the *suibin* and prove I'm the best in the world."

LeClair bit his lip. Give and take. "When's the fight?"

"Starts second week in January. Eliminations will run five, six days, then it's down to the finals. Two guys. One on one. Nothing like it. It's the fucking greatest."

LeClair turned his palms up. "You got a deal. Last fight. Then you and I really get down."

Robbie smiled a small grin of victory, despite his anguish. "I can deliver, don't worry. Can I go now?"

"Watch yourself. You heard the tape. They know. Sparrowhawk's on their side now, not yours."

"I'll be careful. I know they're coming, remember? They won't move until Sparrowhawk tries to set me up. That's how they work, you heard them. Long as he doesn't try anything, I'm safe."

LeClair clapped him on the shoulder. "Whatever you say. Helluva muscle you got there. You leave first. We'll give you a few minutes, then take off ourselves."

When the door had closed behind Robbie the two FBI agents looked at each other in disbelief.

LeClair looked at the tape recorder. "Pick that thing up and let's get out of here."

"Really letting him go to Paris?"

"Have to. He ain't the type you can scare. Probably send a couple of men with him. After Paris he should be somewhat easier to get along with. For a time anyway."

In the elevator going down to the lobby LeClair thought about the possibility of Robbie killing another woman prior to the Paris tournament. That was the pattern, according to Decker. The prosecutor looked at the newspapers he held under his arm, the newspapers which told the world about Charles Fletcher Maceo LeClair bringing down Senator Terence J. Dent.

By the time the elevator reached the lobby, LeClair had forgotten about the possibility of Robbie Ambrose killing again.

32

In the study of his Connecticut home Sparrowhawk swallowed the last of a gin and tonic, and, in a labored attempt to push himself from a deep leather chair, let the glass slip from his hand before collapsing back into the chair, his head rolling about on his shoulders. A worried Valerie Sparrowhawk knelt beside her father's chair. "Daddy, I think you've had enough to drink."

" 'I looked, and behold a pale horse: / and his name that sat on him was Death.' *Revelation.* Bloody world's full of revelations these days."

"It's getting late. Why don't you go to bed and get some sleep?"

He pointed a finger at her. "See here, young lady. I'm the parent around here." He looked at his watch, blinked and tried to focus. "Can't make out a damned thing. Did someone steal my watch? Bloody thieves in me own household. Probably that wretched, foul-smelling monkey of yours, Bixby or something."

"Boadicea. Daddy, why are you drinking like this?" She picked up his empty glass.

He looked at the beamed ceiling. "Pale horse. Death. Started back in bloody Saigon. Dorian, Robbie, Molise, myself. Decker, too. Mr. Decker and his ladylove, to be precise."

"Decker's that policeman you said is after you and your company."

"Ah, but he has yet to catch us." He looked sad. "Someone else has caught us. Robbie, Robbie, Robbie. What am I going to do about you, lad? What ever in this world am I going to do?"

Valerie looked away. "Robbie."

Sparrowhawk turned toward her. "You never told me why you don't fancy him."

Valerie got up off her knees. "Maybe I'd better go to the kitchen and give Mother a hand with dinner."

"I thought you said it was late."

She smiled. "I lied. To get you to stop drinking."

The telephone rang, both in his study and in another room. "Your mother will get it. I can't move. Worried about your old father, are you?"

She leaned over and kissed his silver hair. "You're the best father a girl could have."

"High praise from someone as demanding as you."

Unity Sparrowhawk appeared in the study doorway. "It's from Washington. Mr. Ruttencutter."

"Tell him I'll be there in a minute."

"Yes, love." She looked at her husband and smiled affectionately. No criticism, no questions. Thank God. He smiled back. And blew her a kiss.

Valerie said, "I'll see you at dinner. No more drinking, please?"

As she left, Sparrowhawk managed to stand and on shaky legs crossed the room to his desk, collapsed in a chair and reached for the receiver with both hands.

"I have it, Unity. You can hang up now, love." Then, "Hello, hello, hello. Mr. Ruttencutter, I presume. And to what do I owe this rather dubious honor?"

"You sound sloshed. I'm calling about three dead people. Paul Molise, Dorian Raymond and Michelle Asama."

"Listen, if you must call me at home don't waste my time with half-truths. Her name's not Michelle Asama and you damn well know it."

Ruttencutter cleared his throat. Never could run anything by Sparrowhawk. Ruttencutter, now head of an investigating team employed by a leading Washington law firm, had stayed in touch with the Englishman over the years, primarily by phone. He didn't mind. Sparrowhawk could be scary.

"I called because I've been asking myself questions about recent events, let us say."

"Dear me. Talking to ourselves, are we? Next you'll be hearing little voices in your ear."

"Whatever you do, don't breathe on anybody. Dorian Raymond, Paul Molise and now George Chihara's daughter. Tell you anything?"

"If you're referring to the events of six years ago, events which occurred one rather humid night in that godforsaken land, I've already made the connection. Who's been whispering in your ear?"

"My law firm represents some of the biggest Japanese companies doing business in this country. Far as connections go, I've got a bunch in Tokyo. I want to know how much further you think this thing is going to go."

Sparrowhawk threw back his head and laughed. "If you're worried about your arse, then I'd say forget it. Can't go much further. Chihara's daughter is the last and she's dead. Seems she is the only member of that family we overlooked that rather fateful night. With her no longer among the living, I think you can breathe a sigh of relief."

Ruttencutter did sigh. He sounded anything but relieved, however. "I sure as hell hope so. Tough enough doing business in this power-crazy town without having to worry about somebody creeping around behind me. Christ, I ought to get away more."

"If you say so."

"I have this country home in Maryland. Should get there more often than I do."

Sparrowhawk reached for a letter opener. Bloody bugger was boring him into paralysis. Ruttencutter didn't know what worry was. Try working for the wogs. Sparrowhawk said, "I believe my wife's summoning me to dinner. Thank you for calling."

"Look, you have my number. If you hear anything, anything I should know about, get on the horn, okay?"

"I'll be sure to keep in touch. *Ciao.*" Sparrowhawk smiled. And heard glass break in his kitchen, a window; outside the guard dogs barked, snarled, signaling the presence of an intruder.

He was on his feet instantly, a Magnum from the desk drawer in his hand. Cold sober.

"Daddy, what was that?"

Sparrowhawk was on the run toward the kitchen. "Haven't the foggiest. Where are you?"

"Dining room. I'm setting the table. Mum?"

Sparrowhawk reached the kitchen before his daughter did. And he saw something that made him collapse against the doorjamb, his gun hand useless at his side. "Jesus in heaven, no."

Unity Sparrowhawk lay bleeding on the gray linoleum floor, her eyes staring up at the ceiling. An arrow, tipped with a blue and white feather, had entered one side of her neck and reappeared on the other.

Valerie pushed past her father, stared, then threw herself, sobbing, on the floor beside her mother. "Mum? Mum? Oh, God, please answer me." She looked up at Sparrowhawk, disbelief in her eyes. "We have to get her to the hospital. Help me. We have to do *something*."

Dazed, Sparrowhawk shook his head. "Too late." He had seen enough of death to instantly recognize when there was no hope.

Gently, he pulled his daughter to her feet. "She's dead. Mum's dead."

Valerie, seconds from losing control, shrieked, "You're wrong. We have to take her—"

She broke down and threw herself in his arms, hating him for telling her, hating all of life for being so obscenely cruel. Sparrowhawk pressed her head against his shoulder. His own tears were hot on his face and he felt a cold emptiness steal its way into his heart. He knew, but he did not, could not, believe.

He lifted his head and screamed, "Unity!" and clung tightly to his daughter. She barely heard him whisper, "Why, Robbie, why?"

33

"I'm sorry to hear about your mother, Miss Sparrowhawk," Decker said.

"Valerie." She looked around the almost empty squad room. "Doesn't seem glamorous at all, not the way it does on television."

He looked around, too. "Paint's peeling, the windows haven't been washed in years, the radiator leaks and I think something crawled behind the wall and died. At least it smells that way. No different from any other squad room in Manhattan. Just your everyday, overcrowded, dirty little room."

It was Christmas Eve and Decker, one of only three detectives still in the squad room, was about to leave for the night. That is until Valerie Sparrowhawk, whom he had spoken to twice on the phone, telephoned again to ask if she could see him. Her mother had been killed ten days ago with a steel-tipped arrow. Authorities suspected a deer hunter whose aim had gone astray. So far, no suspects, and no arrests.

She said, "It was good of you to see me on such short notice."

"My pleasure." She was beautiful. And under one hell of a strain. Circles under her eyes, fingers shredding a tissue, eyes looking everywhere at once.

"My father won't talk about it," she said. "He suspects Robbie Ambrose; he mentioned his name almost immediately the night my mother died. Then he never mentioned his name again. I thought after we returned from burying my mother in England, he might open up more. But—"

She shrugged and gave Decker a smile that was more like a plea. "It's my mother, you see. I have to know why a man would do this to her." She dabbed at her eyes. "Someone has to tell me something. I was hoping you, you . . ."

She pressed her lips together and fought to keep from crying aloud.

Decker said, "You mean because we were all in Saigon at the same time?"

"My father's mentioned you once or twice. He says you're investigating his company."

"Was. I've been taken off that case. About Robbie, all I can tell you is what you probably already know. He doesn't like women."

"I don't need to be told that. I've known it for a long time. He tried to hide it, but I can tell. And something just occurred to me. If Robbie killed my mother, then he did it deliberately. My father was nowhere near her at the time. Robbie just deliberately, deliberately—"

She pressed the tissue against her mouth.

Decker nodded. "Yeah. It was his way of getting back at your father. I think it may have something to do with Robbie now being a federal informant. I'd have to think about it more and work it out. Anyway, Robbie's in protective custody at the moment. Nobody can get to him. He'll appear in a karate tournament next month in Paris and after that—" Decker turned his hands palms up.

Valerie cleared her throat. "Tell me something: now that Robbie is a federal informant, does this mean he's going to get away with killing my mother?"

"I won't lie to you. If federal authorities need him badly enough, he'll be allowed to get away with anything. It's happened before."

"Doesn't that bother you, someone like Robbie Ambrose walking around free? You're supposed to deal with people like him."

"Yes, I know that. And believe me, I've tried."

"And you've given up. I'm sorry, I shouldn't have said that."

"No, you have every right to say whatever you want, especially now. But I haven't given up."

She sighed. "At the moment, I don't care who deals with him, just as long as somebody does."

Decker stood up and took his jacket from his chair. "Anything can happen. Look, it's Christmas Eve and I don't have anybody special to celebrate it with. Would you let me buy you a drink?"

She looked at her watch. "I have to meet my father. He's working extra hard to put my mother's . . . this thing out of his mind." Her eyes went to Decker; she saw his sadness and almost reached out to touch him. "Not a good time of the year for anybody to be alone, is it?" She rose. "One quick drink. Maybe two quick drinks. I could use them."

Decker grinned. "Two quick drinks coming up." He held out his hand and she took it.

Inside the dojo, a sweating Decker stopped and looked at the wall clock. Just after ten-thirty, Christmas Eve. Who the hell could be knocking on the door at this hour? On this night. Officially, the dojo was closed until after New Year's. Except for a night watchman, the entire building was empty.

Breathing deeply, Decker, in his *gi*, crossed the floor and stopped at the door.

"Yes?"

"LeClair."

Decker looked down at the floor, hesitated, then turned the key and opened the door.

LeClair was alone. "Would you believe trick or treat? Promise I won't be long. Got a driver waiting downstairs and he wants to get home and trim the tree or something. May I come in? Never been inside a dojo before."

"Keep on the rubber matting. No shoes allowed on the floor."

"You de boss."

He entered and Decker locked the door behind him. The prosecutor looked past Decker at the two unsmiling Japanese standing in the middle of the dojo floor. Both wore sweat-stained *gis*, black belts and short haircuts.

"Santa's elves?" said LeClair.

"They don't speak much English."

"I see. They look like bad news. They any good?"

Decker looked at the Japanese. "You might say so." They were two of Shina's top men, flown in from Japan and under orders to work Decker hard twice a day, every day for three weeks. Early morning, late night and no days off.

Decker said, "They're returning to Japan soon. Have to get back to work."

"Oh? What kind of work?"

"They train people."

"Like who?"

"Oh, like the bodyguards to the imperial family, bodyguards to top Japanese businessmen. They also work with Japanese military intelligence."

LeClair reached inside his overcoat and removed a sheaf of papers. "Well, anyway . . . Robbie Ambrose is going to Paris next month to compete in the *suibin* tournament. Big deal among you big boppers, they tell me. Anyway, we have to take a few security precautions. Well, what do you think happened when we looked over the name of contestants and came to the list of competitors from the U.S. of A? Why, folks, we came across the name of one Manfred Decker."

He folded the pages and returned them to his inside pocket. "You are running a game on me, Mr. Manfred, and I'd like to know what it is."

"Me? Run a game on you?"

"Don't fuck with me, Jack. I can do things to you that wouldn't make you very happy."

Decker shook his head. "Yes and no."

"You mean you and your two friends here are gonna kick my butt?"

"It's a thought. No, what I mean is as of January first, I'm no longer a cop. I've handed in my resignation. If you want to dump on me after that, it might not be so easy. And in any case, I'll be in a position to deal with it a lot better."

"I see. Well, you are going to Paris. And you are going to fight in the tournament. And them two very talkative dudes eyeballing me are getting you into shape."

Decker scratched his head. "Well, I know I should be humble, but the truth is I was in pretty good shape to start. Just needed some tournament brushup, that's all. I'm holding my own." Decker, surprisingly, had done a lot better than that. But then he had reason to.

LeClair pushed himself off the bench. "Gettin' old, Mr. Manfred. I am definitely getting old. Anyway, three strikes and you're out at the old ball game."

"You mean Robbie took me twice and you think he's gonna do it again."

"Something tells me you think he had something to do with your girl friend's death in Paris a couple of weeks ago."

"We both know he did."

LeClair rubbed the back of his neck. "Well, what can I tell you. You ought to understand how these things work. Informants, making cases, all that shit. Man, you been a player. You got to understand."

Decker said, "When you see Robbie, give him a message for me. Tell him *sutemi*. Just that one word. *Sutemi*."

"*Sutemi*. What's it mean?"

Decker stretched. "You don't want to double-park in this neighborhood. They hand out tickets like you wouldn't believe. Merry Christmas."

LeClair said, "I've seen Robbie work out and, Jack, the man's made a believer out of me. Taking him on is like sticking your dick in a Cuisinart. You're bound to come up short. He's got this trainer, an old dude named Seth Robinson, who's worked with three world-champion boxers. Got to tell you, Mr. Manfred, no way you'll take Ambrose, assuming you do make it through the eliminations."

"Then you don't have anything to worry about. Your case is safe. Your informant will be around to hand you MSC."

"What can I tell you. I need him."

"You want him. There's a difference. Anyway, *sutemi*. He'll understand."

Downstairs in his limousine LeClair used his mobile phone to wake up a sleeping Robbie, now in a safe house in the Village. Robbie laughed. "Wow, he said that?"

"He did."

"No shit. Tell him I said, that's cool. I can dig it. Tell him I definitely hope we meet, finals, preliminaries, whatever. *Sutemi*, huh?" Robbie laughed again and hung up.

After Christmas, LeClair had a secretary look up the word. *Sutemi* meant to the death.

34

Paris
Second Sunday in January

In a hotel behind the Cathedral of Notre Dame and facing a tree-lined quay on the bank of the Seine, Decker sat on the edge of his bed and finished threading a needle. The white jacket of his karate *gi* lay across his lap. To his left a second *gi* jacket hung from the brass bedpost. When he had knotted the white thread, Decker reached for a blue envelope lying on the bed beside him and took out several grains of rice, plus a two-inch-square piece of gray cloth. Placing the grains of rice on the inside of his *gi*, near his heart, he covered them with the gray cloth and sewed the cloth to the *gi*.

When he had finished, he turned the *gi* over. Good. The white stitches could not be seen. He reached for the second *gi* jacket and repeated the procedure.

The cloth had been cut from the kimono worn by Michi the night she had been murdered. The rice was *semmai*, specially washed rice offered to the gods in the Shinto burial ceremony, where Decker had first vowed to kill Robbie Ambrose even if it meant dying in the attempt. *I am already dead,* Michi had said. Since her death, those words had become true for Decker, too.

He hung the *gi* jackets in a closet that was bare except for his overcoat, the one suit jacket he had brought with him and a single suitcase. Pulling out the suitcase, he placed it on a luggage stand and opened it. Inside was a metal and leather knee brace and two rolled elastic bandages. Decker thought of Robbie Ambrose. An hour ago the two men had been face to face. But only for a moment.

It was Decker's final run, his last before the start of the

suibin tournament tomorrow morning. In the Tuileries an early-morning fog hid fountains, ponds and formal flowerbeds. Near the Place du Carrousel, Decker veered to the right to allow three oncoming joggers to run past him. One of the three sprinted ahead, closing the distance between him and Decker.

Robbie Ambrose.

The security guard cupped his hands to his mouth. "Got your message." He grinned and kept running. Decker slowed down, turning his head to watch Robbie. The two task force agents, whom Decker recognized, slowed down to eye him. No one spoke. And then the fog swallowed up Robbie.

The sight of him brought back memories of Michi's funeral in Tokyo. Her body laid out in the Shinto temple, her head toward the north and without a pillow. Hands clasped, white cloth over her face. A table near her head, with *semmai*, water and a sword on it as well, to keep away evil spirits. The burning of incense sticks and incense powder. The chanting of a priest and the mourners leaving their seats to approach him to receive the *tamagushi* branch.

Back in his hotel room, Decker looked at the Polaroid photograph taken of him and Michi at the Brooklyn Botanic Gardens. Arms around each other and smiling. A heaviness came over him and he turned from the photograph to stare at a tiny doll resting on a corner of the dresser. The doll had belonged to Shigeji Shina, second in command of Japanese military intelligence. It had been sewn on the black-hooded funeral robe he had been scheduled to wear on his kamikaze flight.

Decker's request for Michi's *hachimaki* had convinced Shina of the detective's determination to avenge her death. Nothing was said directly about the detective's killing Robbie Ambrose. It was simply understood that he fully intended to do so. And so in addition to paying for Decker's return trip to New York, arrangements had been made for two of Shina's top martial arts instructors, traveling under diplomatic passports, to come to New York and work out with him.

The instructors were demanding, uncompromising. They had drawn blood.

In the end, Decker's speedy and steady techniques drove the two Japanese back across the empty dojo floor. There was to be no socializing among the three. Shina's orders. They were to meet only in the dojo, as warriors. At no time had Decker received any praise or encouragement from them. When it was necessary the three communicated in broken English, Japanese and by gestures.

When the last practice session was over, the Japanese changed clothes in the dojo and prepared to leave for the airport. The older one, Daigo, handed Decker the doll from Shina and, for the first time, smiled. Deeply moved, Decker bowed. He had received his praise.

In his Paris hotel room Decker picked up the doll and moved it into the sunlight, admiring its faded but still lovely colors. His mind would have to be in a state of *mushin*, detached, clear, ready to respond to any attack without consciously thinking about it, not bound to any technique. *Shiki soku se ku, ku soku ze shiki.* Form becomes emptiness, emptiness becomes form.

The telephone rang. Decker ignored it. Taking his passport, wallet and room key from the dresser, he left the room to go downstairs for lunch.

After eating and taking a short walk, he returned to the hotel, checked with reception and learned that the caller had been Valerie Sparrowhawk, wishing him good luck tomorrow. She did not know his true purpose in coming here.

There was a telegram from Ellen Spiceland, also wishing him luck. Ellen, who suspected what her partner planned, had said nothing to him about it. She had held him and cried and said, "Do what you have to. Just, just . . ."

And she said no more.

The two task force agents angrily banged on the door of the Champs Élysées hotel suite they shared with Robbie. "Okay, asshole," said one, "open up. We know you took the key from downstairs. Open this fucking door. We want to talk to you."

The door opened and a grinning Robbie bowed, then turned to walk away.

One agent, heavier than Robbie by thirty pounds, grabbed his elbow.

"Son of a bitch, I want to know where the fuck you went

when you ran off like that and left us with our thumbs up our asses. You know you're not supposed to be out of our sight. I got half a mind to put your ass on a plane back to New York. I ain't impressed with this karate shit—"

Robbie pivoted until they were back to back and, in the same motion, drove his elbow into the agent's kidney. When the agent released his grip Robbie smashed his heel into his instep, then dug his fingers into the agent's throat, twisted and pulled. Just hard enough. The agent gasped for breath.

Robbie smiled. "Go for your gun, dipshit, and you'll never talk again. You won't swallow right, you'll have trouble breathing and your neck's gonna look like a dog tried to eat it and gave up halfway through the meal."

The second agent said, "Okay, okay, everybody cool out."

Robbie, nose to nose with the stricken agent, said, "If you ever, *ever* lay a finger on me, I'll break it off."

Robbie took two steps back. "Okay, dipshit, now you can go for your gun. Go on. Take out the fucking gun and blow me away. But the moment I see your hand move—"

Neither agent saw what happened next. In the blink of an eye Robbie threw a kick and stopped with the edge of his foot less than an inch from the stricken agent's face. The second agent's eyebrows rose. He had never seen anybody move like that. Jesus.

The agent who had grabbed Robbie now stroked his own throat. Better try diplomacy. His voice was hoarse. "We were just doing our job. You ran off when we turned to look at Decker and we didn't see you for an hour."

Robbie scratched his temple. "Felt like doing some sprints and being by myself is all. Hey look, I'm here, ain't I? Lighten up, man. I waited for you guys before eating. I'm starving. What do you say we go downstairs and get some steaks."

He clapped the big agent on the back. "What LeClair doesn't know won't hurt him. I won't tell if you won't."

In the elevator going downstairs Robbie touched the gold stud in his ear and thought of the whore he had just killed. Blonde, young, driving around in her own car. Her body was still in the car, parked in the Bois de Boulogne. Well, the lady didn't belong to her pimp anymore. She belonged to *Hachiman Dai-Bosatsu*, great Bodhisatva, god of war.

* * *

In the cold night Decker stood across from the Hotel Richelieu and stared at it for almost an hour. In his mind he heard the liquid and gentle sounds of the thirteen-string *koto*.

Tokyo. Yasukuni Shrine. "Even if we die separately, we shall meet again and bloom in the garden here, which is a haven for all flowers."

"We will meet here after death, Michi. I promise."

At seven o'clock Decker got into a cab and returned to his hotel. After leaving word that he did not want to be disturbed, he lay down on his bed. And wept until sleep brought darkness to blot out the pain.

Paris
8:05 A.M. the next day . . .
***First Day of the* Suibin**
Tournament

Decker sat in the practically empty Arène des Sports, Paris's newest and most up-to-date arena, surrounded by over six hundred contestants. With a capacity of twelve thousand, it was shaped like an amphitheater, rows of beige leather seats rising one above the other. Its thick glass and steel roof caught the early morning sun, filling the gleaming wooden floor below with alternate patches of shadow and soft yellow light. Reporters, photographers, television cameramen and tournament officials gathered in front of the seated contestants. The *karateka*s represented over eighty-three countries. Some, Decker noticed, had brought wives or girl friends. After all, a trip to Paris was a trip to Paris.

Preliminary eliminations would begin at 8:30 sharp and last until six this afternoon. For the winners it would be a test of stamina, fighting several opponents in one day with few breaks in between. For the losers, today could be their last at the tournament. One loss meant you were out, and with it went the seven hundred dollars entrance fee and whatever traveling expenses you might have incurred. By tomorrow at least half of the contestants would have been eliminated.

Semifinals and the final match were to be held Friday, the last day. The two men who survived the semifinals would have a fifteen-minute rest before facing each other. Decker, his knee brace, elastic bandages and *hachimaki* in his hands, listened as the rules were read in English, French, German, Spanish and Japanese. Decker decided not to turn around and look for Robbie Ambrose. But he felt himself being watched.

Each entrant had already signed a waiver exempting tournament organizers from liability for injuries or death. No contact. Repeat, no contact. This tournament was a return to classical fighting, to traditional karate. Light contact was sometimes permissible, but only at the referee's discretion. That stipulation drew a few snickers.

Points were to be scored on effectiveness of "killing blows," based on technique, spirit and sportsmanlike attitude. Deliberately stepping outside the fighting area could cost a fighter the match. A reprimand from the referee meant automatic awarding of two points to the opponent.

The fighting areas were to measure eight yards square. Semifinals and finals would be fought on a single raised platform in the center of the arena. Preliminary bouts would have one referee, with four judges at outside corners of the fighting area. All matches had timekeepers and recorders. Double that number presided over semifinals and finals.

Three doctors and as many nurses would be on the floor at all times, with an ambulance waiting outside.

Since all contestants were experienced black belts, there would be no classification by weight. The *suibin* tournament was a world friendship tournament, promoted by the people of Japan in celebration of the growing international popularity of karate and, Decker suspected, a subtle promotion for Japanese industry. The tournament had drawn Japanese, Korean, Okinawan and even Chinese stylists, but tournament control was in Japanese hands.

Though strictly controlled, the fighting could still be dangerous. There was no protective gear for hands or feet, but contestants did wear protective cups and mouthpieces.

Decker looked to his left. Spectators, some still drinking morning coffee, began to file in.

A woman's voice came over a loudspeaker. "May I have your attention, please. Your attention. Please listen carefully for your name. The following names are to report to area one. Area one." She repeated the instructions in Japanese, French, German, Spanish. Decker closed his eyes. This was the worst part. Waiting.

More than one hundred names were read off and the contestants, in *gis* ranging from white to sky blue trimmed in black, began filing down onto the floor. Some were barefoot, some wore sandals. Few spoke.

At 8:45, when Decker's name was finally called, matches were already under way in two areas. Several men had been treated by doctors. Three men had been carried from the arena on stretchers. Decker was assigned to area three.

He breathed deeply, calming himself. When he heard his name he tied Michi's *hachimaki* around his head and with his knee brace and bandages in his hands, walked down the stairs onto the wooden floor. Over the loudspeaker he heard a man say, "And now will these names please go to area four, the last area to your right. Ambrose. Robbie Ambrose."

Decker kept on walking.

Paris
January, Second Friday
Suibin *Tournament, Last Day*

Sparrowhawk was drunk. His mouth was parched from too many Turkish cigarettes, and the pills he had taken to help him sleep had been a mistake. Pills, gin, cognac. Small wonder he was sick to his stomach.

Unity's passing was part of that relentless logic called destiny, a chain of destruction that began when he met Robbie in Saigon six years ago. And now the chain had come full circle. With Valerie at his side, Sparrowhawk sat in the top row of the sold-out Arène des Sports, torn between the desire to see Robbie die and the strange hope that he would survive.

Robbie, my son. My wife's murderer. The trusted comrade-in-arms who saved my life in Vietnam; who turned *grass*, police informant, to avoid prison for having murdered God knows how many women; who I trusted with my life; who I almost betrayed; and who learned of that impending betrayal and revenged himself by killing the most important part of me.

When it became apparent that both Robbie and Decker would make it to the final day, Sparrowhawk had telephoned Dieter from New York for tickets.

"Two tickets," said Valerie, who was in his office when he made the call. "She was my mother."

"What do you mean by that?"

"Manny's partner says he has his reasons for wanting to meet Robbie in this tournament. I think you know what they are. I want you to tell me."

On the Concorde flight from New York to Paris he did, leaving out his own involvement in Michi's murder.

Valerie said, "And the head of the task force knows this?"

"He does. But Robbie will never be brought to justice for any of his murders. He's too valuable, you see. He's needed to bring down MSC and Senator Terry Dent. And me, of course."

Valerie's expression almost made Sparrowhawk tell her the truth. But he kept silent as she said, "The only person who can deal with Robbie, truly deal with him, is Manny Decker. Otherwise Mum's death—"

She looked away, a fist pressed against her lips.

Sparrowhawk reached for his drink and looked out of the plane window.

In the Arène des Sports, the crowd cheered and applauded. Valerie clutched her father's arm and pointed down to the left. Sparrowhawk nodded. From a passageway that led to locker rooms one floor below, four *karateka*s strode toward a raised platform in the center of the arena floor. As spectators cheered, photographers and film cameramen at floor level moved in closer to the fighters. Uniformed guards prevented exuberant fans from running out onto the floor. Someone threw a rose at the fighters.

Decker and Robbie were two of the semifinalists. Decker was matched against a hard-driving, long-legged German, while Robbie was to fight a man whom some saw as the tournament favorite, a Japanese with blinding speed.

Valerie slipped her hand in Sparrowhawk's and squeezed tightly, her eyes on the fighters now clustered around the officials' table. Sparrowhawk saw only Unity. He looked up at the thick glass and steel meshed domed ceiling and wondered if the right man would die here.

LeClair, who with three members of his task force sat on the arena floor, leaned forward and watched the tall German stalk Decker. It was a four-minute match, three points. Score: all tied up at two points apiece. The German, speedy, and forceful, was damn good at attacking, at leaping in and scoring with punches to the head. Unfortunately for Decker, the German didn't always pull his punches. He'd made contact twice, drawing blood, but no penalty.

The German usually faked, a dip of the shoulder, quick motion of the head, a hand thrown in the air, then a forward lunge and that was it. LeClair was impressed.

Decker, however, impressed him even more. The detective was obviously hurt. He limped. His right ankle was bandaged and so were both wrists. There was blood on his *gi* and LeClair knew about his bad knee. Still, Decker fought a smart, cold-blooded fight. His weapons were his foot sweeps and fast hands. Twice he had swept the German into the air, dropping him hard on the wooden floor, then quickly following up with strong punches to the head and stomach. Mr. Manfred was good, no doubt about it. Too good, maybe.

The idea that he might make it to the finals and harm Robbie was more than a trifle upsetting to LeClair. And more upsetting was what he knew—that Decker was out to kill Robbie. *Sutemi*. LeClair could not afford to have that happen, not when he was so close to making the case against MSC.

As soon as he'd gotten the word that Decker was in the semifinals, LeClair decided that it might be a good idea to hop a plane and maybe have a few words with Mr. Manfred. The prosecutor had even toyed with the idea of having his men grab the detective and sit on him until the tournament was over. Ah, but Mr. Manfred had his own idea on the subject.

He had simply disappeared from his hotel, leaving another

hotel as a forwarding address. When LeClair checked there, guess what? No Mr. Manfred. Seems Decker had known LeClair might make a move. Too late now to do anything about it.

LeClair turned from the action down on the arena floor to look over his left shoulder. Decker's partner, Ellen Spiceland, was here, along with her husband. And so were the Harpers, the couple who owned the dojo where Decker trained. Some of Decker's karate pals were with them and all had their eyes glued to the detective and the German. Yesterday, in the short time left to him, LeClair had ordered his men to question Decker's friends as to his whereabouts. The friends claimed to know nothing. Turned out they had been telling the truth. Spiceland had been the most uncooperative of all, making it clear that even if she knew where her partner was LeClair would be the last man on earth she'd tell.

By the time LeClair had learned where Decker had spent the night, it was too late. Mr. Manfred had slept in the Arène des Sports on the same shiny wooden floor where he now fought for the chance to kill Robbie Ambrose.

A roar from the crowd made LeClair turn back to view the action. Shit, he'd missed it. The German was on the floor, with Decker's fist an inch from his temple.

Ippon. Third point. Decker the winner.

Fuck me, thought LeClair, shaking his head. He looked over his shoulder again. Ellen Spiceland was on her feet, clapping. Decker's karate friends were hugging each other and slapping palms.

Disgusted, LeClair looked down at the arena floor. He saw Decker limp to the edge of the fighting area and use his hand to wipe blood from his mouth. It's up to you now, Robbie baby. *Sutemi*. If it has to be, then it has to be. Just make sure the right man ends up with a tag on his toe.

Decker and the German he had just defeated sat on the edge of the platform and watched Robbie and the Japanese circle each other. For Decker, the past four days had been a painful blur. The eliminations, hard, often brutal fights, had been followed by nights made sleepless by injuries and bad dreams. He had faced fighters from South Africa, Korea,

Brazil, America, Mexico, Russia. He had dared them all to kill him. Some had tried. All had failed.

Decker touched his bandaged right ankle, which had been damaged yesterday by a wild, uncontrolled Cuban fighter, who had eventually been disqualified for clinching, then biting Decker's ear.

The detective's right knee ached. He'd taken a few shots there, some accidental, some not. Only the steel brace kept it from collapsing entirely. One wrist had been damaged blocking kicks from a hulking Russian; the other had been hurt when a Brazilian had blocked Decker's punch to the stomach. Since there was no protective equipment for hands and feet, his face had been scratched and his ankles bled from foot sweeps by fighters who had not clipped their toenails, despite tournament regulations.

How many fights? He had lost count. Ten, perhaps a dozen. All he knew for sure was that each one had been more challenging than the last. But Decker had a secret. He was already dead. He had accepted the way of the samurai and was prepared to die here in the arena. He had given up his body, his mind; the most he could do with his life was to bring justice to Michi's soul.

In this state, with his mind cleansed of all fear, he watched Robbie tie a thin red sash around his waist for identification by corner judges, each of whom had one red and one white flag. You have to win, thought Decker.

Four-minute match, three points.

The referee, a powerfully built Japanese in shirt sleeves, tie and stocking feet, and himself a former all-Japan karate champion, placed a whistle in his mouth.

"Rei!" Bow.

He lifted his right hand, eyed both contestants, then dropped the hand.

"Hajime!" Begin.

In less than a minute the speedy Japanese scored two points on kicks that sent white flags high in the air. The crowd loved it. Decker didn't. "Come on," he muttered. "Go for it, you son of a bitch. Go for it." He willed Robbie to hear him, to react, to fight back.

Robbie, in a *gi* of yellow silk, the name *Robbie* stitched across his shoulder blades, backed away. His hand went to the gold stud in his left ear. He appeared unconcerned, too unconcerned, Decker thought.

The detective thought of Michi. One more point, just one and Robbie would be lost to him forever, swept from the arena by LeClair. Here, in a public place and in front of thousands of witnesses, the detective could kill Robbie and get away with it. Accident. That would be the verdict. Killing him outside of the arena was another matter. For the first time since the tournament began, Decker felt anxious. He saw the possibility of failure. He clenched his fists. Robbie must not lose. "Get him," he whispered. "Get him."

And then almost magically, Robbie responded. His best weapon was the spinning back kick and he used it well. He scored once for a full point, then with only seconds remaining he caught the charging Japanese with a face punch that staggered him. The punch, however, was not ruled deliberate. The Japanese had run into the blow. When the match ended both fighters were tied with two points apiece.

A two-minute overtime was announced. Sudden death. First man to score a single point won. Decker held his breath. He watched both fighters stand on their taped marks and bow. And it was as though Robbie had read the Japanese's mind. A second after the bow the Japanese, always aggressive, leaped at Robbie, who timed his back kick perfectly, spinning around to catch the Japanese in the stomach, stopping him in place. Four red flags went up. Decker, excited and relieved, led the long and loud applause.

From the officials' table in front of the fighting platform, a French-accented voice said in English, "Ladies and gentlemen, kindly remain in your seats. After our fourth demonstration of the day, a series of weapons *kata*s by a team from Hong Kong, we will then conclude with the grand championship. This will be a four-point, six-minute contest between Mr. Manfred Decker of the United States and Mr. Robbie Ambrose, also of the United States. The winner will receive the *suibin* trophy."

As the announcement was repeated in different languages, the audience applauded. Both the German and the defeated Japanese wished Decker and Robbie good luck before leaving the platform. The two finalists themselves left the platform, but stayed on their respective sides. Decker thought of Michi, of dying, of love and duty.

When the Chinese left the platform, Decker and Robbie climbed on it again and began to stretch. After stretching, Decker loosened the screws on his knee brace and flexed his knee. He sat down, removed the bandage around his ankle, then retied it tighter. He tightened the bandages of his wrists and when he looked across the platform he saw Robbie staring at him.

Sutemi.

Neither man said the word out loud. But it hung in the air between them, a reminder that one of them had only minutes to live. The referee stepped up on the platform and the four corner judges found their seats. A half dozen Japanese officials conferred among themselves, while timekeepers tested stopwatches and buzzers. To the right, doctors and nurses moved chairs to within several yards of the platform. Photographers and film cameramen circled the platform, shooting the silent fighters.

Decker touched his nose and his ear. No blood. There was a sharp pain in his ribs, an injury he had forgotten about. He put it out of his mind, and circled his foot to loosen his bound ankle.

The referee motioned him and Robbie to their tape marks, facing each other four feet apart. The *karatekas* held each other's gaze. Neither man would look away. Decker saw Michi, heard her voice, heard her say his name.

"*Rei!*" They bowed, eyes still on each other.

Decker touched the *hachimaki. I am already dead.*

He bit down on his mouthpiece. Robbie did the same.

Sutemi.

"*Hajime!*"

Decker sidestepped to his left, stopped, then began circling to his right. Robbie shifted stance, left foot forward, hands protecting his face in a boxer's high guard. Decker wore the red sash.

Robbie struck first. Inching forward, he suddenly jabbed with his left fist, followed by a quick right cross, both of which fell short, as they were meant to. The spinning back kick was his weapon. That's what he used. He threw it hard and fast, striking Decker's sore ribs.

Four white flags went up.

"Ippon!" One point. Robbie.

It took all of Decker's self-control not to touch the damaged area. He must not show Robbie that he was hurt.

The referee signaled both men to their marks, signaled them to bow, then, *"Hajime!"*

Decker attacked low, using his left foot to attempt a sweep, then spun around and aimed a backfist at Robbie's head. Robbie took one step back, ducked and countered with a right hook aimed at Decker's liver. The detective leaned out of range, then shot the fastest side-thrust kick he could at Robbie's stomach. Robbie, on his toes, danced out of range. Decker pursued, bringing up his right knee to kick at Robbie's stomach. But before the kick could be extended Robbie jammed the ankle, Decker's sore ankle.

Limping, Decker backed off and Robbie circled, stopped, changed directions, stopped again. Waited. The two men stared as 12,000 people silently watched. Suddenly Robbie hopped-skipped toward Decker, and lashed out with a side-thrust kick again to the sore rib. The pain clawed its way to Decker's eyes, then down again to his chest.

"Ippon!" Four white flags. Second point Robbie.

And that's when Decker knew what Robbie was doing. In a four-point match he would first have to prove his superiority. He would score three times. The fourth point would be Decker's death.

I am already dead.

With nothing to lose, Decker gambled. Throwing his right hand at Robbie's face as a distraction, he swung his right leg low, a hard sweep at Robbie's left ankle. Quickly, Robbie lifted the left leg high and out of danger. But instead of backing away, he dropped the left leg to the floor and with his right leg kicked twice at Decker's left side, the ball of his right foot smashing hard into Decker's left forearm. Thigh and hips went into the kicks, making them strong, deadly. The kicks sent Decker to the floor. The roaring crowd was on its feet.

Decker's left arm was on fire. He didn't bother to use it to help himself from the floor. The severe pain racing up and down his left side told him the left arm was now useless. Cradling it with his right hand he attempted to rise but fell back.

"No point!" barked the referee, who also signaled for a time out.

Robbie calmly walked to his mark, dropped to one knee and removed his dripping mouthpiece. He wiped his forehead with the back of one hand. His eyes were on the floor in front of him and he seemed indifferent, almost bored. No need for concern or worry. He knew how the fight would end. It would end as all his fights did, with one exception. Decker would not just be defeated. He would die.

Dizzy with pain, Decker needed the referee's help to make it to his feet and leave the platform. His left arm throbbed. He could barely close the fingers of that hand. The fist he made with it was useless.

As the audience watched, a French doctor examined the arm, then said, "It is broken, monsieur. I am afraid there can be no more fighting for you."

A seated Decker, the arm resting on his thigh, shook his head.

As the doctor and two nurses conversed rapidly in French, the referee and several of the Japanese officials came over to Decker. Decker eased himself from the chair and stood up. His knee was worse. It would give way under him. The metal brace would not be able to prevent that from happening.

"Tape my arm to my stomach," he said.

"I cannot allow that," said the doctor. He was small, bearded, imperious and used to being obeyed. "That is not a game anymore, monsieur. With one arm you will surely be hurt, perhaps killed. No, I cannot allow that to happen."

Ushiro Kanai stepped from the group of officials. He and Decker held each other's gaze, then Kanai said, "This is, after all, a championship match. Its purpose is to remind the world of samurai spirit. Such a spirit does not accept defeat. If Mr. Decker feels he can continue, we must respect his wishes."

Giri. Kanai had paid Decker what he owed.

"Fou," snapped the doctor. Crazy.

The damaged arm was placed inside Decker's *gi* and taped against his stomach, first at the wrist, then at the forearm. He refused medication. Drugs would only dull his reflexes.

When he climbed back onto the platform, a limping, one-armed fighter in a blood-spotted *gi*, the arena rose in a standing ovation. Sparrowhawk got to his feet. A solemn LeClair stood. The building expanded with cheers and soon the cheers became an ongoing explosion. Robbie looked around, then across the platform at Decker and this time the security guard did not look away in contempt. This time he eyed him thoughtfully.

The referee walked over to Robbie. A warning against further roughness. Only the fact that this was the final bout coupled with Robbie's record of clean fighting and sportsmanship in the tournament prevented him from being disqualified. Robbie bowed. Then he walked across the platform and extended his hand to Decker. The detective took it without a word. The applause and cheers continued. Not even the announcer's pleas for quiet could stop the clamor.

"Ladies and gentlemen, please be seated. Please allow us to continue. One minute remains in the match. Only sixty seconds. Mr. Ambrose leads Mr. Decker three points to none."

One minute. Sixty seconds in which to kill Robbie. Or lose him forever. Decker called on his *kami*, on Michi. Help me, help me . . .

"Rei!"

"Hajime!"

Robbie charged, then stopped. Something in Decker's face bothered him. And in that instant *Hachiman* spoke to Robbie. *You cannot kill a man who is already dead. There is nothing that can destroy a man who has accepted the way of the samurai. He is also protected by a most powerful god, one stronger than I, the god that was once Michi, the woman. A god of love, a god that not even war and death have been able to defeat.*

Robbie felt fear. *Hachiman* had always been the strongest of gods. Defeat was unknown to him. There was no god but *Hachiman*. But even as the words flashed across Robbie's mind he felt the god of war pulling away from him. Pulling away . . .

Kill Decker quickly. Yes, that was it. Kill him before *Hachiman* disappeared. Kill the last of the Saigon ghosts and be the *bushi* of all time.

Using his right leg Robbie threw a power front-thrust kick, then withdrew the leg and with all of his strength swung a right cross at Decker's head and cried out, *"Hachimannnnnnn!"*

For Decker, all fear was gone. He would meet Michi once

more, meet her at Yasakuni, at the sacred Tokyo shrine. *Hai,* it would be good to die.

When two tigers fight, one hurts, one dies.

Decker attacked. And never knew that he attacked. His body did not belong to him anymore; his mind no longer existed. He willed no action, made no decision. Later he could only say that he had no memory of those last few seconds.

He ducked under Robbie's right cross, leaned closer and in a vicious counterpunch of his own, drove a right uppercut deep into Robbie's throat. The blow smashed his larynx, crushed all of the cartilage. Instantly, Decker opened his fist, turned his hand palm up and struck again, attacking the throat once more, this time with the thumb side of his palm.

Robbie, eyes bulging and hands at his throat, staggered backward. Decker's *kiai* was hair-raising, and came from so deep within him that it stunned the audience into silence and as Decker yelled he swept both of Robbie's feet from under him. For a second, Robbie, face discolored, hung in midair, drowning in his own blood, then he dropped to the floor with a sickening thud.

Four white flags went up and a cheering audience was on its feet.

The chant began. *"Decker, Decker."* Young Frenchmen tucked their left arms in their jackets or shirtfronts as Decker had done and imitated his uppercut and foot sweep. The applause would not end. It changed into a rhythmic hand-clapping, accompanied by stamping feet. Only those officials climbing onto the platform, along with the little French doctor, even suspected that Robbie Ambrose was dead.

Epilogue

March

Decker walked into the bathroom, opened the clothing hamper and placed Michi's towel-wrapped *kai-ken* at the bottom. Then, picking soiled sheets and shirts from the floor, he piled them on top of the weapon, filling the hamper to the top. He was about to clean his teeth and go to bed when the telephone rang. Quickly jogging to the living room, he picked up the receiver on the second ring. "Yes?"

"How was your trip?"

"Gave me a chance to rest. She did all the work. She had research to do at the Smithsonian, the Folger Shakespeare Library and the Library of Congress. It meant I was left on my own part of the time, but I didn't mind. We spent a pleasant ten days together."

"I'm glad," Raphael said. "God knows you needed the rest after what you'd been through. Well, have you decided?"

"I'll take the job."

"All right! Hey, I'm really pleased. Number-two man at MSC. Hey, I'm excited."

Decker looked at the bedroom. "Sparrowhawk won't like it, but I guess that can't be helped."

"Sparrowhawk's not heading the task force," Raphael said. "I am. By the way, LeClair's out of a job again. His law firm is letting him go. He doesn't know it yet, but he'll get the word sometime this week."

"Why?" Decker didn't care, but he was curious.

"Robbie Ambrose, what else? The wives of two very important clients refuse to have him into their homes because of the way he handled the Ambrose thing."

"Cover-up, you mean."

Raphael said, "Whatever. He really tied the can to his own tail with that one. And speaking of doing it to yourself, Sparrowhawk's getting worse. Heavy, heavy drinking and the powers that be don't like it."

"That's why they offered me the number-two spot."

"Something else Sparrowhawk's not going to like. We just got the news today. His friend Ruttencutter."

Decker sat down and began to twist the telephone cord around his still-sore left wrist. "What about him?"

"Found his body this morning. He'd been missing for a couple days. Wife hadn't heard from him, his office was getting antsy. He's got this country home in Maryland and I guess he went there to open it up for the spring or something. It's not far from Washington. Anyway, they found him there with his throat cut. Looks like B and E, but nothing's missing. Nothing to go on. Sparrowhawk and Ruttencutter were in Saigon at the same time."

Decker said, "I know." He looked at the origami wildlife figures on his desk.

Raphael said, "You know Longman and Davison, the agents we had guarding Robbie, they're still talking about that fight. Said they'd never seen anything like it. Place was in an uproar. Longman's taking karate lessons himself now. They said that fight between you two guys was the best they'd ever seen, including any boxing match in the past ten years."

"Got me disqualified," Decker said. "Almost got me jailed. Took some fast talking by the Japanese to convince the French it was an accident."

Raphael hesitated. Then, "Well, we won't go into that. Look, I have to be upfront with you. We're happy to have a man inside MSC, but your life is on the line. You ought to know that going in. If Gran Sasso ever learns you're still working with the task force, he'll burn you."

"I know."

"Frankly, I don't know why you want to get back in this rat race. You're out of it. Any security outfit would pay a small fortune to have a guy like you on the team. Why do you want to get back in?"

Decker thought of Michi. And of Sparrowhawk.

"Giri," he said. "And don't call me on this line anymore. Gran Sasso will probably be watching me closely, at least at

the beginning. From now on, I'll call you and only you. Nobody is to call me and that includes you. If I have anything I'll make the first move. That's the only condition I have for this job."

"You got it, soldier. By the way, what's this *giri* stuff?"

Decker sighed. "We had a long drive back from Washington today. I'm tired. Think I'm coming down with a cold. March was never my favorite month of the year. I'll be in touch." He hung up.

He returned to the bathroom, cleaned his teeth, then walked to his bedroom. After he had stripped he slipped into bed beside Valerie Sparrowhawk. *Hai.* He would take the job. And she could be used against her father. Decker would find a way. He always had.

He lay in the darkness, his back to her. When he listened carefully there were times when he was almost certain that he heard the sound of the elegant *koto* in the March wind beating against the bedroom window.

ABOUT THE AUTHOR

MARC OLDEN is the author of, among others, *Gossip, Poe Must Die,* and *Book of Shadows.* His newest novel is entitled *Dai-Sho.* He makes his home in New York City.